KT-481-748

YOUR GUILTY SECRET

Rebecca Thornton is a journalist and runs an online advertising business. Her work has been published in *Prospect Magazine, Daily Mail, The Jewish News* and *The Sunday People*. She was Acting Editor of an arts and culture magazine based in Jordan, and she's reported from Kosovo, London, and the Middle East. Rebecca is an alumna of the Faber Academy writing-a-novel course, where she was tutored by Esther Freud and Tim Lott. You can follow her on Twitter @rebs_web

Also by Rebecca Thornton

The Exclusives

YOUR GUILTY SECRET

REBECCA THORNTON

Leabharlanna Poiblí Chathair Baile Átha Cliath
Dublin City Public Libraries

Withdrawn From Stock
Dublin Public Libraries

ZAFFRE

First published as an ebook in Great Britain in 2018
This edition published in paperback in 2019 by
ZAFFRE
80–81 Wimpole St, London W1G 9RE
www.zaffrebooks.co.uk

Copyright © Rebecca Thornton, 2018

All rights reserved.
No part of this publication may be reproduced,
stored or transmitted in any form by any means, electronic,
mechanical, photocopying or otherwise, without the
prior written permission of the publisher.

The right of Rebecca Thornton to be identified as Author of this
work has been asserted by her in accordance with the
Copyright, Designs and Patents Act, 1988.

This is a work of fiction. Names, places, events and
incidents are either the products of the author's
imagination or used fictitiously. Any resemblance to
actual persons, living or dead, or actual
events is purely coincidental.

A CIP catalogue record for this book is
available from the British Library.

ISBN: 978-1-78576-075-4

1 3 5 7 9 10 8 6 4 2

Typeset by IDSUK (Data Connection) Ltd
Printed and bound in Great Britain by Clays Ltd, Elcograf S.p.A.

Zaffre is an imprint of Bonnier Books UK
www.bonnierzaffre.co.uk
www.bonnierbooks.co.uk

Asia Mackay. To many more years of friendship and laughter . . .

Lara King Official Website
Status: Unpublished
August 26th 2018
1500hrs

Now is your chance. Grab it whilst you can. Take a long look at my face. I hope I am how you imagined. I can't shoulder the burden of your disappointment. Not today. So, let's start with my skin. Is it as flawless as it looks on those pages? My hair – the shine – I try hard with that, although I suspect right now it might be looking matted and lifeless.

Lara? Lara? Over here! Look this way!

I know. You've rarely seen me like this. I'm normally dressed so beautifully. My hair blow-dried, my make-up perfect. I'm sure you know already, that even if I'm going for the *au naturel* look it takes a lot of preparation. Day in, day out. Normally I call the shots. But after everything that's happened today, I need to be told what to do. Conor had had to ring me, just before the press conference.

'It's OK,' he had said. 'Listen to me, Lara. I'm handling the media. But for now, do as I say. I've asked Lily to bring everything you need.' And so I had done as I was told. Lily arrived soon after, with a change of clothes for me.

We had been led to the back of the police station into a room with three wooden chairs and a pine-coloured table.

1

There was a mirrored wall too. It crossed my mind I was being watched. But then again, I was always being watched. I had taken off my workout gear and put on a pair of jeans, fingers unable to grasp the buttons.

'Here.' Lily had squeezed my hands. 'Stop. Let me.' She had pulled tight my waistband but then I saw her hands were trembling too. Lily, who could handle anything. I then shook out my hair and took off the remnants of my make-up with a cleansing wipe. It was at this point I was barely able to breathe, sweat trailing down my face. We had walked out together, Lily and I, side by side.

And now, it's time. I watch you, necks stretched high, camera phones tracking my face. Please. Don't judge. Just listen carefully to what I am about to tell you.

I know you'll care. You've always taken mine and my daughter's lives in your hands, and your hearts. Most of you anyway. Some of you dismiss me. You might pretend you've never seen any of our reality shows or clothes ranges. Dissected mine and Matthew's pap shots in the showbiz pages. '*Lara King? She's famous for nothing.*' That's where you are wrong.

Before I go any further, I need to say something to you all. I'm still getting to grips with the fact that this is my reality, but I hope *you* realise this is true life too. That the lines between fact and fiction are no longer blurred. That this is not a show piece for the glossies. It's not some new storyline for the latest television show I may be appearing in.

I watch the trail of lights, immortalising the image of me in cyberspace. A montage for you to watch, on repeat. *Record. Click. Upload.* '*Look who we saw today!*' you might write. '*Much prettier on camera.*' Or perhaps you'll be kind. Say how pretty I am in the flesh. And you might even remark that you are surprised I'm quite tall. Most of us are shorter in real life. And so it goes on. Of course you'll probably assume – just like everybody else that is walking past – that the world's media have been called here today because I've got a new product to launch. A perfume, perhaps. Notes of jasmine. Something citrus. Fresh and light.

But then you'll peer closer, and as the sun stings your eyes, you'll just about be able to see the redness around my lower lids, my hands shaking as I grip the microphone. And then you'll see Matthew next to me, that familiar blond hair and green eyes, his tanned arm behind my back and you'll be comforted by his presence – after all, you've welcomed him from Australia so generously. You'd be awed even. A gasp. A hand gripped around your friend's arm. 'Oh my God. Look who it is. Oh my *God*.'

But then you'll wonder what on earth is going on. You might even be a little frightened when you see my face. It's at this point I think of Ava's nanny, Joan. How am I going to tell her what's happened? The sag of her features as I detail the events of the day. The way she will push back the curls behind her ear, softly, as though her hair might break if she touches it too hard. And then, the things she will say to me afterwards.

I watch as the police usher you all away as we're about to start. I see you at first bewildered and then angry, as though you have a right to my life. Which, I suppose, you do. Or parts of it, anyway.

And so it begins.

Silence other than the rasp of my breath and the click-click of cameras. A magnified screech, as my lips touch the cold metal.

'Hello.' I clear my throat. 'Hello. Thank you. For being here.'

I watch you on the pavement, heads turned towards me. You know something is wrong now, I can see it in your faces. But savour this moment because you don't know, just yet, quite how bad things are going to get. Or how your daily lives will be wholly consumed with what's happened. Yes, and I mean all of you. None of you across the globe will be immune, no matter how you try.

I'm so thankful for those I know will help out. My cheerleaders. But then the memories of today start unfolding in my mind, clawing and strangling my brain. And as the world around me sharpens into an almost unbearably bright Technicolor light, I lift my face to you.

Are you ready?

Today, I need you to put yourselves in my shoes. I want you to imagine what I'm going through. Shut your eyes if it helps. Careful, though. You might want to steady yourselves.

Today, I need you to see me for who I really am.

A mother. A human being. A person with flaws.

Today, I'm not the Lara King that you think I am.

Guys, I'm here. Right near the spot where she disappeared. Well, as close as we're allowed. The forensics, they've taped off an entire area. They're on their hands and knees sweeping up tyre tracks and it's looking like something out of the Burning Man Festival. I'm standing about three yards from the *Sky News* van. You might even be able to see me if you switch on the TV now. I'm wearing a white T-shirt. Denim cut-offs. I'm waving. See me? Look closely, because I'm not sure you'll be able to hear much of the report. The noise, you see. The helicopters with heat-seeking equipment, flying over the canyon droning in and out of earshot.

There are dogs too, sniffing around for little Ava King. I saw them in the distance, over by the police cars. Their noses were pressed into a small pink cardigan and then they were ushered out into the rocks. 'Go. Find her, Cyrus,' I heard one policewoman yell. I saw her fingers, crossed tight behind her back.

They'll be sniffing out a sweet scent, I reckon. Almonds and coconut milk. She looks like she'd smell like that, doesn't she? Pure and perfect and so innocent. Although I have to keep reminding myself that I don't know actually know her IRL.

They're really working those animals, though. They're crawling around the place, going down the ravines, under rocks, mouths foaming white in the heat. The police are scraping the ground with sticks, shouting her name and you have to think that if she's got lost around here, they've ploughed enough resources into giving her the best hope of being found.

Everyone's here too. The public, I mean. Like, thousands and thousands of people. Already. It's fucking crazy and the media vans, they keep screeching up along the road, clanking around to see where they can set up their big satellite dishes, and who can slick on their frosted pink lipstick the fastest.

We're all suffocating with the heat but people are giving out free bottles of water and sandwiches and stuff. 'Feeding the five thousand.' That's what I heard one person say.

The most screwed-up thing is that I reckon when she disappeared there was no one around. For miles and miles. It's endless here. Some of the view obscured by trees and bushes. I'm looking down now at all the shrubs, a patchwork of grey, brown and green. Six years old and all alone. Her heart must be going batshit in her little chest.

All this shouting and screaming isn't gonna be of any use though, not if someone's taken her. She won't be anywhere near here. That's what I heard the *Sky News* woman say. Apparently Lara reported hearing a car drive off.

Women, men, children, they're all weeping, shouting, 'Ava, Ava.' Flies buzz all over the place, their thick black bodies pressing themselves right in my ear. But I'm sure she's OK. She said so, didn't she? Lara. She said in her press conference that she was sure her little girl was fine. That she was clinging on to hope.

It's weird, cos they don't look like they think she's fine. They've blocked all the roads and I heard some detective shouting about the interstate. Three hours he was saying. If we don't find her in three hours.

Then what? I wanted to shout. Then what?

Anyway, they want me to speak! On camera! Imagine that. Me, the school geek always behind my computer and now I'm racking up traffic like a shit-storm and I'm going to be on live TV! Holy shitaake!

OK, so guys, I'm going to be your number one destination throughout the investigation. Check here first for all the latest and I promise you, I'll be here with all the exclusives. You all know how much I love Lara and Ava. I'm devastated but I'll do my best to be a good gatekeeper.

Anyway, gotta drink some water. My mouth is so dry. Be right back after. Tune in.

Here with the latest updates on missing Ava King, brought to you by Lara and Ava King's number one fan.

Twitter: @ryan_gosling_wannabe

What would you do if your child disappeared into thin air? I mean, what would you *really* do? You might pound the pavements screaming their name, breath sour with fear. Air escapes you.

And when you get home, escorted by the police, you might fall into the arms of your husband or wife or a member of your family. Slamming your fists into their chests, your knees dropping to the ground. Pleading. With who, you don't really know. And then with a renewed vigour and a sense of hope, you'd go out again. Back to where your child disappeared. You'd watch as the police knocked on surrounding doors and took witness notes and because you were there, in the action, you might feel you were doing something. Anything.

You might consider me for a minute when I tell you that my child has disappeared, yet despite the world's gaze on me, I have absolutely no control over where I look for her. I cannot open the front door to our home in The Hidden Hills. I cannot press the pattern of small, shiny gold buttons that remotely open the huge iron gates, with the hand-carved wooden sign on it. *Los Palisades*. I cannot use my thumbprint to access the extra security we had installed.

If I *could*, I might for a moment sweep my gaze across the lawns for any sign of her – my eye line darting in and around

8

the uniformly cut grass, the luscious, rare rose blooms spilling down from the clean lines of our house – even though we were miles from where she disappeared. I'd still glance over to the pool – as I always did. A habit I'd been unable to relinquish from before she'd learned to swim. The clench of my stomach just until I reassured myself, two or three times over, that there was no small body, face down in the softly lapping turquoise water.

I would then race down our cobbled drive, lined with newly buffed cars. I'd curse the palm trees forcing me to weave my way around their silvery trunks. I'd ignore the burn of my lungs. The way my legs would barely be able to hold me up. I'd run, purely because I'd be incapable of driving. Or perhaps it would kick-start my senses afresh. And I'd try and think back to where it had all started, my throat swollen with the catch of my breath.

I'd try and revisit that moment we'd left the house, water bottles under our arms. Me, in workout gear despite having no intention to exercise. Her in a navy sundress, embroidered rabbits across the collar. Silver Superga trainers. Her face tilted up to mine, scrunched up against the sun.

'Treat day,' she'd said. 'Can you believe it? Just you and me.'

I'd think about this as I tried to remember, left or right? Which way had I manoeuvred the car?

Had I thought about the paps as I normally did when we left the house? Had I planned my whole route along the back-streets, where they might not be lurking, eyes scanning for my number plate? The way their lenses followed me, like snipers. Or had I just driven aimlessly, enjoying the day panning out ahead of us, with nothing to do. No one to see. Just me and my daughter. But I can't remember the ins and outs of my thoughts from this morning. If I had known what was going to happen, I'd have taken more care to engage with my inner monologue. To remember the way I'd felt a little impatient as Ava had kicked at the tyres of our car before she'd climbed into the back seat. The slight twist of her front tooth as it pushed its way through her gums.

I'd have looked carefully at the way her body was formed. The soft roundness of her stomach. The fine, blonde hairs travelling down her tanned arms.

But of course, I never thought that today would end up like this. I do, at other times. Think the worst. Catastrophise. But there was something so perfect about the way today had been panning out. Just me and her. A special treat. Ice cream. It was the first day in a long while I'd felt able to breathe.

That in itself should have been the first sign of things to come.

It was Detective Mcgraw who sat me down in the police station and told me that he was driving me straight home and that I had to stay indoors. Those green eyes of his, continuously locked onto one focal point a fraction above my right shoulder. White face, a fine tracing of freckles smudged across his top lip.

'I need to be out there though. Looking for her. She's my daughter. Please. There must be a way?'

'I know. And I'm sorry. We can't risk hampering the investigation. Thousands of people are out there, looking. And so we need you to stay inside your house.'

I knew he was right. That it was for the best. You see, I wanted you to be looking for her, without distraction. Surely I had learned by now – stay out of view in times of trouble. After all, a wrongly placed smile, a casual lift of my eyebrow could set you off, and that's not what I need right now.

I'm getting ahead of myself. I suppose I should tell you the things that happened less than six hours earlier. Just after we had pulled out of our drive, sun beating down through the windscreen.

I'll tell you as much as I can remember. The same details I told Detective Mcgraw in my oak-panelled study after he'd told me they'd taken my computer and mobile phone. We'd sat, me at my desk with my leather in-trays and stationery drawers all in straight lines in front of me. He was opposite me, in an ergonomic swivel chair that kept twisting from underneath him.

'I'd planned a special day out,' I told him. 'Just us. It's such . . . It *was* such a beautiful day,' the words spill out my mouth.

'Any reason for the outing? An occasion, perhaps?'

'Yes. It was my way of saying thank you. For the way Ava behaved for the announcement. Did you see it?'

'I read about it.'

'She had been so good,' I continued. 'So I told her that I'd take her out.'

'And then what? We've pieced together as much as we can of your journey, mapping the CCTV footage. You hadn't pinned any of your locations on your public social media accounts. Any private ones we need to know about?'

'No.'

'OK. If you could tell me what happened this morning, then?'

'At nine forty-five this morning we drove to Laurel Canyon. To go for a walk. On the way there, Ava grew tired. She lay down and fell asleep in the back of the car.' My voice took on a robotic quality as I became more and more disassociated from myself.

'What time was that?'

'About ten fifteen, I suppose. We were nearing Laurel Canyon and the drive is about thirty minutes from home.'

'What time did she wake up this morning from her night's sleep?'

'I can't remember exactly. But she was exhausted from the past few days. And the heat. Why? What relevance has this got to do with finding her? Please, Detective Mcgraw.' I sat forward, trying to get some air into my lungs.

'Just trying to get a clear picture of everything surrounding her disappearance, Ms King. She fell asleep and then what?' He waved his hand in front of his face as though swatting flies except when I looked, there was nothing there.

'When she fell asleep, I drove from Laurel Canyon, back to Laurel Canyon Boulevard which is about halfway back to home. I drove around there for a bit, and then when I thought she had been asleep long enough, I turned around and drove back to the canyon where we were going to go for a walk.'

'And why did you do that, Ms King? Drive around the Boulevard, I mean. Instead of perhaps waiting at Laurel Canyon, given that's where you were about to go walking?' His eyes rested on a large black and white picture of when I had been eight months pregnant with Ava.

'I was just killing time, Detective. Have a few moments to myself. I rang Matthew at about a quarter to eleven or so. I like driving. I find it peaceful, when there are no paps around. With my job it's time to be alone with my thoughts.'

'Right. And there were no paps around today? Or your security?'

'Not as far as I know. And I'd kept it just me and Ava. I felt OK about that. We weren't going anywhere with lots of people. Look, I know I shouldn't have been on my phone when I was driving.'

'We just want to find your daughter. That's our main focus right now. So you were speaking to Matthew. For how long in your estimation?'

'Twenty minutes, I guess? You've got my cell. You'll be able to tell, won't you?' There was a level of irritation in my voice that I tried to contain.

'Chat about anything interesting, did you?'

'What we had planned for the rest of the week. Our work. And then Ava was awake, asking to go to the toilet. She said she was desperate.'

'You got off the phone at this point?'

'No. I just stopped the conversation for a bit. I'm sorry. I just, it's difficult. Like I told you, I don't have much alone time.'

'So, you pulled over and Ava got out the car to go to the toilet. How long had she been awake for at this point?'

'I can't fully remember. I'd looked at her in the rear-view mirror before. I think we'd smiled at each other.' I thought of my daughter, a fist lodging itself behind my breastbone.

'And before she went to sleep, she was fine?'

'Totally fine.' I started to cry. 'We had a great time. Singing Katy Perry songs along with the radio, chatting about her school friends. Laughing, joking. She was happy we were together.'

'So by the time you stopped and pulled over so she could go to the toilet, it was, about what time?'

'Eleven thirty or thereabouts. I pulled over straightaway. There was no one around. We were just by the side of the road, so I thought she'd be fine. I thought she was right behind the car. But then, then I was back talking on my phone. I guess at some point, I realised it had been too long. I heard a car. Another car. I hung up. And that's when—'

'Slow down, Ms King, and try and breathe.'

My mind pulled back to that moment. I had craned my head around, waiting for her to pop up. *Mommy. I'm here.* Everything had shifted on its axis when I realised she wasn't anywhere to be seen.

'I looked. I looked and looked and looked. I screamed. I screamed her name over and over.' *She's hiding,* had been my initial thought. Funny girl. And then as time went on, my heart had started to race.

Game's up now.

'And you heard a car drive off?'

'I did. I can't tell you if it was near or far. I heard it though.'

'How long after you realised she had gone did you hear the car?'

'Oh, God, I don't know. I just don't know. Five, ten minutes? Fifteen at a stretch.'

'So by this point it was about eleven forty?'

'I don't know. I think so. Please. I can't remember.'

'You heard any signs of a struggle? Screaming?'

'No.'

'Do you think she would have gone into someone else's car willingly?'

'No. Oh God. Well, Joan, her nanny,' I could barely get the words out now. 'Matthew. Lily. That's all.'

Silence.

'Fine. Let's go on. You then got out to look for her?'

'I did.' I felt winded. 'I looked for her for about fifteen or twenty minutes. You know, I really thought she was coming back at that point. Otherwise I would have called earlier,' I heard my voice getting faster and faster. 'I rang Matthew back. He told me to ring you. She wasn't anywhere. I had forgotten about the noise of the car I heard. I was in such a state, I didn't know what was going on.'

'Look, I really think you should have one of our family liaison officers present. I think it would help.'

'No. Please, I'm fine. I can't. With my situation . . .' I looked around the room at all my awards, the framed magazine front covers with me on them, hoping he'd understand.

'Fine. Of course. Would you like us to call your friends? Family?'

'No.' I thought of my friends. My skin itched at the thought of anyone being near me. And then he pulled himself upright, as though he'd realised he'd been giving me too much power, been too acquiescent towards me.

'All right. Listen, we need to search Ava's room too. You might like someone with you when we do.'

'Search it? That's not necessary.'

'We need to get a clear picture.'

'Fine. Just don't be disruptive with her things.' I then thought about Joan and how much time she spent in Ava's room. I thought about how she would ask me again and again how Ava was there one minute, and gone the next. And I'd tell her the things I was sure about. Which was this: that I do not know. I do not know how my six-year-old daughter could have disappeared like this.

I would tell her the things I do to safeguard my little girl. I would remind her that I check the swimming pool every time I leave the house. That we have the best security – including her favourite bodyguard Adrian – whom we trust with our lives.

But for the moment, what I would leave out is that I am guilty of doing what most parents must have done in their lifetime. If you happen to be one, please, do me the honour of reassuring me.

Tell me that perhaps you might have got over-involved in a conversation with someone whilst your child was over in the other side of the park. Looked over. Realised you couldn't spot the heft of their body. Their little legs waddling over to the next set of swings. What clothes did you put them in this morning? God. You can't even remember. Ah – that's right. Green. You'd be looking for a green anorak. And then you'd see a flash of pond-water-coloured material and your muscles would relax and you'd vow never, ever to lose concentration again.

Or – perhaps you've sent a few WhatsApp messages when you thought your little one was busy playing with their toys. You'd been caught up in a conversation with your mates. Wanted to have the last words with a partner with whom you'd been rowing. It's OK, you told yourself. Nothing to harm them. *I've got this.*

Please. Work with me here. Tell me you've done one of the above.

Because perhaps, only then, would I be able to admit to Joan when she asks me, that I made a mistake.

A terrible, unforgivable mistake.

'Lara, come here, hurry.' Conor had pulled out his mobile phone and waved me over. 'Look at this.' My heels clipped over the shiny hall floor as I walked towards him. Everywhere else in the house was off-limits whilst preparations for our big announcement were under way.

'What is it?' My voice wavered until I saw him, one leg hoiked over the other in a pale pink scallop-edged armchair, finger pressed up to his mouth. *Thank God.* His relaxed pose. As Head of Lara King Publicity he had the power to turn a good day into something hellish, with only a few words.

'Everyone's going shit-crazy online.' He tapped his phone. 'They're all wondering what the fuck is going on.' He gave a triumphant nod. 'Look – all the showbiz blogs have published the photos of the events company setting up outside yours. The surprise for the public was a genius idea. And so was the media blackout.' Not wanting to crease my black Lanvin dress, I perched on the wood-carved arm of the chair, and peered across at the picture on the screen.

'Look,' he went on. 'Papa Razzle dot com. *Lara's Big Secret,* they've called it. It's a massive front-page splash. That will mean all the news sites will soon follow.'

Although I was used to being headline news, my stomach still swooped. He was right. They were fuzzy images, obviously taken with a paparazzi drone, but I could still see aerial shots of the vans outside the property, navy curlicue writing on the bonnets. *Bear Productions*. I could see the clear blue water of our swimming pool, the twelve state-of-the-art, solar-powered white sunloungers along both sides and the gold-plated cherub statue given to me by a Saudi prince, that held trays of drinks.

If I looked closely I could also make out Matthew, one leg folded up, his beautiful, golden body roasting in the sunshine. Conor read my thoughts.

'Matthew – he's scheduled to arrive about an hour before the announcement. Is that right?'

'Yes,' I told him, excitement zipping up my body. 'That's right.'

'Oh, wait, look here.' I felt the coolness of Conor's arm on mine. 'All these comments under your latest Instagram post, speculating on your *surprise announcement*. Millions of them. Some of them have called it. But other theories are crazy.' I skimmed through them and couldn't help but soak up the excitement spreading around my loyal fans. I thought about Ava and the big day ahead. How things were about to change for everyone.

'Hey, what's the time?' Conor flicked his eyes down to the silver Rolex I'd given him last year. He wore it well, even with his usual outfit of plain white T-shirt, ripped jeans and red Converse boots. 'Manny's about to arrive, isn't he?'

'Yup.' I stood, smoothing my hands down my dress. 'He'd better be on time.'

'He will be. He's got too much riding on this. Just don't tell Ava he's writing a big feature on you guys.' Conor lifted himself up. 'She'll freak. Just say he's a friend, or something. Got it?' I nodded.

I'd seen Manny's byline picture many times. He looked like the uncle out of that *My Family and Other Freaks* show that Ava loved and I knew for that reason, she would warm to him. I just hoped not too much. As for the rest of the day – well, she'd never let me down but this was bigger than anything we'd ever done together before. A new chapter. The promise of something glittering.

Conor and I had timetabled every second of the announcement, and his team back at Conor PR headquarters had scheduled everything seamlessly. Ava and I had practised every spare minute.

'Mom, OK, so listen,' she had asked me as she sat on the ostrich-feather stuffed ottoman at the end of my bed each morning. 'Have I got it right?' She had cleared her throat. 'Hi, everybody, I'm so excited for what's ahead,' she repeated. 'You've all been so supportive of us, and we are so grateful to you but everyone needs a change, in order to grow and be nourished.'

'That's it. But back straight.' I had thought about the media training I'd been given by Conor when I'd first arrived in LA.

'You need to be familiar yet distant,' he had told me. 'And number one rule. Always authentic. Anything else and they'll smell it a mile off.'

'And remember, Ava,' I had whispered. 'No ruining the surprise.' I held a finger up to my lips. 'Our secret. OK? We want it to have the biggest impact it can and so no telling.'

'I know, Mom.'

'Good girl. I can't believe how lucky I am.' She sat bolt upright then, hands in her lap. I willed her to stay in that position, because since we'd told her about the announcement she'd been fidgety. I silently prayed that when Manny turned up, she'd be on best behaviour.

'Right,' said Conor, after the doorbell went. 'Manny. You go into the living room where they're setting up everything. I'll say hello to him, bring him to you and then leave you to it. Remember. Your narrative for today is . . .' He rubbed his hands together.

'Yup,' I sighed. 'I got it. Everything is shiny and golden.' Conor looked around, his gaze settling on a huge gold statue of Buddha on the hallway table.

'That's the one. Now quick. I'm going to answer the door. Go. Get Ava too so we can introduce them.'

I started to feel hot. It was all beginning. I took one last look in the hallway mirror. I considered what Manny would make of me in the flesh, when he had a proper chance to scrutinise me. If he'd notice the three tiny freckles, triangulated on the top of my left shoulder. Or the shimmering flecks of gold in my otherwise green eyes. If he'd wonder whether my caramel-streaked hair, beautifully plumped pink lips, and thick eyelashes were the real deal. *All mine*, I'd shrug when people asked, my voice laced with false apology. Or if he'd be able to help himself wondering how much the diamonds round my neck were worth. And quick as a flash, I thought of back then. The snarl of her mouth. The glare of my hands under the bright lights. I snaked my hand up around my throat and pulled at the necklace.

Not now, I breathed. It was over ten years ago. *Not now.* No need to think of any of that. And bam, it hits me. A creeping sadness, a boa constrictor squeezing itself tight around my chest and I thought I was going to cry. No, I told myself. *Not now.*

I readjusted the diamonds, pulled my back straight, and walked into the living room.

One side of the room was filled with people in black T-shirts and trousers, all preparing for the announcement by setting up chairs and live-streaming equipment. There was a brief silence when I walked in, people side-eyeing me – some open-mouthed – before a flurry of movement started up again. I focused on Marco under one of the skylights, holding his camera in different positions, so that I didn't have to make eye contact with any strangers. Still shaken from the earlier memories and feelings, I inhaled and reminded myself of what today was for. How this was going to be a defining moment in my life. I couldn't see Ava anywhere and so I pressed zero on the intercom dial and called for her.

And then I heard Conor.

'Lara,' he shouted across the room. 'Manny's here. Time's pretty short.' He looked around and gestured across the room. 'As you can see, we've gone big.' I walked towards them.

'So nice to meet you, Manny.' I extended a hand, firming my grip around his thick, rough fingers. A fleeting look of surprise crossed his face. I saw his eyes, behind brown tortoiseshell glasses, scan the space around him; the shiny black baby grand piano next to the marble fireplace, the six Damian Hirst spin paintings I'd had commissioned and the long rows of pale grey sofas with their sumptuous cushions, arranged at exactly the same angles. He walked up to the stone sculpture in the centre of the room. I went to join him.

'That's a Henry Moore,' I said. 'Listen, Manny. I'm about to introduce you to my daughter. But I haven't told her why you're here. I don't want too much from her, given the changes that are about to happen.' He had nodded, his fingers spread across his middle.

'Sure. I get you. Any heads-up on that? The announcement, I mean.' He pushed his glasses even further up the bridge of his nose. I expected him to laugh but he remained silent, a serious look crossing his face.

'No. You'll have to wait. But let me introduce you to everyone before I get you a drink.' I waved a freshly manicured hand towards the end of the room that led into the kitchen. I sneaked a peek at our schedule book Lily had left open on the top of the piano. In it were the headshots and names of all the production staff. Each second had been rehearsed over and over again and there was no room for error. But then I saw Joan, standing by the sofa, an odd expression on her face.

'Manny, this is Joan.' I waved her over. 'Ava's nanny.' She looked pinched. I knew that expression – she saved it for when she was angry at me, something she seemed to be more and more these days. Normally I ignored it but today when I was already on high alert, I felt a surge of rage. I didn't want her poisoning the atmosphere.

'Joan,' I said. 'Please could you be an absolute dear and gather together Ava's home learning for later? And tell her to come up if you see her.' I turned to Manny. 'School of course starts soon. Joan has been Ava's nanny since day one. She's indispensable and we've been trying to keep Ava on top of things so that she's prepared when she goes back. Isn't that right, Joan?'

'Yes,' Joan replied, turning her back to me.

'Right then. Moving on. Let's begin, shall we? Music, lights and action?' I clapped my hands and just on cue, the room went silent. *Ava*.

She walked towards me, her legs making small, precise steps, as though she was on a tightrope.

'Darling!' Pride flooded my voice. 'Come here. I want to introduce you to someone.' She stepped neatly into the space I'd made for her, brown eyes shining up at me. 'I'd like you to meet my friend Manny.' She squashed her lips tight, like she was trying to stop herself from laughing.

'Hello.' She went quiet and then spoke again. 'Manny.' She clamped her hand over her mouth.

'Hello, Ava,' he said. 'It's a silly name isn't it. *Manny*.' And she opened her mouth and I saw the pink of her tongue, the flash of her small white teeth.

'It's a nice name.' She laughed again. 'I like it.' He laughed with her, his whole body softening.

'Well, thank you. It's lovely to meet you and I very much like your name too.' He turned to me. 'May I use your restroom?' he asked.

'Of course,' I said. 'Just don't go stealing our cashmere quilted toilet paper.' A dig at reporter Eva Borthwick, who'd managed to swipe a roll or two at a previous press day. I expected him to laugh with me as he had with Ava, but he'd already resumed his serious face again. I felt stung. I called over to Joan, who was standing by the door ready to leave.

'Joan, before you go, please show Manny where the bathroom is, whilst I get some last-minute make-up done. Thank you.'

I watched the back of him as he stooped under the door frame – a strange habit, given he wasn't particularly tall. Conor called over from the other side of the room.

'Guys, quick. Ava, Lara. Whilst he's in the bathroom, we need to Insta this moment. To get everyone pumped.'

'I need my make-up redone.' I beckoned them both over to the make-up station that had been set up for the day – a plain white table, in front of a huge, gilt-framed body-length mirror set up with lighting around the edges.

'Fine,' said Conor. 'Ava, sit with your mom whilst Tavie does her make-up.' At first, Ava sat on my knee.

'Ava, off of me, darling.' I pointed to Tavie, who was dabbing collagen gel onto my skin. 'Just until this is done.' Ava did as I had asked, but then got back up again.

'Mom,' she said, pressing her face into my neck. 'I'm scared.'

'You'll be OK.' I tilted my face away from hers, not wanting to ruin my make-up. 'You've been doing brilliantly.'

'No, I mean.' She lifted her head. 'It's going to be different around here after we do this, isn't it?' Her eyes swept across the room. 'Just, everything's gonna change.' The room went silent and Tavie stood, make-up sponge in mid-air. I held my breath, thinking that any minute now, Manny was going to walk through the door.

'That's OK,' I told her but really I was getting agitated to keep things going as they were. I should have realised, though, that Ava was finding it stressful too.

By the time Manny returned from the bathroom and Conor had uploaded a picture to Instagram, Ava was back to her usual self. I watched as she threw herself at the zebra-skin chaise longue across the room. I looked at the contours of her face that had been brushed with a very light powder. A small, round apple of blusher on her cheeks. She looked blissful. I knew the public would be so excited to see us, to see what the new future would hold.

'Are we ready to go?' I called over to Manny who was flicking through old editions of *Vogue*. 'And if so, where's our guest of honour? Must be here somewhere.' I forced a laugh but looked at my watch. It was later than I had thought. Even a few minutes out of schedule and the whole day would collapse. The announcement was due soon and it certainly couldn't be done without a full house.

'Anyone? Conor? Could you be an absolute love and help me have a look for Matthew?' I pulled out my phone and checked WhatsApp. Offline. And he had been for the past two hours. What the hell?

Where are you, darling? We're all here waiting. See you soon?

'One minute, everyone. I'm just going to use the bathroom.' My heart was pounding. I could see Ava in the corner, her eyes following me across the room.

Please, Ava, I begged inwardly. *Don't start asking where I'm going*. Thankfully, she stayed put, although I could see her limbs twitching to get up and follow me.

'I'll be right back.' I blew her a kiss. 'Mummy's just going to be five minutes. You're doing so well.'

I walked out the room, my jaw set tight. Someone had started pumping up the music. Rihanna. The beat sliced through me, putting me even more on edge. When I reached my study, I sat down in my custom-designed sleek orange swivel chair and WhatsApp'd Conor in the other room.

Lara: *What is going on? He's not answering my messages. Have you spoken to him?*

Conor: *I don't know. Sit tight. It'll be OK. Just get back in here and carry on as normal. Manny doesn't suspect anything. We'll just stall.*

Lara: *We can't stall. All the press are coming in about two hours. They expect me to be a diva. I don't want to give them any unnecessary ammo.*

Conor: *I'm on it. Don't worry. Sometimes it's good to show them you're a bit of a diva. Beefs up the narrative.*

Lara: *But I'm not*

I started to type and then deleted it. I had better things to be doing. I wondered whether to warn Fantine, the events manager, that things might be running late. No, leave it. Don't cause unnecessary panic.

I put down the phone and looked around the room. The oak panels were shiny and clean with no smudge marks on them. All my books, awards and blown-up magazine covers were in their right place. Except I could feel something was off. For a minute, I couldn't quite put my finger on it. I glanced around again and that was when I saw the key-box was half open. It was a padlocked box, gold-leafed and attached to the wall to the left of my desk, so that each set of keys hung down neatly on hooks.

My name was etched on the outside. On the inside there were around forty bunches of keys kept under tight security. Only Favio the estate manager and Joan had spares.

Strange, I murmured. I didn't recall opening the box. At least not in the past week and even then, I was sure to close it. And if I hadn't, Joan would have noticed, given it was on her list of things to do at the end of each night. Maybe I had opened it and forgotten. After all, my mind had been on other things for the past few days. I got up and swung it open fully, tracing my nails down the hooks.

I skimmed through each key. Everything was in its place except for the one labelled *'swimming pool annexe – indoors'* which had been put back at a different angle. I readjusted it. Weird. I shut the box, except I knew something wasn't right; an uncomfortable sensation in my stomach.

It was then I thought to check the main security system. I logged on from my phone, panning to the swimming pool annexe. The screen was blank. Someone must have obstructed the camera's view. No one could have derigged any of the recording devices without the system going off.

What the hell was going on? I thought about the last time I had used the indoor pool. Probably over a year ago, the weather was always too nice to need it. It was cleaned and maintained once a week and that would have been last Tuesday along with the outdoor pool. My mind started reeling.

Not the time to think about it, I told myself, checking my phone again. Nothing, but just as I got up to leave I got a text.

Conor: *Lara, come back. Looks weirder you having gone to bathroom for ages. We'll sort it together.*

I took a deep breath, trying to clear my mind, but at the same time anger uncoiled itself in me, at the thought that something could go wrong on my big day. Everything had been organised with such precision and now *this*. I wondered about my plans for next year. How they'd be affected if this didn't go as I'd predicted. I steeled myself against any such outcome and strode right back into the room.

Ava was in the corner playing with a small Tamagotchi toy she'd got as a present the week before. Everyone was busy setting up. Manny sat on one of the sofas on his phone.

'Ten minutes,' I said to everyone. 'I'm so sorry. Things have been a little held up.'

I walked over to Conor who was sitting showing Marco something on his phone.

'I can't carry on like this,' I hissed. 'Pretending everything's normal.'

'You're doing a good job. Just focus. You're a master at this. OK? And the gossip blogs are going mad trying to find out what's going on. Everyone's on tenterhooks. So this isn't such a bad thing.'

'OK but, Conor, come on. Do something, please. This is all going to shit. This is the start of everything. You said so yourself. How can you be so calm? It's your reputation on the line too, don't forget.'

'Ten minutes.' He pointed at his phone. 'Let's just give him ten more minutes. I'll set a timer and if Matthew hasn't arrived by then we'll think again. Yes?'

'Fine.' I gritted my teeth, all the while the lights seared right through me. I barely noticed Ava, still in the corner. Marco got up and was checking angles and lights and held up his wrist for me to see his watch.

I looked over at Conor's phone. Ten minutes. I could do this. I relented and ended up chatting to the production staff for what felt like hours, for want of anything else to do, all the while feeling more and more like I was going to combust. And then Conor's phone alarm went off. Ten minutes was up. He shook his head at me. I took that as read that he still hadn't been able to get hold of Matthew.

'Right.' Conor clapped his hands. 'I know you have all been so patient and so good, but I'm afraid our guest of honour, Matthew Raine, has had to deal with an emergency at home. His father.' I saw Conor fumbling on his thoughts, trying to work out if Matthew had ever mentioned his father in public, whether he even had a father who was still alive. And then I realised that despite Conor's earlier nonchalance, he was now nervous, his smile frozen onto his face, blinking as though he had a piece of grit in his eye. He'd prepared this day so that hundreds of press turned up. We'd have to give them something else big if Matthew didn't show. My mind sped up trying to think of possibilities.

I thought of Derek Raine, and wanted to reassure Conor he was OK. That Matthew's dad was not going to be in the spotlight anytime soon. And then I made a mental note to get Conor to stand outside and intercept Matthew when he finally showed his face, so he didn't blow our cover.

'Manny, I'm sorry about this.' I clasped my hands tight. 'It's awful form to do this to you. Keep you waiting when you've come all this way. Look. Do you want to, I don't know, sit?'

'Oh please, I'm used to waiting around for interviews. This is nothing. I've left my laptop charger in the car anyway,' Manny said. 'I'll just go out and get it whilst we wait.' He jangled his car keys at me. 'Do I just let security know I'm going out?'

'That's right. They've got your name and details so they know you're on the property. Rosa will see you out and deal with our security keypad.' I pressed the intercom and dialled into the kitchen.

'Rosa, if you could just see Manny Berkowitz out the house, I'd be very grateful.' I turned to smile at him and as I did so, I caught sight of a Hermes 'H' keyring he had hooked onto his finger. On it was a white and silver fob. My heart jumped and at first I didn't know why. Then I realised. *That was it*, I thought. It was meant to have a fob. The swimming pool annexe key. It was meant to have a golden fob and it was gone. It was possible to use the fob to open the door to the annexe. I started to feel light-headed but knew I had to hold it together. Why would anyone want to go to the indoor pool when it wasn't even in use? I was absolutely certain it hadn't been me. I gripped my fingers around the diamond necklace again, feeling unable to breathe, that familiar feeling wrapping itself around me.

'I'll see you in just a minute,' I called out, looking at Conor. It was only then that I realised Ava, at this point, had also disappeared. All that was left was her Tamagotchi, its eyes blinking and mouth grinning at me, from the chaise longue.

You know when something bad happens? Like, real bad and there are some people that just get super loud? Like, the more foghorn their voice, the more they think they are going to erase every shitty feeling they've got? It's like that here. Online and offline. A massive echo chamber of thoughts and emotions. It's like everyone's personally offended by this awful shit that's going down.

Let's take a deep breath. Concentrate on what's at stake here. A small girl's life. Not some shitty grudges you guys have been holding about something totally unrelated. Yeah?

In terms of news of Ava there's been nothing so far. I'm still here, in the canyon. It's hot. So hot. I keep peeling my clothes off me. We've all given up and the sweat's now just running off our faces into our eyes, and down our faces. Everyone's blinking like there's some crazy dust storm about. If you wanna help, bring fans. Those small plastic ones.

Lara King hasn't come out her house since she left the press conference, but I can tell you now that in the past few minutes, the film star Matthew Raine has made a statement, through his people, to say that he will keep us all posted. We'd all been keeping our eyes peeled (try admitting you don't care about seeing

31

Matthew Raine in the flesh even at a time like this. I promised Granma I'd try and get a photo. He's in that new sci-fi series on Netflix too. Oh my God. Meeting him is top of her bucket list!).

'I'll be in and out,' he said through his people, 'helping the search but also trying my best to support Lara. She's doing the very, very best she can under such awful circumstances, and we thank you from the bottom of our hearts for all your support.' But then people tell me that he's made his way back to the police station, so we're not sure what strange things are going on. I'll be sure to keep you posted as and when.

Here with the latest updates on missing Ava King, brought to you by Lara and Ava King's number one fan.

Twitter: @ryan_gosling_wannabe

Forgive me. I'm not thinking straight. I haven't even introduced myself. I'm guessing most of you already know who I am. For those of you who don't – who truly don't – given that I'm begging you all to help me find my daughter, I think it's probably a good place to start.

My name is Lara King. I'm thirty-six years old. I'm a star. A celebrity. If the papers are to be believed, I'm a global phenomenon. Whatever that means to you, to me, to any of us. My daughter is six. And well, you'd have to have been hiding under a rock in the past few hours not to know what's happened. You won't quite know the finer details surrounding her disappearance yet. But I'm coming on to that.

When Detective Mcgraw finished asking me about the events of the day, and went on to ask about Ava's father, I almost forgot where I was.

'Ava's father?' I placed a hand on my chest. 'She doesn't know him.'

'And you, Ms King?' I looked at him, the answer on the tip of my tongue but then I remembered I was here. In my study, with the huge windows, the crystal chandelier, the globe that Ava loved to spin, and the smell of old books. I was here, and my daughter was missing. This wasn't a chat show where I'd laugh and tell the host that some things had to be kept secret, whilst fluttering my hand in front of my eyes. 'I'm aware that this might be sensitive.' He took a breath. 'But if you could give us a name. Details. Some insight into his character, how you met.' His eyes swivelled across the room at this point and rested again on the photo of me when I was pregnant. 'Please.'

'But, Ava's father? Why would you need to know?'

'We need to just really explore every single avenue and make sure that no stone has been left unturned.' He took a breath. 'It might help us look into new areas.'

'This is sensitive. You're right. She doesn't know him. And nor do I. He was an acquaintance. At a party. I don't even know whose party it was. I ended up there after some awards ceremony.'

'Don't worry, Ms King. Please. No judgement. A name is all we need.'

'I'd had too much champagne,' I told him, shaking all over. 'I don't normally drink. I guess it was just a stupid mistake. Except, of course it gave me Ava.'

'So you don't actually know who he is?' Detective Mcgraw said lightly.

I thought about the due diligence that had gone into finding Ava's birth father. That no one had as yet succeeded. Not the public. Not the most eager of press who'd found a blank space on her birth certificate where her paternity should have been.

'It was an Oscars after party. Hosted by Lucy Wigmore. That's what I can remember. The guy – he was called Tom. Weston, I *think*. Or Westfield. Westburt. I've never been able to properly recall.' I swallowed. I'd never said those words out loud before but of course, everything was at stake here. 'I've googled variations. Looked for him. I remember he was a Brit. But no, he doesn't know.'

'OK. Thank you, Ms King. Ever hire someone to help you find him?'

'No,' I snapped.

'You never wanted to tell Ava who he was? Was she interested?'

'No.' I rubbed at a small stain on my desk. I didn't know why. It had been there for years and was ingrained into the wood. 'Look—' I felt he wasn't going to stop until I gave him some sort of explanation and I wanted him off my back. 'In my position,' I said slowly, 'I need to be careful about who I trust. Who I let into my life. That kind of thing. Ava and I are happy as we are. We've built up a team of people around us that we trust. Most of whom were with us before we got into the public eye.'

'All right. Thank you, Ms King.' I thought about the press. The lengths that they had gone to, to delve into my life. Very imaginative, some of them, I had to say.

'Whilst I'm on the subject,' said Detective Mcgraw, 'is there anyone else you can think of who might've known your whereabouts today?'

I shook my head, thinking back to this morning.

'No. It was just us. It was all meant to be perfect.' I thought about Joan. How pleased she'd been when I'd told her it was mother-daughter time.

'All right. Anything you can think of that didn't seem right to you in the past few days?'

'I don't think so. The only people that would have known we were out are those who normally know our schedule. Matthew. Joan. Lily. She's my PA. She knew. I'd signed off for the day. And Conor, too, my publicist.'

'Has Joan been with you long?'

'Six years.'

'She's good with Ava?'

'Yes. She is.' I wanted to say lots of things. How she'd said some hurtful things lately. But that I'd managed to keep myself from getting too angry. But my throat got all closed up, and all I could do was nod.

'Right. Thank you, Ms King. That will do for now. I'm going back to the station for an update meeting and I'll be speaking to Conor. I'll ring you straight back.' He walked over to the door of my study. 'Nice picture.' He pointed to a black and white shot of me and Matthew behind the door, both of us facing the camera.

'Thank you.'

'Is he good with her too?'

'Who? Matthew? Yes. He's good with Ava. She loves him. Where is he? I need him back soon.'

'I believe he's down at the station helping out with some enquiries.'

'Why?' I said, standing up from my seat. 'Why isn't he here?'

'Ms King, I'm sure he'll be home soon. I'll make a call. Nice he's good with her.' He motioned his head towards the picture again. 'She saw you two getting on lately? Ava?'

'Yes. She did. She was excited about the announcement and the changes it would bring.'

'You ever fight?' I was about to answer when we heard footsteps. Conor. I recognised the shlump-shlump of his baseball boots and then the door started to open. Detective Mcgraw took a step back.

'Conor. Thank God you are here—' But before I could get much further, he was holding his hand out to Detective Mcgraw.

'Sorry. Let me introduce myself. I'm Conor. Lara's publicist. I couldn't help overhearing you. They are the perfect couple.' He looked right at me, as though he was trying to tell me something. 'Aren't you, Lara? I haven't seen them fight yet. God.' He turned to me. 'Lara. I'm so sorry. I really am.'

'We don't fight.' I looked at the picture of us. It had been taken for *Vanity Fair* only six weeks after we'd first got together. Our first front cover. We'd shifted a lot of copies. I remembered the way I'd leaned back into Matthew. The way he'd kissed the top of my head. 'We bicker,' I said. 'But we don't really fight.'

'Listen.' Detective Mcgraw guided Conor out the room and started to shut the door. 'Conor, if you could give us one minute alone. Thank you.' He turned to me. '*Fight*, Lara. By fight I mean aggressive behavior towards each other. That Ava would pick up on.' I thought of my girl. How she'd been when she first found out that I was going out with Matthew Raine. 'Can I bring him in for show and tell?' she'd laughed. I hadn't been surprised. The perfectly structured face – that smile – the one that held the world alight.

'There's no way,' I tell him again. 'There's no way she heard us fight, because we didn't fight today. Or anytime recently. You saw how happy she was during our announcement.'

'I did.'

'Please, are we finished now? She's out there. Ava's out there. Somewhere. And you're in here asking me questions that aren't relevant.' I'd managed to control myself before, but the words started to come out in great gasps.

'OK. Thank you, Ms King. So you wouldn't say you and Matthew are having a slightly tricky time together?'

A slightly tricky time. Joan's phrasing. It was *exactly* the type of language she'd use. She must have said something to Detective Mcgraw. I could hear her voice now, her quietly clipped English tones, the slow nod of her head.

'Me and Matthew having a tricky time? How strange.' I repeated, 'No.'

'And would you say you are a good mother?'

'Yes. Yes, I would.' What had Joan been telling him? I didn't want to start asking myself such big questions at such an awful time. I knew I would start to spiral even more. I told myself to put Joan out my head, and concentrate on my daughter.

'OK. That's all. Thank you. I expect Conor will be wanting to discuss press strategy with you. I'll leave you now. And, Ms King?'

'Yes?' Images of Ava flooded my brain. The soft ebb of her breath. The way she'd kick her right leg out when she was getting tired, or hungry. All the earlier adrenaline seeped out of my body. I felt heavy and absolutely sick with longing to see her. I ached all over. I wanted to look for her around the house. Imagine the way she'd run up to me as she heard me at the top of the stairs. 'Mom. Mom, can I wear some lipstick?' she'd shout. I pressed my knuckles into my chest. The pain was becoming unbearable.

'I know how difficult this must be for you. Given the position you are in too. But we're doing absolutely everything we can to find her.'

Again, I found I couldn't speak.

'I'll make sure that Matthew gets back to you soon. Anything else you need?'

'No,' I wanted desperately to scream but I just about managed to control my voice. 'Just my daughter back. Please.'

Detective Mcgraw left the room, his gaze sweeping the walls as he walked out the door. I sat back down at my desk but the pain was too great to sit still, so I got up. And then I couldn't do that either, so I sat back down. And then I saw Joan out the corner of my eye talking to Detective Mcgraw. She was doing that thing where she tucked her hair behind her ear, but over and over again like she was on fast-forward.

I tried to peer through the door to make out what she was saying but her mouth was obscured by Conor's arm. I leaned right over my desk and as I did so, everything fell to the floor.

'All right?' The door crashed open and Detective Mcgraw, Joan and Conor watched as I bent down and scooped up the items that had fallen to the ground. I started to cry again. The small blue glass dolphin that I'd bought back for Ava from filming in Toronto, the paperweight from *The Larry Bauer Show*, the small silver statue from England, with my name engraved on the bottom. The one I'd been handed the moment my life had changed forever. The very moment, in fact, that it had all started.

'Tell me the story again. Please,' Ava would beg, pirouetting with it above her head. She loved nothing more than hearing it, over and over. My rise to fame. 'Please.' I held it to my chest, pleading for her to come home. But when I could bear it no longer, I put it in a drawer and slammed it shut, layers of sadness clamouring for attention.

'Come on.' Conor picked up some papers that had floated to the other side of the room. 'I'll help you. Do you want something? I can get you stuff. To help you, I mean. Take the edge off.' I thought about the last time I'd taken some downers after a bout of insomnia. Over a year ago – and how out of control I'd felt and how much I'd disliked it. Despite feeling as though I was climbing the walls, I would be doing Ava a disservice if I wasn't fully compos mentis now. I shook my head.

'Fine.' He shook his phone up at me. 'If you change your mind just tell me. And in the meantime you can give me the answers to some stuff the press have been asking.'

'The press? Please, can you just deal with it?'

'I'm sorry, Lara. I need you here to strategise with me. We can't get anything wrong.' He put his face right up to mine. So close I could see small bumps around his jawline and smell the scent of fresh mint gum. 'I know this is traumatic for you but we need the public onside. To get this absolutely one hundred per cent right. It's probably one of the most important things that we can do in the search to help her. Given you can't go out there looking for her. This is something we *can* do. Do you see? You've got the entire world watching.' He unwrapped another piece of gum from his pocket and bit into half of it. 'You've got all of this at your fingertips. That's more than anyone else has. So we cannot put a foot wrong now.' I felt galvanised by the thought that there was *something* I could be doing. I knew we had to be careful. I did know that. I knew a hundred per cent.

Because I knew how it all worked, you see? I knew entirely that this was up to me and the way I played it.

I knew, right at that moment, that the entire world could choose to love me or hate me. That they could choose to help me or vilify me.

I inhaled and shut my eyes.

The idea of it scared me though. More than anyone would ever know. Because I was aware that if I put one foot wrong, one tiny step out of line, a mistimed breath, or an ill-judged word and something bad happened to my little girl – people lost interest in looking for her – moved onto the next story – or even worse, turned on me, then really, I would only have myself to blame.

August 23rd 2018

1030hrs

I thought about what Conor had said. *Everyone's going shit-crazy online*. Everyone was watching, waiting with bated breath for the big announcement. Millions of people. I'd set everything on this announcement and was desperate for it to run smoothly. And yet the compulsion to find out what was going on in the swimming pool annexe had become too strong.

It would take a couple of minutes to get to the pool to find out why the key fob was missing and why someone had obstructed the CCTV. I needed to make sure everything was in order before Manny started snooping around. I'd promised that he could have a brief look at the house.

'Conor,' I shouted across the room, as though I didn't have a care in the world. 'I'm just going to my study. To call Lily in the office. OK? Check she's confirmed a few last-minute things.'

Before he could stop me, I left. On the way back from the pool, I'd call Joan on the intercom to ask her to bring Ava back immediately, because I had no idea where she was. I knew she wouldn't have gone far. She didn't like being alone or far away from us both.

I walked out of the living room to the back of the house. I opened the door and walked through a large Tuscan-inspired courtyard, used primarily as a walkway to the outdoor swimming pool. This opened up to a back lawn. I thought I heard footsteps behind me but when I looked, it was silent. At the very bottom of the garden was the swimming pool annexe. It was a sleek, low white building but given it was never used, I had plans to develop it into a beautiful white and airy third guest house.

I could already see that the door was ajar. Fear pulsed through me. There were strange, tinny noises in the background. The thud of footsteps and then urgent whispers. And then the sound of faraway music. Someone must have brought their own speakers which meant that either they wouldn't have known about the Sonos sound system that was installed in the building, or they didn't want anyone to know they had been using the place.

I took my shoes off, my feet hitting the soft spikes of grass. The garden had been freshly watered and the drops cooled my soles.

Leaving my high heels on the ground, I tiptoed towards the door of the pool. I could see someone had tried to wedge a chair under the door handle to keep it shut, but for some reason the chair had fallen to the floor.

It was open wide enough that I could just about see through the crack in the hinge, although when I looked I could only see a flash of blue and the mosaic tiles surrounding the pool. It was at that point, though, that I heard a rustle, and a cough and something that sounded like someone sobbing.

Weird, I thought. But surely only one of the staff, taking advantage of their day off, using the facilities on their own time.

I thought of who I had hired lately that might do such a thing. Rosa and Marcy had been with me for five years and I trusted them implicitly. The gardener? He was pretty new and Marcy had told me he'd been helping himself to a suspicious amount of coconut water from the fridge but he was in Mexico for two weeks. I resolved to go through everyone's employment contract again. No personal use of the facilities without explicit permission from myself.

I pushed the door open a fraction to see what was going on inside. I watched, for what seemed like minutes but could have only been seconds. The more I saw, the more I wanted to scream, my body alight with fear. And then I felt a soft tapping on my back. I nearly jumped, but something stopped me. Instead, I turned around and that's when I saw Ava's face behind me. Her golden hair was tied back and her eyes looked huge, and she was trembling all over. She looked very young in her white dressing gown. Almost like a ghost of herself. She was peering around me, directly into the pool house, watching the entire horrific scene unfold. I turned back round again to look inside the annexe. The actual pool was empty. The only signs of someone being in there was a small black box by the side of the water and then the strange sounds again, coming from the corner of the room. Howling. Crying.

I pushed Ava back as hard as I could and slammed the door shut. My skin tingled. I thought about what I'd just seen and how I would explain it to Ava if she asked. Sex, drugs – all of that in its many guises – I could talk to her about quite easily – but *this* – no. Not this. I'd have to shut her down if she questioned me. That split-second image had the power to destroy my entire life if anyone found out. And given everything that was about to happen – the announcement – it made it, if that was possible, even worse. I tried to control my fear but the slithering knots inside my stomach, the drill of my heartbeat, meant I was right on the edge of a full-blown panic attack.

'Ava, get up,' I hissed, because she had slipped over on the wet grass. I knew I had to keep calm, otherwise I'd start screaming and I couldn't alert anyone to what was going on. Mud and grass had stained Ava's dressing gown and my breath was now coming in jagged waves.

'Did you see it?' I said smiling as broadly as I could, despite the fact I thought I was going to pass out. Oh God, I was thinking. Please, let no one come here now. I thought of who might find us. I listed through the possibilities in my mind. At least that gave me some feeling of control. Marcy and Rosa were in the kitchen. Joan was the only person who might have come and tried to find Ava. I prayed she'd be waiting in the house. I wasn't sure I would be able to pretend everything was normal after what I'd just seen play out in my own home. The place that was my haven. The walls that were meant to protect us.

Ava didn't speak but her neck made tiny movements to the left and to the right like a baby bird.

'Ah, just wondered if you had noticed the new painting in the pool house. Did you see what was going on in there? I was just checking it had gone up. They might want to do a . . .' I looked around and thought for a minute I had felt rain, but realised that was ridiculous, 'photoshoot in there. Good lighting. Let's go back, darling, shall we?' I thought I heard a noise again then. The light shushing of soft-soled shoes on the grass but when I looked, I saw no one. I must be going mad, I thought. *Fear.*

Ava looked at me then. Her skin had paled underneath her tan and I wondered what I looked like. Whether my eyes had taken on that sunken look that they do when I go into shock. I reminded myself to ask Tavie to redo my make-up.

'What was that?' she asked. 'In the pool annexe? Why did you push me like that?'

'A surprise, my darling.' I clapped my hands together, trying to forget what I'd just seen, and trying to get her to do the same. It was countdown time until now and I needed calm and perfection. 'I can't tell you now. But I promise you'll love it. Now shall we go back inside?'

'Yes.' She grabbed at my hand. 'Yes. Let's.' Her arm was still shaking. 'Please—' She pulled at my hand. 'What was happening?' she said over and over. 'I saw. Is that . . . was that someone . . .'

'I don't know,' I told her. Because in part, that had been the truth although fragments of conversations were now coming back to me and then it all made sense. I started to piece things together and it meant that unwittingly, I was a part of it all too. *Oh God.* 'You didn't see anything, did you now?' I looked down at her. 'Did you?' I repeated. I could feel the crack of her knuckles in mine. 'Did you, Ava?'

She shook her head.

'But what was that—'

'Shhhhh,' I snapped. 'Because if you did see anything, or you told anyone, bad things might happen.' I knelt down, careful to pull up my dress. 'And you don't want very bad things to happen, do you, darling?'

'No. What kind of bad things?' She rubbed at the side of her tiny, freckled nose. I thought of her laughing earlier with Manny, and how different she looked now, the things she had just witnessed seeping up from her subconscious, casting a different light in the black of her pupils.

'Just, bad stuff. You're too young to really know. But you must forget everything you just saw. OK?'

'I want to tell Joan,' she cried. 'She told me I should tell her. Everything that goes on. She could help?'

'Did she now,' I said, keeping my voice light. 'Definitely not Joan, because then she might leave us. OK? That's the thing. If she finds out, she might decide to go. Do you want that?' I thought back to when Joan had first arrived from England six years ago just after Ava had been born. The way she had stood at our front door with one, large metal suitcase that she'd padlocked twice.

'Joan said she'd never leave me,' Ava said.

'But she will. If she knows what you saw. OK? So you have to promise not to say anything. Or she'll pack her bags tomorrow. All right? We don't want her to go, do we? We couldn't manage without Joan.' It was true, I thought. She'd made herself totally indispensable to us now with Ava crying and crying if she took more than three days off in a row. I knew it was cruel to scare Ava like that, but there was no other way. I couldn't risk everything being destroyed. We were at the cusp of greatness. *True greatness*, I told myself. The pinnacle of fame. And it had to be kept that way.

'No.' Ava shook her head. 'No. I never want Joan to go.' And the expression on her face at that point told me everything I needed to know – that I was safe. That despite the horrors of it all, despite the fact that this would probably give her nightmares for the rest of her life, Ava had weighed things up in her head and her heart, and would never, ever breathe a word of the things she'd just seen.

Ryans-world.com

Entry: August 26th, 1730hrs

Author: Ryan

The cops – they're still running all about the place. They're everywhere. Stationed all over the road. Stopping cars, banging on the roofs. 'Wind down your window, ma'am. We want to know where you were earlier, if you happened to have seen this little girl.'

I can see heads shaking. 'No, no I haven't seen her.' Nothing.

Word has it that Matthew still hasn't been to the house again. He didn't speak to any of the paps like he normally does, or give his trademark wave when he left the police station; in fact, he gave the paps the runaround, so no one knows where he is now. He just got into a black sedan with this dude who looked like a plain-clothed police officer and drove back into the direction of *Los Palisades*.

And now I'm wondering, if he's not there, then who is looking after Lara? So let's dissect things here and talk about what we do know. There's that PA of hers, Lily. There's Conor. Ava's nanny, Joan. And a couple of her security. All those same faces that I recognise from the pap shots and the show. It's good to know she's got a loyal entourage. Those that have been with her since day one.

But so far, I can tell you from a pap contact of mine that there's been absolutely no one else going into her house apart from the detective running the case. And that's what I'm finding so heartbreaking. Where is her family? Where are her friends? She's lost her daughter and for all intents and purposes, she's all alone. Seventeen million followers on Instagram. Sixteen million on Twitter. And not one person with her when she needs it the most.

Here with the latest updates on missing Ava King, brought to you by Lara and Ava King's number one fan.

Twitter: @ryan_gosling_wannabe

I thought about how much everyone knew of the 'real me'. How much *I* knew of the real me. I certainly didn't know that if my daughter ever disappeared into thin air, that I'd actually feel it in each and every cell of my body. That I'd be unable to sit still. That Conor would be talking to me about strategy, about public image, and all the while, I'd be twisting and turning, desperate for some relief from the searing pain.

I didn't know, either, that my thoughts would race faster than my heart. I didn't know that I would be capable of conversation. But it seemed that I was. I well and truly was, because words were streaming out my mouth. I couldn't make sense of them, though. It was like my body and mind had become two separate entities – trapped in those fleeting moments before an opioid painkiller sets to work.

'What can we do, Conor?' I pleaded. 'We need to think of something. Anything.'

'Look, Lara.' He was so close I could smell the hot tang of his breath over the gum. 'Firstly, I've bought you a laptop.'

'Thank you,' I said.

'I've been thinking about it,' he said as I loaded it up.

'And what?'

51

'I think we need to add a more real-life element to things. To keep the public engagement high. So perhaps we need to drip-feed a few pictures of you when you were younger. Not quite so manicured. Maybe just after you gave birth.'

'Manicured?' I started to tell him that I'd had my nails done only yesterday and then I almost laughed. He's not talking about nails.

'We just need to be totally authentic. Show you as a real person now. A mother who has lost her child.'

'She's coming back though,' I told him, but the words sounded uncertain even to me.

'You as in the real Lara King that no one else has access to. Not even your family,' and then he shut up before he said too much. 'I mean your family over here. So photos from your past. Not from when you were young, though. We don't want them getting you confused with Ava. I mean you look so similar.'

'No,' I snapped. 'That's not happening.'

'Look, Lara.' He held up his hands. 'No one will be looking at your past mistakes.' In the years I'd been in LA, I'd told Conor bits about what had happened in England. Nothing close to the full story, though. 'Believe me' – the tone of his voice became more forceful – 'your humility about everything that happened before you got here was what made people love you over here, so let's keep to that narrative. And anyway' – he waved his hand in the air – 'no one remembers that. Look at you. Bad girl gone good. It's how you built yourself. People saw you had to work at it. That you' – he looked around again, pointing at the hi-tech music system and touch-screen controls in the corner of the room – 'weren't just some rich girl who never lifted a finger. You reinvented yourself after all that crap in England.' I heard the tap of his fingers on the side of the desk. 'So don't worry. They'll be right behind you. OK?'

I thought back to 'all that crap in England' and what Conor would say if he knew everything but at the same time felt a surge of pride at everything I'd achieved.

'OK,' I told him. 'OK, fine. I'll think of something.'

'Good. And, Lara, is there anything you need to tell me? I don't want any surprises in the press. All right? I like to think I know most of the skeletons in your closet, but if things are going to be leaked, I need to strategise in advance.' He twisted a small gold ring on his little finger. I thought about the ways in which he'd 'strategised' before, and how inappropriate that would seem now.

The time I'd been caught speeding. 'Look, don't do it again, please,' he had warned me. 'But I've got something that will distract the public.' It's when I'd first really seen how it all worked. 'This one never fails, let me prove it to you.' Conor had photographed me in front of a black and white marble bathroom top at a party, with a twenty-dollar note on the side. #crazytimes, he had captioned it and loaded it onto Instagram. The more eagle-eyed viewers had posted right away. They had circled the white threads of marble. '*Is that DRUGS?*' they had written. '*Jesus. I never had Lara down as a coke-head.*' And that's where Conor had worked his magic. Zooming in on the detailed lines of marble. #thatsitalysfin-estmarble #saynotodrugs. Bingo, everyone had forgotten about my brush with the law.

'There's really nothing to say,' I told him. 'You know everything.'

'Good. Because if there was, it might fuck up the investigation.' As he said this, I started to feel dizzy. 'And,' he went on, 'how about we focus on the announcement too? I think the public will be even more receptive to helping find Ava. Don't you? If they are reminded of how happy you were and how much you both had to look forward to?' I thought back to this time three days ago and how much I had to lose if things went wrong. About the things I'd seen in the pool annexe, and how they had nothing to do with me. I wasn't prepared to let other people's lives get entwined with mine.

'Wait, Conor.' My hands shook and I blinked away the stinging liquid from my eyes. 'No.'

'Lara? Are you OK?' Conor slid off the desk. 'Lara? Is there something you need to tell me? We can sort it out. Whatever it is. Especially if it might impact the investigation. What is it? The announcement? England? Tell me. Whatever it is, I can help.'

I thought of England. Me on the stage. The cheers of my name. *Lara. Lara.* The screams, the echoes, the whistling. My spine, infused with the blissed-out warmth of love being heaped upon me by the crowds.

'No,' I said, again. I noticed three lines of sweat trail down Conor's forehead. I thought of the small silver statue in my study. The way it felt in my hands. Cold. But it made my blood feel hot. And then a flash of my daughter. '*Mom. Tell me. Please. Tell me the story.*' Her face enraptured, her breath hot, as I went through the details over and over again.

'There's nothing I need to tell you. Release some more pictures from the announcement day,' I told Conor. 'The ones from backstage.' If I gave him that much, he might stop snooping around. And as for what had happened in the pool annexe, I had made up my mind then and there not to think of it again. I had to focus on finding Ava. What we saw on the day of the announcement had absolutely nothing to do with our lives. *Nothing.* That's what I was telling myself, anyway.

'Thanks. Listen. I've got to go and meet Detective Mcgraw now. You all right here now for a bit? I'm going to go and get Joan and then I'll be right back later on.'

'I'm fine,' I told him. In truth, I wanted a moment alone to unravel all the thoughts going on in my head.

I knew that public scrutiny was going to be at full pace. That probably right about now, instead of helping me find Ava the press would be approaching people from my old life. Unearthing old friends from school. Offering money to those who needed it, for a kiss and tell.

There was nothing I could do about that, though. Stuck here in my home. I thought of what Conor had told me when he'd first signed me.

Control what you can. Leave what you can't.

I thought about what had happened in the past three days, since the announcement. The public reaction. How absolutely extraordinary it had been.

And so with that in mind, I went online to Media Spy, where I could get all the latest information on every celebrity. And that's when I first saw people talking. Just a few discussion threads at first. One entitled *England.* One entitled *Ava's dad.* I felt sick. Neither thread had gained much traction. After all, there were more pressing topics that were at play but I could sense that something might stick and that it'd multiply like a virus.

Unable to bring myself to open any of the threads, I slammed my computer shut. Surely there was something more useful I could do to help find Ava, than trawling through useless gossip forums?

So I set to work calling people in high-profile places; heads of missing people charities and other celebrities who had been ambassadors in that field. If people were surprised to hear from me, they didn't show it. A couple of times I had to hang up, because it all got too much, and I couldn't stop thinking about England and the things Conor had said to me. That if I didn't tell him everything, it'd fuck up the investigation. How could it? From back then. From all those years ago? On top of that, I couldn't shake the sense that there was something else I could be doing to help find my daughter. Something that was much closer to home.

England, July 2004

I didn't see him at first; the man who would change my life. My senses had been elsewhere: the tang of sweat, citrus aftershave and bubble-gum perfume, the bitter smell of chemicals in the air. The floor had pulsed to the sound of Shapeshifters' 'Lola's Theme', juddering up and down as though it might suddenly give way, and we'd drop into nothingness. A great drunken heap of us mangled and bloodied on the concrete below. Just as I'd been thinking about the news story – how my friends and family would react to the headlines – I saw him next to me, haloed by a bright white light behind him, like I was staring right into the tunnel of my own death. The crowd parted and there he was, hands in his pockets, white, flashy trainers on, like he's king of the fucking world.

'All right?'

Of course, I couldn't hear him over the music, so he had come up close.

'All right? These guys giving you trouble?' He was covered in a rich, wooded scent. He looked around the room, and then settled his gaze back on to me.

'No,' I told him, willing him to go away. 'I'm fine,' I shouted again.

'New to London?' he asked.

'No,' I lied, wondering how he could tell.

'What's your name?'

'Lara,' I told him. 'I'm with someone.'

He watched as I peered around him through the red curtain, trying to make out the bodies inside. We'd had a heads-up earlier from a mate of Hannah's who worked on Dancing Buddha's guest list.

'They're all going to be there,' she had told me, swaying her hips side to side. 'All of them. Straight from the match. You in?'

I hadn't even bothered to reply and we'd spent the day preparing – me, watching Hannah put on make-up and then both of us getting dressed. Her in a bodycon dress, pink with white stripes, me in a black strapless number with a sweetheart neckline.

'What?' I said to him. 'Please—' I turned to look for Hannah but she was already at the bar. I pulled the top of my dress up, my hands flat against my chest, so my skin was fully covered. 'My mates, they're all over there,' I told him again. I pointed over to Hannah, who was standing, elbows right back against the bar top, right leg kicked out, and the glint of gold as the taller of the two men gestured to the bar staff.

'I've got to—'

He took my hand and I felt the lights, the heat burning me up. 'It's not what you think,' he said. 'I don't . . .'

'You don't what?'

'Look, I've got a girlfriend. A fiancée, rather. Her name's Kaycee.' He started to rummage around in his coat pocket. 'Here.' He opened his wallet. 'She's beautiful. Anyway, see, there's this thing' – he sounded more animated now – 'this competition. *Idolz*. I thought that you . . .'

'What on earth are you talking about? *Idolz*?' The name rang a bell, I just couldn't think where from. 'If you're so set on building your life together with this Kaycee chick, then stop following me.' I had been bolstered by Hannah, waving me over. *Competition*. I'd been warned about men like him. Probably wanting to charge me the earth for some seedy shots in my underwear, with the promise he could make me a model. I thought of Hannah's earlier insistence that she put some more make-up on me. I'd told her no. I looked over as she pointed to a green bottle with a bright orange label. He slipped his wallet away and grabbed at my arm again. 'Wait. I need to talk to you,' he said. 'I heard you.'

'You heard me?' The inside of my lips had caught on my teeth, and I licked my lips. 'No you didn't. You can't hear a thing in this place. Now please—' I swivelled around as best I could and was about to grab the hand of a total stranger for help, when he leaned in close to my ear and started to hum so I could almost feel the tickle of small hairs deep down in my ear canal.

'Recognise that?' he said. And he did it again, this time a bit louder, faster. He was smiling, clicking his fingers and nodding his head as though he'd been proven right about something – but I didn't know what.

'No idea.' My ribcage clamped around my heart.

'You do.' He had sung again. 'See?' And I listened to the song. The lyrics.

'If only, if only I could . . .'

And I'd thought back to three hours earlier. On the graffitied bench outside Hannah's one-bed in Greenford, an old raincoat covering the wooden slats, vodka bottle being passed from hand to hand. Hannah, blowing smoke rings and me singing, *'If only, if only I could*,' and I wanted to shout for help but I was frozen to the spot.

'Did you follow me?' I walked off as I was shouting. I could feel the thud of my pulse right through my neck. 'What the fuck.' I was flooded with anger, 'You followed me. You freak.'

'Look, I'm not here to hurt you.' He grabbed at my arm again. 'I'm really not. I want to help you. Seriously, I want to, look, wait—' but over the sound of his voice, my words, *my* song, echoed right through me and before I knew it, I'd pushed my way into the crowd.

'Lara,' said Hannah, 'who's that guy?'

'No one,' I told her. If I ignore the fact he'd followed me, he'd disappear. We managed to get rid of him soon after. Hannah had worked us closer to the VIP lounge. And it was there that we'd been waved right in behind the hallowed red curtain. The players, they were all there. Frank. John. Didier. All of them from Hannah's favourite team. And as the night wore on, I forgot about the man who had been following me. Despite the players whistling me over, I stood back, still feeling uncomfortable from my earlier exchange. I watched Hannah down drinks until the whites of her eyes skimmed her lids. She'd been taken by one of the guys into the very back of the VIP lounge into a dark corner that had been cordoned off completely. I saw limbs of strangers, shifting, shaping; heads bent right close to the table top, one nostril shut tight with a rigid finger. I had gone after her, but had been pushed back by another guy in a suit. 'She's fucking hot, mate. But she's jailbait.' He had pointed at me and then there was a gust of cold air as a back door to the club had opened, and all I could see was a dark alleyway, a hem of pink. And then, the slam of a car door, red lights glowing in the dark, the sound of splattering road-water and Hannah had gone.

I was alone, wondering if I was safer here without my friend, or whether I should go back into the other room where the guy had a chance of finding me.

Then I wondered how I was going to get home. I had precisely one pound in my pocket, no wingman in Hannah, and my bedsit was at least a four-mile walk from here. I picked up a drink from the table next to me, the warm dregs of a flat Red Bull and vodka and sipped it as a slow, black emptiness swallowed me whole. Perhaps the guy wasn't such a bad bet after all.

I took another sip, the liquid tasted soapy on my tongue. I had no choice really, but to sit and wait.

Wait for someone to come and save me.

La, I'll be there soon xxx

Matthew had texted five minutes earlier. At that point, I had almost laughed and gone hysterical with relief. If I just managed to put the pool annexe to the back of my mind until we finished, everything would be fine.

'So.' I twirled my hair around my fingers. 'Manny, given you've been kept waiting, you have carte blanche to ask me anything you like.' I wanted him to take away a good feeling from the day. I tilted my head as we both leaned against the side of the baby grand. 'What's the thing you most want to know about me? We can have a nice, cosy chat whilst we wait for Matthew.' Although I felt anything but cosy, at least I knew there was soon going to be an end to the discussion if Matthew kept to his word.

'He'll be here soon so you don't have long. I love your T-shirt.' I went to a cupboard to the left of the fireplace which contained all the samples for our fashion ranges and pulled out a similar blue V-neck. 'Here,' I said. 'Off-record, this time,' I laughed. 'But Matthew is working on a range too. I think this colour will suit you.'

'Cool,' he said, looking pleased. 'Thank you. So, do you miss England at all?' I stood stock-still. Although I had told myself not to think of it again, I couldn't help but question what had just happened in the annexe. I thought I'd pieced together parts of a puzzle I'd been missing for a long time but what I'd just witnessed couldn't have been real. And now, here was Manny asking me about England.

'Bits of it.' I tried to sound casual, twisting my thumb around the gold bracelet that Matthew had given me. 'I mean, you know. It was so long ago. And I'm here. In LA. How could I miss England with all of this?' My voice sounded strained and high-pitched.

'True.' He looked around, nodding his head. 'And Ava's father?'

'Ah,' I laughed, glad he had changed the subject onto a topic I'd had lots of practice answering. 'Only a matter of time, wasn't it?' I sounded friendly but at this point, I was desperate, waiting for the seconds to tick by. 'Well, as you know, I don't divulge any of that information. All I can tell you is that he has some quite spectacular genes.' I nodded over in Ava's direction. She had now resumed her previous position, tanned legs dangling over the arm of the chair, Tamagotchi beeping in her hand. I noticed she still looked slightly pale. There were red lines across the bottom of her thigh, where she'd pressed her nails into her skin. I hoped they'd go away soon.

'He's not part of Ava's life but he's given me the greatest gift, so for that, I'll be enormously grateful.' I prayed Ava would behave. Forget about everything that had just happened but then I looked over again and she was doing a strange movement with her throat as though she had something stuck in it. *Tic, tic, tic*, it went. It looked familiar and then I remembered I had gone through a phase of doing it myself – after everything that had happened in England. It was my way of trying to suppress the nausea that was constantly swilling around in my stomach.

'Do you want him to be a part of your life?' Manny interrupted my flow of thoughts.

'Well.' I stood up at that point, checking my reflection, patting my face. 'I, well . . .' I felt incredibly thirsty. I thought of what my media training had taught me. *Don't look as though the question has fazed you. Don't um. Don't ah. Bring it back to something you want to talk about.* 'Interesting you should ask me that' – I grabbed at a lip gloss from the mantelpiece – 'because Matthew, oh – wow, and would you look at that, there he is—' and then the door swung open and Matthew bowled in.

'I'll carry on this conversation with you later,' said Manny. He was standing behind me and I caught his reflection next to mine. There was something in his face at that point. A drop in his features. I couldn't work out if it was desire, or disgust.

'Yo, guys.' Matthew bounded across the room. He clapped his hands together and went up to all of the production team, high-fiving them. 'Sorry I'm late. My dad got taken ill. He's in the hospital. But he's OK.' Thank God he'd got the memo, I thought. *Thank you, Conor, for catching Matthew in time so he kept up with the story.*

'You just had a shower, dude?' Manny asked. 'Thought you were at the hospital?'

'Nope. Sadly didn't have time.' Matthew lifted up his arms and laughing, inhaled. 'Ran all the way here from the car. Just shoved my head under the tap. Didn't want to subject all of you to a real stink.'

'Well, you smell pretty good anyway.' Manny gave a strange laugh and then music started playing again and people started dancing and zipping around as though it was a party. He had that effect. Even Manny looked like he was loosening up.

'Ready for this, my beautiful darling superstar?' Matthew kissed me smack bang on the lips in front of everyone, bending me backwards, which normally I hated but I got swept up in it all and then as I dipped towards the floor, I thought he might drop me. I looked at him and then I felt him shaking.

'You OK?' I whispered.

'OK? I'm great,' he shouted but his eyes looked slightly red, his gaze distant. 'Come on, sexy mamma, dance with me.' He swung me around and I caught Ava looking at him, her lip curled to the side.

'Come on, Ava,' he said. 'Dance with me too.' But she shook her head and looked back down at her Tamagotchi. There went the movement in her throat again and I thought she might cry. I saw Manny catch the exchange, and so I went to Ava myself.

'You OK, darling?' She'd taken off her white robe by this point and she was wearing a beautiful navy dress with a lace collar. 'You look amazing. I know you're nervous,' I said loudly, so Manny could hear.

I noticed a faint pink scar across her kneecap. My mind traced back to any accidents she had had. And then a fleeting memory. Joan, rushing in whilst I had been on a photoshoot.

'Not to worry.' Joan had held her hands up. 'Just a small cut on her knee. She's been on her roller skates. I'm just grabbing her a plaster.' I remembered hearing Ava shout for Joan. How

I'd wrestled with holding up the fifty-person photoshoot so I could go and console her myself.

'I've got it in hand.' Joan had run past me. 'Don't you worry. Leave it with me.' And I had. I had told myself that it would be more confusing for her if both of us had been there. That one person should take charge. That if it had been anything really serious, Joan would have come and got me and stopped the magazine shoot. And that had been my last memory of it.

Until now. My first thought was that she should wear a pair of fine white tights for the announcement, especially with the three red lines she'd pressed into her leg. But then on second thoughts, I remembered Conor's words and realised it showed an authenticity about her that people could relate to. I'd keep it in shot and hope that the rest of her leg went back to normal. After all, it was part of her.

'Can we do it just us two?' Ava said. 'The photo.'

I took a small stem of lavender from a ceramic bowl next to us and held it up to my nose.

'No. We can't. That's not the point of it. But if you are a good girl.' I stripped the plant of its buds and squeezed it into my hands. 'Smell this.' She inhaled. 'If you are a good girl then I promise I'll spend an entire day with you doing whatever you want. How about that? Ice cream?'

'Really? But you never let me.'

'Shhhhh,' I held a finger up to her lips. 'I promise,' I whispered and she looked at Matthew and then at me.

'Caramel?' She smiled then. 'Sprinkles?'

'Anything you like, my dear,' I told her, a perfect smile wrapped around clenched teeth. 'Anything at all. Just let's get this shot done. Marco's ready for us.' I looked over and Marco was waving us over, pointing at the camera.

'Just remember, Ava, our day together. I promise. Just you and me. On Thursday. Forget about everything else. And remember our little secret about Joan,' I whispered. 'We want her to stay, don't we? Just do everything we prepared for and everything will go as planned. OK?' I stroked her neck, just by her throat, hoping it would alleviate some of the anxiety that had manifested itself there. 'Joan?' I said again and she nodded and got up just like that. She put her arms out and we had danced to 'Please Don't Stop the Music' and I silently congratulated myself for distracting her.

'Ready for the photo of the decade?' Matthew shimmied his hips and whooped and the whole room clapped. 'Let's get this show on the road,' and Matthew, Ava and I walked across the room, hand in hand, smiling at everyone as we went. The photo of the decade, I thought to myself. Let's just get this done. It didn't matter what I'd promised Ava to get through the day. Somehow, I'd keep to my word.

'Here.' Joan placed a silver tray onto my desk. 'You must eat. Keep up your strength.' She looked at my stomach and then my arms. Her judgement left me winded.

'Thank you.' I didn't look up. I needed her to leave the room. Her presence made me think too much of Ava. I noticed how my little girl had even started taking on some of Joan's mannerisms. The way her tongue pressed down in the corner of her lips whilst she was thinking.

'Salad. Eggs.' She pointed to each item on the tray.

'Thank you,' I said again. I made a big show of typing, looking at my watch but she still didn't get it.

'Listen.' She shifted from one foot to another. 'Lara, I need to speak to you.' Her eyes filled with tears. I didn't acknowledge her request. I couldn't take on anyone else's grief and fear, even those closest to Ava, but she carried on anyway.

'Please,' she whined. 'Detective Mcgraw. I heard him. He asked you a question.'

'Yes?'

She started to cry. I looked straight at my laptop, unable to move or say a word.

'He asked you a question about you and Matthew.'

'Look,' I said, 'I can't talk about anything. I've been told to keep shtum on everything. I'm sorry, Joan.'

'But it's not to do with . . .'

'Joan. My daughter's life is at stake. Please. Stop asking questions.'

She was quiet then.

'Did they look in her room?' I asked. 'Ava's? Detective Mcgraw, I mean, I haven't been able to go up there.'

'They did. I waited outside. I told them to be respectful. Keep it as was. They didn't take anything.'

'Thank you.' We both went quiet. 'I miss her. I miss her so much.'

'Me too,' whispered Joan and then I felt the energy in the house shift. I knew immediately. He had that effect, like a whirlwind. I felt it in my bones. Joan felt it too. Her body went rigid. Matthew was home.

'Lara,' he shouted from the hall. He looked at Joan who was still standing at the door to my study, and waved. 'Lara. God, I've been down at the station.' Somehow he'd changed from his earlier clothes into an untucked white shirt, beige shorts and a pair of black flip-flops. He looked tired and unshaven, but still beautiful. 'What's been happening? They took my phone. They've had me down there for hours.'

'Matthew, I'm so glad you're back.' I pushed my plate away and put my head into my hands. 'So glad.' I looked up, hoping Joan would have got the message but she was still standing, staring at Matthew.

'Joan, if you could leave us,' I said. She nodded and pressed her back to the door as Matthew walked past. 'Thank you, Joan.'

She walked out and shut the door behind her.

'Lara,' said Matthew, over and over he repeated my name. I could do nothing except stare at him.

'Where is she?' he cried. 'Poor thing. She must be . . .'

'Stop,' I shouted. 'Stop. I can't bear to think about it. I told Detective Mcgraw I was on the phone to you. He didn't think it was the reason for her disappearance. I'm not to blame, am I? Please. Tell me I'm not.'

'Listen, Lara. We're going to find her. OK? This is all going to be OK. I have no doubt that she's lost. They have to find her with half the country out in force.' He scanned the room, as though looking for her. 'She can't go unnoticed. A six-year-old girl? She can't just vanish like that.' He scraped his hair back and turned around in a full circle. 'God. Lara. Jesus.'

'What if someone took her? What if someone kidnapped her?'

'No, Lara. You can't think that. She's lost. And she'll be back soon.' He sounded so convincing that she'd be returning any minute now, that I almost believed him. In fact, I did believe him. For a minute, I almost took a step outside myself and wondered what all the fuss was about. Of course she was going to walk through that door. Any second now, and she'd be right there, laughing. Smiling.

'Sorry.' She'd throw her arms out to me. 'I'm sorry I scared you.' It was totally inconceivable that she wouldn't be coming home.

'Any updates online?' He nodded towards my computer. 'Perhaps we can find something there. Want me to look?' I pushed the laptop towards him.

'I can't. You look. I've just been on our favourite site,' I told him. 'Media Spy. I don't want to read anymore. Look at the official ones. The news. Let me know if there's anything.'

He took the computer from me. I watched as beautiful fingers tapped the keyboard, blond hairs glinting in the light. He went silent, his eyes scanning the screen. I watched the flicker of his right temple. It reminded me of the day of the announcement. The way he'd tried so hard to hold it together when he'd seen Manny, his muscles giving way when he tried to hold me. I watched the way his mouth was moving, as he read the words in front of him. And then he stopped.

'What?' I said but he just carried on smashing at the keyboard. 'What is it?' I repeated but he didn't answer me. I heard him, then, whisper something under his breath and I wanted to ask him what he'd said but my blood had started to race around my body so fast that I felt my ears ring.

'Matthew,' I shouted after a few seconds. 'What is it?' I was too scared to drag the laptop towards me so I could see the screen. I felt that my body couldn't cope much longer with being in this perpetual state of panic. But then I realised that this journey had probably only just begun.

'Lara,' he said. 'Listen.' As he turned to me the landline rang. The only person I'd given the number to outside of the house, was Detective Mcgraw.

'Yes?' I picked it up. I assumed he was calling me with the same thing that Matthew had just discovered. Better to hear it from someone official, rather than reading something from the press.

'Lara,' said Detective Mcgraw. 'I want to apologise on behalf of LA police.'

'What? What's happened? My daughter?'

'No, we haven't found her. I'm sorry. There's been a leak. To the press.'

I almost laughed. Was that it? The reason for the blood draining from Matthew's face? That didn't matter. I was used to it. What could be worse than my daughter going missing? And surely it was nothing to do with my past, or what had happened in the pool annexe. But then I realised the ramifications of what he was telling me. That if it was serious, it could have an effect on the investigation. He read my thoughts.

'Don't worry,' he said. 'It won't have any impact on the case. We've made sure of that.' I listened to him drone on, willing him to talk faster but when he didn't, I snatched the computer from Matthew's grasp and turned it towards me. I could feel Matthew staring at me as I digested what was in front of me.

I recognised the website immediately. The familiar splashes of red and pink. The bubble writing at the top. I knew what was coming when I saw a telephone icon in the corner of the screen and a play button in the middle of the article. I scrolled down to the picture of myself. My mouth was open and my hand raised up to my face. It had obviously been lifted from my show and captioned to make it look as though it had been taken today.

'I'm sorry,' I heard Detective Mcgraw down the phone. 'I'm really sorry and we're dealing with this right away,' but I had put the phone on the desk before he could finish. I had absolutely no control over my hands at all. Before I knew it, I had clicked on the cursor and I was scrolling down to read all of the text. I was frozen, but I could still hear Detective Mcgraw's voice, echoing from the receiver.

'It's all right,' he was saying. 'We're going to fix this.'

I leant over and pressed the red hang-up button on the phone receiver. My most vulnerable moment, out there for the taking. I looked at the comments, the counter racing upwards. And then I looked at the number of people that had pressed play. Nearly two million so far. It had probably only been up for fifteen or so minutes. Maybe I should listen to it. Punish myself even more. Because that's what they wanted, wasn't it? These people? To punish me?

I hit play and listened as my voice echoed around the room.

'Hello?'

'What's your emergency?'

'My daughter. She's gone. Vanished.'

I clearly hadn't been aware of what I'd been saying at all. It was like I had not been responsible for the call. I listened on as though this was all happening to someone else, fresh bits of information being drip-fed to me as the audio played. Did I really say that? Did that really happen? And then I saw Joan standing at the door, hand clamped around her mouth, trying to contain her horror at the parts that came next.

England, July 2004

I wasn't saved by anyone. I left the club alone, facing the four-mile walk home. I figured it would be about five in the morning before I got to bed. Maybe earlier if I took the back streets. But then, I weighed up the chances of an eighteen-year-old girl being murdered in some dark alleyway. How I'd have scuppered my chances at a bright future before they'd even begun. Main roads it was.

But then I saw him again, wearing white trainers, leaning against the wall by the exit. I had thought about calling for the bouncer but when I had turned, I could see they were busy, ushering people home. I could see the lights filling up the club as people weaved out. Groups of friends, new couples, lips glistening in the moonlight.

'Thought I'd find you here soon. Your mate?' My stomach had pivoted.

'She's . . .' I nodded my head over to the entrance. 'Just coming.'

'I thought I saw her. Leaving. With them guys. Out the back.'

'You were spying on us? What do you want?' I asked him loudly. I took out my mobile and unlocked it, ready to dial nine-nine-nine.

'I told you.' He pulled out a cigarette and offered me one. 'I'm not here to hurt you.'

'Then what?'

'Just like I told you before. I—'

'You followed me?' I moved closer to the front door and I was thinking about how I was going to get rid of him before I walked back. 'I followed you because . . . wait . . . I'm new to this too.' He rummaged around in his pocket and I took a step back, my heart going shit-crazy, my thumb hovering over the dial pad of my phone.

'Don't look so freaked out,' he laughed. 'It's this,' and he handed me a white business card. 'Look, lady. I'm no smooth operator. But just hear me out. Or give me a chance, rather. Read the card. Call me. OK? I might be new to all this but I've got good instincts. Believe me. I know something when I see it. I know it's no use asking you for your number now. You look like you think I'm about to do you over. So I have to hope you'll ring me. Please. It might change your life. I think I can. I think I can change your life.' He watched me turn the card around in my hands and then turned and walked off, the night mist trailing him into the distance.

'Don't forget,' he shouted back at me. 'I can change your life.' And then he was gone.

I read the card, typing his name into Google with the last of my data before my internet was cut off for the month, but nothing came up. Just a picture of an old dude and his dog at Crufts.

Loser, I thought.

Both him and me. It was time to go back to my small bedsit. But then I scrolled down and there was a makeshift website.

Ben Finn.

Bolt Enterprises.

Talent Management.

And then I thought about what he'd said earlier. The competition. *Idolz.* And then a flash of memory. A segment that I'd seen on *Entertainment Now!* About a new show launching, called *Idolz.* That was it. They had been looking for people to audition for the next big thing in pop. Spearheaded by Felix Brandlove. The winner would be the proud recipient of a million-pound recording contract. It all came flooding back to me. I'd remembered sitting in Hannah's flat, turning up the volume on the telly.

But I stared at the card again and then I started to hum my song. '*If only I could. If only I would.*'

Something inside me shifted at that point. I felt lighter, and everything sharpened. Maybe things would change after all. Maybe it was meant to be. Maybe my future was written in the stars and that's how white-trainers Mr Ben Finn had found me. I had always known I was different. Even when I had been younger.

The street lights cast their glow. A taxi thundered past, its lights bright and electrifying. Goosebumps raced over my skin and all of a sudden, the world made sense and I started the long journey home. One foot in front of the other. But all of a sudden, I didn't care.

This was going to be the start of everything.

Ryans-world.com
Entry: August 26th, 1945hrs
Author: Ryan

So, guys, big news. Here's a link to the audio of Lara King's leaked 911 call. I don't know how I feel posting it here. It just feels well, wrong. But if it reaches people then that can only be a good thing. For those of you who want to read the full transcript, see below.

PAPA RAZZLE ONLINE EXCLUSIVE!
BREAKING NEWS:
08/26/2018 1800hrs
214,575 Facebook shares
675,438 Retweets
935,885 Comments

FILED UNDER – AVA KING, LARA KING, MISSING CHILD, 911, POLICE FILES PAPA RAZZLE has managed to obtain the audio of Lara King's call to the police at midday today, after her daughter Ava went missing.

911 Call Handler: Hello? What's your emergency?

Caller: Hello? (heavy breathing) My daughter. My daughter is missing. I'm in ... I'm in Laurel Canyon. Send someone. Quick. Please.

911 Call Handler: Could you tell me your exact location?

Caller: (Inaudible) Laurel Canyon . . . by . . . (inaudible)

911 Call Handler: Can you tell me your name please, and give me your number in case we get cut off?

Caller: Oh God. Hurry. Please. My name's Lara and my number is . . . Oh God, I can't think. It's it's— (Number redacted)

911 Call Handler: Lara, can you tell me how long your daughter's been missing?

Caller: Ten, fifteen minutes? (heavy breathing) Please. Oh my God. I don't know. I was on the phone at the time (inaudible). I don't know. Please (inaudible. Gasping) I don't know. Please. (Caller starts to scream)

911 Call Handler: Please, could you try and keep calm so we can locate you.

Caller: I'm, God, I don't know.

911 Call Handler: Can you see any landmarks, anything we can use to locate your whereabouts. I'm dispatching a team out now to Laurel Canyon. Stay on the phone with me so we can pinpoint your location.

Caller: Ava (caller is screaming at this point), Ava, where are you? Oh God. Please hurry. I drove past a (inaudible) I think.

911 Call Handler: Which sign?

Caller: God, I think, I drove from Laurel Canyon Boulevard. We're here. By . . .

911 Call Handler: Can you get an exact location from your phone?

Caller: Hang on, hang on (breathing hard, takes cell away from ear). I'm near a sign. I passed a sign. Highway (inaudible) it says (heavy breathing from caller). Going north towards Laurel Canyon Boulevard. That road. I think.

911 Call Handler: Great we've dispatched someone who will be there shortly. And you say you were on the phone at the time of your daughter's disappearance? Can you tell me how long you were on the phone – how long you think she's been missing for? Stay on the line. Stay talking to me. Someone will be there very soon with you.

Caller: I don't know. I was on the phone. She asked to get out the car. To go to the toilet. And then when I realised she had been gone for too long I went to look and she wasn't there (very heavy breathing). I screamed. Screaming (inaudible), Jesus Christ, she's gone. I heard a car. Someone must have taken her.

911 Call Handler: OK. It's OK, stay calm.

Caller: Tell me you'll find her. Please. It was just a normal day. Driving. Singing to Katy Perry on the radio. Happy. It was normal. Nothing to indicate . . . (inaudible) from one minute to the next. Here, now (inaudible) gone. Please.

911 Call Handler: We'll have someone with you shortly.

(Sound of a siren in the background.)

Call goes dead.

Comments on this section will be moderated.

#Methree: Oh my. She was on her fucking CELL when her daughter went missing? She presents herself as this perfect mom, but she wasn't even watching her child? That bitch gonna DIE.

Meghans_Sparkle: All these celebrities think they can do what they want. She's probably never looked after her kid in her life despite making billions pretending to do so. Doesn't deserve to have one. Especially that cute little Ava, who has probably been taken away by some lunatic.

Blake_Lives4eva: Come on, guys, she took her eye off the ball for one second. I've got two little hunnies myself, one boy, one girl, and often I lose concentration. Or answer my cell. Don't you? Give the girl a break. She might have been answering an important call. She's an amazing mom. Look at that little girl Ava. Kudos to Lara, she's raised a beautiful little angel and we should give her credit for that.

Katy_Perry_No1_Fan: Guys, has no one picked up on the biggest exclusive in this story? Katy Perry! Ava and Lara singing along to Katy Perry! MWAH I FUCKING LOVE YOU, KATY PERRY.

Here with the latest updates on missing Ava King, brought to you by Lara and Ava King's number one fan.

Twitter: @ryan_gosling_wannabe

'I'm sorry, Ms King.' I felt the blood drain from my face as Detective Mcgraw rang the landline again. I waved Conor away, so he could deal with the Papa Razzle fallout. 'I'm really sorry,' said Detective Mcgraw. 'We couldn't stop it. Papa Razzle, they . . .' I could barely hold the receiver. 'Look. I'm sorry.' I felt dizzy, remembering how I'd wanted to scream, waiting for the call to connect after I'd dialed nine-one-one. How careful I'd been not to touch the screen of my mobile with my face, in case the sweat disconnected the emergency call. The way the responder had asked for my phone number. *Hurry up, just damn well hurry up,* I'd been thinking as I'd looked around the empty landscape for any sign of my daughter. Why is this fucking necessary? But of course, as everyone knows, it was necessary.

I thought of all the Papa Razzle audio calls I'd listened to myself. Housekeepers calling for paramedics for their famous dying employees and the like. 'Oh, Ava,' I said, shutting my eyes. I prayed nothing else would come out.

'Did someone leak it? Someone on your force?'

'That we don't know, Ms King, but we are looking into it and we'll do everything we can to resolve it.'

I felt my heart thud right down to my feet.

'There's been some positive steps, though,' said Detective Mcgraw. I heard an intake of breath down the receiver and then realised it was my own.

'We've managed to piece together some CCTV. We're trying to trace the cars around you at that point. But we've got some really good clear footage of you and Ava at a red light. You'd stopped on Laurel Canyon Boulevard. The time as stated on the footage is exactly ten a.m., so this footage is your journey from your house to Laurel Canyon fifteen minutes or so after you left for your day out.' I imagined Ava's face and curled my hands around the handset. 'So,' he continued, 'this was before she fell asleep. Before you drove around waiting for her to wake up.'

'Oh God. How does she look?'

'She looks, she looks OK, Ms King.' I thought of what she could have been thinking about. How she'd had that anxious tic in her throat and that I hoped she didn't have it in the video. I only wanted to see her relaxed and content.

'Can you send me the footage? To my email.'

'Yes, Ms King. We were hoping to release it. With your permission, first, of course. We hope it might trigger someone's memory.'

'Thank you. As soon as you can.'

'And, Ms King, we're going to need some more info on the drive that you took when Ava was asleep. The route. We've got some footage of you driving around but there's a lack of CCTV and speed cameras in parts of the canyon so if we can piece together your journey, that would be helpful.'

'Of course.' I swallowed, thinking back to the day's events. How long ago it seemed, how time seemed to be stretching, collapsing in on itself. She was six. Surely there was a good chance she was still alive? I shut my eyes. 'But if I'm not allowed out?'

'We've reconstructed your journey so far using Google Maps and our own tracking system – we've run your licence plate through the recognition system caught on the cameras so we've managed a fair bit but if there are areas you can tell us about, we'd appreciate that. We're on a really' – he paused, 'limited time frame now,' he said. 'So if we could go through it now. Over the phone?'

'Of course,' I said to him. We spent half an hour going through the route I believed I had taken. I tried to piece it together but I could barely type the keys on the board.

'I'm so sorry. Oh God I'm in such a muddle,' I said. 'I hope that's accurate,' but the more I tried to think back, the more everything seemed hazy, the memories of earlier shrinking like I was watching them through the smaller end of a telescope. I started to feel hysterical.

'It's OK,' Detective Mcgraw said. His voice sounded kind then and I felt calmer. Like the information I'd given him had turned out to be useful and I'd gone some way into helping my daughter.

'On the whole it seems to fit.' His voice sounded far away. I could hear him tapping on his computer. 'I'll need to give this to the team. And then I'll come back to you if we need more.'

'Fine,' I told him. 'Anything I can do to help. When will you next be here?' I tried to keep the neediness out my voice because I really knew that I needed to let the police focus and get on with their job without feeling like they had to look after me, especially given I hadn't wanted anyone around me. Detective

Mcgraw must have read my mind again, though. He seemed to be good at that. Surprising, really, given he could barely look me in the eye.

'I've got a briefing with the team in five minutes. I'll be over after that. As I said to you before, please let us send over a specialised officer. Our family liaison officer can keep you informed of every part of the investigation. I know you said you didn't want anyone.'

'Fine, OK. No. I don't. Can you send it to me? The footage you got of us?' I couldn't keep the impatience out my voice. The longing to see my daughter's face was painful. 'Before you release it? My private email is foreverlara at Lara King dot com.'

'Got it. You gave it to me earlier before the press conference.' I had absolutely no recollection of doing so and I wondered if that was the way my shock was manifesting. 'We'll aim to send it out now. Before the morning broadcasts. I'll speak to Conor too, discuss how to play things. Our comms team are planning things now but of course we need to liaise with you.'

'Thank you, Detective Mcgraw.'

I put down the phone and went back to my laptop. The footage was there already, waiting in my emails.

To: foreverlara@laraking.com
SUBJECT: Laurel Canyon Boulevard CCTV

I had suspected I'd open it fast, greedy to see her face. But I found that I couldn't do it. My body froze and I started to cry but when I least expected it, my hand moved, fingers pressing on the touchpad. *Click.* The cursor froze. '*Please, Ava. Please, come back to me,'* I whispered. *'Please. I need you here.'* The email flick-ered, opened. The white *play* arrow obscured her face at first, but I could see that the picture was clear. There was my daughter in the back. I could see her face in all its glory. She was looking out the window, into the distance. I tried to imagine what she'd been thinking. I remembered the announcement and how she'd reacted to it all. Thank God, I thought, thank God I'd taken her out alone. Made it up to her. I stroked her face on the screen, static prickling my fingers. I felt totally empty. *She's coming back,* I told myself. *She is. She's just got lost. And she'll be found.* Pain gnawed away at me. I thought about my conversation with Detective Mcgraw from earlier. The expression on his face was etched into my mind.

'I heard a car,' I'd told him. And the way he'd tried to pull together his features.

'It's OK.' He had rubbed at his eyebrow. 'It doesn't have to mean anything,' but I could see in his face that he thought the exact opposite. Celebrity. Celebrity's daughter. Obsessed fans. Enemies. Blackmailers. The stakes were high. And then him asking if she would get into any car willingly.

No. Only Joan, Matthew, Lily. I could almost see his brain ticking through each scenario. I told myself to focus on the things I could do to help find my daughter. Finally I managed to press *play*.

I watched as our shiny black Bentley rolled up to the red light. There was one car in front of us. A red soft-top convertible with a brown-haired woman in the driving seat, in some huge white sunglasses. It was at this point I had a vague memory of a car driving too closely to us, earlier that morning. Or was it the day before? I was so muddled, I couldn't quite grasp the memory. Time was elastic. I couldn't even pinpoint when I'd been at the press conference. I kept hovering over the thought and questioning whether I was making things up now. I watched as the light flashed amber and then green. There she was. A straight-on image of my daughter. She looked so perfect, the whole scene like something out of a Chanel advert. Her conker-brown hair with natural golden highlights flowed straight down her back, her eyes wide with excitement, taking in everything around her. I looked at her throat. No sign of her anxiety tic. She just looked perfect. An ache burned in my chest.

I watched myself staring at the road. My bespoke personalised dashboard and the front of the car were both in focus, the lights glowing like a mini-spaceship. My hands were spread across the steering wheel, fingers laced with diamonds.

I focused on the screen again. I hadn't remembered what we'd been talking about. I hadn't even remembered taking that route but I thought about her again and everything that had happened in the pool house. Whether she'd been replaying the scene in her head. A six-year-old, trying to make sense of the things she'd seen. I knew I should have discussed it more carefully with her. But then I thought I'd make it worse. It was Joan who once told me to be careful with any anxieties. 'Validate them but don't indulge them,' she'd said to me when Ava started telling us she was afraid of the dark. And so I'd thought it best just to leave it. Make her think it was all acting. She was young – she'd forget about it. *Surely.*

I knew she hadn't run off. It wasn't something she'd do. It just wasn't. But a seed had been planted. Maybe . . . just maybe. I played the CCTV footage over and over searching for any clues. I watched our car pull up to the traffic lights, slowly, and tried to get an insight into Ava's mind, what she'd been thinking. Each time, the light turned to amber, then green. Our car pulled away and I watched the back of her head slowly pull out of view and then, that was it.

She had gone.

Just as I was about to press play again, someone knocked on the door.

It was Joan.

'Conor,' she said. Her voice was calm but she was doing this bullfrog breathing and her eyes were bulging out of her face. 'He's back and asked me to hurry. To get you quickly. He needs you. Can he come in? He won't take no for an answer.'

'He can come in.' I motioned towards the laptop screen. 'But I need you to stall anyone else. I'm busy at the moment.' Before I could finish talking, Conor was right next to me, and my fingers minimised the screen on my laptop.

'We're in trouble,' he said before I could admonish him. Joan stood near us wringing her hands which made me feel even worse. I'd wanted her to leave the room before Conor started talking.

'Wait,' I turned to Conor, my finger held to my lips. 'Can we do this in private?' I nodded – imperceptibly – towards Joan, hoping Conor would get it but he didn't pick up on my cues, touching everything in sight like an overwrought child.

'Joan. If you could give us some space, please,' I said. I wanted to pummel her, to tell her that she had no right to my daughter's life in this way. That I was her mother.

'Five minutes.' Conor held up his right hand in Joan's direction. 'And then I'll fill you in too.' He smiled. Since when had he felt like he needed to defer to her? When she shut the door, he came and sat down on the corner of the desk and covered his mouth with his hands.

'They're turning,' he said. I could tell he was trying to keep calm, trying to keep his voice steady, but I saw the way he blinked. I'd seen him do it only once before, when one of his big clients had been caught in a hit and run DUI scandal.

'The leaked audio, Lara. They're going fucking *mad*. I don't know what to do. I need your help on this one. I've tried not to bother you. But the police – they've been useless and I'm losing confidence here. It's their fault this happened in the first place. Of course they don't want to get involved and as far as white-washing this, they're not interested. So I need a plan of action now. Like I told you, we need to get this right.'

'Who is going mad?' I asked, despite already knowing the answer. I just needed a few more moments pretending every-thing was fine, so I could process it all. And hearing Conor say that he was losing confidence filled me with dread.

'You were on the phone when Ava went missing. They know. The public. There's been a shift in mood. We need to do some-thing. Before this all goes to shit and we can't pull it back.' He rested a hand on my shoulder. 'Before we lose all hope of finding her.' I shut my eyes and tried to stop the sinking feeling deep within me.

'Well, they've got nothing to do with it, have they?' I said, knowing how untrue this was. 'I don't give a damn anymore. I don't care. I just want her back.' Conor didn't move. 'I don't give a fuck!' My voice echoed across the walls. Conor looked shocked. I was so aware of the paps and the television cameras constantly following me that my default behaviour was to be on 'form' even within the privacy of my own home. It had been many years since I'd been so unaware of how I was behaving. But my eyes felt all dry, my throat was sore and still I carried on.

'Cruel. It's just cruel.' I heard my breath coming in waves. 'I don't need them,' I said. 'I just need Ava.'

'I know, Lara. I'm sorry,' said Conor. 'You do, though.' He looked at his watch and then at the window. 'You'd be stuck without them. You can't move. Trapped. You need to listen to me. You need them now. More than ever.' He took a deep breath. 'You might think you hate them right this minute but don't forget, Lara, they've been good to you. Really good to you.' His eyes roamed around the room and settled on the large framed award I'd been given for the best television show, voted for by the public. 'And I know sometimes it can be a love-hate relationship' – he paused – 'but you have to forgive them for this. They're in shock too. After all, everyone loves Ava. It's hard on them as well. And they've forgiven you in the past.' I steadied myself on the desk. I thought that somehow he was going to bring up England. 'I mean, not that you've done anything to forgive. But just . . . anyway, who cares. We need to focus here.' Conor was one person who could keep me level and tell me things frankly but even he knew when to stop. 'So let's just figure this one out. If you were a member of the public and this had happened, what would make you feel better? I'm thinking maybe show them your charity appearance backstage shots? The ones you did for that safe driving campaign two years ago? That could work?'

We both went silent. Conor pulled my laptop towards him and started tapping away.

I didn't want him to see the things I'd been searching. *Is Ava King alive? Did someone kidnap Ava King?* But he seemed totally involved in what he was doing and not the least bit interested in my previous search history.

'Fuck, Lara.' He scraped his fingers down his cheeks. 'It's gaining traction.' His phone rang and he disappeared outside the room. 'Right,' he said when he returned. 'I've just spoken to Faye from the office. It's gone mad on the front pages online. *LA Times* says: *Lara distracted on phone. New York Times: Lara takes eyes off daughter whilst on phone.*' He shook his head. 'She's just sent me a rolling list of the headlines.' I grabbed his mobile and scrolled through them.

'How do we get a grip on this?' I said, my voice pitching higher.

'I don't know,' he sighed. 'I think we should release something. A story, or pictures that haven't been seen before. What about Joan? Would she speak? Talk about what a wonderful mother you are?' I felt defensive at this point and I wasn't sure why. 'I just need to let Faye know. She's waiting to hear from us and push the button. This is going to be a mammoth task.' I wished he'd stop reminding me. Usually he was so calm and would just take things off my hands and get them done.

'Maybe,' I said, thinking Joan was probably the last person I'd ask, unless I spun it that it would help find Ava. 'The police are releasing the CCTV footage, if they haven't done so already. That will help. Look at this. *The Times* of England. They're saying I shouldn't be vilified. That every parent does it.' I started to read out the article. *'Let's not berate Lara King. She took her foot off the parenting brake for longer than necessary. Yes, but it shouldn't have been calamitous. In most normal situations, the girl would have returned to the car quickly and without trouble.'* I stopped reading, thinking that she hadn't, though. She hadn't returned to the car quickly and without trouble. I couldn't read on. The defence of my actions made me feel even worse. If that was at all possible. But it give me an idea.

'How about we get people to talk.' Conor rubbed his hands. 'About you as a mother? Like, teachers and parents from Ava's school? Everyone will want in. They'll all want to admit to knowing you. I mean, of course, they'll want to help find Ava too,' he added quickly.

'We don't need to do anything.' I slammed my hands down on the desk. 'It *was* a bad thing to do. I *was* on the phone. I'm going to come clean,' I said to Conor. 'I should have gone with her. I shouldn't have been distracted.' And I meant it.

Because, you see, I realise that despite my earlier words, despite my screaming and shouting about you being cruel, I know you. I know you *deeply*. You may think I don't. After all, we don't have much in common. Or so you think.

I know your reactions. I know how you feel when I post on my social media that I've had a difficult day with my daughter. That things aren't always perfect. *Thank God*, you think. *She goes through it too.*

And then when I post the other stuff. The perfect stuff. *God*, you think. You cannot help but stare at the clean, crisp clothes that we are both wearing, after a day playing among the golden leaves, the smiles laden with love and happiness. Or the sun, speckling our bodies as we do yoga together on the lawn, limbs supple and tanned. It sickens you, yet you delight in it all and you can't seem to get enough.

And so I know now that if I deny any wrongdoing, or try and whitewash my actions, *you'll turn even more.*

I put my head in my hands to block out all light and sound and the other thoughts crashing around my head, and I thought about what Conor had said. *What would make you feel better?*

And after five minutes or so, I realised.

'I know,' I told him. 'I know exactly what to do.'

Gutted. I mean I'm not a parent, am I? (Unless any of you special ladies want to tell me something!) No, seriously, I didn't think she'd be the type of person who'd do that. Be on the phone. Not notice her kid had gone missing. I know most of you tell me that it's a mistake. That sometimes you take your eyes off the prize. I get that. Fair enough. But to not notice your child had gone? That seems careless to me, but then I keep thinking – she must have been having some pretty heavy-duty conversation not to have thought that it was weird Ava had been gone for so long. What if something had gone wrong? Maybe she was real upset? Who knows. I try not to judge too much but tbh, it's going round and round in my head. Whirring, whirring. I know I won't be able to sleep tonight. And then I think, whoa – poor Lara. She must be feeling so shitty and surely that deserves some compassion?

Maybe I'm biased. Maybe if I had better home circumstances, I'd feel differently. My mom, she left me. I've been living with my granma since I was ten, so you know if I had a daughter, I think I'd cherish her, and dote on her and really, not let her out of my sight.

Signing off now for some peace and quiet but I wanted you to come here to find info you haven't yet had from anywhere else, so I've uploaded some pics of Ava that y'all might not have seen before. A friend gave them to me. They're out-takes from a fashion shoot she and Lara did last year. Look how goofy she looks.

This is breaking my heart.

Here with the latest updates on missing Ava King, brought to you by Lara and Ava King's number one fan.

Twitter: @ryan_gosling_wannabe

'I'm going to say sorry,' I told Conor. 'That's what I need to do. It'll help. I promise. Please. Let me say something. In a blog post. On Instagram. I need to make that connection.'

'Yes.' Conor looked up at me slowly and then nodded. 'Bring the focus back onto Ava and the search. That's genius.' His voice sped up and he started pacing the room. 'It'll make them feel like they're needed. Wanted. That can only be a good thing where support for the investigation is concerned.' He pulled out a pen from his back pocket, clicking the top of it. 'We don't have long until it's pitch . . .' He looked towards the window. I couldn't follow his gaze. Ava hated the dark. 'Please, leave the side-light on,' she would beg whenever I left the room before bed. Joan had bought her a small ladybird lamp and she'd count the spots with her small fingers pressed on each one. One. Two. Three.

'OK. Good,' he said. 'We'll do that. Set it live. And then we'll start to work out next steps. OK?' He started talking about something else. Your reaction. This, and that. Tomorrow. Next steps.

'OK,' I told him but I wasn't listening. I was thinking that she'd be home by then and that I wasn't going to sleep until she was back in her bed.

When Conor left to speak to his office, I allowed my gaze to look at the window. Light was fading. I tried to keep my thoughts distracted, or I felt like I'd go crazy and in the end, I did what I'd promised myself I wouldn't do. I looked online. It was the only way I could feel involved in the investigation. I flicked to the official Facebook groups that people had set up. Millions of followers. I looked at the search routes that were being posted. I imagined her then, wandering around in the dark. My eyes followed the trail of the blue lines that had been digitally drawn onto maps. Her small feet balanced as she tried to make her way home in the dark. I skimmed through the messages and posts. I couldn't keep up with it all. Messages of support. Some of hatred. I closed the website. I couldn't still my mind, though. I needed another distraction. My body seemed to be totally restless, trying to keep up with the traumas of my mind.

And so I decided to look on Media Spy. To see what people were saying about the case. I flicked quickly through the threads I'd been previously monitoring. *Ava's dad* and *England* had a few more discussions on it, but nothing like the most recent ones about me being on the phone. I hoped and prayed they'd stop, when they read what I had to say.

Just as I was contemplating writing an anonymous thread, Joan came in with some tea. I noticed she'd forgotten the teapot, though.

'Lara. I couldn't listen to it, you know. Your phone call. I couldn't. I'm sorry it leaked.' She spoke quickly and then looked down at the tray, realising her mistake.

'I'll get the teapot in a minute.' She put the tray down on my desk. 'But I need to talk to you. What we discussed earlier. You and Matthew?'

I kept one eye on my computer screen, on the forum counter. Three hundred thousand people were discussing a thread that had been posted exactly seven minutes ago, labelled 'Lara and the Papa Razzle call'.

'Me and Matthew? He's upstairs now, I believe. He needed a breather.'

'I can't stop thinking about what Detective Mcgraw asked you.' She drew breath and started speaking fast, so I had no chance but to listen what she had to say. 'If you and Matthew had been rowing at all in the past few days.' I snapped my head up. She looked frightened then. 'I didn't mean to overhear.' She held up her palms. 'I was coming to ask you guys if you wanted any food. The door was ajar. I'd just let Conor into the house. I wanted to see if you all wanted to eat, given Anthony's not here.'

'And?' I injected a breeziness into my voice but I felt the air being squeezed out of me.

'And, well, I heard you.'

I moved my finger around the rim of the glass Joan had placed on the tray.

'You heard me what?'

'I heard you and Matthew after the announcement. The row you had. Before I showed Manny around.'

'Oh God, Joan,' I sighed. 'That. I thought you were here for something serious. To do with Ava.' I patted my chest. 'You scared me. You want me to tell the police that Matthew and I had a row about the fact he was late for the announcement? And the photoshoot? A lovers' tiff?' A shadow crossed her face.

'But,' she said as I thought back to her standing by the fireplace threading her fingers through her hair. *Listen to me*, she'd been saying. *Listen to me*. 'It sounded like it was more than that.'

'I know. I was so stressed out with coordinating that huge surprise for the world. Millions of people tuning in. I mean I was so angry with him.' I lowered my voice conspiratorially. '*Men.* I would have had it all in hand if he hadn't been late.' She seemed to be pacified by this. 'I'll quite happily tell them,' I told her. 'But I don't want them to start looking in places that aren't relevant. A small row because Matthew was late doesn't warrant police time looking for Ava.' I almost choked on her name. 'Don't you think? I mean, if I thought it was going to help . . . It'd just be awful, them wasting all their time. What do you think, Joan? You tell me what you think.' It was an effort just to keep my voice steady and to keep myself from hurling the glass at her.

'Oh, well now you put it like that.' She looked down at the floor. 'I guess you're right.'

'I am. I just need for them to focus. I had a long chat with Conor just now. That's what he thinks. That they need to focus. The press. The public.' If there was one person Joan trusted, it was Conor. He'd stopped the paparazzi from publishing a picture of her at Ava's fifth birthday party after she'd begged him to keep her anonymity. 'He thinks that if they lose interest then we'll lose momentum. Look what's happening now. With the Papa Razzle phone call.' I wondered whether she too was going to start berating me for being on my phone.

'Well, that's a bit different,' she said. I detected a hint of accusation in her voice and then I remembered one of the points in her contract was that she wasn't allowed to use her mobile whilst she looked after Ava.

'I was . . .' I shut my mouth. I didn't want to defend myself to her when I felt so broken already.

'Anyway,' she said. 'I'm going to get the tea.' I knew she wanted to say more. She didn't move, except to mouth something, as though she was rehearsing for a play. And then she came out with it.

'Detective Mcgraw. He was asking me so many random questions. I couldn't work it out. But he said my alibi checked out. I mean I didn't think for a minute he'd be investigating me.' Joan had a smug look on her face that made me feel furious. 'All is fine from that end. So are we missing something else?' she asked. 'Something obvious?'

I almost laughed but then she corrected herself. 'I mean, she *was* behaving strangely. I told Detective Mcgraw that she was not quite herself.' I thought back to the words Mcgraw had used when asking about me and Matthew. *Quite a tricky time.* Joan had started making me look bad. I wondered if I should speak to Conor about it.

'Do you think she ran off?' Her lips were trembling. 'She wouldn't have done that. She just wouldn't. I told Detective Mcgraw that too. That there was just no way she'd run off in a million years and I know her better th . . .'

Better than anyone. I could sense were the words on the tip of her tongue. I snapped my laptop shut. 'Better than *he* does,' she saved herself. She was getting out of hand, Joan. But then perhaps she'd hit a raw nerve. Perhaps Joan *did* know my daughter better than anyone. I remembered how she'd begged for me to spend more quality time with Ava before the announcement. I prayed to God that she hadn't told Detective Mcgraw all of that and made me look even worse.

Her words crashed around in my head, making me feel sick.

Better than anyone.

Do not question yourself as a mother, I told myself. *Focus on Ava*. And then I felt angry towards Joan for making me feel this way. But I couldn't shift the sense that she was somehow trying to inveigle herself into number one position in the search for my daughter.

Mother's guilt. Always going to be there, no matter what we do, I'd remembered the midwife telling me when I was at the hospital.

And I had an uneasy feeling that should anything have happened to Ava, she'd somehow manage to make me feel I was at fault. The thought that Joan would somehow find out about the annexe too, or that Ava had said things to her made me terrified.

And then I thought of what Joan had been about to say. *Better than anyone.* Had she been right? Were there things she knew about my daughter that I didn't?

A mother always knows best, I consoled myself, but the words faded in my mind. Pebbles, sinking into the deep black ocean.

'The perfect shot.' Marco waved his camera around like it was a raffle prize. 'I've got it. We're done. Here, want to take a look?'

We had both leaned over as he had pointed to the image, Ava, right in the middle, smiling. Matthew sat to the right of her, one hand on her shoulder, and the other arm around me.

'Yeeha!' said Matthew, rubbing his hands. 'We look hot, hot, hot. Don't we?'

'Well, I hope it's a nice photo,' I said, looking at Manny.

'Sure is. It'll look great alongside my profile of you guys. We'll use one of the frames that you don't use for later.'

'Fantastic,' I said, hoping Ava hadn't cottoned on to the fact that Manny was here to write about us. 'Now is there anything else I can get you, Manny? Anything else you'd like to ask?' In truth, I wanted him gone. 'Because we'll have to get ready soon for the press conference.' I looked towards the door but he stayed right where he was and then he leaned forward to Ava.

'You enjoy all this press stuff, little one?' he asked. My skin started to burn, especially after I'd told him not to say why he was here. 'Ava's got to go do her home study now.' I bustled everyone out the room. 'Haven't you, darling?' But she just kept staring at the floor.

'Oh, I'm sure she won't mind putting that off, would you, Ava?' He looked at her Tamagotchi. 'You fed your pet today?'

'Yes.' She looked up and smiled. 'He's full now.'

'Wow. You know something? I kept a Tamagotchi alive for months once.'

'Seriously? That's so cool.' She handed him the plastic toy and pressed a few buttons. 'Look. He makes this funny noise if I do that.'

'That is mega cool,' said Manny. 'You know what, I bet you can't be bothered to do your home study. How about you show me round your house? Your mommy already said I could. If there was time.'

'Oh no. I'm sorry. It's a bit late now. And Ava has to do her study, I'm afraid. Another time,' I chipped in, trying to keep my voice controlled but before I could say another word, Ava had leaped up and grabbed Manny's hand.

'Please, can I? Please. Just before everyone gets here,' and she turned to Manny and dragged him to the door. 'Will you tell me more about your Tamagotchi pet?'

'No, I'm sorry,' I told them both. 'I'll have to escort you. It's not that I don't trust you, Manny, It's just that—'

'You don't trust me. I get it,' he laughed. 'But this is all off-record. Unless, of course, there's stuff you don't want me to see.'

'No, no. It's not that.' I thought about the indoor swimming pool. How I was no longer sure of what was going on in my own home. How I needed to be in control of who went where in my house. And I didn't want Ava saying anything by mistake, after all, it hadn't been long. But then Joan walked in.

'I'll take them both,' she said, airing out a tea towel. 'No problem, Lara. You get ready. I know you've got a lot on.'

'Oh, Joan,' all the earlier irritation receded, 'are you are sure?'

'Of course.'

'Please, remember her home study, though,' I said. 'She's got to finish it before the announcement.' Joan looked at me and frowned.

I glanced over at Manny and widened my eyes.

'Oh, sure,' she said.

'And wait.' I grabbed Joan's arm and pulled her towards me. 'Not the swimming pool,' I told her. 'The indoor one. It hasn't been cleaned this week. And don't let Ava answer any intrusive questions,' I said under my breath.

'Of course, why do you think I'm going?' Joan winked. 'You get your make-up done. See you in a bit.'

When Joan, Manny and Ava left the room, I switched off the music.

'Everyone out,' I shouted. 'Now.' Within two minutes the room was empty, apart from Matthew.

I walked over to him, a tight smile on my face.

'What the *fuck*,' I hissed when I made sure that the last person had well and truly gone. 'This has been planned for weeks.'

'Listen, I'm sorry, sugar.' He took both my hands in his and for a minute, I nearly melted. I was annoyed with myself for having been sucked in by his beauty. 'I'm so sorry.' He started stroking the fleshy part of my palms. 'I promise it won't happen again.'

'You're damn fucking right it won't happen again.' My voice was perfectly steady but the inside of my body felt like someone had set fire to it.

'I went into the indoor-pool annexe,' I told him, my voice quiet and hard. 'Very interesting what I saw. And now everything makes sense. Some of the things you've told me. Some of the things I've pieced together. I get it now. Jesus Christ, Matthew.'

'Oh God, Lara. I'm sorry.' He pulled my hands up to his face. 'I can explain.' I looked around.

'No. You aren't to explain. You are never, ever, ever to speak of this in my house. Do you understand? I'm going to pretend I never knew.'

'Yes,' he said. 'But, please, I need to speak to someone about it . . . I didn't mean to . . . I had to – there's a part of me that . . .'

'Stop. If you mention it one more time, you and I are done.' Then he got defensive.

'Look, you don't have a fucking hold over me,' he started saying. 'You don't own me.' He pushed his blond hair back and even after knowing him as long as I had, I was still struck by him.

'We have a bigger problem. Ava was with me.' I grabbed his hands, pulling him towards me. 'She saw things she shouldn't have done. You understand? Couldn't you have been doing normal things that Hollywood actors do? Sex, drugs and rock 'n' roll? This, though? It's fucked. More fucked than anything I've ever known. And the consequences? How can you live with yourself,' I spat. He looked like he was going to cry but I carried on. 'So you need to make it up. To both of us. You'd better be on time for the announcement.'

'Oh God. OK,' he said.

'You do everything I say from now on,' I told him. 'Or . . .'

'Or what? You'll go to the press? Tell everyone everything?' He put on a babyish voice.

'Shut up.' I raised my fists up to his chest. 'Just shut up. Please. You still don't understand. My daughter. I won't have you . . .'

'Don't speak to me like that.' He grabbed my shoulders and held me square to him.

'I'll speak to you how I please, do you know what's at stake here?' I turned and gestured my arm across the room and it was only when I looked round that I saw Joan by the door. Matthew and I both started.

'Oh, Lara.' She pretended to jump, 'I just came back because I wanted to ask you what time you needed us back. That's all,' she said, but she was looking as though she might cry. She was pulling at the front strands of her hair, over and over, curling them into thin ropes.

'Twenty minutes,' I sang. 'That'll be fine.' I turned my back.

'OK.' She narrowed her eyes at us before walking out of the room.

'Look. I'm sorry, Lara.' Matthew drew me in tight. 'I'm sorry. This whole thing, it's messed with my mind. So much. You can see, can't you? The horrors of it. The nightmares. That's why . . . that's why. I can explain. Everything.'

'No. Last time this is mentioned. Ever.'

'Fine,' he said. I thought he might explode, so I had to switch off every single emotion, to try and ensure that the atmosphere was calm. If I pretended all was fine, and that I was happy, all would be well.

'OK, Matthew. All forgotten,' I said, clapping my hands. 'Let's just make this fun, shall we?' He looked pleased and relieved but inside I was still churning with anger, fear and shock.

It was nearly another half an hour before Joan, Ava and Manny returned. Ava and Manny were giggling and discussing real pets.

'I would really like a toy poodle,' said Ava. 'They're so cute but Mom worries about the hairs on the furniture.'

'I would like a sloth,' said Manny. 'So it would make me feel less lazy.' Ava threw her head back and laughed.

'Hello, you three,' I said as they came into the room.

'Thanks for the tour,' said Manny. 'I'll be off now. But just to let you know, you have quite the daughter there.' He patted Ava on the shoulder. 'You know that? You are one very cool little six-year-old.'

'Oh, thank you.' She grinned. 'Will you come back another time?'

'I sure can. If your mommy will have me.'

She looked at me then and tugged at my arm.

'Can he? Come back?'

'Sure,' I said, knowing full well I wouldn't allow it but so relieved he'd managed to calm her down. Manny grabbed a denim jacket from the armchair where he'd left it.

'By the way,' he said, slinging it over his shoulders. He leaned forward and spoke right in my ear. 'Your daughter.' He looked over at Ava. 'I meant what I said. Off-record.' He laughed. 'She's a cool little cookie. You take good care of her.'

'I will,' I told him. 'I will.'

'No.' He grabbed my arm. 'I mean it. You've got something amazing there. Cherish her. She's very close to her nanny, isn't she? Called her Mommy by mistake.' He said it with a slight laugh, but as soon as he said those words, my stomach dropped. If I reacted I'd look defensive. If I didn't, I wouldn't be acknowledging Joan's efforts and I'd look mean.

'Joan. We couldn't live without her. We really couldn't.' Even my teeth stung.

'Well. Anyway' – he waved – 'just, you know, take good care. Ones like this don't come along very often. Make sure you spend time with her.' He held out his hand. 'Thanks again for the access.'

'No problem at all.' I watched him leave the room, thinking about what he'd just said – how one damning piece could destroy everything – and then I felt enraged that he was judging me like this. How dare he. How *dare* he. I spent more than enough time with my daughter. I knew her from back to front. I knew the things that upset her. I knew that she was happiest in the garden whilst I sunbathed and read. I knew that she itched her nose three times before she went to sleep. I felt something swell inside me. I wanted to stop myself but before I could rationalise any of it, I had stepped right forward.

'Wait,' I called him back. 'I'm a good mother, you know. I do spend time with her.' I was aware I sounded desperate and needy but there wasn't enough time to find another way into the conversation. 'I'm a good parent. I single-handedly raised her to be who she is now. With Joan's help, of course. And our housekeepers, Marcy and Rosa. And everyone around us. But it's me. I am a good mother.'

'Hey.' He held up his hands. 'Slow down, Lara King.' He let out a long, slow exhale. 'Hey, lady.' He looked at me then, eyebrows meeting in the middle. 'Cool it. I never said anything. I never said you were a bad mother.'

I watched him walk out the door. Everything felt like it was moving in slow motion. I hadn't been able to charm him like

I had with most of the others. One thing that I could control was people reacting well to me when they met me.

God, we thought you'd be so, well ... *different*, they'd say, searching for the right words. And then I'd make sure I pulled back a bit. Just enough that they didn't think they could get *too* close. Or I'd signal to whoever was on security duty that day to step forward and move me away. *Sorry, Lara's got another meeting now. Thank you.*

But Manny – I thought about the inscrutable expression on his face. I wasn't used to it – people not being taken by me. Yet he hadn't done any of the other things that people normally do when they see me in real life.

Even if they try and hide it, I can always detect something: a quickening of breath, a slight flush, a dart of tongue licking a lower lip. Or the way they pretend not to know *anything* about me. Ever so careful with what they say, should they give the game away. *Play it cool, cucumber. It's Lara King but I'm going to pretend I don't care.* But with Manny – with Manny, it was all too strange. None of that mattered. It felt like he could see right through me, deep into my bones. It scared me and I wanted him out of the house. The thought he could see all the things that I kept hidden.

My fans,

This is truly the most difficult thing I've ever had to write. As I'm sure you all know, today, my daughter Ava went missing in Laurel Canyon. There has been no sighting of her since this morning. For those of you who follow us, and have supported us from the beginning, I know you will be finding this devastating.

There have been many, many leads and for that, we are so, so grateful. Please – keep them coming. Click **here** for more details.

The police have been doing an amazing job, although we've been told to keep details to a minimum, so officers can concentrate on the search for Ava because at the moment, we have no idea what's happened to her. They've been following up every line of enquiry but until she's found and safe with me at home, I won't rest.

Before I go any further, I wanted to set straight a few of the events from that day, so there will be no more speculation about what happened.

Ava and I drove to Laurel Canyon. At that time, I made a phone call, during which Ava stopped and asked me if we could make a pit stop. I pulled over and she got out. I carried on my phone call. I know, already you must be thinking: stupid woman. I'm thinking it too, believe me.

It was after some period of time that I realised Ava had been gone for too long. At this point I got out the car and tried to find my little girl. The pain and guilt I'm feeling is like nothing I've ever experienced, and I'm desperately sorry for what's happened.

I know that some of you may be thinking that I left my child. I was momentarily distracted. I should have gone with her. But it was a spare moment to finish my phone call, a chance to chat to someone without distraction, which as you know, can be all too difficult to do when we are constantly under pressure.

But I just want to ask you one thing. Please. Don't punish her for my wrongdoing. Please, don't turn against us when she needs you the most.

I know you miss her. I miss her.

I miss her so very, very much. I need her back and she needs to be right here, home, with those who love her the most in the world.

Yours, with all my love, hope and affection,

Lara King

England, July 2004

I woke up, fragments of the night before flitting through my mind. White-trainers guy. *I can change your life.* The long walk home filled with hope and promise, propelling me forward step by step. I could still taste Red Bull, sweet and cloying in my mouth. I couldn't bring myself to get up; my bedsit had no heating and I was shivering in my T-shirt. I reached over to the old wooden stool I'd found on a pavement among other rubbish, and grabbed the business card, turning it over and over in my hands. *Ben Finn. Talent Management.* It wasn't until after lunch that I made the call. I'd dragged it out on purpose, ignoring the excitement billowing in my stomach.

'It's Lara,' I said, when he answered. 'From the nightclub.' There was a silence on the line that made me think he'd hung up. 'Hello?' I said.

'Hi. Sorry about that.' I heard a whispering down the line. 'I'm pleased you rang. I'm sorry if I freaked you out last night. I just wanted to speak to you. Properly. Not in those surroundings. Bloody awful club.' He laughed. 'Nice to meet you, Lara. Listen. You've got something. That's what I wanted to tell you.' I heard the click of a pen and then the scratch of lines on paper. 'Look, loads of people can sing. It's not just that. You've got *something*. I can't explain it. When you were singing. I couldn't ...' He'd gone silent. 'I couldn't take my eyes off you. Not in that way,

I have a fiancée, remember? I mentioned it last night. I'm not interested in you like that. It was something else. A quality.' I had gone quiet too, my cheeks flooded with heat. 'Anyway, there's a singing competition soon,' he said. 'That's what I was trying to explain to you in the club. I just couldn't focus. With all that noise. *Idolz*. It's new. On ITV. It's going to be big. I want to put you forward, Lara. I sat listening that whole time you were with your mate. So would you be up for it?'

'I guess so.' I shrugged but pressed the handset tight to my face and my surroundings took on a dream-like quality.

'Right. OK.' He'd slowed his voice down. 'Let's not get ahead of ourselves,' he added, as though he'd read my mind.

'I'm not,' I snapped, bringing myself back to reality but he didn't seem to be listening.

'So, let's get sorted. After we've had an initial meeting and gone over contracts, all that kind of thing, we'll need to work on your story.' I took a deep breath. 'We need to be quick. Deadline for application is soon. So start thinking about it. Your narrative. Before I start filling out all the forms. The producers like that kind of thing. For example, is there anything I need to know about? From your past? It'll come out, if you get through. I don't know much about the format yet but my contact at the production company says they're trying to make it quite personal. Get the audience hooked on each contestant. That kind of thing.'

'You can tell them that I have a happy life,' I started. 'We aren't well off or anything. We don't have much. Tell them that I want to make good of myself.'

'You aren't well off?' he asked. 'I need to make them really sit up – give you the whole Cinderella backstory.'

'Fine,' I told him. 'Go the whole hog. Tell them that I suffered badly when I was a child. That my parents are really excited about this. You know what to write, surely.' I was getting carried away, thinking about how I could become the nation's poster girl for turning my life around. London being paved with gold. That I am 'just an ordinary girl who has made it and look, so can you'.

'OK,' he said. 'I'll fill it in later after we've been through all the boring stuff. This will be good,' he says. 'And apart from that, if anything does happen, we need to make sure that you don't have any . . .'

'Any what?'

'Well, skeletons in your closet. Put it that way. Anything that could come out later in the press that might, well, destroy your reputation. You know if you ever became big people like to betray you. Lure of money. Of power.' I couldn't believe he was already talking as though I was going to be a star. 'So at least if you tell me if there's anything you've done, I can manage it before it gets to that point. All right? You don't need to tell me now. I just want you to think about it for the time being. That's your homework.' He went quiet, waiting for me to say something. *Anything.*

'No.' I heard his breath stop down the phone. Because at that point, it had been absolutely true. 'No,' I tell him again. 'Nothing on me. I'm as good as gold.'

He laughed. 'Lara King. As good as gold,' he chuckled again. 'That's what I like to hear.'

'I can't believe this.' Conor rushed into my study. 'Your website has crashed. Too many people visiting it after your letter to the public went live. I've got IT on it now. But it's worked.'

'Thank God.' I looked at myself in the mirrored part of a photo frame on my study desk, as I thought of it being read. 'Should we do anything else?'

He massaged his earlobe. 'No, we don't want overkill. We need to leave it now. We need to leave the narrative to breathe. There's going to be people looking into your past, though, so we need to be careful. They're going to use this as an opportunity to find other things they see as *inadequate parenting* from you. So we have to prepare for that and anything else.' He gave me an odd look at that point, narrowing his eyes, his head tilted to the right.

Flashes came back to me then. Ben Finn in the nightclub, wearing white trainers, his eyes fixed on mine

And then afterwards, leaving England. I thought about how people had turned once. How I'd managed to rein it back in. How I wasn't going to let that happen again, because when my daughter came back, we were going to carry on as we had before and I was going to make sure everything was absolutely perfect for her. I felt better now, after my chat with Joan. We'd done something proactive that had had a positive effect for the search. I told myself not to play to the earlier guilt. That it was good that Ava had a female role model to look up to in me. But still, my heart clenched when I thought about what I'd do if she didn't come home.

'Lara?' Conor said. 'Are you with me? Listen. If there's something you need to tell me, you need to let me know now. Before I get any more of these.' He showed me his phone. I looked over, skimmed through a load of phone messages from his office.

'What the hell are these?' I asked.

'I've just been talking to you about them. Haven't you heard a word I've been saying?' I shook my head. 'Messages saying they had to talk to you. About England. They've been talking about Be Squared?' At the mention of it, my mouth filled with a bitter taste. The throb of music. The sparkle of diamonds. I started to feel like I was going to throw up.

'Some nutter,' I told him, pleased he hadn't googled Be Squared and found all the old headlines. Even though the press had only managed to get a fraction of the story, I didn't want him thinking there was more to things than had initially been reported. 'Ignore them. There's nothing to tell.' I passed back his phone.

'OK, good,' he said. 'So I can tell the office we're good? Because obviously now the police have released the CCTV footage of you and Ava at that red light.' He crossed his arms. 'And I want the public focus to remain on that now. I think it's going to be useful.'

'Fine. All fine,' I said. 'Anything else?' I wanted to be alone to do more online searches on Media Spy and see what was going on.

'No,' Conor said. 'We need to keep quiet for a while. Don't want the public to think we are in any way capitalising on anything.' He bit his lip when he realised the implication.

But I hadn't exploded. Because I knew it would be a possibility you might think that. See? I told you. I know you. I know how your minds work. And although I like to think that such cynical behaviour wouldn't enter your psyche, well – somehow, just somehow – it might be planted in there by the things you read, the images you see. The headlines you skim when you're on your way to work.

I've been guilty of it myself, you see.

So I know.

I'm sorry for earlier. Cardinal sin. Bringing myself into the story. Back to the important things.

Wow. Just wow. It's eerie here. But beautiful. The canyon's lit up with the back glare of cell screens. Every motherfucker here is watching that video of Lara and Ava at the red light.

Play, rewind, repeat. Because we're all thinking the same thing. What the hell happened to Ava King? She just vanished and that was it. No clues, no nothing.

'Oh my God, there she is,' everyone's whispering and pointing to their screens. 'Look. That might be the last time any of us ever see her alive.' I've watched it too, over and over. The way Ava looks right out the window as they stop at the lights. She's perfect. And Lara, in the front seat. Those diamonds. Freaking hell, those diamonds! She looks so beautiful too. I wanted to reach right out and touch her face. And they looked so happy together. I guess it was. They searched Lara's car. Took all the fingerprint swabs. All was exactly as it should have been. Clean, perfect and lovely. Just like both of them.

There are candles everywhere too, and Chinese lanterns, floating up into the sky. Beautiful fire, orange against the black night. The stars are out too. I wished for Ava on one.

People are singing, praying, chanting. It's like a shrine here and it's gone all quiet. If you listen carefully you can hear songs too, from across the canyon. People have stopped shouting for Ava now. Occasionally there's a scream, echoing across the place. The bark of a dog. But otherwise there's this weird atmosphere. Like people are just waiting, waiting for the call that they've found a body.

'She's not dead yet,' I want to shout. 'Come on. Don't give up. Don't give up on her.'

I'm still here, by the media scrum. If I'm quiet, hunched over behind their vans, I can hear the news reporters talking in their hushed, urgent voices. It's where I'm getting most of my updates from because they don't know I'm there.

'We can't release that yet,' they're saying. 'Police orders' and all that shite but Ryan_Gosling_Wannabe is here to give you the dirt, all the juicy stuff I've been collecting on the way. Titbits from Casey Lane, hack extraordinaire. She's been talking to her friend at the *LA Times*, apparently. Manny Berkowitz.

Casey says there's something on Matthew that Manny's hiding. 'That fat bastard,' she was hissing. 'He knows something. I'm going to fucking find out what it is if it's the last fucking thing I do on this godforsaken earth.'

Word also has it (sorry, Case, I know that earwigging isn't the done thing but I also know that you would do the same thing in my situation) that Matthew was being questioned earlier as a 'person of interest', whatever that means. Apparently, the big whisper of the day from the *Sky News* van is that perfect Matthew Raine wasn't where he told police he was at the time Ava disappeared. They can't trace his phone signal for a part of the day. Something about someone knowing someone at the telecoms company but it's not set in stone, folks. Need two sources to verify and all. (See, I'm getting the hang of this!)

Anyway, that's all I got, folks, from behind the scenes. But I promise to let you in on the scoop as soon as I have it here.

As for the police, they're still here, trailing the area. I saw the forensics shaking their heads earlier too. 'Nothing,' they said to the weirdly staring detective who was here earlier. 'We've found nothing.' Ha! There's good lip-reading for you.

Btw y'all see me on *Sky News*? They're repeating it on the hour every hour. If you like it, please feel free to retweet and share! Ryan_Gosling_Wannabe bringing you the latest on Ava King.

Click **here** for the link.

Here with the latest updates on missing Ava King, brought to you by Lara and Ava King's number one fan.

Twitter: @ryan_gosling_wannabe

'I'd like to be famous,' Ava once told me, her brown eyes search-ing my face. 'Like you.' And then she'd asked me how everyone knew who I was. 'All the paps that chase you all the time. Why do they want to do that?' I wanted her back here now, so that I could tell her that soon she'd be more famous than she could possibly imagine. She might laugh. See the irony in it all. That her face, right now, was probably one of the most recognised on the planet. I wanted so desperately to tell her that that was a mad thought. That I was sorry she had got what she wanted and that she wasn't here to enjoy it.

Conor came in again. Darkness had settled and he looked more agitated than ever, blinking three, four times in a row on repeat.

'I have a feeling things might start unravelling,' he said.

I battled to keep from losing myself entirely. 'Conor. Please, you're meant to keep things calm for me.' I battled to keep from losing myself entirely.

'OK.' He inhaled a great gulp of air. 'OK. Let's start again, Lara. Manny, he's got something. On Matthew. He wants our statement before he releases it. But it doesn't look good.' His voice had sped up again and I could barely make out what he was saying to me.

'Conor. Stop it.' I was angry. Wasn't I going through enough? 'Conor. Stop. Please. I can't keep up. There's a million things going on in my brain right now. Just start from the beginning. I'm trying to pick up a thread halfway through.'

'I'm sorry, Lara. I'm sorry.' He stopped and pressed his fingertips to his lips. 'OK. I'm sorry. I'm ready. Do you remember at the announcement, Matthew was late?' I didn't like where this was going. But then I thought there's no way Manny could have any idea about the swimming pool.

'I remember. Yes.'

'We told Manny during the announcement that Matthew was late because his dad was in hospital.'

'God damnit.' I held my hand up to my chest. 'God damnit. Seriously. I don't need this now. There's a missing child. Why's he pestering about a small white lie?' But as I said it, I was thinking about everything else that Manny could uncover.

'I know. He rang me just now. He'd been to find out what hospital Mr Raine Senior was in. To try and get him to make a statement about Ava. Or something. Who knows with Manny.'

'Well, he could have still been in hospital? Couldn't he?'

'Well, I tried that. But Manny's ferocious at his job. He's like a fucking parasite. Apparently he thought something was dodgy when Matthew came back with wet hair, smelling freshly washed.' I remembered then, Manny asking if Matthew had been for a shower and that he'd said no. That's apparently when he became suspicious.

'Well, I couldn't very well tell him that I'd been to have a shower whilst everyone was waiting, could I?' he had told me.

'It wouldn't have taken Manny long.' Conor leaned his head back and massaged the bridge of his nose. 'He traced Raine

Senior to Fremantle Prison in Perth. Somehow managed to get out from the guards that he'd been right as rain.'

'We can't let this get out.' I thought of Matthew's father. It had been one of the first things he'd told me. 'Of course, no one knows,' Matthew had said, as he'd sat next to me on the large cream sofa in my lounge. 'I've never really told people this before but I need to tell you. Just so you know everything. My dad. He's locked up. Behind bars.' He had wiped his mouth.

'Oh God,' I'd said.

'We were out drinking at this watering hole in the middle of nowhere back home in Perth. Me and my old man. Anyway, there was a brawl. I can't remember what it was about. Then my dad – I followed him outside to the back of the pub in this small square. Thought he was going for a smoke. Turns out he . . .' Matthew had swallowed then, unable to go on. I had held my hand out to his.

'It's OK,' I'd whispered.

'He punched this guy. He'd said some things. About me. My dad was steaming angry. Went at him. And, well . . .'

'Well?'

'That was it. One punch. It was over. The guy got airlifted to hospital but he died a day later. He never meant to hurt him badly. He's a good man, my dad. A real good man.'

'I'm so sorry.'

'It's OK. It's weird. He's the softest guy, Pa. He's not some crazy' – he'd bitten his thumbnail – 'murderer. He loves me so much. Was being loyal. But to see the family of the guy. I had to look them in the eye. I was the only one there to be a witness. Against my own father. Anyway. It's all in the past. They never want to talk of it again.' He'd read my mind as to whether it would ever come out in the press. 'Come on, drink up.' He passed me an alcohol-free beer. 'Let's go crazy.'

I looked at Conor, thinking about the conversation I'd had with Matthew about his father and wondering how much Matthew had told him. 'I know this cannot get out,' Conor replied. It seemed he knew more than he was letting on. 'Look. I don't want to be bothering you with this. Normally I'd deal with it. As you know. But I need your input here, Lara.'

'And I'm giving it to you.' I felt strangled. 'Aren't I? What am I doing? Oh God. I'm sorry. Yes. I'm here.'

'Shall we give him something in return? He's suggested something.'

'What?' Although I already knew what was coming, thinking back to Manny asking me questions about Ava's father before the announcement.

'No, no. I'm not going into Ava's paternity. Not now. At the very least that would be of the height of disrespect to Ava. And how on earth would that look?' I clung to the edge of my desk begging for some form of respite or some good news. I wasn't going to put myself in the firing line where Matthew and his father were concerned.

'Ring Mcgraw,' I said. 'Tell Manny he'll have to stop under police instructions. That it will impact the investigation.'

'Done that. Didn't work. As if Manny gave two shits. He's pissed you lied to him.' I thought back to the panic that had overwhelmed me. The swimming pool. The big announcement. Mine and Ava's future. 'He says that under the circumstances, it looks dodgy you lied about why Matthew was late.'

'What the hell does that mean?' The pit of my stomach fired up. 'What's he insinuating? I don't like that. I lied to him because he's a member of the press and I don't want them knowing every single in and out of our lives.'

'Listen.' Conor chewed his lip. 'OK. I shouldn't have asked you. Don't worry about that. I'll sort him out. I'll figure it out. But, Lara, you need to tell me. You need to tell me about Ava's dad. So I can—'

'You need to know nothing,' I said in a breezy voice. I squeezed the edge of the table again, thinking about Ava's father.

'It wasn't' – he swallowed – 'non-consensual, was it? Because—'

'No. No it wasn't. But it was a mistake. It was someone I met at a party here in LA. I'd never met him before. But we both clearly fancied each other. I drank too much. So did he. That was it. There's no crazy secret. No one from my past who is going to sell a story on me. No one who knows about Ava.' I thought back to Detective Mcgraw's face when I'd told him the same thing. The way he'd looked just past my cheek and chewed at his lip, and the way my mind had immediately filled the gaps into what he'd been thinking of me.

'Fine,' he said. My mind started jumping from thought to thought. Ava, Manny, Matthew. 'Leave Manny to me, then,' he said. 'That OK?'

'Yes. I don't care. Just think about it. Think about what's at stake here,' I said. 'Please.'

He turned to leave but then looked back at me. 'Why so secretive then? About Ava's father?' *God, not you now too, please, Conor.* He was the one person I could rely on not to ask questions and to get on with his job.

'Because—' I thought about how to answer him. 'Because mine and Ava's relationship is sacred. Something special. Mother and daughter bond.' A sharpness twisted in me. 'And I don't want that ruined by anyone else. She's mine, you understand? I don't want someone I barely knew at the time sullying it. Reminding me daily that I slept with a stranger. And who knows what he'd want from me.'

'OK.' With that, he left the room. 'I'll go and deal with it. I'll speak to him again. See what I can do.'

'Thank you, Conor.' I thought back to Ava, how she'd never really asked about her father until Matthew had come onto the scene, and how I'd told her that it didn't matter. We had all we needed here in our home – with Joan and Rosa and Marcy – and that we were strong.

But all these questions were setting me on edge. People demanding too much from me, wanting to know this or that when really, they should be thinking about Ava. And then I thought about someone else who might be affected by Manny's line of questioning. I picked up the intercom. I realised I'd have to tell Matthew about his dad.

'Matthew?' I said. There was no answer. 'Your dad. Things are going on. You might want to prep him.' But still he didn't answer. Perhaps I could ask Joan to find him. Perhaps I could get up and look. But something paralysed me to the spot. I felt too fearful to move, like a child scared to get out of bed in case there was a monster underneath it.

But then I remembered the house security cameras. I could log on. If he wasn't answering the intercom, I could search for him that way. Detective Mcgraw still had my phone, so I opened up the browser on my laptop and logged in to the HomeCam website. I flicked from room to room with the cursor, but he didn't seem to be anywhere in the house. But then I scrolled to the downstairs cameras, Joan's part of the home, where Ava also had her bedroom. And there he was.

Peculiar, I thought. He and Joan looked like they were talking. They hated each other. Or so I thought. Weird. I watched the back of his head and then he looked up, right at the cameras, and walked off. I thought about using the intercom downstairs to alert them to the fact I knew they were together, but something stopped me. I felt like I was being untethered in space. I couldn't work out if things had taken on sinister overtones because I was in shock over Ava, or whether there really was something odd going on. And then I noticed a message flashing up on the screen of my computer.

Warning: Security tapes have been removed from the hard drive, back-up copies available only.

The hard-copy security tapes. Removed? Someone had taken them. Detective Mcgraw. *It must be.* After all, they'd taken the computers, phones, and my car. *Everything.* I tried to remember when there'd been a time I hadn't been around to see what Detective Mcgraw was doing. He'd told me about when he'd taken the computer and my phone. I hadn't even seen him go into the utility room. Perhaps he hadn't wanted to give anyone any prior warning they were being taken for analysis.

I couldn't ask anyone, as I didn't want to alert people to the fact that they'd gone, or that they were available and that I was even thinking of them at all.

But then I thought about the swimming pool. The way someone had covered the annexe security camera.

If someone inside the house had taken them, it meant they were trying to hide something. And if Detective Mcgraw had taken them for analysis, he'd also find out that someone had tried to cover up the footage of the pool.

I sat very still, thinking about monsters under the bed. Except at that point, they felt like they were crawling all over my house.

'What shall I wear?' I asked Hannah, looking down at my jeans – ripped, but not in a cool way. 'To the audition?'

'*Audition?* Fuck, never thought you'd say those words so soon. You want to look done up but not too try-hardy. Don't you?' she said as we lay on the damp grass drinking wine outside her parents' home.

'I guess.' I looked at Hannah, moonlight shimmering over her face. 'I don't know. That's why I was hoping you'd help me?' She leaned over and squealed.

'Shall we go inside? Let's look through all my clothes.' She got up, sliding the wine bottle under her arm. 'You can take whatever you like. Mum and Dad aren't back till Monday, so don't worry about them.' I got up after her, and we went inside.

'Come on.' She opened the drinks cabinet and took out a bottle of Malibu. 'Let's go upstairs.'

Her bedroom was neat, with fluffy carpets, and photo frames of her and her sister Mae, their faces drenched in sunlight, smiling and laughing in every snap.

'OK. You.' She pushed me on to her bed. 'Sit down. Have you ever even worn make-up before?'

'Nah.' I touched my face. 'Not really. Apart from when we went to Dancing Buddha. And you made me wear that mascara.'

'Jesus Christ. You really are quite something.' She opened her wardrobe, pulling out piles and piles of shiny black boxes. 'Make-up course,' she said. 'I wanted to be a make-up artist but got the job I have now instead. Thought it would be a quicker way to get noticed.' I think about her work as a receptionist at a nightclub and how she was going to pull rank there.

'No wonder you always look so perfectly made-up,' I told her. She got to work on my face, priming and powdering. She smeared an iridescent white cream over my cheekbones, then dabbed some juicy pink gloss onto the back of her hand, and patted it onto my lips.

'Go *mwah*.' I did as she asked. 'God. You really don't know what the hell you're doing, do you? Right. Setting powder now, some mascara and eyeshadow and then we're done. Look up?' I blinked as she slid the black wand over my lashes.

'OK. Let me look now.' She stepped back. 'Fuck me. You ever seen yourself done up? Look in the mirror. Actually, wait. Let me get you dressed first.'

'What? What do you mean?'

'Nothing. Just that I think the camera will love you. Can't wait for you to see.'

She'd thrown a pair of jeans at me. 'These and, hmmm, these.' She chucked some high heels at me and an off-the-shoulder top. 'These will look cool.'

I slid them on, and then stepped into the black patent heels. I took off my bra and put on her top. She'd stood, puffing out her cheeks, letting out a long, slow whistle.

'Jesus, you look – fuck. Look in the mirror.'

She swivelled me round and we both looked at my reflection. I wasn't expecting much. But when I saw myself, I felt a loosening in my chest.

'I know you're not meant to put any importance on looks, blah, blah.' Hannah peered over my shoulder. 'But holy cow. You're gonna knock 'em dead. You'd better bring me with you.' She cupped her hands under her bra. 'I've only got these babies to work with.'

'No you don't,' I told her. 'You are beautiful.' I wanted to look at her, but I couldn't stop staring at my own reflection. I looked like those girls on the telly. Glammed and glitzed, spruced and shined and I opened my mouth to start humming my song. *'If only I could, if only I would.'*

She rested her chin on my shoulder and we both stared in the mirror. 'I know we haven't been mates for long. But I'm so excited I met you.' I thought back to the promotions job we'd both done for a party night at a club in Essex. How we both vowed that we hadn't left our families behind for nothing and that we were going to find fame and fortune whatever the cost. 'You did it,' she said. 'I really am gonna be friends with a famous person.' She went on. 'Just remember, I knew you before.'

I wanted to tell her that she was wrong, that she mustn't jinx it, but the words felt like velvet draped over my body and I stayed silent thinking about the audition and meeting the TV producers, and backstage and the cameras. And then she sighed.

'And your voice too,' she said. 'You've got it all. Bitch.'

I had it all, I repeated her words in my head. *And I wasn't going to lose it.*

Nothing was going to get in my way.

'I'm tired,' Ava told me. 'My tummy hurts.'

'Have something to eat. There's all the food for the press,' I pointed to a table that was laid out beautifully with canapés on silver platters. 'Just don't touch the ones that have been styled. Look, there's the vegetable tray.' I looked at her stomach. 'Have one of those. Not the carb stuff.'

'Can you come with me?' she asked. 'I don't want to go alone. There are too many people.'

'Ask Joan.' I looked over but couldn't see her. 'We've got an hour before the announcement so I'm just trying to keep calm.' I nodded towards the huge cameras that would broadcast the live feed to millions. 'Just don't get filmed piling food into your mouth,' I said. 'Oh, Ava, I'm joking,' I told her when I caught sight of her face and she crumpled.

'I don't want to do it,' she cried. I pulled her out of the way into my study and thanked God that Manny had gone and that the rest of the press hadn't been allowed in yet. I dabbed at her eyes with a piece of tissue paper from a small black and white mother of pearl inlaid table. I could hear Joan talking to Matthew in the other room.

'What?' I said. 'What is it that you don't want to do?'

'I don't want to do the announcement. With everyone watching.' She had moved over to one of my office chairs. She climbed into it and span it round, her knees knocking the side of my desk. I walked over and placed my hand on the edge of the chair. I thought about Ava and how much she loved doing things for the public. How much she wanted to be like me. 'Famous, Mommy, so that everyone knows me.' And so I wondered why on earth she was behaving like this. The earlier debacle in the swimming pool had all been sorted in my mind and she had seemed happy enough after Manny left.

'Stop,' I told her. 'It's not a toy. What's wrong? You've been like this all morning. You know what today means to me. *Us.*' I swallowed.

'My real dad,' she said. 'I want to know about my real dad.'

'Now, Ava.' I gripped the edge of the chair again wondering if Manny had managed to say something to her when no one was listening. 'We've talked about this before, haven't we, sweetie?' I looked at my watch. It was nearing time. I thought about the hashtags gaining momentum. The way Conor had promised me that the media and public interest would be ramped up right about now. 'We'll set things viral about half an hour before. That way we know the whole world will be tuned in. And then bam!' He'd wiggled his fingers right in front of my face.

'I know you said that my real dad doesn't want us. But I don't want Matthew. He's not my real dad and he . . .'

'And he what?' My voice sounded sharp.

'He—' I pulled out my mobile phone. 'He— nothing,' she said. 'Actually, he's a horrible man.' She looked at me, her lower lip stuck out. I put my phone back onto the table. I had to play this right. If I indulged her too much she'd get worked up and ruin the announcement. Not enough and I risked her getting agitated.

'Oh, you don't mean that.' I made sure not to ask her what she knew. 'Actually, you know what, Ava. Matthew is a good man. He really is. You may think some things about him. But he is a good man.' I couldn't even begin to explain to her everything that had gone on. I thought of Matthew. How the things he'd been through had led him to act strangely at times, and now, after seeing what I had in the annexe, it all made sense. But despite it all, he was good.

'Listen, darling. If I thought Matthew was bad, I wouldn't be with him. I wouldn't let you near him. Of course not. I'm your mummy. You know that. You might have seen things that *look* bad. But you don't know the full story.'

She nodded then. That's all she needed, I told myself. Some reassurance now and then. It's all anyone ever needed.

'OK? You understand? So remember – it's not Matthew's fault that things are changing here. Change is a good thing. New beginnings. Listen, Ava . . .' I pulled her hands towards me. 'It's always been you and me, hasn't it?' We both looked over at the photographs scattered around the room, her eyes in each one, shining out next to mine. 'Hasn't it? Am I right?' She put her hands back in her lap. 'So don't you think it would be nice if someone else came into our family. So that we had someone else to look after us?'

'But we've got Joan,' she said, flicking a bit of cotton off her knee. 'And Rosa and Marcy. They're our family.'

'Me,' I tell her. 'You don't want *me* to be lonely, do you? What happens when you grow up, Ava. When you leave me?

I'll have no one then. It'd be nice for once to have someone looking after me.'

'I look after you.' She looked down into her knees, her voice small. 'I try to.'

'I know but sometimes I need more, you know?'

'Do you love me?' she asked. 'Tell me the truth. Do you love me?' I frowned. Where the hell was this coming from?

'Yes. I love you. Of course I do. You shouldn't be asking those types of questions, Ava.' Matthew appeared at the door. 'You guys, we ready for this?' He looked at me first and then Ava. 'Cos I'm ready. We're gonna do this together?'

Ava looked at me then, her eyes scanning my face so I bent down and whispered into her ear.

'You wait,' I said. 'You wait and see what it will be like. And don't forget. Our day out together. *Alone.*' I grabbed her hand and lifted it into the air but she snatched it back. 'Ava,' I sang, but there was a warning tone in my voice. 'Ava. Now come on. We know how to behave in front of our guests, don't we?

'I don't want to. Matthew.' I reminded myself that she just needed reassurance.

'Look. It's OK, honey. The swimming pool. Just . . .' I flicked my hand. 'Just remember, your day out. I can't take you if you don't cooperate with me now, Ava. So one more time. Are we ready?' And she looked at me, her chin set forward. I held my breath, although I wanted to shout at her that we were actually keeping millions of people waiting. That this wasn't a game, but I knew if I did, I'd scare her. And I needed her onside. The bridge of my nose started to tingle.

'Fine,' she said as I released my breath.

'Yup.' I held our arms up and waved them around. 'We're ready everyone.' I pulled Ava along and I could hear Joan whispering from down the hallway. 'Ava,' she was hissing. 'Come here. You don't have to do this, you know.' I wanted to scream, but we were in a public space and people were walking around carrying vases of flowers and chairs. I had no idea if the paps had started arriving for the announcement. 'Joan, I've got it,' I said in as firm a voice as possible. 'Thank you. I'll take it from here.'

'She says I don't have to.' Ava looked up at me and Matthew was busy looking down, swiping his finger from left to right on his phone. 'Joan says I don't have to.'

'Joan doesn't mean that,' I told her. 'You're coming with me.'

'No,' said Ava. 'I want to go with Joan.' She stayed right where she was with her hands on her hips.

'Now come on, Ava, this is not like you at all.' I looked over at Joan who shrugged her shoulders.

'I'm so sorry,' she said. 'I didn't mean for her to go against you. I just thought I'd try and make her feel more relaxed.' She squeezed Ava's shoulders. 'She seems, well, tense. Peculiar.' It wasn't like Joan to be so forthright about Ava. She was normally good at disciplining and guiding her without being too much in our way.

'She's fine.' I thought of all the people waiting to tune in and then my phone beeped. Conor.

Hashtag the announcement is trending. We're all set to go. Live feeds sorted. Everyone's geared up and excited!

'We're all a bit tense.' I clapped my hands trying to lighten the atmosphere. 'So, come on, Ava,' I told her. 'You're the star of the show. You know that, don't you?' I looked at Joan, tensing my jaw. 'So don't please make her feel anything but.'

She nodded at me and gave a small grimace to Ava, as if to say, *Sorry, I tried.*

I took my daughter by the hand and I turned to Joan.

'This is a happy announcement,' I said to no one in particular. 'So I hope everyone is going to be on board.'

'I hope it's a happy time for Ava,' Joan said. She had no idea what we were going to announce as Conor had told us to keep it quiet but she still looked like she wanted to hurt me. 'It is.' I worried then that I was going to let rip. 'So please help me with Ava.' *As is your job*, I wanted to add. And then I thought about the vast amounts of money I pay her.

'I will,' said Joan. 'And, Lara, I know you're busy now.' She started pushing her hair back from her face. 'But after the announcement I really would like to talk to you about something.'

'Fine.' I hoped that would shut her up for a bit. 'Ready, little one?' I turned to Ava. She nodded and I could see she was back to her normal self again. I had never had this problem with her before. She was usually so acquiescent and well behaved. I knew it must all be down to earlier.

'Good girl, Ava. You don't want to show yourself up, do you? In front of millions of people?' A look crossed her face then – terror mixed up with determination. It reminded me of myself when I'd been younger, back in England, and then I squeezed her hand. As I did so, I felt something cold wrapped within her fingers.

'What's this?' I said, lifting her arm up. I tried to uncurl her fingers but her grip was too tight. 'Show me. Show me now what you've got.' But she shook her head. It looked like a piece of metal. 'What is it?' I pulled harder but as I did so I saw some press walking past. They were all looking at us.

'Well, we don't have secrets in this house,' I said, loud enough for everyone to hear. 'But I'm sure you want your privacy. Just as long as it's not going to hurt you, isn't that right?' I pushed her hand back down, thinking that I was going to find out what she'd got but that it would have to wait.

'You're just like me.' I tried to distract us both against my own feelings of helplessness. 'You can do this. OK? Just think about our future. Because that's what we're working towards.'

I supposed I had to be grateful to Joan. Because if she hadn't been here, Ava probably wouldn't have played ball. But she was getting far too involved in Ava's life for my liking. Manipulating every situation against me. I felt stuck. And out of control.

'Come on then.' My voice was shrill. 'I say what goes on in this house, so you come with me.' I looked up at Joan to see if she'd heard me, but she'd already gone, leaving Ava looking anxiously at the empty space she'd left behind.

I scoured Media Spy for any details into the investigation. Nothing, apart from one new posting on the England thread. I clicked on it. There was no profile picture. Just a small avatar of a fork of lightning. There was no discussion, just a few question marks. Weird. I shut it down and contemplated going upstairs. Detective Mcgraw had told me I needed to sleep. I knew I wouldn't be able to. But at least, if I did manage to get upstairs, and into my pyjamas, then I'd be able to pretend it was a normal night. That Ava was asleep downstairs. The rest of the house was quiet. Conor had gone somewhere. I hadn't heard either Joan or Matthew in a while.

But then Detective Mcgraw came through the door. Joan must have let him in. Usually the heavy front door made a loud noise and the beep of the security keypad would have gone off but today, I'd heard nothing.

'Lara?' He looked parched. He clearly hadn't had so much as a drop of water.

'Joan,' I intercommed the kitchen. 'Please bring Detective Mcgraw something to eat and drink.' I didn't want the guy in charge of the investigation keeling over.

'This man.' Detective Mcgraw pulled a photograph out of a plastic folder in a small, black briefcase. 'Do you recognise him?'

He showed me a picture of a surfer-type dude with long brown hair in a topknot, a neatly-shaved goatee and a silver safety pin in place of an earring.

'No.' My blood had run cold. 'Why are you asking? I've never seen him before in my life. Do you think he has something to do with Ava's disappearance?' I peered closer.

'It's something we're looking into, among others. Now, please, look. Look again.' He pressed his finger into the paper, as if his action would push me into instant recall.

'I'm sorry, Detective Mcgraw,' I said. I wanted desperately to know who he was. 'I feel like I'm letting you down but—'

'Don't worry. You're doing great. What about this one?'

'Now, this other guy?' I looked at the picture. It was a front-on image. He had tiny auburn dreadlocks, alabaster skin and piercing green eyes. 'Know him?'

'No,' I said. 'I don't think so. Who is he?' I leaned forward. I had never seen him before, but in my line of work, I came across hundreds of people in a week. Hair stylists, make-up artists, the general public, business colleagues, designers, our sponsors. The list was endless. Detective Mcgraw stayed silent, picking at his left thumbnail. I noticed the rest of his hands looked manicured and very clean.

'They're from your announcement day. We've been through everyone that was in your house. There were a couple' – he rubbed his eyes again and I wondered if the strain was getting too much – 'that weren't background checked properly by the events agency.'

'Bear Productions?'

'Yes. We're just looking into those leads now. Might be nothing. One has a few convictions. The other is an out-of-work actor and gave a false name, so we're trying to locate him. But we've already questioned everyone who was in the house that day. No one saw anything strange. Or if they did' – his voice sharpened – 'they're not talking.'

I thought about Bear Productions. How they prided themselves on being the most discreet and security-conscious event production agency that all high-profile people used. Their employees hadn't even been allowed phones on my property, with everyone handing in their cells at the door. They were then searched for any recording devices and their social media profiles checked to make sure they hadn't disclosed their location.

'Please let me know if you find anything at all on them. Who are they? What are their names?' I thought about doing my own due diligence on them.

'I'm afraid I can't tell you that, Ms King. Data protection and all that. Nice picture . . .' Detective Mcgraw pointed to a photo of Matthew on the wall, with me next to him. It had been taken at Nobu, on our first date. I had been wearing a large sun hat, denim jumpsuit and heels. Matthew wore casual khaki shorts and trainers. The paps had been out in force that day.

'Yes. It was from a while ago.' I thought back to the first time Matthew had met Ava. '*The* Matthew Raine?' she had gasped. 'Just wait until I tell my friends.'

'Where is Matthew now?'

'Upstairs.' I told him.

'He hasn't come down to be with you?'

'I asked him to leave me,' I snapped. 'I want to be alone at the moment. Why?'

'No reason,' he said. 'I just thought you might want company. It's often the night-times that are the worst in these situations.'

I thought back to the fact I'd always been watched, and how this was the first time I'd been behind four walls and not on display to anyone.

But then Detective Mcgraw cleared his throat.

'I'm sorry. So as I've said, we've got no concrete updates for you. But we're looking into a few leads. We've got a few licence plates being put through the system. Cars in the area that might have taken a similar route to you.' He walked over to me again. 'I'll speak to Conor but I think another press conference is needed. A formal one. Police-led. It might focus the public again. They're going a bit off-piste. We need to keep them on this. Your absence is fuelling them. They keep going on about some old stuff. Headlines from the past. Something's rearing its ugly head.' He looked at me. I wondered what he was talking about. I didn't give him the satisfaction of asking.

I lifted my face and pushed back my hair. A habit, I told myself. Or a reflex movement at the thought of being looked at.

'Oh,' he said, 'by the way, Ms King.' His tone had changed, become almost jovial, like we were strangers at a cocktail party. 'Matthew's father. Derek Raine. Do you know him?'

Matthew's father? I went cold. Why was he asking about Matthew's father? I kept very still but then I got the sense that perhaps Detective Mcgraw had been watching me in my own home. It was too much of a coincidence that we'd just been discussing him, Conor and I, and here he was minutes later, asking about Derek. My eyes darted around the room. Had they bugged the place? Were they somehow watching the feed from the security cameras from outside the house? But how would they know my password, which had been encrypted to the highest level?

Don't be ridiculous, I told myself. *Now you're getting totally paranoid.* But I could feel my vision begin to tunnel. He had absolutely no reason at all to be asking about Matthew's father. I took a breath. I didn't like the idea of being watched by him at all.

'God, Matthew's dad. There's a disaster,' I started to say. Then I realised that Detective Mcgraw might have been talking to Manny, somehow. That Manny had been quizzing him. As Conor had said earlier, the man was a parasite. Perhaps Detective Mcgraw had been alerted that something was off. Or perhaps Conor had mentioned something whilst they strategised together about press. But no, Conor wouldn't have done that. But anyhow, either of those two options were better than the thought I was being watched. In my own home.

'A disaster? Why's that?' Detective Mcgraw lifted his chin. As though he *knew* something and just couldn't wait to spring it upon me.

'Well, I'm not sure if you are aware,' I called his bluff, 'but he's in prison. You must promise me not to say a word.' I spoke in a loud whisper. 'I don't want the public getting distracted. Unless, of course, they need to be.' He nodded his head. 'He's in Perth, Western Australia. He had some awful experience with a bar brawl. Punched someone who later died. Poor Matthew took it very hard. He was there. Had to be a witness against his own father because there had been no one else around. It's really messed him up.'

Detective Mcgraw went silent. He'd clearly been expecting a cover-up from me. I'd say he almost looked pleased. Relieved, even. Like he'd been proved wrong about something.

'Awful,' he said, looking around the room again. 'Well, glad he's not here to give you any trouble. I'll be off. Get some sleep.'

I buzzed Conor from the landline.

'You spoke to Detective Mcgraw about Matthew's father?'

The phone went silent.

'What, about the fact that he's in jail? No, course not.' I looked around the room. Silly, ridiculous thought. Of course I wasn't being watched. I was watched for a living. I knew when people were looking at me.

'You think that Manny and Mcgraw have been talking? That Manny could have set hares running with Mcgraw?'

'No. I don't. Why?' I shut my eyes and squeezed the handset. Not the answer I'd been hoping for.

'No reason,' I said. Along with my daughter's disappearance, things were sliding more and more out of my control. And Ava's disappearance or not, there was nothing I hated more than being out of control.

England, August 2004

The audition was the first time I'd ever been stared at. Scrutinised. Initially, I'd felt skinned. And then something inside of me had come alive. I remembered walking out the door of the television studio.

Ben, staring, eyes prowling for something. *Me.*

'It was good,' I told him when he'd asked. I had started an edited version of what had happened at the audition. The real version had been mine to keep. The real version, which involved me walking into a room filled with cameras and stagehands and stylists and microphones.

Me, standing under those bright lights, a surge of elation shooting through me. Nothing else in the world had mattered.

Me, clasping that cold metal microphone.

'Lara,' I told them. 'I'm Lara King.'

'And why are you here today?' they'd asked, their faces smiling at me from behind their table.

'I'm here because this is where I'm meant to be.' I had clutched the microphone hard at that point, smiling as though my life depended on it.

'She's pretty,' I had heard one of the judges say. 'A real natural beauty. And look at the monitor. Look how she is on screen.' And then I'd heard a collective gasp from the rest of the production crew as they'd all looked towards the image of me.

I had told them where I was from. A glossed-up version that I knew they'd want to hear – more of the stuff Ben had filled out on the application form after I'd signed the contract. My story. But as soon as I'd opened my mouth, I started saying things I didn't mean to.

About my parents. My background. And then I saw their faces. The way they looked at each other. The way the man with an earpiece beside the camera gave them a muted thumbs up. They leaned forward. One of female judges shook her head and looked sad.

'Gosh, so you've really had a tough time,' she had said. She had white-blond hair in a middle parting. A smiling ice queen.

'I have. But I really want this. I really want to turn my life around.'

'So go for it,' they'd said. 'Good luck. You know if you win, you get a million-pound recording contract, don't you? So sing your heart out. We're all rooting for you after what we just heard.'

And I had opened my mouth, and heard the roars, and cries of an audience far away inside my head – and I had sung.

'Well, come on then,' Ben had asked me. 'Did you get through? Do they want you back?' He was terrified. The new TV concept had been all over the news. Everyone had been talking about it. He knew that this could be the start of his career, and mine. *A million-pound recording contract.* I could make him rich.

I thought about the things I told the judges. The lies I had told them when I realised that the story they wanted from me was a hammed-up version of my own life.

'We had absolutely nothing growing up,' I told them. 'Nothing to eat. My parents couldn't even give us scraps.' They had looked pleased about this.

I thought about after I had finished my song. The echo of my voice had filled the room, and the moment that they had told me my fate.

The way that the cameras had zoomed right in close, lapping up my face. I had seen it. On the monitors. Just after the judge had pointed it out. My face on screen. He was right.

My own face, I thought. I had tried so hard to hold it together. To stop the surge of feelings; the warmth in my veins, the joy, change my features into something else entirely. I had felt a rush through my entire body, better than the time Bradley Dartmoor had fingered me until I was dizzy. Better than the time I'd jumped off the pier with my school friend Tam, the wind hissing and howling in my ears.

Better than any fucking thing I'd experienced in my whole entire life.

August 23rd 2018

1400hrs

The Announcement

'Welcome to you all,' I started to speak. 'I know you've all been watching, waiting for the big surprise announcement.' I scanned the room and paused. 'We've gathered you all here today' – I looked over at Matthew, his golden hair shining in the sun – 'to tell you something.' Ava had been sandwiched between us. 'If you want to tweet, it's hashtag the announcement. Firstly, we'd love to say thank you so much for sharing this moment with us. You've all been so supportive and we are overwhelmed with gratitude. Thank you.' We all smiled as everyone clapped.

'Now before the announcement itself, darling Ava would love to say a few words.'

I gestured towards my daughter, holding up my hands in a clapping motion. A chorus of aaahs rippled the press.

'Hi, everyone. My mother and I are working on a new chapter now,' she said. Then she stopped. I pressed my thumb into her back and she started again. 'It's just that . . .'

For a minute, I thought she looked like she was going to be sick.

'She's very nervous in front of you all,' I interrupted. 'She thinks so much of you. But you'll all be kind to her, won't you?' I put my arm around my daughter. She was looking at Matthew out of the corner of her eye.

'Go on, darling,' I whispered. 'You're doing just amazingly.' I started to feel sweat dripping down my back. Please. *Please*, I thought. Not now. Not after all of this. I turned to see Joan, her hands over her eyes. The room started to shrink. I held my breath, and then she started to talk again.

'As you all know, it's just been me and my mom all this time. But, we'd like to . . .'

'She's so excited she's lost her voice,' I laughed. 'Go on, darling.'

'We'd like to announce that I'm getting a stepdad and that Matthew and my mom are getting engaged.' Matthew reached over and kissed Ava on the forehead. I held her hand down before she wiped away the fleck of spittle that he left on her skin. I thought I heard a noise escape from Joan's mouth.

'And so, our next series,' I continued, taking over from Ava, 'will be starring your favourite Matthew Raine too.'

'That's right,' Matthew continued, as rehearsed. 'From now on, I'll be putting my film career on hold for these two lovely ladies. One of whom I will soon be calling my wife. The other is going to be my new little girl.' He waited a beat before he squeezed Ava's cheeks. 'Isn't that right?' She wrinkled her features.

'And so the focus will be on building our family as a unit. And, who knows' – he looked at my stomach – 'perhaps there'll be some more little additions to the family running around soon.' He did an exaggerated wink to the crowd. I laughed and held my hands over my cheeks.

At this point, the crowd went wild. People were standing up. Whooping. Cheering.

'OK, OK,' I laughed. 'We knew you'd be so excited about the Matthew bit. But we'd also like to thank you, our fans, for treating us so well and with such respect. We wouldn't be where we are today without you guys and so.' I lifted my hands and started clapping. 'A round of applause for all of you lot.'

I looked around the room and saw everyone full of smiles and joy for us. I thought about the sponsorship deals on the horizon too. Matthew, Lara and Ava. *The perfect three*. But then I looked to Ava's right and there was Joan, statue-still. I looked at the cameras that had been placed on us three, praying that she was out of shot and then to my horror, Ava got right up and moved towards Joan. I thought about stopping her for a minute, but instead, I gave a big thumbs up to both of them, as though that had been part of the plan all along. I couldn't afford for anything to go wrong.

The live feed would now be being watched all around the world. Trending on Twitter. It might even have reached the news. I put my arms around both Matthew and Ava and pulled them tight to me.

'Right,' said Conor when everyone was quiet. 'Wow. Well done, guys. That was something really special. I think that's it.' Conor leaned over and switched off the live feed. He then turned to the audience.

'Guys. Thank you so much. To all of you press and to the select few bloggers we hand-picked to join us today and of course the special friends of Matthew and Lara – please go and eat. There's plenty of food for you.' There was a rush of bodies as everyone got up.

We mingled with the guests for a bit. Matthew slung an arm around me and passed Ava some food. 'My future *wife*,' he said, over and over. He'd then handed round trays of canapés to the press.

'You don't need to do that,' I said. 'Look.' I grabbed one of the waiters. 'Excuse me,' I said. 'Would you mind taking this?' As I approached, the waiter flushed red and I thought I saw him put something in his pocket. Don't tell me he had managed to smuggle in a phone, I thought. Or he was another one nicking something inconsequential from my house, so he could go back to his friends and show off. 'Look,' he'd say. 'I've got a piece of Lara King's napkin.'

I thought about confronting him. Asking him to empty his pockets but as I looked closer, I thought maybe I'd been wrong. I blamed the adrenaline from earlier. *Calm*, I told myself. Everything's over now. It's finished. I could get back to normal.

'No, of course not,' he stammered. The poor thing went even redder and then I realised he'd probably just had posters of me all over his room and was stunned by seeing me in the flesh.

'Thank you,' I said. I noticed he was wearing a small blue plaster over his left ear and a thin, black hair net over his hair. Good to know the events team were being thorough about hygiene but also I wanted to tell him he should take out his piercings. The blue tape looked ugly and next time, I didn't want that in my house. But I thought if I spoke to him anymore, he'd combust. 'Let me take that off you right away.' He then looked like he was going to ask me something. *Please, don't.* I thought. Otherwise I'll have to get rid of the events company. But he'd taken the tray and walked off and by the time I'd turned around to find Matthew again, the waiter had left the room.

'Guys, Ava's going now to finish her home study. But thank you again for everything,' I said, hoping they'd take their cue to

leave but no one moved a muscle. 'Back to school next week.'
I saw my daughter's shoulders had slumped.

'Oh, do I have to?' Everyone laughed. She went down with
Joan and everyone shouted goodbye. 'You're brilliant,' came the
cries.

An hour later, Conor started shifting everyone out. Then
he turned to me and Matthew who had been in and out all
afternoon.

'A quick look online tells me that, holy shit' – he showed me
his tablet – 'we're trending. Millions of people talking about it.
Oh my God. People actually think you are already pregnant.
This couldn't have gone better.' Matthew kissed me. 'The lady
of the moment,' he said, bringing me close to him. 'You've saved
me. My heroine.' We all laughed.

'No, seriously.' He looked at me again. 'Thank you.'

'Well, you didn't exactly help me out, did you? Earlier? When
I had to come and find you.'

'Darling, I'm so sorry. I am. I'll make it up to you, I promise.
I'll arrange something amazing, just for us two. A surprise.' The
earlier anger had lessened after the success of the announcement.
Conor punched both fists into the air.

That evening, Conor arranged to take Matthew and me out.

'A lovely celebration supper for the newly engaged couple.
One shot of you two, together,' he said. 'And that's it. Then you
lay low, for the moment, OK?' I nodded. 'Right. Supper. Holly
restaurant?' he said, referring to the most exclusive place
in town.

'Let me just say good night to Ava. She did very well today.'
I had been expecting to see her all happy and pleased with

how she'd done but when I made my way into her bedroom, she was with Joan. I thought I heard Ava say something about Matthew.

'Are you sure?' Joan was saying. 'Don't be daft.' She had her arm around my little girl.

'One moment,' I said to Joan. 'I'm just going to say goodnight to Ava.'

'Fine,' she replied and then she started, 'Wait.' She threaded her fingers through the front curly strands of her hair but they kept getting stuck. 'Wait. Lara – I want to talk to you about Ava. Just a quick word.' She pushed the door ajar so Ava was out of earshot, and lowered her voice.

'Look,' she said. 'I had no idea that was going to happen. I find it quite surprising, actually. That you didn't warn me. It's a big thing, getting engaged. Ava's out of sorts.'

I wanted to ask her if she was sure she wasn't just peeved she hadn't known in advance about our surprise.

'You think she was out of sorts?'

'Yes,' she said, a touch defensively. 'I think you should spend some more time with her. It's been very unsettling lately. And now you've gone and announced you're going to get married in front of' – she threw her hand in the air – 'all these people?'

'Unsettling? I'm trying to do the exact opposite. I'm trying to create a settled family life for us all. Things were just fine before I met Matthew but now he's in my life, I'm trying to make things work best for all of us. This engagement – it was part of it all,' I told her.

She looked like she wanted to say something then, but she pulled on her bottom lip with her teeth.

'Fine, then maybe you can explain that to her? She's only young. She doesn't really know what's going on. This is all a big change for her. And she keeps saying strange things. About Matthew. Saying that she wishes he wasn't around.' She faltered but I could see she wanted to continue. I wasn't going to give her that opportunity.

'I'm taking her out for the day on Thursday. Just me and her. So why don't you take the day off. Treat yourself. You can go swimming. Sunbathe. We won't be around.'

'That's good,' she said. 'But you need to spend time with her alone. Not as a treat. Just because you're with her.' She took a breath and her eyes started to water. 'You're her mother, you know. She needs a break from all of this.' She guided her hand around the room. I followed her arm, tracking the beautiful artwork, the silver that had been polished and brought back down since the announcement. 'She just needs to experience being a child.' The space between us went heavy with silence.

'When was the last time you hung out with her, when it wasn't to do with work? Or your show? Or your . . .' She looked like she wanted to be sick. 'Brand?'

'OK. Stop,' I said.

My head felt stuffed. I wanted to defend my actions but deep down, I knew it was true. I just didn't need to hear it from Joan.

'OK. Please have a lovely day tomorrow,' I said, signalling the end of the conversation. 'I'll go and see to my daughter now.' I hurried into Ava's room where a heaviness descended over me.

I felt angry with Joan. *Don't shoot the messenger*, I told myself. *Don't do anything rash. Don't get rid of her. You need her.*

'Are you going out?' Ava looked at the wall behind me, unable to look me in the eye.

'I am. Not for long. You did very well today.' But she didn't reply. I kept silent until eventually, she turned her gaze to me.

'Why did Matthew do those things?' I thought about the pool house. What exactly had she seen or heard?

'Oh God. I don't know. He's acting. He's an actor, remember. That's what they do – test out scenes for films.' I said, pushing her shoulders down. 'Go to sleep.'

'No. I saw. I saw what happened. He wasn't acting. It was real. It really scared me, Mom. I don't understand. I need to know.'

'Look, Ava, sometimes things are just too adult to understand. And that's all there is to it. Matthew's a good man. He's just had a tough time. We need to feel sorry for him,' I told her again. 'Look.' I pulled out my phone. 'Here's what they are saying on Instagram about you.'

I flicked through my Instagram account for her to look at but she barely moved her head. She just caterpillared her way down under the duvet.

'Fine,' I said. 'I'm going then, if you want to be like that.' I was still hurt from Joan's words and I had begun to question my every movement.

'No.' Her head shot up. 'Can you stay?' she whispered. 'Just for a bit. I hate the dark. I'm sorry. I won't ask again. I promise.'

'No,' I said.

And then she went on. 'I'm hungry. I'm hungry.'

I thought about the huge table of canapés laid out – all the delicious food she'd had access to – and the way she often said she was hungry as an excuse to stay awake, but tonight I wasn't having any of it.

'No, you aren't hungry, Ava. Not after all that food earlier. You aren't having anything to eat.' She opened her mouth to speak but I held my finger up to her lips. 'Shhhht,' I said. 'No more. Sleep.'

I willed Joan to be quiet; she was outside Ava's bedroom, opening and closing drawers, banging and crashing around.

'OK but please, Mom, just stay.'

'No, Ava. You've upset me. Do you see what happens, when you upset me? I don't want to be with you.' I felt all the emotions and nerves from earlier rise up to the surface. The things we'd seen at the pool annexe, me having to pretend it was fine. Trying to process it all in my head – the fact it had shifted my whole view of everything I knew into disarray. That I would have to keep this quiet for the rest of my life or risk everything. The announcement. Manny. The fear of Matthew not turning up. All of it was jostling for space in my mind and I felt my synapses on fire.

She started to cry and I thought that she was about to shout for Joan.

'OK then,' I told her, getting up and shutting the door. 'Five minutes.' I felt bad then. 'Oh, Ava, I'm sorry. I just had it all taken out of me today.' I thought then that she was about to ask me some more questions about Matthew, so I shut my eyes and pretended to go to sleep. But then a few minutes later, I opened one eye and there on her side table was the outline of something heavy. Metal. My mind flicked back to what Ava had had grasped in her hand so tightly just before the announcement.

I didn't want to move an inch in case it disturbed her going to sleep. Every fibre of my being willed myself still.

Eventually I heard her breathing slow down and the light whistle of air fill the room. I leaned over and rested my hand on her head. She was fast asleep. I rolled over and pulled the object towards me. Weird, I thought. I recognised it. Perhaps some lucky charm? I strained my eyes against the light and pulled it closer towards me and that's when I realised. The fob. It was the key fob to the indoor swimming pool.

What on earth was she doing with it? Why had she been clutching it so tightly? I thought about waking her up but then I'd have to deal with the fallout and really, I had to get going. I slipped it into my bra and told myself to remember to put it somewhere safe, and of course, to quiz her about it first thing in the morning.

'Night, my little girl,' I whispered as I let myself out of her room. I felt the cool metal against my skin. I was pleased I'd found it but its presence near me made me feel even more uneasy. 'Sleep well.' I smiled at Joan.

'Lara?' she said. I turned back towards her.

'Yes, Joan?'

'Congratulations.'

Ryans-world.com

Entry: August 26th, 2245hrs

Author: Ryan

There's so many crazy theories going on. Some people are still saying she's run away. But if you want my opinion, there's something sinister going on.

Something's in the air, no doubt about it. But the worst thing of all? This whole thing tonight seems to have turned into a massive, crazy-ass party. I swear there's all these groups of people out with kegs, and everyone's juiced up, and when I went for a wander earlier, there were some high-school dudes smoking joints. It's like this has done something crazy to everyone.

I guess I'm feeling it too. The craziness.

Here with the latest updates on missing Ava King, brought to you by Lara and Ava King's number one fan.

Twitter: @ryan_gosling_wannabe

August 26th 2018

2300hrs

Once the thought that I was being watched had been seeded in my mind, I couldn't get it out. I knew there had to be a plausible reason for Detective Mcgraw asking about Matthew's dad just after I'd been speaking about it to Conor, but the more I thought I was being watched, the more I felt my skin crawl. I wanted to go upstairs, but couldn't move from my seat.

Had Detective Mcgraw been in my study before I'd arrived? Surely I'd just watched too many drama series. I wanted to google it, to see if it was even legal, but I was even too scared to do that. In my heart, I knew that Detective Mcgraw would have done nothing of the sort. But it was too late. The idea had clawed itself into my brain.

Anyway, even if I was being watched, I needn't have cared. I'd been doing nothing wrong. 'Stop,' I shouted down the persistent thoughts, but they erupted even more. *Maybe this is trauma*, I told myself. I thought I'd been managing so well before and now I knew why. My body had been in fight or flight mode. And now, the gears had shifted.

I managed to calm myself down by going online and distracting myself. I kept looking at the England thread on the forum to check it hadn't changed. Open, flick through, close. I did this on repeat until my arm ached.

'Lara.' Conor appeared at the door. 'I'm sorry. I'm going home soon for a rest. I just wanted to see if you were all right.' I always teased Conor for looking young. But right now he looked like he was being dragged down by an invisible force. 'Detective Mcgraw wants us to report to him now every time we do anything.'

'Fine,' I told him, not caring who knew what any longer, or who did what. My mind felt bruised. Conor walked over to my desk.

'I will but, Lara, what the fuck are you hiding from me?' He was leaning over me, right up close. I could see the thin hairs that he normally took such pains in shaving.

'What?' And then he stopped and covered his face with his hands.

'Jesus. I'm fucking sorry. I'm sorry. I know. This thing – it's like a beast and I know I should be more sensitive but it's getting totally out of control.' He rubbed his forehead. 'If I don't control it then I'm as responsible as . . .'

'As who?' I snapped. 'What's wrong with you? You're a machine. You're not meant to be behaving like this. Come on.'

'I mean, just, I feel responsible. For that part of her safety. I know that much. I know that if I fuck this up, oh God.' He leaned over my desk with his elbows right close to me. They were all chapped and raw. He normally looked after himself so well. 'Fuck. God damnit, where is she?' I started to cry. 'It's OK, Lara.' He steadied himself. 'It's OK. They'll find her. They honestly can't not. Not with the number of people that know what she looks like. Or the amount of police presence around here. OK? I truly believe that.'

'Do you?'

'Yes, but, Lara, look, you have to help me out. You have to. I know there is something going on. Something you're not telling me. The way you keep dismissing me when I ask. I know what you'd normally do.'

'And what's that, Conor?'

'You'd tell me where to go.'

'Conor, my child is missing. I don't expect there's any correct protocol with which to behave under these circumstances. Do you?' I wanted desperately to tell him how scared I was. How I thought someone was watching me but I struggled to get the words out.

'No. But it was those messages. Those emails I've been getting from England. Something in your face. Panic. I know you, Lara.' I started to shiver. 'I know your exact movements. I know when you don't want to tell me something. I know because you have this weird smile on your lips. A half-smile. As though you can't quite keep it inside but you know you have to. You've got it now. If you don't tell me, it's going to . . . Ava. I don't know how else to get through to you.'

I thought back to England and how he was wrong. It wasn't going to help Ava. What was going to help Ava was what we'd been doing.

'Look at the way the public reacted to my letter. About me being on my phone,' I said. 'That's how we help her. More of that. Just let me deal with it.' I imagined people finding out the whole truth. And then everything else leaking out, somehow. Matthew. The pool. Ava.

I heard Conor shouting at me and the distant sound of a phone ringing. A samba, which felt entirely inappropriate.

'Lara.' He grabbed at my arm. I felt the press of his fingers around my elbow. It hurt. 'Lara, what's up? It's Detective Mcgraw on the line. He wants to speak to you.' He passed me the handset. 'Lara. Come on,' Conor was saying. 'What on earth is the matter? You need to speak to Detective Mcgraw. You look like you're totally dazed. Disconnecting.' And then he took the handset from me. 'She's not with it,' I heard him say, 'I think she's gone into shock,' and really, at that point, I almost started to laugh. I felt it bubbling up inside me but then I went all cold, deep into my bones, as though my blood had frozen over.

'Yes, yes I'll just pass you over,' he said. 'I don't know why she wasn't answering the landline or her emails. She's, no, something's not right. Shock. I think. yes. No. Here she is.' I took the phone and pressed it to my ear.

'Yes?' I said. I felt that dropping sensation again. The feeling that I had felt earlier today, when I realised Ava was gone. I credited myself with being so pulled together earlier. Now I knew why – this was on its way. I told myself to pull myself together. That Ava deserved my full attention, even if I could barely put one foot in front of the other.

'I've been trying you,' said Detective Mcgraw. I mumbled something about talking to Conor and then I realised I'd switched my landline onto silent when I'd been looking online. What if my little girl had been found and I hadn't been there to answer the phone? What was I playing at? And the worst thing was that I hadn't even been aware of what I'd been doing.

'What is it?' I asked.

'I'm coming over to talk to you. That OK? I want you to get some rest. I'll be over soon.'

'Fine,' I told him. 'Anything, though? Please tell me you've got something.'

'We're looking into all avenues. Those two guys from Bear Productions. We've looked into them. They're clean. Just in case you were worried.'

'Fine.' I couldn't stop fidgeting. 'Thank you. See you in a bit then,' I said, shifting around in my seat. I couldn't get comfortable, or ease the sensation of dread in my stomach.

When Conor left, I looked online again. Theories abounded about my daughter. Some ludicrous, some painfully realistic. And then I worked up the courage to log on to my official website, where I looked at pictures of us together. The beautifully crafted shots we'd posed for. Her with a rattan basket stuffed full of homemade pumpkin muffins. We'd done a video montage that day, with the ingredients sent to us by Eco foods. They'd paid us four million dollars for a year-long endorsement and Ava had been so happy to see her face and mine on the back of the baking box. A black and white photograph, her nose smudged with cream-cheese icing, me laughing.

I scrolled down some more, except it made my heart hurt too much to stay on any one image for too long. I flicked through, briefly pausing over a beautiful black and white picture of her swimming. And then with a start, I remembered, the key fob. The coolness of it on my skin after I'd taken it from beside Ava's bed, before putting it at my own bedside.

I had the idea that I was going to return it to the key holder right that minute. My paranoia gave way to urgency. I switched off the laptop and ran upstairs to the bedroom, past Conor who was on the phone in the hallway.

'I thought you were going,' I said.

He held up a hand to signify that he was busy.

'You can stay,' I told him. In fact, the idea of him here was sooth-ing. 'Please stay.' I clasped my hands together and he nodded.

'Shhhh,' he mouthed.

'I'll tell Joan,' I mouthed back and then I ran up the stairs. I was going to get the key fob and I was going to put it back. I didn't know why. Just the mere existence of it gave me the creeps. It made me think of Ava and the swimming pool and the awful things that must have been going through her head.

And how I'd done nothing to stop it.

I was certain Ava hadn't run off but now the possibility that she may have done, just as a little defiance, had started to intrude into my thoughts. Maybe she just wanted to scare me a little. Get me back for the way I'd spoken to her the night before. Or maybe I was reading too much into it. Projecting my own fears about my parenting on to the situation. I felt sick.

All these things crowded into my mind as I thought of my little girl, unable to find her way home. Frightened, alone. Hyperventilating as it got dark. It's OK, I thought. I'd put the fob back where it belonged. Everything would be back to nor-mal and she'd come home. I knew it. The fob had started to represent some sort of talisman – a symbol as to what was going to happen next.

But when I got up to the bedroom, the fob wasn't there.

I opened all the drawers around me slamming them closed. 'Everything OK?' I heard Matthew shout.

'There you are,' I said, after I hadn't been able to find him earlier. 'Where have you been?'

'Here,' he replied, 'in the upstairs den.' I was going to ask him if he'd been downstairs to see if he'd admit to having spoken to Joan, but I couldn't concentrate. 'You OK?' he called. 'What's with the banging sound?'

'Everything's fine.' I opened the drawers of the beautiful mahogany chest that had been shipped over from Provence. The silver and enamel ornament tray that had been given to me as a thank you present for appearing on *The Larry Bauer Show*. I threw all the contents into a pile in the middle of the room. But I couldn't see it anywhere. *Where the hell was it?* I crawled under the furniture, the swinging hammock chair that looked out onto the view outside. I clawed my hands into the carpet, my nails digging into the thick, cream fibres, but it wasn't anywhere to be seen.

'Nothing,' I screamed. And then I remembered his father. I hadn't told him that Manny had found out about him being in prison. One tiny lie and now all this.

'By the way,' I called, pulling at my hair. 'Manny's onto us about your father. He's found out that he's in prison. And weirdly.' I took a breath to shake myself of the memory and the paranoia. 'Detective Mcgraw was asking about it too.' I expected that Matthew would dismiss it, given there were more important things at hand. But he turned to me then, his eyes blazing.

'What the fuck—' He ran into the bedroom from the den, his T-shirt collared with sweat. 'What the fuck do you mean?'

'Matthew.' I tried to calm him down but I felt petrified that he was going to smash up the room. His whole body was tense, a criss-cross of veins rising up from his neck.

'Shut it down.' he ripped off the silken oyster-coloured eider-down from the bed, and held it to him. He was shaking. 'Get it shut the fuck down, or someone will pay.' I realised then why he was so angry. I kicked myself for not having seen it earlier.

'Fine,' I told him calmly. 'I'd like to remind you that my daughter is missing. So please, let's just concentrate on what matters.' He sat and put his head in his hands. 'OK?' But he didn't reply, he just shook his head and cried. I was watching everything collapse. Me. Matthew. My daughter had vanished and I was now being put under pressure to get Matthew's dad out of the limelight. I didn't care. I wasn't going to put myself under scrutiny instead.

So now, more than ever, the key fob had become fixated in my mind. If I found it, then Ava would come home. That's all there was to it. It sounded irrational. I knew that. But nothing about this situation was rational.

If it was in the house somewhere, it meant she hadn't been taken. There was no weird link between her going missing and the events of three days earlier. She had got lost at best. She was coming home soon. And if I alerted Detective Mcgraw to the fob and the fact it had gone, they'd start getting unnecessarily distracted.

She hadn't run off, I told myself over and over. We'd had so much fun, I remembered telling Detective Mcgraw. She was in a good frame of mind. *Singing, laughing, chatting.*

Matthew left the room. 'I'm going to my room,' he said. 'Don't disturb me unless necessary.'

'Fine.' I picked up the eiderdown and folded it up. Then I bent down to see if the fob had slid underneath the bed but it wasn't there. I reminded myself to check if Marcy or Rosa had seen it. I gave myself an hour. If I hadn't found it then perhaps I'd tell someone. It had to be around. It had to be somewhere in the house. It became all consuming. Overtaking all the previous paranoia, or perhaps because of the paranoia.

Just the thought of getting the fob back filled me with a sense of relief and control. Ava had had it before now. She was, or so I thought, the last person to have touched it. I thought of the way her small hands had clasped it so tightly in her bed.

And then it crossed my mind that perhaps Ava had found the fob in my bedroom after I'd taken it from hers. Perhaps she'd found it in the morning before we'd left, when she came up to my room. Perhaps she'd carried it with her on our day out. I thought back to when we'd left the house. What Ava had been wearing: one of our designs, the navy dress. It had one pocket on the front of it that she could have slipped it into. The thought that I wouldn't be able to find it in the house filled me with such a sense of foreboding that I had to sit down.

Just as I was working out what to do next, I heard the doorbell. Joan answered. I could hear echoes of Conor's voice.

'Detective. Hello. Yes. She's behaving . . . oddly . . . definitely sinking in now.'

And then the house intercom went.

'Lara? Detective Mcgraw's arrived,' said Joan.

'Send him up. I'm not coming down,' I said although I wasn't really aware of what I was saying at that point. I would never, ever normally let anyone near my bedroom. But I wasn't interested in anything, other than the damn fob.

I held my breath as I heard Detective Mcgraw coming up the stairs. I jumped, and pushed everything back beside my bed. I didn't want anyone to see what I'd been doing. It was my little secret. Everyone clearly already thought I was losing the plot. And maybe I was. I wanted to scream, *Wouldn't you?* I thought I'd been pretty sane so far. But perhaps Conor was right. Perhaps it was only just sinking in.

Detective Mcgraw knocked on the door. It felt all wrong: him being in my bedroom, his black lace-up shoes soiling my luscious carpet, but I didn't say anything. I just continued to push all the items I'd ripped out from my dressers under my bedside tables in case I found the fob.

It appeared that, just like my daughter, it had vanished into thin air.

England, December 2004

'Follow the red light,' one of the production crew with spiky hair and baggy trousers told me. He held up his finger. 'There. Just look into that.' I stared at it as he moved the camera up and down the stage. 'For the record,' he said. 'I think you're going to win.'

'Ten million people,' he shouted after me, as I left the stage. I needed some water. 'That's the forecasted viewing figures for tonight. So . . . break a leg.'

I had not been thinking of any of that when I had been prepped that they were going to announce the winner of *Idolz*. Two finalists. I had been chosen from over ten thousand entries and sixteen contestants. Me and Sarah Dunne.

My mind was blank as I stood on the stage, holding Sarah's hand. Looking down at the floor whilst Daryl, the show's host, waited for the final public vote to be counted. We listened, the air heavy, waiting for his voice to tell us that the numbers were in.

He started to speak but I knew before he'd even opened his mouth to make the announcement. A shift in my energy. And then he called it.

Your winner.

Lara King. I felt my eyes go first. Drawn across the crowd. Watching arms pumping the air from the audience. My ears rang, hot with the screams, the roars, the heavy bassline.

'And now up,' he said, 'singing for the very last time, your champion, the girl you voted to win *Idolz*, please give it up for . . . *Lara King*.'

I felt the tears press heavy against my lids. Then the golden glitter rained down over me and I looked at the silhouetted figures, raised in their seats, and I felt truly, totally invincible. Afterwards, when I'd left the stage, people were pulling at me from every angle, until I felt someone tugging at my sleeve. It felt familiar and when I looked up I saw Ben. I moved over to one side and hugged him.

'We did it. You and me, Ben. We did it.' And just as I was about to tell him what had happened on stage, he stopped me.

'Wait,' he said. He had a serious look on his face. *Shit.* My first thought was that they'd somehow found out I'd not quite been so truthful about my past. But then I knew they wouldn't care about that anyway, given how much money Ben had estimated I'd make them.

'Listen,' he said. 'Don't freak out. But I've got to leave.'

'Fine,' I said. 'Go. It's late. Don't be silly.' Although I had expected him to come and celebrate with me.

'No. I mean, I *really* have to leave. I'm so, so sorry. My fiancée, Kaycee, has gone into labour earlier than expected. I've got to leave for a while. But I'll make sure the team look after you well.' He stopped and tilted his head back. 'Oh God,' he said. 'I'm sorry.' The show had already catapulted me into the public sphere. The free stuff, the team of people, the work on my appearance, it was all getting out of control. And now I'd actually won and Ben was deserting me.

'It's OK.' He held his arm out, not quite touching my shoulder. 'I've asked Joanne to look after you.'

'My publicist? But that's not her job, is it? I mean, she does my publicity, right?'

'We've made a deal with her and the record company that she'll divvy up her job brief between doing your publicity and managing you. The reason I've sorted that with her is because I've worked with Joanne on other things. She's fantastic. Knows what she's doing and will be supporting you one hundred per cent. She'll become a true friend.'

'OK,' I said. I ended up speaking to her, and Ben was right. She was great and I knew we'd get on. But something sat uneasily in me. I wasn't sure what it was. A sense that something was going to go wrong.

'It's all OK,' Joanne soothed, after Ben had sent his paternity out-of-office email to everyone. 'I promise, I'm here to help. We'll have a laugh – there are some amazing Christmas parties coming up – but we've got some serious business, too, and we're going to get you the best publicity known to man. OK?'

I had laughed and told her I was going to hold her to her word but still, I felt uncomfortable about Ben going.

And I was right. It *had* all started to go wrong. Slowly at first. The first thing was a beauty treatment. I suppose, that's when it all really went tits up. It sounds ridiculous. A beauty treatment. So innocuous. But it had some dreadful consequences. And just when I was least expecting it, which is how it goes for most things.

'Just a treat,' Joanne had told me. I had heard her tapping on her computer whilst she was talking to me, which annoyed me. 'I've booked you in for a small session before your big interview on *This Morning*.' I wanted to tell her to focus on me. That if the interview was so big, that she should not be doing two things at once. But then I gave myself a talking-to. *Don't get ahead of yourself.* She might have had important stuff to do. It might have been to do with me. So instead, I told myself to relax. That I hadn't had a moment to myself since I'd started this whole thing.

I had a driver to take me straight from the hotel where I'd been staying.

'The Beauty Clinic?' he said, tapping at his SatNav. 'I've got it here, let me see.' He looked at his screen. 'Just off Chiswick High Road.'

'Yup.' I shut down the conversation, ignoring him when he told me his twelve-year-old daughter was a huge fan. The air was freezing when I got out the car, and everyone had that pumped-up energy they get just before Christmas. I walked in to the warm, jasmine-scented beautician's, where Joanne had booked me in for an 'all over pampering session', as she had called it, 'somewhere quiet and out the way.'

The lady behind the counter got off her stool when I walked in. She was dressed in a crease-free white uniform, with a row of silver pens lined up in her front pocket.

'I'm Iris. So lovely to have you,' she sang, taking my coat. 'Please, come in.' She looked at a bunch of notes she had on a clipboard. 'Right, you're booked in for eyebrows, hair extensions, botox, and I'll be doing a facial technique today too. It's a new laser therapy treatment.'

'Are you sure, I'm only just coming up to nineteen,' but then I shut my mouth thinking about conquering the world. I had a sudden thought that it must be my birthday soon. I had been so tied up in the competition that I wasn't even aware of the date.

I let Iris work on my body, toning my face, adding extensions to my hair, laying me down on a reclining chair, the smell of antiseptic filling the air.

'Now for the small injections in your forehead. Just the tiniest of sensations,' she said, pricking at my flesh. 'Ten tiny injections. That's it. You won't see the effects for about ten days,' she told me. 'But then you'll look much fresher. My clients love it. It just means that you'll stave off the wrinkles later on and, well, the camera loves you anyway but it'll love you even more now.' She wiped at my skin with a tissue. 'Don't touch your forehead or massage it until tomorrow.'

I left feeling rejuvenated. Like the old me had been swallowed up and a new one had taken its place. I could take on the world now, as I made my way to the dental surgery.

When I arrived at the red-brick building in Harley Street, I was ready, gunning even, for more work to be done. I walked there, strolling along the back streets of the West End with the Christmas lights twinkling above the buildings, hoping that no one would recognise me. A brown Vauxhall Astra stopped and started alongside me. I turned, facing the road, trying to peer in the front window, when someone wound it down. A large camera lens pointed in my direction. Wow. I was being papped. I rushed the rest of the way to the dental surgery, careful to keep my hair in one place, and not to trip up. Everything was different now, I realised. I had to think about my actions, and every single movement I made.

'I'm sorry,' I told the receptionist. 'I'm early. I was going to walk around a bit but . . .' I stopped myself explaining the full story.

She sat up straight when she saw me, pretending to look at her computer screen, but I could see her glancing at me every few seconds.

'I'll see if Dr West is free now before the next patient turns up,' she whispered. I started to say no, I'm not in any hurry, but then a feeling came over me. The first feeling like it and my stomach felt all airy and light, and then I felt strong.

'Thank you,' I replied, tossing my hair out of my face. I had just been papped after all. I deserved a bit of special treatment. 'Yes, that sounds ideal.'

I texted Ben.

Just got papped. I think. Not at any showbiz event.

He replied:

Congratulations, then. You've made it big.

Hope everything going OK at the hospital!

Elation hit, followed by a slump of emptiness that leached into me. I was called upstairs. Exiting the old-fashioned lift, I was welcomed into a huge, airy room. I put down my bag on a large brown leather chair by the door.

'I'm a bit frightened of needles,' I told the nurse but she patted me on the back and laughed at me.

'You got up there and performed in front of all those people and you can't hack a small thing like this?' She pointed at a tray full of wrapped syringes. 'Don't you worry. Lynn here is the best dentist around so you're in safe hands. Anyway, go on then. I'll give you something so you won't feel a thing.' She had unwrapped a small pill, putting it in my hand. I took it and waited for five minutes. 'Nothing's happening,' I told her.

'It won't. Not quite yet but . . .' She patted me on the arm. I liked being around her, so I allowed her to inject a tranquilliser into my veins. 'This will do the trick.'

Just as my limbs had started to relax, my phone went off. I tried to lift it, but my arms felt like jelly. I let out a small giggle. 'Jeez,' I told the nurse.

'Good. You won't feel a thing now for your procedure.'

I looked at the screen, struggling to lift the phone to my face, squinting at the message.

It was Hannah.

Coming out tonight? Come on. You owe me. You've ditched me the past three times. You told me you'd kept it free. So you and me. You can get us a table at that new place that just opened last week? Be Squared? I've got something I need to tell you. Something mega important. I would lure you with the promise of loads of celebs. But you are one.

Fine,

I texted back. I'd been looking forward to a night in the hotel, but I had started to feel like I could go out and have some fun.

But I'm recording tomorrow. With that hottie Mark. So gotta be on top form.

Whatever.

Fine, Missy. You'll be on top form. But tonight, we're going to cause some havoc. You and I – cocktails and shots.

I texted back:

C u later x.

I didn't even notice the sound of the drill. Or the sawing of my teeth. 'First phase,' the dentist had said, 'that smile of yours will be just brilliant.' I could barely feel my head moving. It felt like it was sliding all around the black leather headrest.

When we finished I saw Hannah had texted again.

Book the table. We need to celebrate. Holy shit. I've just seen you on the TOP OF THE MAIL ONLINE PAGES! Getting your teeth done? Snazzy! You've properly made it now. U'll be on the front of all the mags soon.

Top billing of the Mail Online for walking to the dentist. I couldn't believe it. I'd made the headlines when I'd won the show, but I never in my wildest dreams thought this would happen.

OK, I will. I'm in the mood for havoc too.

I had been thinking that I'd better come round from the medication before anyone saw me. And then I picked up my phone again and sent her another text.

Just as long as the cameras aren't watching.

They're always watching. Better get used to it now you're mega famous. Someone. Is. Always. Bloody. Watching.

'Here.' Matthew handed over a plate of buckwheat pancakes. We each lay on a sofa in the living room, papers and magazines spread around us. Anthony had left us strong coffee and freshly squeezed orange juice on the counter, along with three jugs of cucumber-spritzed ice water in the fridge.

It was warm in the house, but I had spread a large shawl over me for comfort.

'Fresh and Wild made these, especially for you,' said Matthew. 'I went and collected them yesterday so we could celebrate. Here's to' – he pulled off a section of blueberry pancake – 'us,' then put some in my mouth. 'Let's go and get Ava and then I'm off for the day and night.'

'Where are you going again?'

'I told you. Didn't I?' I felt the familiar drag across my chest.

'No.' I tried to control my feelings. 'You didn't.' I was cross, mainly because he hadn't spent any time with us since the announcement, and I wanted him to connect with Ava, after she'd been behaving oddly.

'I'm sorry. I'm going to Jenna's. For the script run-through? Remember?' Jenna was Matthew's mate from way back who was now a casting director. I could sense Joan overhearing our conversation – the stall of her movements as she tried to listen.

'Yes, I do. I remember now.'

I turned to Joan who had been preparing Ava's timetable for the following week at school.

'Is Ava downstairs?'

'Yes, she's finishing off her study. I'll call for her.' She looked at Matthew.

'Good,' I said. I was getting sick and tired of the way she was behaving. Her mood swings and constant passive-aggressive remarks. I wanted to shake her and tell her that she'd made herself clear last night. That I understood what she'd been saying and she didn't need to be so childish. 'If you could go and get her, I'd be grateful.' The tone of my voice was remonstrative.

'She's being odd,' I said to Matthew after she'd left the room. 'Any idea why?' But he shrugged and put another piece of pancake in his mouth. 'I hope there's no sugar in these,' he said.

'Sugar? You really care about sugar,' I started but I felt the pressure of his hand on my thigh.

'Shut up,' he said. 'You don't know who's listening.'

'Fine. Anyway, are you sure about Joan?' I said. 'You don't know anything? She hasn't—'

'No,' he said. 'Now, quit. These taste sweet. Motherfuckers. I'm going to complain so much if there's sugar in here. Oh, Ava.' He chewed on his pancake. 'hi.'

We both looked over to see her clutching Joan's hand. She was wearing a smocked pink jumpsuit and white espadrilles.

'Ava, you look tired,' I said. 'I hope you aren't getting ill.' Joan raised her eyebrows at me in mock surprise.

'She's been a busy girl, haven't you, Ava love?' Joan reached down and tucked Ava's hair behind her ears. 'Very busy.' Joan glared at me.

'Right. Enough,' I said. 'Matthew. Ava. In the kitchen. Now.'

Ava followed Matthew. She knew better than to argue when I spoke like that. 'Joan?'

'Yes, Lara,' she said, facing the mantelpiece. She wiped her hands across the marble, around the BAFTA statue that we'd won for best documentary. She inspected her hands, blowing on her fingers. 'Hmmm,' she said to herself. 'This needs a clean.'

'Joan,' I said again. 'Do you have anything to tell me?'

'No,' she said, still trailing her hands along the ornaments. She started to walk to the other side of the room.

'Joan,' I shouted once she was at the other side. 'Come back here. I need to talk to you. Enough. You don't get to behave like this in here. You said your piece yesterday. If something's troubling you, you say so.' But she carried on looking around the room. 'Look.' I changed tack. 'We value you so much. Ava loves you. We can't do this without you. You hold us together but clearly there's something wrong.'

'I'm sorry.' Her shoulders sagged. 'I've been keeping it in all this time. I wanted to say something yesterday. When I asked you to spend more time with her . . .' She walked back towards me and sat down. I moved over a bit.

'What? What is it?'

'It's—' She pulled a bit of fluff from the shawl, which I had kicked off on to the sofa. 'It's Ava and Matthew. You and Matthew. It's not just you spending time with her. It's more. Things are different. She's being affected by it and I don't know how to help her.' And then she stood up and walked towards the mantelpiece, threading her hair through her fingers. 'It's not right,' she went on. 'And she's been saying some odd things since the announcement. Really odd things. Something about you, Matthew, you at the swimming pool. All this weird stuff. It's like . . .' she trailed off.

'It's like what?'

'It's like the time the last kid I nannied for had watched a horror film by mistake. It had been playing on the television whilst his parents were having a dinner party. I wasn't there,' she added. I thought of what Ava had seen. How it had been like a horror film in itself.

'And?' I could hear Matthew in the kitchen, singing 'Ain't No Sunshine'. 'What's that got to do with anything?' I yanked a thread off the blanket and wound it around my fingers.

'Well, that's how Ava's behaving really. It's not right.' She started to rake her fingers through her hair again, harder this time. 'I can't describe it. It's like she's seen or heard something and she can't get it out of her head. I think you need to speak to her. And she keeps asking about her father too. Her biological father and if he's coming to get her. I don't know why she thinks that he would. I've just been so upset by it. And if you don't mind me saying.' I could tell it was all coming out now. 'I think Matthew should start behaving more like a proper father. If that's what he's telling everyone he is.'

'Oh God,' I said lightly. The swimming pool. I thought of the fob and the way Ava had clutched it in her bed. And then I thought that I should go and call someone to come in and change the locks to the annexe, so that I didn't have to worry about it any longer and so that it couldn't be used for anything like that again.

'Probably something she's seen with one of her friends,' I said. 'I'll ask them to hold off screen-time. And I get your point about Matthew,' I said, biting down on the flesh of my lip. 'Any tips on how to welcome him into her life?' I knew this would open Joan up, give her a sense of power, change the direction of the conversation. And it worked and then I could stop feeling so angry. I'd just listen to her drone on and zone her out.

'Well, I'm so glad you asked my advice,' she started. 'Now, I've been thinking . . .' and she did go on and on and on. I tried to listen. Really, I did. But my mind kept dragging back to the swimming pool and Ava's face. As though the vision had burned itself on my brain, searing itself deep, like a thorn embedded right into her soul. I had tried not to think of it. To tell myself that all was OK with the world. That these things happened. Move on. Ava would be fine. After all kids are resilient little things. Joan herself had said as much only a week ago, when Ava had said she wanted the corridor light on.

'These children,' she'd continued. 'They really do hold up a mirror to their parents, don't they?'

I had wondered then, what I was meant to see in myself, when I looked at my daughter.

You know when you see footage of crazy Justin Bieber fans, the Beliebers, crying, screaming, rattling their ribs for the boy himself? That's what it's like down here now.

People have lost their shit entirely. The TV crews are giving off light but people are also here with head torches, portable lamps, the works. There's a whole campsite been set up, not far from where the forensics were doing their initial search. It's like some weird, fucked-up festival. Like this macabre, shadowy party where people are simmering with fear. Fear that something terrible will happen. But fear also that she'll be found, and then they won't know what to do with the news.

I heard they are scaling up the search. Even more, if that's possible, when you've got the entire world looking for you. That's what *Sky News* is reporting. And I'm hearing more whispers about Matthew.

The 'Find Ava King' video that the police did has racked up nine billion views. How fucking mental is that? That's more than the three billion previous record holder: 'Despacito' by Luis Fonsi. How's that for a bit of light relief from this nightmare that we're all living. Because that's what it is, isn't it?

It's our story. It's all of our story. It's like she's everyone's little sister, Ava King. And we all need a bit of light relief now and then, don't we? From the horror that this universe keeps throwing at us.

Anyway – the response I'm getting for these updates has been a little bit crazy. You guys love them. I've had thousands of tweets wanting more info. So please, feel free to retweet and share the hell out of these updates. I'll be broadcasting soon, too.

Like a bat outta hell.

Signing off,

Twitter: @ryan_gosling_wannabe

August 27th 2018

0000hrs

Detective Mcgraw stood over me, like a looming shadow. I felt like his presence was polluting the sacred space where my daughter was meant to be.

I wanted him to leave, so I could go and search for the fob in Ava's room, to see if she'd found it and taken it back. I needed to work up the courage to go in there, knowing she wasn't in her bed. It's OK, I told myself. I'll pretend she's at a sleepover at Misty Banks' house. I'll run down quickly. Look through her things. Tell myself she'd forgotten her favourite T-shirt for tomorrow morning. I'd grab that too, to make the scenario more real so that I could trick my mind into believing she hadn't really gone.

'Lara?' Detective Mcgraw pushed the door ajar. I could see him, shifting from one foot to another. 'Shall we go elsewhere?' He took in the belongings strewn on the carpet. I looked down to check there was nothing too personal.

'No. Here, please,' was all I could manage.

'Fine. Listen, Lara.' He shut the door fully at this point. 'It's good we aren't downstairs. Because I'm here about Matthew. I need to talk to you about him. In private.'

'Again?' I wanted to say, but I saw the look on his face. The tic in his left cheek. I could see the way he was now looking just above my shoulder but somehow, he'd be taking in everything about my face and my personal belongings.

'You knew of his whereabouts during your phone call with him?'

'Not this again.' I started picking up everything I'd dropped. 'We've been through it. Please.'

'We spoke to Joan earlier,' said Detective Mcgraw. I stopped and looked up at him.

'And?'

'She said she overheard you and Matthew talking. Apparently Matthew was telling you that he was staying with a friend the night before Ava went missing.' *Jenna*, I thought. I prayed he hadn't been lying about that. For all of our sakes.

'We've checked that all out, Ms King and that's all in order. He did indeed stay with Jenna Bromfield, who told us they were doing script run-throughs together.' I breathed out. I thought about Jenna and her husband James and their twin girls, Dini and Della. I looked down again and picked up an old ornament I'd bought from Paris. A small ballerina that I was going to give to Ava but she had asked me to keep it by my bedside. I felt something in my chest, punching to get out.

'So he must have told you where he was when he was on the phone to you?' He kept his voice light. I sensed he was trying hard to control his patience. 'You chatted for a while. Makes sense that someone would ask where their other half is?'

'For the very last time, Detective Mcgraw. I don't know where Matthew was when I called him. Now I need to go. I need to do something.' I couldn't keep my mind off the fact that I was going to search for the fob in Ava's room.

'Then can you explain this, please?' He pushed a piece of paper in my direction. It showed a long list of telephone numbers, with three lines highlighted in neon pink. *Mine.* 'Matthew told us he was at his friend's house this morning after he left Jenna Bromfield's,' Detective Mcgraw went on. 'Lucas. He told us afterwards he went to a raw juice place in Laurel Canyon Boulevard. That all fits. But—' He dragged his finger across the paper.

'But what?'

'According to our records, there's a whole lot of time when he's not accounted for. His phone was off until the signal reconnects at just before midday when you called him, just before Ava went missing and he drove towards you. Except we can't find any CCTV of his car. Ms King?'

'Sorry, yes?'

'Do you have anything to say? About Matthew? Where he could have been in that time?'

'No. No. Ask him. Sorry. I don't.' I nearly pushed Detective Mcgraw out of the way but he sidestepped in front of me, his shoulders squared.

'Ms King. Please. I need your cooperation here. If you are hiding something from us, if you are in any way covering something up for Matthew Raine . . .'

Then what? I wanted to ask. 'If he was in any way doing anything' – he coughed – '"unsuitable",' we need to know.' I thought of Joan again and whether she'd been talking. 'Because there's more,' he said. I knew what was coming.

'We've been analysing all your security tapes. There's footage. From the day of the announcement three days ago that has been tampered with. I'd like to ask you if you knew what was happening in the indoor swimming pool annexe on that day.'

I thought I heard movement outside the room. We both looked towards the door but it went silent. I slid my hands across the carpet. So warm and fluffy. Ava loved to lie on it and stretch out her arms and legs, leaving her imprint in the fibres, like a small snow angel.

'Annexe?' I coughed. 'The swimming pool annexe?' I thought about Conor telling me he knew when I was up to something. The smile that played out on my lips and I worked hard at keeping my mouth in a straight line. 'What do you mean? Anything to do with the staff?' I played dumb. 'The events staff?'

'We don't know what was going on but someone deliberately obstructed the view of that security camera from ten that morning. We're going to be asking everyone if they saw anything.' If he found out that either Ava or I had seen what was going on, that would be it.

'My team are on it, though,' he said. 'Looking closely at the blank footage and what happened at exactly the moment the cameras were tampered with. You'd be absolutely amazed at what goes on these days in telecommunications forensics. How much information we can pull from seemingly nothing.'

I wanted to tell Detective Mcgraw at this point not to antagonise me but I was scared then at what they might find. If somehow they were going to trace my and Ava's route to the pool via the security footage. I mentally calculated where the security cameras were in the property and I didn't think there were any leading up to the annexe from a certain point in garden but I couldn't be sure. And this was when I realised that it was all getting out of hand. That I couldn't come clean now. It would look too bad that I hadn't admitted it all before. I had to keep going and pray that Ava would be home soon so I could put this whole sorry nightmare to bed.

'OK,' he said. 'I'm going now. I suggest you get some sleep. I'll bring him back later.'

'Bring *him* back? Who?' He nodded towards a large photograph on the wall. I looked over to a huge black-and-white image of my husband-to-be.

'Matthew,' he said. It was only when he'd gone, that I realised what he'd meant. *The missing time*. Matthew was in trouble And I hadn't even had the chance to say goodbye.

England, December 2004

Be Squared nightclub. I was ready for the night out. All charged up from the shouts and flashes of the paparazzi. '*Lara. Over here. Lara.*' There were crowds of them. Blue flashes threaded my vision. I'd dressed up and despite the freezing temperatures, I didn't feel the cold. After the beauty treatments, I felt like a million dollars. New dress, new face. I lifted my chin to show off the large diamond necklace that had been loaned to me by Lavelli jeweller's. I could see the light sparkling off it. I held my hand up to it, smiled. Chin up.

'*Lara! Lara!*'

They felt good, sitting heavy on my skin. Just right. I had been told to have security with me if I was going to wear them in public, but there wasn't a moment that I was going to be alone.

I was taken through to the VIP section by the manager. He led me in, pulling back the red curtain.

'Security here,' he said. 'Lots of them so you're in good hands.' And then he stopped and stared at me. 'But you'll probably need your own protection soon judging by this lot.'

'Oh and by the way.' He leaned towards my ear. 'We've got others coming in later. Justin, Usher, the works. They all like their privacy. Just so you know, this bit. There's no cameras here. Nothing. You can do what you' – he looked around him and then back at me – 'want without anyone, you know. So, just get your friends in and come back, yeah?' His hair had smelled of sweet lime, all slick and shiny under the laser lights.

It was dark in the VIP room, but I spotted Ben's outline first. Shoulders rounded, a white cap on his head. The first time he'd been out since the baby was born. He was holding some-one's hand. I squinted towards them and realised it must be Kaycee. I'd seen her in the photograph Ben kept in his wallet but in real life she was so much prettier. She looked up, eyes shining, arms open.

I didn't understand what was going on and then I saw Hannah, galloping over with a bottle of champagne. A sparkler fizzed from the bottle neck. A tray full of Moscow Mule bottles with paper umbrellas sticking out of them. The sofas were covered in purple satin cushions, curls of smoke filled the air.

'Your birthday,' she'd squealed, jumping up and down. Her hair was tied back in a topknot and she was wearing a slinky black dress, her hips swaying gently. 'Tomorrow. Or had you forgotten?' I clutched at the date in my mind and then I remem-bered telling the beauty therapist that I was eighteen. God. Nineteen and I hadn't even registered. And then I remembered Hannah's text:

I have to tell you something important.

'Div.' She flicked me on the arm. 'I didn't have to tell you any-thing. Just it was so last minute had to make sure you didn't flake out. Just about managed to get these guys together.' I looked around, smiling.

'You told me that by the time you were twenty, you hoped you'd have a job in a club or something. Now look.' She held up the bottle, removing the sparkler and swigging from it.

'And holy fuck.' Her eyes focused on my neckline. 'You haven't just done things by half, have you? Can I touch them?' I let her hold up the diamonds in her hands, twisting them in the pulsing lights. 'Jesus,' she whistled. 'Can I try them on later?' I didn't want to sound like a killjoy, or too up myself after all she had done for me, so I nodded and looked over at the rest of the group.

'Oh yes,' she carried on, dropping the diamonds back against my skin. 'Look who else I gathered up. I told them you were expecting us all.'

I looked over at Ben. 'Kaycee wanted to come out. Her first night out since having Isabella, so let's give her a few drinks too. Show her a really good time.'

'Hi, Kaycee. Nice to meet you,' I said. No wonder Ben was so keen on making a life for his family. Making things good. She looked glorious and kind and my heart twitched with something I couldn't put my finger on.

'The baby?' I asked, looking at them both.

'She's with Kaycee's sister.' Kaycee punched the air and laughed. 'Freedom. Just for a few hours.'

'And, Joanne, hi.' She stood up and air-kissed me, holding her hand over her newly fixed chignon.

'Hi. Lara, guess what?' said Joanne. 'We've also got something else to celebrate.'

She was smiling, looking over at Ben and I knew what was coming next.

'Is it my song?'

'Yup.' She stood up and grabbed my arms and then everyone else joined in and we danced around in a circle, shrieking and screaming. The best night of my life.

'And there's more,' she said. 'There's more. Ben? You tell her.' I looked over at Ben who was sitting rubbing his hands up over his knees. He stood up and put his arm around me.

'They want you to do the opener to the . . . wait for it . . .'

My mouth filled with warmth. 'What?' I said, because I was looking from one person to another and no one was answering me. 'What?' I shouted again over the sound of TLC's 'No Scrubs' just in case they hadn't heard me the first time. They were all standing there looking like they'd been struck dumb.

'*Charity Aid.* They want you to appear on *Charity Aid*. As one of the headline acts and as the lead for their charity single that will come out in the New Year.'

'Jesus no,' I said. I felt as though my body was lifting off into space. A vacuum between where I'd meant to be and where I actually was. 'Oh my God,' I said, looking at Hannah, 'did you hear that?' My voice barely audible.

'Come on,' she motioned for the bartender to bring us some more champagne flutes. 'Let's get hosed,' she laughed.

I didn't drink very much. But by the time midnight rolled around, the floor seemed to be being pulling out from underneath me. I concentrated very hard, putting one foot in front of the other, imagining my legs had steel rods through them. Jesus, I thought. And all those paps outside. I'd better pull it together.

'Hey,' I shouted, to no one. 'I think I'd better go,' but they were all over in the middle of the dance floor. Ben was dancing with

Hannah, doing some funny, robotic movements that normally I'd have laughed at.

I looked for Kaycee, but I couldn't see her. She wasn't on the sofa where we'd been sitting all night. Joanne was in the corner, snogging someone I recognised from a soap opera.

'All right?' said one of the security guards.

'I'm fine,' I told him. And then I was being hemmed in from every corner by total strangers.

And then this girl appeared in front of me. She was small, tiny in fact, with peroxide hair in a pixie cut and black eyeliner, flicked up at the edges. She was wearing a leather jacket and silver studs and stars decorated her ears.

'I just wanted to come and say hi.' She gripped her hands around her stomach. 'You were amazing on the show. We all fucking loved you.'

'Thank you,' I said, moving around her. I wanted her to go away, but then there were others, pushing and shoving me.

'I really did love you. I mean really loved you. We were so glad you won. I voted for you.' When I looked at her again, I noticed the rim of her nostrils glowing white under the UV lights.

'Hey,' I shouted to the bouncer. 'Can you come and get me?' But my voice was lost and I shouted again. He looked over this time and led me back to my seat, pushing everyone else away. 'Here. I'll put a rope around your table,' he said. I noticed the girl again. She'd followed me. She was signalling for me to come back, but I shook my head and turned away from her. When I glanced back, she was banging the edges of her fist together in the air. 'Fucking little stuck-up bitch,' she was shouting. I squeezed my stomach muscles tight and swallowed back a glass of champagne. Ben came dancing up to me, moving from side to side.

'Hey.' He sounded slightly breathless. 'Where is she?'

'Who?' I looked around. The peroxide-haired girl had gone.

'Kaycee? Where is she? You must know, you've been with her all night.'

'No,' I tried to tell him I hadn't. That I'd been on the dancefloor but he wasn't listening.

'Where is she? Kaycee?' Ben was all sweaty, the grin ghosting his face. 'She's not here? With you?' I shook my head.

'Haven't seen her for a while,' I told him. He turned to me. 'Bathroom? Can you just ...' He flicked his head towards the loos.

I stopped, thinking about all the crowds I'd pushed through. All the people who'd stopped trying to get a piece of me. But then I thought – this whole fame thing. It can't stop me from helping people out. It can't stop me from going about fifteen steps to the bathroom to go and find someone on behalf of someone who'd been responsible for me getting all of it in the first place.

'Of course.' I got up, making my way to the loos. They were sparkly black granite, with purple UV lights casting a forensic glow all over the room.

'Kaycee?' I shouted but there was no response and all the bathroom cubicles were shut, except one.

A lady sat in the corner, perfume bottles and sweets spread out across the surface and a change jar next to her.

'I'm sorry,' I told her as I walked over to the closed cubicle. 'I've got nothing on me,' which was the truth but it sounded hollow, given the thousands of pounds of jewels slung around my neck.

'No worries at all,' she said. I felt someone come up behind me.

'Yeah right,' the person behind me said under her breath. I twisted around and saw her. The pixie girl from before. I noticed for the first time how dark her roots were. My *fan* that supposedly loved me so much. Who had turned on me when I hadn't given her what she wanted.

'What did you say?' I moved closer to her. I could smell something on her breath. Like nail polish remover and gum. But she just shook her head.

'Stuck-up little bitch,' she hissed, shaking a fist at me. 'Say you can't spare any change.' She was grabbing at my diamond necklace. I forgot about everything for that moment. I forgot who I was. Who I'd become.

'What the fuck did you say to me?' I moved closer, my hand clasped around the jewels.

At this point, I knew I should have stopped, but it was like something inside of me had come loose – a plug in a certain area of my brain and the thoughts and actions were splurging out and I no longer had any control. *Stop*, I thought to myself. *Just stop*.

But it was too late for that and I walked forwards, inhaling her cheap scent and the minty fumes from her mouth. *Just too late*. And I knew that if I took one – just one more step forward, that this would be the beginning of the end. *Stop*. I told myself. *Just stop*. But it seemed I had no control over myself at all and before I knew it, I was close enough to see the way her eyes had started to glint, and I could see her gums and teeth, snarling right at me. *Step back*, I told myself one more time. *Be sensible. What would Ben do?*

But as I looked at the smudges of black under her eyes, the slight scar on her right cheek, I knew it was too late.

It was too late for any of that. And then it came.

I keep wondering if Ava's scared. If she knows her mom is waiting for her.

I didn't. When my mom left me. I was a few years older than Ava but still, I thought she was coming back.

Always.

I still do.

But she never did. She never has. So I keep thinking about what that feels like and wanting to tell Ava it's OK. Never before have I wanted so much to tell someone that. That it's OK.

Here with the latest updates on missing Ava King, brought to you by Lara and Ava King's number one fan.

Twitter: @ryan_gosling_wannabe

Happy_Styles: Aw man, shucks. Stay happy, man.

Becky_with_pink_hair Bitch is probably dead by now get a life.

Selena_Gomez_Kidney My mom left me too. It doesn't mean they don't love us. Maybe they had to do it. Let's stick together.

August 27th 2018

0100hrs

For a minute I forgot where I was. The idea of sleep was ludicrous. When I was sure that Detective Mcgraw had left the house, I rushed downstairs to Ava's room.

I had forgotten that I'd asked Conor to stay over. I saw his belongings strewn all over the hall table. I'd never seen the house look anything less than perfect. It set my teeth on edge. I stopped for a second wanting to tidy up and make everything look as it normally did but the pull of finding the key fob was too strong.

When I reached Ava's room, I heard Joan sobbing in the room next door. I briefly thought about going in there and talking to her but instead, I opened Ava's door. I felt like I was doing something wrong. As though Joan would burst in like a great protector. *I'm her mother*, I told myself. I have every right to be here. But I felt like an intruder in my own home.

When I opened the door, everything looked in its correct place. The unicorn duvet was pulled up over her pillow, neatly pressed and crease-free. I felt nothing. I think at this point it was too much to process. I opened her wardrobe. Everything was in its place. And then I saw, sticking out of her pillow, a pyjama sleeve. I lifted up the pillow and saw her little pink top and bottom scrumpled up, as neatly as she could have made it, and pushed right into the middle of her bed, just as she'd been taught. Since she'd gone missing, this broke me the most. The thought that little over fifteen hours ago, my daughter had tried to be a grown-up. She'd got undressed, thought about what she should do to be a good girl. She'd done it all alone, her small fingers rolling up the material. And then she'd got herself dressed in the clothes that Joan had laid out for her the night before.

I sat down then, and cried for a very long time.

When I gained enough strength to look for the key fob I went through all her drawers, pressing my fingertips right to the back to check I hadn't missed anything. When I'd finished looking everywhere, I crawled under her bed and found a small padlocked toy. It was a little bird that had a keypad on its tummy that served as a lock. Just as I was about to start trying to open it, I heard Joan on the intercom.

'Lara?' I took the bird and stuffed it up my top. I didn't want Joan asking questions. 'Lara,' she called again. 'It's Conor. He needs you upstairs.' I hadn't heard her leave her room. She must have gone when I'd been crying and hadn't noticed. Always creeping up on me somehow, wherever I went. It was starting to freak me out.

I walked upstairs, careful to leave Ava's door open a notch, just like she wanted it when she went to sleep.

'One second,' I shouted to Conor, as I ran up to my room and hid the bird under my pillow. When I got back down, Conor motioned towards the kitchen. I hadn't been in there since Ava had gone missing. I couldn't bear to see her empty space at the table but when I followed him in, I found the light and airiness made me feel less hollowed and stuffy than my study.

'Where's Joan?' I asked.

'Don't know. She brought me up here then disappeared.'

I looked around and then went to the door and pressed my ear right up against it.

'What are you doing, Lara?'

'Checking.'

'Checking what?'

'That Joan's not here. I think she's listening. Or something. Strange things keep happening.'

'Lara? Are you OK?'

'No,' I shouted. 'Conor. I'm not OK. My daughter has . . .' I leaned on the kitchen island and wept some more. 'I'm sorry. I don't know what's real and what's not. I can't tell what's going on. I'm questioning everything. Second-guessing.'

'It's OK.' He came closer and stretched out a hand towards me. 'It's OK.'

He was blinking and looking around the room. I didn't have the energy to absorb his awkwardness.

'Look,' he said. 'I just wanted to discuss these.' He held out his phone again. I shook my head.

'No, Conor,' I whispered. 'No. I'm tired.'

'There's something going on,' he said. 'These emails. They keep coming. You told me it was OK. But they seem to know things. About you.'

'Like what?' I hiccupped.

'Like your real birthday.'

I went silent. When I'd first been launched in LA, Conor had told people I'd been born on Valentine's Day. 'Just makes you that bit sweeter,' he said. 'It's coming up soon and I'm going to tie you in with a couple of campaigns. Heart-based things. All right?' I'd agreed unthinkingly, even forgetting my real birthday of December the twelfth.

I thought back to who knew my real birthday. My friends from England. My family. Everyone who knew me back then. People I'd worked with.

'But it would be easy enough to find my real birthday,' I said. 'Wouldn't it?'

'Well, only if they knew to look. Right?' His eyebrows lifted. 'Right, Lara? Listen, I need you to help me out here. Something's going on.'

'Nothing's going on.' But all the paranoia from before, the thought of Detective Mcgraw watching me, the CCTV from the pool house, Matthew talking to Joan, the key fob, let alone Ava's disappearance – the list was endless – it all started to seep in and I began to lose control of my mind. My thoughts kept slipping from my grasp, fading into nothingness before I could make any sense of them.

'Lara. What are you doing?' Conor asked, looking over at the door. I followed his eyeline and then strode over.

'Did you hear something?' I asked.

'No. Lara. Listen to me. Stop it. I need you to stop this now. I need you to focus. Look at me, Lara.' He stood up and walked over, placing a hand on each of my shoulders. I'd never felt Conor touch me before. He seemed to have an aversion to physical contact of any sort, and would go rigid if I ever tried to kiss him hello but here he was, exerting great pressure on to me.

'Focus. Now. Please.'

'OK.'

'What are you hiding from me. These emails. They're not right. I've read enough to know the shit some of your obsessed fans come out with. Declarations of never-ending love. All that shit. But this is different, Lara. It's scaring me. The tone of the emails. They're desperate. Asking you to contact them. I'm afraid that something big is about to happen and you know what it is and you won't tell me. Tell me. Now. Please.' He took a sharp breath inwards.

'Do they give a name?'

'Just a number. The email address is some gobbledegook shit.' He tried to pass me his phone so I could take a closer look but I swatted his hand away.

'Lara. Please. Help me. I'm sinking here. We need to find Ava.'

'I know,' I snapped. 'Don't you think I'm desperate? I just need some time to think.'

'No. Time is something we don't have. You need to manage this. For me.' He walked away from me. 'For Ava.'

'Everything I do is for Ava. This is for Ava. I'm trying to protect us. Don't you see?'

'As am I.' His blinking was so fast I could barely see his eyeballs.

'Lara. Listen. If you're embarrassed about something, I don't care. I couldn't give two fucks if you killed the Queen of England. My job here is to protect *you*. My client. That is my job. My one and only job.' He wiped his forehead. 'You know those journalists? Who shoot poor, dying orphans with their shit-hot cameras? And everyone says, *why didn't you step in? Why didn't you help them? Why didn't you give them some bread?*' He walked back over to where I was, and shook me again. 'Because that's not their fucking job. Just like it's not my job to care about what you've done. My job is to be the best at what I do, which is to keep your reputation squeaky clean and to keep you universally adored. So whatever' – he scraped his hands through his hair – 'the fuck it is you are hiding from me, you need to tell me. Now. You're behaving strangely. Something's not right. This is not just worry over your daughter. There's something else.' He collapsed in a wooden chair opposite me. 'I can tell from the way you're acting. The weird disconnected looks. I don't own this industry for nothing, Lara, and I need to know.' He was quiet then, his brown eyes pinning me down.

I wanted to tell him, mainly to see how he'd react. Just the abridged version, of course. The papers had got a fair bit of it anyway. And obviously he knew the bits Joanne and I had told him when I arrived. I wondered if the paranoia would go away a bit if I did tell him. Problem shared, problem halved and everything, but then the idea of losing control over that portion of my life tightened my chest considerably.

'It has nothing to do with Ava's disappearance,' I told him. 'Nothing.'

'What doesn't?' He got up and stroked my arm. It felt good to have some physical comfort after having been alone all this time. With Matthew gone I had no one else to really turn to. Perhaps he would help. I'd tell him, he'd get rid of it all. I should have trusted him at the beginning. I started to cry.

'Do you promise, Conor. Not to be mad?'

'I promise.' He nodded and I felt his fingertips squeeze around my upper arm. 'Go on.'

'England. The night that everything started going wrong. There was more. Much more. The press never got the whole story. I think it's her emailing.' I thought of the peroxide-haired girl snarling at me and then shut my mind off before it went any further. 'She probably wants money.'

'Well, we can give her money,' said Conor. 'We can give her however much she wants. Just tell me. Tell me what happened.' I opened my mouth, wondering which bit I should start with. 'Wait,' I said, and I walked to the door and opened it.

'Just checking Joan's not listening,' I said. If he was shocked, he didn't show it. That's why you are so good at this, I thought.

'It was at about midnight, I guess.' As I started talking, my whole body felt lighter. This was a good thing, I told myself. I already felt better. The paranoia started to settle, my thoughts flat-lining into something altogether more coherent. We were interrupted when the doorbell rang, making us both jump.

'What the . . .' Conor looked at his watch. I stared at him, willing him to answer. I was too frightened.

'Can you get it? It's after midnight,' I said. 'Do you think it's Detective Mcgraw? With news?' I sat down.

'Oh wait,' he said, looking at the video entry phone. 'It's Anna.'

'Anna? Who's Anna?'

'Anna Devon. She's a lawyer.' He spoke quite calmly, but he rubbed at his eyes. 'I'll answer it. But if you don't tell me now, the end of this story, before she gets here – this could be very, very bad indeed.' He was whispering now, right up to my face. 'And the truth. All of it.'

'I was telling you the truth just now,' I said. But I started to tell him. The very final parts. I could feel the memories threatening to overflow. Shame swirled around in my gut and then

I stopped because I thought if I told anyone the worst part, my entire career was going to be over. Just like that. And that would also mean that when Ava came home, we'd both be finished. I'd have done her a total disservice.

'What, Lara?' he hissed. 'What? You need to tell me. Quick.' But I'd changed my mind, and with that, I'd already started to run to the front of the house, before Joan could get there first. I could hear her coming up the stairs. I opened the door and looked at the woman in front of me. She was all made-up. Red lipstick, softly smudged brown eyeliner, as though she was about to go for a night on the town. I was about to show her in, when she pushed past me and made her way through to the kitchen and sat down. She'd put a large folder on the table and was busy thumbing through its pages.

It was only after she'd introduced herself, stiff in her red suit and oxblood briefcase, that I realised I'd never called a solicitor. It was the middle of the night. And she looked ready to start an entire day of work.

So that meant it was someone else who'd got her to come over. Conor. And by the looks of things, he thought I was about to be in an awful lot of trouble.

England, December 2004

The peroxide-blonde girl was right up close to me now, the slash of her red lips opening and closing, flashes of white gum on her tongue.

Stuck-up little bitch, she said.

'What did you just say?' I repeated to her. I got right up close. I could feel her breath on my cheek.

'I said, *yeah right*, you don't have any money on you. Don't say you've got nothing. You filthy little liar.' *Keep cool*, I told myself. Joanne had told me all along. Don't let people rile you. The press – they'll do it on purpose. Shout nasty things to get a reaction. Don't rise.

I took a breath. *Don't rise.* But then she leaned forward again.

'I saw you. Earlier,' she said, her nails tapping the surface. 'I saw you all by yourself. Think yourself popular, but everyone hates you. None of your so-called friends would even sit with you,' she snarled. I looked down at her hands. The tips of her fingers were stained brown and I feel something shift, but at that point, I could still control it. I swallowed. And then she leaned even closer, grabbing tightly at my wrist.

'Bet your parents don't even like you,' she whispered. I stood there, my mouth dry. 'Am I right? You hoped they'd be proud. Instead they just see you for who you are. Mummy and Daddy think you are a slag,' she had been singing then, 'a dirty, little, slag.' And then she took a swig from a bottle she'd taken from beside the sink. She swilled it around in her mouth and then spat the liquid into my face.

I wiped at my skin.

'What the fuck have I done to you?' I screamed back. 'You're a disgusting cheap whore.' Everything around me felt like it was spinning around, and I was caught in the middle – a centrifugal force. 'You fucking ugly, cheap whore.' I got right up in her face to show her I wasn't scared. 'You stalked me on the dance-floor,' I hissed. 'And now, when I didn't give you attention, you turned like the filthy little slut that you are.' And then I saw it. A small, red light moving around in my vision, her hands holding a mobile phone down by her waist, following my face, my hands as I moved around the room.

Fuck. I think. *Fuck*.

Why would she pick on me? Why? When there were countless other high-profile people in here. I was an easy target, I thought. That's why. She saw me coming a mile off. And I wonder how much money she'd make from that little video of hers.

'You'll only get a couple of thousand for that,' I told her. 'I'll give it to you. You nasty piece of work.' But she just gave me a small, triumphant smile. And then I caught sight of myself in the mirror. My eye make-up had started to run and I looked all sorts of crazy, a dead-eyed stare with the promise of fame and glamour. I stepped back, grabbing onto the diamonds around my neck. I started to feel alert.

'Look,' I said. 'Stop filming. Like I told you. I'll give you some money, if that's what you want.' I pointed to the door.

'I've got . . . let me just go and get my bag.' But she was now holding up her phone.

'I don't want your money,' she said loudly. She was jittery, her limbs jerking around. 'I just want a bit of respect.' She wiped her nose. 'But now people are going to know the truth about you.' My heart sank. I wanted to explain. I'd had too much to drink. The people – the noise. It had all got to me but she was staring, eyes glittering. I heard a gagging sound coming from a toilet stall and I jolted suddenly remembering why I was here. *Kaycee.*

I ran over, knocking on the door of the locked cubicle. It was only a half door, with space at the top and bottom, so I crouched down and peered underneath. It was Kaycee, hunched over the loo, totally passed out. Her hair was spread around the porcelain like some kind of Medusa. I slid myself underneath and pulled myself up the other side, opening the lock and then dragged her out, pulling her up over to the sink.

'Here,' I said. 'Here, cold water.' I started running the tap, turning towards the blonde-haired girl but there was no one else in bathroom. Just me and Kaycee. How strange, I thought. It was almost as though I'd imagined it. An empty space where she had been, only the flicker of low lighting over the sink. Even the bathroom attendant had gone.

Just me, myself and my thoughts. As though none of it had ever happened.

August 25th 2018

1850hrs

'Mommy,' she said. Ava rarely called me that. 'Can I talk to you before bed?'

'Sure,' I told her. I was sitting on the large grey sofa outside her bedroom. 'Want to see my Instagram?' But she shook her head. 'Why not?' I asked.

'Because Joan said I wasn't to look at it too much. That I needed to get affir-something elsewhere.'

'Did she now?' I said, putting down my phone. I had been thinking about Joan a lot in the past few hours. How much she'd been taking up my time with her moods and lectures about my parenting. How much she'd been intruding on my mental space. I'd told Joan to finish work early today and even though she was off the clock, she had still been hanging around, sapping my energy.

'Ava,' I said. 'Do you think you are getting a little old for a nanny?' She shook her head and started to cry.

'No,' she said, her bottom lip sticking out. 'I'm only six.'

'Fine,' I said. 'Well, she'd better watch herself that's all,' I muttered, to no one in particular.

'What do you mean, Mommy? Watch herself?'

'I mean exactly that.' I watched her face crumple again. 'It's OK. She just has to remember who is in charge here.' As I was talking, I felt more and more angry. Angry that Joan had been questioning me, hovering around judging and watching. Implying I wasn't looking after my daughter properly.

'She said she's worried about me,' said Ava, sitting down on her bed.

'The announcement,' I said, steering her mind into a different direction.

'I saw everything,' she whispered. 'The swimming pool. I was there. The whole time.'

'Don't be ridiculous,' I said. 'Saw what?' I gave a tinkly laugh but she turned her head and wiped her eyes.

'I tried not to make a big deal of it, Mommy. Because I didn't want you to be cross. But I saw. I think I know what was happening. It *was* real, wasn't it.' I thought back to how she would have reacted if I'd explained to her exactly what she'd seen.

'I hope you didn't tell Joan.' I patted her on the head, thinking about how Joan would go straight to the police if she knew. I dreaded even thinking about it. For a start I'd have to say goodbye to absolutely everything I'd built. I sat upright. One way or another, I'd make sure Joan didn't find out. The way she was about Ava at the moment, meant that I didn't trust her not to do something impetuous.

'You know what, Ava? Joan told me a little secret,' I said. 'She told me that you have a big, big crush on Daniel at school.' I thought back to how I overheard them talking one day in the kitchen, the giggles of my daughter as she told Joan how handsome Daniel was and made her pinky promise to keep it quiet.

'She did? Why did she tell you that? I told her not to say anything.' She started to cry again.

'Don't say anything to her, will you, Ava? About me telling you. She thought it rather sweet actually. Thought I should know since I'm your mother, after all, but she did tell me that you'd asked her not to say anything. But she does tell me things. Quite a lot actually. So I'm a bit worried about how to trust her. Do you see?' She nodded her head and looked sad. 'Because you'd asked her not to say anything but she still did. That's no good, is it? That she can't keep a secret. She has quite a big mouth.' I stopped myself then. I wanted to say more but I knew I had to keep it controlled if Ava were to believe me and my plan was to work out. 'So you mustn't say a thing to Joan. OK? Not about whatever it was you saw in the pool. Nothing. We need to keep some things quiet.' I put my finger to my lips. 'Remember when Conor gave you that talk? About never, ever saying what goes on in our family?'

'But Matthew's not . . .'

'Shhhhh,' I said again. 'Shhhhh, little one.' I pulled her towards me. 'He is. Do you realise how very powerful you are, my little Ava? You, me and Matthew together? How much we can do as a three?'

'I want to go and play with my dolls,' she said, twisting herself away from me.

'No, Ava, come here and listen to me,' I called, but she'd gone. I heard the patter of her feet on the stairs. Something let loose inside me, the sting of anger curling itself around my stomach. I dug my nails deep into my palms and wondered if I should do something differently. Poor Ava. Thinking Joan had betrayed her. I knew it was wrong, but I was desperate. I thought about how we could work on this together. How I had her best interests at heart alongside the pressures of my job. I wanted so desperately for her to be happy and comfortable and for everything to be OK. More than OK. I wanted us to thrive. I thought back to my own upbringing. How there'd always been a hole inside me that couldn't be filled. I didn't want the same for Ava.

Tomorrow, I thought to myself. Special mother-daughter bonding time. I vowed not to have any social media.

I texted Joan and decided I'd be straight with her too. Perhaps then I'd be able to trust her again.

We've already spoken about your day off tomorrow. Confirmed. I'll need you back by tomorrow night at five.

A reply came three seconds later.

I'm so pleased you're having some proper time together. I'll be back for five. Enjoy.

All of a sudden, the feeling of high-pitched anxiety and stress disappeared, despite Joan's behaviour. Perhaps I'd misread things. Perhaps I was being too defensive as a mother. Perhaps she was doing the right thing. Perhaps I was being too hard on my daughter. It was my fault. I was in charge here. I was the one that was going to have to change everything. Matthew could take over some of the sponsorships. I'd bring in someone new to help Lily with the business side of things and the organisation. I'd delegate more, so that I could spend precious time with my child without the glare of the media.

That's exactly what I planned to do. Make everything OK again. I'd obviously ceded too much control over what was going on under my own nose, in my own house, and because of that, bad stuff had started to happen. I rubbed at my arms. That would have to end.

I couldn't wait to see Ava's face when I told her everything I was planning to do. She'd stick her tongue in the gap between her teeth and squeeze her little fists together.

'Yes,' she'd say. 'Yes, just you and me?'

And I'd tell her over and over, 'Just you and me. And we'll have to start getting used to Matthew being around too, like I told you. But I'm going to concentrate on you, and you alone, Ava. My beautiful, funny girl. OK? I promise you. I promise you that.' And then she'd forget about the swimming pool. She'd forget about asking who her real father was. And then things would be on track for our future. A perfect family of three.

The sun would rise again and I was being given a sign. A chance. And if I didn't want my daughter traumatised in her own home, I had to make sure I had control over everything – absolutely everything – that went on inside it.

August 27th 2018

0120hrs

I needed everyone in my house to disappear, so I could continue my search for the fob and find out what was in the small bird I'd found in Ava's room.

'Anna, if you'd like to freshen up I'll ask Joan to show you the spare room,' I told her. 'You can use that as your base.'

'Thank you, Ms King. But that won't be necessary just yet.' She looked at her Rolex. 'I normally have a few hours of sleep a night so I'll be up for a while – I'd like to talk to you for a bit then I'll have a sleep when I've got the important bits done. Sound good?'

'Yes. Thank you.'

'Now, I'm dreadfully sorry about your daughter,' Anna said, looking anything but. She was flicking through another pile of papers that she'd pulled out of her bag. 'Sit down,' she said, not looking up. I did as I was told. But then the doorbell rang again.

'Jesus,' I said. 'That must be Mcgraw.'

I was right. He stood there, alone, holding a laptop. He walked right on in too, towards Conor. It seemed I had no control over who came in and out of my house. I thought I was going to start hyperventilating.

'Detective Mcgraw.' He nodded towards Anna.

'Anna Devon.' She stood up and held out her hand. 'I'm Ms King's lawyer.'

'Do you need to talk to my client?' She turned to me. 'Would you like to talk to Detective Mcgraw alone?' When she referred to me as her client, I started to feel frightened. It seemed that this whole thing surrounding the disappearance of my daughter had taken on an entirely new life of its own.

'No,' I replied. 'What are you doing here again?' I said to Detective Mcgraw.

'There's nothing solid,' he replied. 'We've got some leads with a few cars that were seen in the area, witnesses coming forward but nothing to warrant me disclosing anything more, Ms King. I'm sorry.'

'Then . . .' I looked up at the clock on the wall. He interrupted me before I could go much further.

'I *am* here for a quick chat about something that may or may not be relevant though. In my mind, it probably is. So, in absence of you being down at that station, do you mind if I record this?' He held up a small black dictaphone. I felt sick.

'No,' I whispered.

'Good. Now. You ready? For the benefit of the recording it's now one thirty-five in the morning, August twenty-seven, twenty eighteen. Ms King, do you want to watch this video footage?' he said, opening up his laptop. Conor tripped over towards the desk and looked at me. I wondered if somehow, he'd got footage of me and Ava at the swimming pool annexe, the day of the announcement.

'Sure,' I said. *Keep calm*, I told myself, but I leaned forward and held on to the edges of the kitchen table for support.

He opened up a media player program on his computer and pressed *play*, a triumphant stab of his finger on the keyboard. I felt Conor push me slightly out the way, his breath heating up my neck.

We watched the footage. The flickering date in the left-hand corner was from May twenty-fifth of this year. Three months ago. I had no idea why this was relevant. We watched the whole seven and a half minutes and I was growing sicker by the minute. Matthew snorting line after line of cocaine off someone's stomach. His face was pixelated, but I knew it was him.

'What do you think?' said Detective Mcgraw.

'I . . .' I looked at Conor.

Anna was busy scribbling notes on a piece of paper on which she'd drawn three makeshift columns.

Detective Mcgraw picked up the laptop and held it to his chest. He leaned backwards on the kitchen island.

'Interesting,' he said. 'This has been circulating for a while. On Dare or Die dot com. Apparently. But no one realised it was your boyfriend. Until of course someone came forward and pointed out to us all the evidence that it *was* him. Which of course we've cross-referenced. The main evidence of course being his own admission.'

I looked at him. I'd heard of the site Dare or Die. It was where celebrities posted anonymous footage of themselves doing illegal, or nearly illegal things. The thrill of the chase apparently. Things they could never, ever do in public for fear of being found out. It was where a lot of sex tapes were uploaded. Masked A-listers with grainy footage of themselves.

I replayed the video in my mind. Although his face was blurred out, those arms, those beautiful, perfect arms were his and his alone.

'Is he down at the station?' I asked.

'Yes. We're still asking him about his little escapade during the hour before Ava went missing.' Detective Mcgraw was talking fast again, as though he was spewing out the words.

'I came here tonight, now,' he went on, 'instead of waiting until the morning because I wanted to see how you'd react to watching the footage before the identity of the *actor* in the starring role got leaked to the general public. Which I'm pretty sure it will. We've taken measures to get it down but you know – you can't control much on the web these days.'

'And?' I said, wondering where he was going next with this.

'And, I'm guessing you like control in your home – that you're someone who likes to know exactly what's going on and I wanted to know if you knew about this. It appears you didn't. You're looking quite shocked, Ms King. Genuinely shocked. I think I've got a handle on your expressions now. What's real and what's not.' This was an entirely new Detective Mcgraw to the one I'd been privy to during the case so far. The slow-talking man who could never look me in the eye had turned into a ferocious beast who was staring like he was about to launch right at my face.

'I didn't.' I looked him straight in the eye. 'I had no idea that he had videos of himself taking drugs.' I wanted to check Anna's reaction, but I didn't want to break eye contact with Detective Mcgraw, in case he took that as a measure of guilt.

'Did you know about Matthew's narcotics use at all? His partying? If you do, Ms King, and you allowed your daughter to be surrounded by it, it puts a very different light on this investigation. The things Matthew gets up to. The type of people he surrounds himself with. We've checked into this video a bit more. The people who he was with that night. We had an interesting chat with the witness who came forward. Not the type of people one might want to fraternise with. Especially given your profile and the fact you have a young daughter. It puts a slightly seedy slant on the whole thing. Wouldn't you say?' I looked over at Anna, who gave me a slight nod.

'I didn't know about this.' I gestured towards his laptop. 'I've told you. He's had difficult times. What he gets up to is none of my business. And I'd never let Ava be surrounded by it.'

'Really?' He almost laughed. 'We have a lovely little idea, you see' – he cleared his throat – 'that Ava knew all about Matthew's activities. That all of this had something to do with the blank tapes from the swimming pool. And that somehow you covered up for him.' I almost wished, for a brief moment, that I had seen someone doing drugs in the annexe. It would have been easier to explain, at least. *Anything*, would have been easier than what Ava and I had witnessed.

Detective Mcgraw went on. 'You and Matthew argued about this on the phone just before Ava went missing. Perhaps you asked him to stop doing what he was doing. For the sake of your reputation? Beautiful couple. Great brand. How much are you guys worth together? I'm guessing it has to be in the region of a couple of billion. Let alone the influence and power you both wield. Am I right?' I gripped the table harder.

'Between you, over two hundred and fifty million Instagram followers. I heard that your advertising fees on social media have reached millions of dollars per post. Quite a little racket you've got going on, Ms King. Impressive indeed.'

'No,' I said, my voice level. 'No. You're wrong. I would never put my reputation before my daughter.'

'Might I carry on? Whilst you were having this argument, Matthew left the juice bar. He drove towards you to finish off the discussion in person. Away from prying ears. Ava asked to go to relieve herself but instead was distraught. She ran off. We're not quite sure what the next piece of the puzzle is, Ms King. But we'll find out.'

'That's quite enough,' said Anna. 'If you want to question my client like this you'll have to take her down to the station.'

'OK then,' said Detective Mcgraw. 'We've got hundreds of people on this. The manpower being taken up is huge. Millions of dollars chasing up leads from crazy fans when the answer' – he jabbed his finger at me – 'lies right here. In this house. Ms King? As I said, a nice little theory. Except I have a hunch it's a little more than a theory. Now would you care to enlighten me?'

'I don't think I'll say anything else,' I replied. 'I believe you can't find anything substantial. That you're trying to pin this on Matthew and by extension me, with your half-baked ideas. But let me tell you—' I smoothed my hands over my stomach. They were shaking. 'You're looking in the wrong place. I've told you about the car. That's where you should be looking. I think you seem to have forgotten there's a missing child here. My daughter.'

'All right.' Detective Mcgraw clicked his fingers. 'Let's go.' Anna and I both snapped our heads up. 'Station. Now.' We all sat without moving. 'Come on.' He gathered up his dictaphone and started walking towards the door. 'Conor? You seem to be following Ms King around with great interest. You'd better come too. Ms King, you're going to need him when the public see you being hauled in. I've been doing my best to keep you away from prying eyes. To make sure that your presence doesn't distract the investigation. But I'm not going to any special measures to keep this quiet now.' I could hear two chimes of a clock in the distance.

'Wait.' I leaped forwards. 'Wait. For God's sake. Just stop.' Mcgraw turned back around and looked at me, waiting for me to speak.

'Yes?'

'It was silly,' I said, pushing my tear ducts shut with my fingers. 'Stupid, really. Our discussion. We did have a row in the car. We did. But it was nothing. It had nothing to do with my daughter's disappearance. I didn't mention it because I didn't want you to start looking in the wrong place. I told you.' I was crying properly now. 'You kept getting side-tracked with the conversation between myself and Matthew. I don't think Ava was even aware of the fact I was on the phone. I've told you already, she'd only just woken up.'

'You told me,' Detective Mcgraw stated, 'that you weren't sure at what point your daughter woke up.'

'Stop putting words into my mouth, I'm trying to speak. To tell you what happened. We had a discussion on the phone in the car. Me and Matthew. It was a little bit heated.'

Detective Mcgraw walked towards me and put his things back down. I noticed the dictaphone's red flashing light, still recording.

'Good. Now, finally, we're getting somewhere,' he said, his eyes searching my face. 'Please, Ms King. I'm listening.'

England, December 2004

'Lara,' Kaycee hiccupped herself awake. 'I'm gonna ... oh my God. Please, please help me.'

'Listen, it's OK. Just have some water.' I held a glass to her lips but she vomited all over me and the sink.

'I'm not used to it.' she said. 'Baby, Isabella – it's made me ...' She hiccupped again.

'It's OK. Let's get out of here.' I felt more grounded because I was looking after someone else and didn't have to think about what had just happened with peroxide-haired bitch. I waited for a bit. I told Kaycee that Isabella was at home and that she needed to sober up.

'OK,' she said. 'Oh God. Oh my God. I'm an awful mother.' Her eyes went blank. 'I've let her down already. I'm just the worst.' She cried great racking sobs.

'Don't be silly.' I smoothed back her hair. 'Come on. We're gonna go home now. You need to stand up straight. Sort yourself out. Just for five minutes whilst ...'

'Please. Let's go. Now,' she said to me, pulling at the waistband of her shiny green skirt.

'Ready?' She stood up and we opened the toilet door to a wall of banging music and loud voices and she leaned against me.

'You're a good person, Lara. Thank you, for helping me.'

'It's OK,' I said, scanning the room for Ben. I saw him, exactly where I'd left him. I felt like I was going to cry. Devoted fiancé and father.

'Kaycee!' He bounded towards us. His cap was on backwards and he'd rolled down his sleeves. 'Jesus, I was worried.' He looked around. 'Come on. Let's go home.'

'Wait,' I told him. 'I can't leave out the front. I'll go out the back.' I remembered the back entrance from the last time we'd been clubbing at Dancing Buddha. There had to be something similar here. I scanned the back wall and spotted a fire exit, guarded by a large bouncer. I recalled something Joanne had said to me when I'd done my first paid club appearance, when she was running through all the publicity with me.

'When you do your club appearances, they'll want you to be papped as much as possible so you earn your fee. Twenty thousand pounds for the next one.' She'd put on some dark lipstick and smacked her lips. 'So go out the front when you leave, unless you're too drunk, in which case there's always a back exit. Normally it takes you down an alleyway but you can get a car to pick you up. The paps may have cottoned on but if you're careful you should be OK. Normally there's other celebs around anyway.'

'You go out the front and distract them,' I told Ben. 'Tell them I'm coming. They know you're my manager. Order us a cab. I'll take Kaycee out the back so no one paps us. OK?'

'Fine.' He twisted his cap the right way round. 'Hannah and Joanne have already buggered off. You can come back with us tonight.'

'What about—?'

'Isabella?'

'Yeah, won't she . . .'

'She's staying with Kaycee's sister.'

'If you're—' I swallowed down a lump in my throat. The day's events had caught up with me. 'Thank you.'

'Yes. Quick. I'll meet you out the back in five. I'll be in a cab.'

'Fine.' A crowd had started to form around me but then someone else came into the room and everyone moved towards him instead. Justin Farrer, actor of the moment. He waved at me and I waved back.

'*Now*,' I said, propping Kaycee up using my right arm. 'Come on,' I told her. 'You can make it. Just head to the back door.'

I asked the thick-set club bouncer to open the back door, so we could leave the premises. He nodded, looking from side to side, as if he was doing some illicit drugs deal, and finally opened the door a fraction. Kaycee and I both squeezed through, into a freezing cold alleyway that opened out into a square back-yard. I waited for my senses to recalibrate from the smoky, strobe lighting to the silent blackness of the night, before casting my eyes across the place to check there was no one around. I looked for any CCTV: there was an old camera set up above the door frame of the club but when I looked closer, I saw that the cable had been cut, with several wires poking out. *Phew*, I thought. Finally. No one watching. No cameras, no strangers. We were alone.

I inhaled. It smelled of rubbish, stale sweat and urine. And then I heard a small, sad hiccup from Kaycee.

'It's OK,' I told her. 'There's no one here to see us, you can relax now.'

'Are you sure? Is Ben coming soon?'

'He is,' I reassured her. 'And then we'll be on our way home.' I thought of bed. Shutting my eyes, I grabbed Kaycee tightly and longed for sleep, and the soft comforts of their family home. Only then, I told myself, would everything be all right. The flashing red light, the nasty girl – all of that could be dealt with in the morning.

OK – we're gonna look at a few things. Let's talk about what we've seen in the past hour:

1. There's a vid circling the web. One that's dated from three months ago. Someone on a massive drugs bender. It's yet to be confirmed but apparently it's none other than Matthew Raine himself. (Yes – I've seen it. Seriously, you gotta believe me when I tell you that man is a machine.) I'm not gonna link to it here, cos I've got a feeling it's not legal but if you look hard enough, you'll find it. I'll give you a clue. Start by searching the username RagsKnight212. I DARE you or DIE. (Dot com. Geddit?) Take it from there. Be shocked. Be awed. It's a frightening sight.

2. In that vid, if you look very, very carefully, there's a reflection of someone in the window. She's wearing a bikini. Light blue with gold ties at the side. And it's not Lara King. Anyone with information, please DM me.

3. Lara King has got the Rottweiler lawyer at her house today. Anna Devon. She arrived with just a briefcase, wearing a smart suit. NB she's hired by all the A-listers for their scandals.

4. No one from #TeamLara or #TeamMatthew has commented on the video. It's all being kept suspiciously schtum. What does this mean?

Here with the latest updates on missing Ava King, brought to you by Lara and Ava King's number one fan.

Twitter: @ryan_gosling_wannabe

'Where's Joan?' Ava stood at the bottom of my bed. 'I can't find her. Where is she?' Her voice was getting more and more high-pitched.

'Oh, she's gone.' I lifted up my eye mask and pulled down the covers. Rosa had left my breakfast on the side. 'Could you just . . .' I pointed to the tray which had hot coffee, kefir yoghurt with strawberry puree and a smoothie. She walked over to the tray.

'Gone where?' I could see the judder of her bottom lip as she inhaled. I was going to push it. Tell her she'd gone for a while, just to see how she reacted but then I remembered my vow. Connect with my daughter. Have fun.

'Oh, darling,' I said. 'She's just got the day off because of our special day together.'

'But she's coming back, isn't she?' She swallowed frantically. 'I didn't tell. I didn't say a word. About the swimming pool. About anything.'

Anything? What else was my daughter referring to?

'Yes. She is. Am I not good enough for you?' My voice had an edge to it that I tried to control. She picked up my cues.

'It's just that' – she picked up the smoothie and sniffed at it before handing it to me – 'she said she was going to help me with something. That's all.'

'With what? Anything I can do? Or am I not capable?'

'Nothing,' she whispered.

'Look, come here.' I took the smoothie glass from her. 'Try some of this and let's Insta it. Get people to caption it. See if they can guess the ingredients. You try first.' Her nose wrinkled as she sniffed it again and she put the glass back down. Then I remembered my vow not to use my phone today.

'I'm hungry,' she said.

'Fine,' I said. 'We'll go and get something in a minute, when I'm ready. How about we look in my walk-in? Choose an outfit for later.' I pointed towards the room adjoining my bedroom. A huge space that was kept ordered and colour-charted by my stylist. Every piece of clothing was labelled, itemised and dated from when I last wore it. There was row upon row of shoes too. Hundreds of pairs. Manolos, Louboutins, the works. Half of them were unworn and there was a huge back-lit mirror on one wall, where Ava and I would stand on the thick cream carpet, and play dress-up. She loved it. 'Choose something for me?' But she shook her head.

'Go for a walk?' she said. 'And then you said I could have ice cream.' She sounded defiant, as though she was testing me.

'OK. We'll do exactly that. Let's aim to leave at nine thirty or so? It's eight fifteen now. I need to get ready.'

'OK.' She didn't move. 'I'm already dressed. So I'll wait here.'

'Wait downstairs,' I said. 'And I'll be down soon. You look tired. What time did you get up?' She shrugged again.

'Where's . . . ?' She nodded to the other side of the bed, unable to bring herself to say Matthew's name.

'He said he was going to a friend's house, I think. He'll be back later.'

'So it's just you and me?' Her eyes started to shine. 'No security today? No paps?'

'Just us, sweetie.' I felt better then. 'Although if the paps see us they might take photos. They don't know where we're going but they might be out in force. Who knows.' I often wondered how many times Conor rang them with tip-offs. Or bouncers, or shop assistants. I thought about how sometimes it was just random and today, there was some part of me that hoped they might just catch us, nipping into the ice-cream parlour together, or somewhere along our walk.

A true mother-daughter moment that was totally natural. How it would show Joan that I was a good mother. She would be able to tell, after all, that it hadn't been a set-up shot.

'Quick then,' I shooed her out. 'Go downstairs and I'll be with you soon.'

She scampered out of the room. I moved the smoothie and the coffee onto the end of my bed and took a few photos. I toyed with uploading them.

#Guesstheingredients, I was going to write. The more I thought about it, the stronger the pull. I swiped my camera onto the screen and positioned the lens in the right place, setting the correct filters, but then I told myself no. If I was going to make this work, get Ava back to her old self, I needed to concentrate on her and her alone, so I put my phone on the chest of drawers, and got dressed.

'I'm ready,' I shouted down a little while later. 'Come on, it's nine forty now. Let's get the car. Rosa? Marcy? We're off.' My mind pulled back to Ava – she said she was hungry. She must have grabbed something to eat, but before I could ask her, Marcy shouted up at me, interrupting my train of thought.

'Oh, there's water. I left it by the front door,' Marcy said.

'Thank you. Ava, hurry up.' I was keen to get on now. The paps usually roamed the area near the ice-cream parlour in the early afternoon. If we left soon, we'd have a chance of finishing our walk and being there whilst they were still hanging about. I told myself not to think like that, but just in case, I pulled out a lip gloss which I kept in the top drawer of the sideboard cabinet in the hallway and slipped it in my pocket. *Just in case*, I told myself.

'I'm here, Mom.' Ava presented herself at the bottom of the grand staircase. She looked lovely. She'd changed into a navy cotton dress and silver shoes. Her outfit complemented my clothes: too-white running pants and Nike trainers paired with a workout top that I thought would absorb any sweat. Relaxed enough that should the paps see me, they'd know I hadn't dressed up just for them, but flattering enough that it showed off my figure beautifully.

'You look great, darling.' I pulled out my phone again but stopped myself. 'Come on. Let's go. Don't forget the water. It's meant to be over one hundred degrees today. You take one, I'll take the other.' She picked them up and handed one to me with a smile. A real, Ava smile.

'Lovely,' I said out loud and took her hand.

This was more like it, I thought.

'He has, well, he had someone.' I stared first at Detective Mcgraw and then at Anna. 'A friend. That he liked to see.'

'What kind of friend?' Detective Mcgraw sat down at the kitchen table, like he was about to get stuck into a bottle of beer and a chat. He draped his arm over the back of his chair, swung his left leg across his right one and jacked up the volume dial on his recording device.

'A friend. She, well, she and him.' I was still standing. I buried my head in my hands for a second and then looked up at Conor.

Go on, he mouthed. *You're doing great.* Concentrate, I told myself but then this whole thing with Ava – her disappearance – had traumatised me so deeply it seemed to have triggered the memories of every bad thing I'd done.

'Lara?' Detective Mcgraw said. 'Are you OK? You were telling me about Matthew? That he was seeing someone?'

'Yes,' I told him. 'It's just that, it's a little sensitive. Upsetting to me. That's all. He's been seeing someone. Has been for a while. Just for . . .' I glanced over at Anna.

'Look. It was an arrangement that he would get his' – I wrung my hands together – 'his *satisfaction* elsewhere. What I couldn't give him. He needs a lot. And I don't. You must be laughing at me now.' I flushed and looked down, remembering how

Matthew had brought up the subject when I'd told him I was too exhausted to be physical with him. In truth, ever since Conor and I had chatted about stepping my career up a notch, I hadn't wanted any contact with anyone really. It felt like I was giving my all to my career and I didn't have time for anyone, or anything else, apart from Ava.

'I do love you, Lara. But I'm a man.' He'd prodded me in the ribs. 'With needs.' We'd both laughed but I knew there were serious undertones and that was when I'd come up with the idea. It had been brilliant, because in a way, despite him not being faithful, at least I was in control of knowing that he was cheating. No nasty surprises. Nothing. That in itself had made me feel better. Off the hook where bedroom antics were concerned and there was no way the press would find out anything before I did. He hadn't been keen at first, until he knew I was a hundred per cent serious. 'What if they find out?' he'd asked. 'Ava, or Joan?'

'Look,' I replied. 'They won't. And if they do. Well, we'll cross that bridge.'

'So you had this agreement going. Was it Jenna?' Detective Mcgraw looked at his dictaphone.

'A friend of Jenna's. I don't want Jenna getting involved. She had nothing to do with it, really.'

'She just facilitated things? At her house? This was all quite carefully executed, wasn't it? I mean to say, you're quite on top of things, aren't you?' I didn't reply. 'And then you argued about it the morning of Ava's disappearance? You said you didn't mind. You'd given him permission under your own admission. Then why did you argue?'

'Careless.' I looked at Conor. He knew everything. Had been on it from the beginning and had plans drawn up in case anyone should find out. But I'd trusted Matthew to be discreet. 'He was getting careless. I got cross. Said that people were going to find out and humiliate me. In our line of work, well, I wasn't happy.'

'And am I right in thinking, Ms King, that Matthew was busy with someone in the swimming pool, the day of the announcement? Was that what prompted the row in the car?'

'I don't know.' I was getting all tied up in knots. I couldn't remember what I'd told Detective Mcgraw about the swimming pool already, except that I hadn't seen anything or been near the annexe for over a year. No one had even confirmed that it had been Matthew in there.

Take a moment, I told myself.

'You knew what Matthew was up to in the swimming pool. You saw him? So what was it?'

'I didn't.'

'Ava saw him, didn't she? Was he with another one of his women then? Was that what he was up to? Was that what he didn't want anyone to see?'

'No,' I screamed, thinking of what had really been going on in the pool and what would happen if Detective Mcgraw ever found out the truth. How it wouldn't just be some salacious gossip for the press, but something much, much darker. 'Stop it. I don't know.' I worried that there was CCTV evidence of what had gone on in the annexe being analysed. That Detective Mcgraw knew everything already and I'd be caught out. I decided to call his bluff.

'No,' I said again more firmly. 'No. I have no idea what happened in the swimming pool.' Again, I thought of the fob and where it could have got to.

'Stop.' Anna stood up and took the sheaf of papers from the table. 'Enough questioning my client like this. This conversation ends now.'

'I haven't finished yet.' Detective Mcgraw stood up. 'I know you know more than you are letting on. It's late, we all need some rest but I'll be back first thing in the morning, to finish this. As I said earlier, we need to organise that press conference too. Get the public focus back. This is turning into a fucking circus with everyone trying to sell their story and all of this stuff being leaked everywhere.'

I couldn't believe what I was hearing and how much he'd changed in his tone of questioning.

'And Matthew,' he said. 'Don't expect Matthew back tonight. OK?'

I said nothing. By the time I got upstairs, I was too wired to think about sleep, too fearful to even shut my eyes. I waited until I could hear no more sounds in the house, and then I took the bird I'd found in Ava's room from under my pillow, desperately hoping I might find the fob in there. I shook it around. There was definitely something quite heavy inside. I tried various different codes but each one drew a blank.

So I ran downstairs to the utility room and grabbed the tool box, looking around in case Joan, Conor or Anna found me but all the lights had been switched off apart from in the hallway.

I took the toolbox to my bedroom and pulled out the screw-driver, prising open the plastic seams of the toy. By the time I'd managed to get it apart, I'd given up hope. There was no fob hidden inside. Instead, I opened a small note, in which I recognised Ava's handwriting, and an old ring that I'd had from England. The ring was inlaid with small rubies and sapphires. How strange, I thought, that she had it. It wasn't like her to steal. But then I remembered a story I'd told her about how I'd worn it when I'd met her daddy. It was when she'd been particularly curious about his identity. I slid it on my finger and squeezed my hand tight. I looked at the note, sobbing at the sight of her small, neat handwriting, with the looped letters. *Ava King*, it read. *Paternitey unknown.* How cute, I thought. She must have heard me use that expression before.

I felt bad I'd pried into her private life. I put it back. I'd buy her a new bird and replace it all. But then I'd turned the piece of paper around and saw in tiny pencil writing in the corner, a small picture of a family of three. My heart melted. How sweet, I thought, but when I looked closer, I saw she'd written something underneath. I read the words over and over, my heart feeling like it was about to escape from within me. At that moment, I ripped the note up into tiny shreds, crumpled it in my hands, and with her words going round and round in my head, I went to lie down.

England, December 2004

'OK,' I said to Kaycee, 'we're going to get you home. Back to your daughter. OK? We'll be in a warm car soon.' I felt a prickle of fear because we were all alone until I heard a cough, as though someone was trying to get my attention. I looked around and then I saw her.

The peroxide-haired girl, from the bathroom.

She was standing at the top of a large flight of metal steps, which must have been the fire escape to the top floor of the club. She was hunched over, a biker jacket slung over her shoulders. She was licking a Rizla paper held in one hand, phone in the other. I looked around. There was still no one in sight and then I remembered the club manager's words. That all sorts go on in the nightclub and I presumed this meant out the back too. Kaycee put her arm around me and it was at that point that my neck felt wrong. All naked as the cold air hit my skin. I looked down and realised what had happened.

The diamond necklace.

It was gone. The diamond necklace that had been loaned to me with strict rules attached, because it was probably worth close to a million pounds.

My breath started coming in shallow waves. *Fuck*, I thought, grabbing at my top. Fuck. Fuck. I'd have to pay it all back. I didn't have the money. How could I have been so fucking stupid. Lavelli's had told me to take security with me if I went out. Or I was to leave it in the hotel. Then I realised that they would have seen me wearing it earlier in pap shots anyway so I was going to get done for however I played it. My mind was all over the place. What the fuck was I thinking? *I wasn't.* I squeezed the flesh between my thumb and forefinger whilst I worked out what to do.

I frisked both arms in case it had slid down my sleeves but it wasn't there and then I remembered the girl, eyes black as she pawed at the necklace.

Don't react, I told myself. I'll think of something. I always do. I'd tell Ben. Ask his advice. Or Joanne. But it was too late and my body started to move before my mind caught up with it and before I knew it, before I could even process that I was about to do such a horrendous thing, I'd climbed the stairs and was right next to peroxide-haired bitch. I could smell body odour mixed with peppermint. A fresh spritz of fruity perfume. I almost gagged.

'Give me my necklace back,' I hissed, my breath catching. I grabbed at her bag, tipping out the contents but it wasn't in there.

'Stop,' she shouted. 'Stop. What are you talking about?' She was looking around, her eyes settling on Kaycee. 'What the fuck are you talking about?'

'My diamond necklace. You stole it.'

'I didn't.' She looked scared, peering around in the dark.

'Hurry up.' I could hear Kaycee. 'Ben's coming soon. Hurry up.'

'Give me the recording then. Where's your mobile?'

'No.' She lit the cigarette she'd been rolling. Her top lip curved into a half-smile. 'That you are not getting.'

'Lara,' Kaycee pleaded. 'Please.' I thought I heard her retch.

'I'm coming,' I shouted over my shoulder, and before I knew it, my body reacted to the situation. I felt my hands connect with the girl's chest. And then the thump of her body as she tumbled down the metal steps. *Fuck*, I thought, bringing my hands up to the weak light. *How could I have done that?* I thought. *How could I? Was I going mad? Was my mind telling me to do things that I could no longer control?*

'Oh God,' I whispered, shaking. But by then I'd run back down the stairs to Kaycee, who was staring me, her whole body trembling.

No one saw, I told myself. No one saw. Except Kaycee. She was sobbing now, clawing at her face. 'Oh my God,' she cried. 'What did you just do?'

'Forget it,' I told her. 'She ... Just forget what you saw.' It absolutely wasn't a big deal, was it now? I'd seen worse. I rubbed my hands together and told Kaycee to stand up properly but she kept looking over to the corner of the court-yard, piled high with rubbish.

'Stop,' I told her. 'It's fine, for God's sake. She's just drunk.' I heard the vibrations of a taxi's engine, swinging into earshot.

Kaycee let out a cry.

'Come on, guys,' Ben sang as the taxi appeared at the end of the alley. 'Jump in. Quick. Before anyone sees you. It's your birthday now by the way,' he said to me, waving his hands out the window, the slur of his voice loud and loose.

'Happy birthday to me,' I sang, shivering as I pulled Kaycee towards the car. She was crying still, black smudges of kohl streaking her cheeks, her head still turned to the corner of the courtyard. *It's fine*, I thought. I was still rubbing at my arm, thinking about the necklace and then I felt woozy, as though the dental medicine and alcohol had caught up with me all at once.

'Oh, babe,' Ben said, 'it's OK. Jeez, you're only drunk. It's not like Isabella's going to remember this.' He turned to the taxi driver. 'Walthamstow, please. Radbourne Crescent. And as for you, missy.' He poked me in the ribs. 'Don't you start.'

Kaycee kept looking at me, pulling at her hair.

I remembered again the video footage that was on that bitch's camera but by that point, I was so tired. The warmth of the car wrapped around me and I leaned into Ben's arm. The necklace. The girl. The recording. It could wait. I'd sort it out in the morning. But when I did shut my eyes, I could hear the thump of my heart, fierce and strong. I didn't know how I was ever going to rid myself of the guilt leeching into my bones.

So I know you guys are going to accuse me of clickbait here. That the links to this blog said I had the biggest scoop of the century?

Well, I really wasn't lying. So, guys, this is the big one. The big scoop! And I know, I know, we have to still be really mindful that there is a small child missing, but as each minute passes, it just seems that more and more about Ava's disappearance is not right, or that things are unfolding that shouldn't be.

Lara and Matthew have a lot of secrets they're hiding. This one for a start . . . now I know you've all been waiting for this announcement and that I told you I had something huge. So you ready?

But firstly, props go to the amazing Manny Berkowitz, who is on a roll and was the one who worked and worked to get this story. He's an all-round genius.

So you know that there's been speculation about Ava's father for, well, years really. That TMZ did those funny sliders where you compared Ava's face with likely candidates? Well, they seemed to have missed one person off and when I tell you who it is, y'all going to say . . .

OH MY GOD.

Ready? Her dad is none other than the Hollywood film producer Frankie Spearman. I can hear you collectively go silent. Go on then, let that tick over your brains. Wind the cogs. Do you see it? Do you?

Boom. There it goes. The lightbulb.

OH MY GOD, HE IS SO HER FATHER.

YEAH?

Got it now?

Frankie Spearman – I bet everyone's feverishly rooting around for his name online. Looking up his credits. And bam again there it is. His main credit.

Yup. You guessed it.

Lara and Ava's TV show.

Right. So, let's continue with this.

The headlines are as follows and I've summarised the piece below which I got early dibs on, thanks to my contact at the *LA Times*.

Please find the full article here and once again, hand claps to Manny Berkowitz.

PRODUCER AND DIRECTOR WHO CAST LARA KING IN HER REALITY SERIES DEVASTATED TO HEAR OF DAUGHTER'S DISAPPEARANCE VOWED TO HELP FIND HIS CHILD

Despite the film producer's insistence that he is 'distraught' the *LA Times* can reveal that he has shunned all meetings with his daughter since her birth. (Asshole – Ed.)

His name also does not appear on her birth certificate but the *LA Times* can reveal that a number of cheques have been deposited in Lara King's account, with the name of Frankie's company. (Yikes. I'm guessing someone's going to get in a whole heap of trouble from Frankie.) The amounts do not match the ten-million-dollar pay cheque that King received for the six-series show that she broadcast with her daughter Ava and the *LA Times* has seen email exchanges between Frankie, Lara and their legal teams, discussing the nature of their relationship.

Frankie Spearman spoke exclusively to the *LA Times* to say that he was sorry someone felt that they could sell him out. And he had no choice but to clear his name and that Lara King had 'aggressively pursued him' when she had arrived in LA with promises of sexual favors, in return for fame and roles in his movies.

'I don't like to speak ill of people when they are going through such awful pain, but I know how the media works and I know how all this will unfold. Given the recent #metoo campaign, where more and more women are speaking out about sexual molestation in this industry, I need to defend my name and good honor, before another Hollywood smear campaign ruins careers and lives. I would also like to say that for the women who have been put in horrible positions, and have spoken out about it, I salute you, and admire you.'

He then goes on to wish Lara King 'all the best' and is 'desperately praying for the safe return of their daughter'. He finished off by saying that he hoped to 'get to know Ava when she returns. It's at times like this that you realise that blood is indeed, thicker than water.'

I'm guessing now we realise that there is more at stake here than we originally thought. That there are other players in the whole thing, with different agendas and the disappearance of Ava King might involve those who are closer to home than originally thought.

Here with the latest updates on missing Ava King, brought to you by Lara and Ava King's number one fan.

Twitter: @ryan_gosling_wannabe

I'd eventually fallen asleep with fractured images of Ava's drawing in my mind. The small stick figures. The determined lines of her writing underneath each person. *Ava King. Daddy. Joan.* She saw Joan as her mother. The completion of her ideal family image. The memory of my own mother started to pull at the edges of my mind. I woke with a start, knowing that something awful had happened before my mind had even time to process that I'd been asleep.

Ava. Guilt smothered me, that I'd managed to sleep when my daughter was God knows where. I wondered what the temperature had been in the past few hours. I imagined her outside walking, or curled up somewhere. Or if someone had taken her, I prayed they were looking after her. I got up from my bed to stop my mind from segueing onto more unpleasant images of where my daughter might be, or the things that might be happening to her.

I got dressed in a pair of sweat pants and a light cotton jumper and tied my hair up in a low bun. I couldn't contemplate showering, keeping clean or putting on any make-up, even though I knew I'd have to face the press soon.

When I went downstairs, Conor and Detective Mcgraw were already up and waiting. They lowered their voices when I walked in.

'I came back early.' Detective Mcgraw slammed down a newspaper on the table. 'Because my wife woke me up to this.'

'Show me the article.' I held out my hand but he shook his head.

'No. I want to speak to you first,' and then Anna appeared, wearing a new, belted navy suit and freshly applied lipstick.

'I'm here,' she said. 'If you need me.' She made her way over to the corner of the kitchen.

'The question of Ava's paternity' – he covered the paper with his forearms – 'has been revealed. Some pretty shocking news for all concerned,' he went on.

'I tried to come up and tell you,' Conor interjected. 'But . . .' He nodded towards Detective Mcgraw.

'But what?' I snapped. 'All of you colluding to spring this on me? During the worst time of my life? What does it say?'

'You know exactly what it says,' stated Detective Mcgraw. 'You know, because you were one of the only people that knew who Ava's father was. And you lied about it to everyone.'

Conor looked furious and upset. I realised he was still waiting for me to tell him about England and that I hadn't given him the chance to be alone with me. No wonder he was so agitated.

'Look, Lara,' he said. 'We can turn this into a good thing. If any of the other stuff comes out, this will take the focus off.' He looked like he wanted to tell me more but his sideways glance at Mcgraw told me he was too worried.

'A good thing? It's like a circus to me. I can tell you one thing.' Mcgraw sounded resigned, and quiet, after his earlier aggression. 'Manny Berkowitz has really made a name for himself now. And, Conor, you say that you can use this to distract from negative press, yet you have no consideration about what this might do to the actual case? When there's a missing girl at the heart of this?'

'Of course I do. At least it wasn't me who leaked stuff from my own workplace,' he retaliated, referring to the audio call.

'It concerns me, Ms King' – Detective Mcgraw turned to me, after a couple of seconds – 'that you have lied to me consistently about the paternity of your daughter. You told us that you met someone at a party held by a Lucy Wigmore.' I watched as he pushed the dial on his dictaphone and placed it near me. 'Whom we've been chasing for God knows how many hours – sending us down totally the wrong path.' I tried to interrupt, to tell him that I'd warned them that Ava's paternity had nothing to do with her going missing.

'Lying to the police during the investigation of your own daughter?' He looked over at Anna. 'Yet if reports here are to be believed, and I've never known Manny Berkowitz to make a bad call, you've known all along that Frankie Spearman is her father. You told me that you didn't remember who her father was. So please, tell me, what else have you lied about?' His voice was steady and quiet but suddenly he slammed his hands on my desk. 'Lies,' he shouted. 'What other lies?' His face went pale, the skin around his eyes dry. His demeanour was beginning to frighten me now.

'Please,' said Anna calmly. 'Leave my client alone for a moment.' But he stood up and walked around the table, doing his usual trick of not looking at me at all. His tongue kept darting in and out, touching his bottom lip.

'It had nothing to do with Ava. I didn't want things distracted. Everyone looking the wrong way.' I glared at Conor.

'It has everything to do with Ava,' Detective Mcgraw replied. 'Things are not looking good here, Ms King.' He tapped the dictaphone. 'You've deliberately tried to obstruct the investigation into your daughter's disappearance by hiding the truth about something that could have a direct impact on finding her. The swimming pool annexe, Matthew's drug taking and now Ava's father. What else have you hidden from us?'

'I can explain. I can explain it all. I can explain Frankie.'

'Then before I start thinking, I suggest you tell us.'

'Fine.' I sounded like a sulky child which I hated myself for but I was furious with Detective Mcgraw for being so aggressive when I was so vulnerable. I saw Conor shift forward.

'My singing career back in England was over,' I told him. 'Things had gone wrong over there. I wanted to start a new life over here. But it had got to me. The showbiz side of things. I wanted to reclaim what I had.' I looked at Conor, trying to work out if he hated me or felt sorry for me. 'Can we open the windows?' Conor got up and pulled down the large window behind the table where I was sitting. The fresh air felt like poison to me. 'I moved over here to LA,' I went on. 'To start again.'

'And so what then? What happened?'

'After having settled down here for a few years and taking bit-part jobs, the head of this film production company told me he'd make me a star. That I was to go and see him. He liked me. He held my hand in his office. He told me to . . .'

'He told you to what?' asked Detective Mcgraw.

'Nothing. He said he'd make me famous. That he'd give me my own show. He told me he was going to give me a special audition and . . .' I closed my eyes.

'And you . . .'

'Yes. I did. A few times. But eventually he gave me the part. In fact, he gave me a whole show and I don't think any of us realised how amazing and successful it was going to be.' I stopped and thought about how quickly I'd managed to erase everything that had happened in England. 'Then, well, after that, Ava arrived and he said if I kept quiet, he'd make a mother and daughter show for us. It was brief. One month we were, you know, and the next we weren't. We never went out or anything. It always happened in his office.' I shut my eyes and the memories came flooding in. The large leather sofa in the corner. Posters of his films and TV shows hung on the walls, in huge, glass frames. The breathtaking view, scanning right across the Hollywood hills.

I thought back to the times he told me to look out the window. 'Over there,' he had said. 'The Hollywood sign. Look, that could all be yours.' I had felt him then, thrust against me. 'Look, just imagine . . . your name . . . God . . . you're . . .' And then he'd grunted and buckled up his belt. 'Beautiful,' he'd said, waving me back to the sofa. 'Sit down.' I'd done as I'd been told every time, my legs sticky against the leather. 'Come back next week,' he'd said, reading his emails on his computer. He had never even bothered to look up after that. Not even when I had said goodbye, except to hurry me out the room. 'Did you hear what I said? We'll get you sorted,' he'd snap, and I knew then that he was getting pissed off with my presence.

'And that was that, really.' I stood up. 'He's her father. Ava's.'

'Are you saying,' said Detective Mcgraw, looking down at his hands, 'that in your opinion, he took advantage of you? Used his power in return for sexual favours?'

I looked around me. My house. I thought about the sparkling blue pool outside. I thought about my life. The show he'd produced, that had turned me from a fading star in England into a global celebrity. The power I now wielded with my Instagram account. My Twitter. My endorsements.

'I don't know what that has to do with anything, Detective Mcgraw.'

'Right,' Anna interrupted. 'Enough. My client is done.'

'It has everything to do with everything. I'm trying to work out if there's any motive at all, you see, for the disappearance of your daughter. Whether someone did take her.' Detective Mcgraw slowed his voice right down. 'Maybe Ms King here was about to sell her story. Maybe she had contacted Frankie Spearman. A ploy between her and Matthew to gain *more* fame. *More* money. Spearman thought he'd given you a little warning. Who knows? But we're looking into it. Looking into it very, very closely.' He came right up to me and stared into my eyes.

'No,' I said, shaking. 'Please, Anna. Get him out of here.' I wanted to speak more but I was afraid of the feelings that were about to erupt inside me. It felt like I was back in England again, at the top of those metal steps. *Hands out. Push. Thud.* I didn't want to do anything I might regret, so I let it drop. 'Just leave. Please.' As Detective Mcgraw left the room, I shouted after him. 'I had Ava. I'll never regret that.'

'You didn't answer the question, Ms King.' He didn't even bother turning around. 'About Frankie Spearman taking advantage of you.'

'I did. I answered it. I told you, it doesn't matter. It doesn't matter at all. He gave me Ava. And so I don't care. I don't care what happened. I just care that you find her.'

Detective Mcgraw walked off. I was left alone with just Conor and Anna in the room. I signalled for them not to talk. I needed time to think. Weirdly, I wanted Joan here. I wanted someone to make the house feel normal again. I wanted quiet, to think about Ava's father and whether I should get in contact with him. How I'd emailed his PA when I'd given birth.

Mr Spearman thanks you for the email and would be pleased to offer you a meeting with his lawyer at three p.m. tomorrow afternoon at their offices.

He had kept to his word though. He had made stars out of me and his daughter. I wondered what had happened to Isabella, too, Ben and Kaycee's daughter. The last time I'd seen her she'd been a few weeks old, in Kaycee's arms and now she'd be nearing eighteen. I thought about the temptation Frankie had lured me in with. 'This' – he had pointed to the Hollywood sign – 'could all be yours.' I had got them, I thought. My dreams. They had come true. And now, here they were – once sparkling and filled with promise, blackened to the core.

England, December 2004

'Isabella's been crying all morning,' Kaycee said. 'She must know something's up.' I walked over with a cup of tea and handed it to Kaycee, but she pulled the baby close to her and turned her head away.

'Please, let me,' I began, but she buried her head into the small, soft scalp and let out a cry. 'Kaycee. Please. Let me explain. Please.' I wanted to tell her how it just had got all too much – everyone staring. How the dentist's anaesthetic had affected my judgement but I'd known as I had been reeling through everything, it sounded lame. That Kaycee had probably never even raised her voice and there she was, harbouring me in her beautifully warm house, for something awful I'd done.

'I need to feed her.' She undid her top button and turned her back to me. I looked at the back of her plaid collar, the shield of her long, brown hair. I felt myself about to cry. Kaycee. Kind, lovely Kaycee who wouldn't even let me near her child in case I polluted the air between us.

'Kaycee, listen, she . . . she made me do it. She pushed me to it . . . let me just explain what happened. Please. It's not what you think.' But I just heard the soft tut and shhhh as she fed her baby.

I stood watching Kaycee, waiting for her to give in and look at me so I could talk to her. Ten minutes later, Ben walked in and my phone rang. Joanne.

'Hello?' I sang. If I styled this out, it would be OK.

'Lara,' she replied. 'Where are you?'

'Walthamstow,' I tried to sound casual but there was a waver to my voice that I couldn't disguise.

'I'm coming to get you. Message me the address. Straight away.'

'What—'

'You know what.'

I thought back to the red light on the video camera, following me round, as I had leered into her face. *You fucking ugly, cheap whore.* And then afterwards. Kaycee's eyes as I'd walked towards her in the dark. She'd seen everything. She'd seen what I'd done. It hadn't been so bad, I told myself. That bit would never get out. It was just a small act. The things I had said in the bathroom – they will all die down. I didn't need to worry about what happened afterwards, did I? And anyway – she deserved it. It made me feel better saying that.

That stupid bitch. She totally deserved it.

August 26th 2018

0946hrs

The Disappearance

'OK, favourite boy in your class at the moment,' I said, as we swung out of the drive. The palm trees lining the roads always made me happy. Always reminded me of how far I'd come since England. I had promised myself that I'd tell Ava bits about her background today on the car journey. I'd explain where I'd grown up. That despite my attempts at trying, my parents no longer spoke to me. I felt the familiar drag on my solar plexus. The thought that they'd culled me after they'd seen me tell a few white lies about my background on live TV. Despite all that, I think about how unremarkable my background had actually been. Except for me, I thought. Something had always felt hollow inside of me, for reasons I could never work out.

'Um, I haven't seen any boys this summer,' she replied.

'Stop sucking on your hair.' I pulled her long ponytail out her mouth. 'Are you going to be like this all day?' I patted her leg but she didn't reply. 'OK. How about you tell me . . .' We drove down the roads of The Hidden Hills. 'What flavour ice cream are you going to have?'

'Strawberry?'

'Strawberry. Good idea, me too.' I wanted to tell her that the paps might be around. I carried on driving, trying to rid myself of the mental tic that kept telling me to make the call. *Don't do it. Don't do it.* I gripped the steering wheel.

'How about sprinkles and those jelly baby things too, Ava?'

'Can we?' She turned and looked at me. 'For real?'

'We sure can.' I swung out of The Hidden Hills drive and soon we were on the freeway. Peace, at last. 'Nice,' I said. 'Being just you and me, isn't it?'

'Yes. Nice not having *him* around. Sometimes you act funny in front of him.' I'd never heard Ava talk like this before. *Joan.* I swerved the car a little. What was happening to my sweet little six-year-old? I opened the window, leaning my face into the breeze. I slowed down a bit and that's when I saw a car right behind us. The road was otherwise totally clear. I took no notice of it except I sped up slightly so that we were on our own. I wondered if somehow the paps had got hold of our whereabouts.

'Well,' I said, taking a deep breath. 'He is rather good-looking, isn't he?' I laughed but inside, my blood was boiling. I was going to have to have a word with Joan. Put her in her place and tell her to stop filling my daughter's head with things she didn't understand. But then Ava laughed too.

'He is,' she said, 'that's why all the girls in my class love him so much.' Her face flushed and she smiled but then she got all serious. 'Is that why he can do whatever he wants?' she asked. 'Because he's so good-looking?'

'I don't know what you mean, Ava. Look over there.' I pointed at a random building I'd never even seen before now. A wooden-planked shed. 'What on earth do we think that is?' I carried on, talking, hoping she'd get distracted. My voice got lost in the wind and I could tell that my daughter's mind was far away and it was OK, we were all alone now, there were no more cars in sight, and I decided then to keep my mind focused on the now and to enjoy the view. I thought it would be a comfortable silence between us but a strange feeling kept nipping at my stomach. Keep driving, and it will go away, I told myself, so I pressed my foot on the accelerator and hoped for calm.

First and foremost, I'd like to say a massive, massive thank you to everyone who has contributed to this so far. I'd like to say that I'm not paying for people's tip-offs and sources as of yet. This blog was created out of a love for Ava and Lara King and so any tips that come through are taken with the same sense of gratitude and willingness to share – the same spirit in which this project was started.

Secondly, I've been talking to people on the ground all night. I know it's a scorcher today. But last night when I did the rounds – wow. It was pitch-black at about four in the morning and there were still kids camped out drinking and waiting. Then, the hardier among you were still out with torches and supplies, still searching each path and under each bush in the canyon. 'For anything at all that might lead us to her. We'd want everyone to do the same if it were our kids,' said Peter Manray, 57. 'If any of you would like to donate food or water there's a campervan parked up by Laurel Canyon.'

As far as the investigation is concerned, I can tell you that tempers are frayed in the *LA Times'* office. Manny Berkowitz has a scoop that the editors say is not 'in the paper's best interest' to run just yet. What is it? I hear you ask. Well, I can tell you that some of the journalists here are on the scent and have been looking at Casuarina Jail in Perth, Western Australia. And who is from Perth? None other than our favorite film star, Matthew Raine. Update to follow.

And thank you all, for your leads on the female with Matthew Raine in the video footage. I'll be chasing up a few suggestions soon.

Here with the latest updates on missing Ava King, brought to you by Lara and Ava King's number one fan.

Twitter: @ryan_gosling_wannabe

When Joan appeared, it made me feel worse. Like every bad thing I'd done was mirrored by every good thing she'd done for my daughter.

'What's going on?' She'd pulled her hair into a tight ponytail and, rather strangely for Joan, had put on some blusher and lip gloss. She looked at the newspaper on the table. I saw her taking it in, then look at me with something close to disgust.

'Tea or coffee?' she said. I hadn't offered anyone anything to drink since they'd arrived. I'd been used to Marcy and Rosa doing all of that for me. I wanted to punch her for making me look bad.

No one answered her. I desperately wanted a coffee to kick-start my senses but I'd be damned if I was going to ask Joan for a thing. She was busy pulling out a large silver cafétière.

'Look,' said Detective Mcgraw. 'We just need the truth now, Lara. For the best chances of finding your daughter. No one here cares about what you did. Or what you got up to. Please. Just tell us everything. We'll take you inside the station after the press conference. Privacy. You can tell us there. The conference is being held on the corner of the next block to the station. So you don't have to go far. We'll tell the public that you are just coming inside to help out with some of our enquiries. That way it won't look so sudden. All right?'

'Fine. Look. I just want you to find her.'

'Good. So we're on the same page.' Joan was staring at me now, she'd paused halfway through pouring the coffee. I wanted to warn her that she was about to burn herself but then I realised what she was wearing. It was a large knitted jumper that looked handmade. It had two pockets on either side, and she kept burying her hands into the pocket on the left-hand side. I saw a flash of silver through the material. It suddenly hit me what she had on her.

'Conor.' Detective Mcgraw took charge again. 'Please deal with the press. The press conference is at ten a.m. Lara will come to the station with me after that. OK?'

'Fine.' Conor grabbed the mug coffee Joan held out to him. She slammed down the handful of spoons she'd been carrying.

'Ava,' she said, her voice harder than I'd ever heard it. 'She never deserved this. She's a good girl. With the kindest of hearts. Yet all of this, surrounding her disappearance . . .' She held her chest and sobbed and sobbed, unable to carry on talking. 'Please bring her home,' she wailed. 'Please bring my little girl home.' No one moved an inch. After what felt like hours Detective Mcgraw cleared his throat.

'Best get moving soon.' He nodded at Joan with a small smile. 'Lara? Conor? Anna? Are you coming?' Thank God, I thought. She wasn't going to bring the fob up in public. But I was damn well going to find out what she was doing with it in her pocket.

No one said a thing, but then Joan shouted. 'Stop,' she called. 'Wait. I forgot, Lara.' I turned towards her. She was all hunched over like she had a bad back. 'This, I found this.'

I was about to pounce on her but she held it up for everyone to see. I grabbed it.

'Oh, thanks.' I put it in the top drawer of the kitchen island. My legs felt weak. I wanted to ask her where she'd found it but I couldn't risk any questions. 'Right. Let me get ready,' I announced. 'Anna, I know this is not your remit but my stylist isn't here. I don't suppose you might come and help me choose something suitable?'

'Of course.' She nodded but before she had a chance to get up, Joan walked over to the kitchen island and opened the drawer.

'Wait.' She pulled it open. 'That doesn't belong there, does it?'

'I'll put it back later.' I grabbed the fob from her again.

'Let me then.' I wanted to ask her why she hadn't just put it back herself and then I realised she wanted me to be caught out in front of Detective Mcgraw.

'Fine. You know where it goes,' I said, like I didn't have a care in the world. My knees were beginning to buckle.

'Sure.' She was using that annoying sing-song voice she had when she was about to try and prove a point. 'Whoever was in there last must have forgotten to lock up. I know you've sealed everything off, Detective, but I hope you can now lock up properly.'

'Lock up what?' Detective Mcgraw was staring at the front of the newspaper.

'The annexe to the swimming pool. This is the fob. I found it in Lara's bedroom when I was tidying up yesterday. I meant to say' – she turned to me – 'that I'd taken it. Just in case you'd been looking for it. It was on your bedside table. I don't normally go in there as you know. But I thought given Marcy and Rosa weren't here, I'd make your bed. And that's when I saw it.'

'Lara?' questioned Detective Mcgraw. 'The key fob? You told me you hadn't been in the pool for a year? Any reason why it was in your bedroom? I know that all the other keys and fobs are kept in your study.'

I started to really panic now. And then I remembered Matthew and Joan talking on the CCTV. I wondered whether somehow they were in cahoots.

'No idea.' I controlled my voice spectacularly well but Joan interrupted.

'A *year*? You haven't been there for a year?'

'Yeah,' I replied. 'Come on, Anna. Let's go. I've got a black trouser suit that would be perfect. Not too smart. Just right.' Detective Mcgraw's breathing sped up.

'But I saw you,' Joan continued. 'I saw you there. The day of the announcement.'

'No, you didn't. Don't be ridiculous. I haven't been in there for months.' I slammed shut an open drawer. 'Now, please. We're in a hurry. I really need to get washed before I face the public. I've got to get moving. For Ava.'

'I did. I saw you.'

'Anna?' I sensed Detective Mcgraw looking at my back but I didn't turn around. I just started to walk out the door.

'Wait,' he said. I flipped my head back.

'What? Are you going to help find my daughter?'

'You said you hadn't been near the annexe for over a year. What does Joan mean she saw you there the day of the announcement? That was four days ago. When the CCTV footage was obstructed.'

'I saw you,' Joan went on. 'With Ava. Right outside the door.' I realised she'd been waiting for this moment. Any moment, in fact, to catch me out. To show me up as a bad mother. She must have known all along that I'd told Detective Mcgraw I hadn't been in the pool annexe. One of the many times she'd been silently eavesdropping.

'I was trying to find Ava,' she went on. 'I followed her. She must have followed you. Right before Matthew came back into the room. You went looking for him, if I recall.'

'Right. I'd like to go with my client to get ready now, please.' Anna pushed Joan backwards lightly.

'Stop,' commanded Detective Mcgraw. 'I need your *client* to stay right where she is. I'd like to hear the rest of this before we leave.'

'I went after Ava. She must have followed you. I wanted to make sure she was all right. She was beside herself. Had been all morning, except you barely noticed,' she spat. 'I tried to tell you that she wasn't coping. That she'd been asking about her father. Her *real* father. If you'd just taken the time to explain.'

I felt close to tears. I *had* wanted to tell Ava. I just hadn't wanted her to ask too many questions.

'She was nervous about the announcement. Yet you hadn't prepared her for that either. She was nervous about Manny. You didn't even tell her who he was. Just this stranger turning up, asking questions, watching your every move. For God's sake. She's a child.' She started to sob again. 'And then I saw you. I watched you go into the swimming pool annexe. Ava was right behind you.' I hear Conor gasp. And someone else made a noise but I couldn't quite be sure who it was.

'I was going to shout out to you. But you looked scared about something. I didn't think anything of it really. Until I overheard a conversation between you and Detective Mcgraw about the annexe. And then this morning. This morning I remembered I'd found the fob when I'd been tidying up. It all fitted together. That you'd lied. I'd been so distracted thinking about Ava. Thinking about how awful everything is. Grieving, if you will, that my mind had been a complete fog. But you saw something. Didn't you? You saw something in the pool house. And so did Ava. And that has something to do with why she's gone. It all makes sense now.' Her breath's juddering, her mouth pulling all sorts of strange shapes. And then she collapsed on to the floor pounding the marble with her fists. 'She's gone and it's something to do with all this horrific' – she gestured around the kitchen – 'fame. You're always chasing for more. Like a drug. As for Matthew. He tried to shut me up too.'

'What?' I asked. 'I have no idea what you are talking about. None of it.'

'Matthew. He knew I had the fob. He saw me looking at it from outside your bedroom. Came down to my room and told me to give it to him. Said that I'd lose my job if I said anything. But I figured I don't care anymore. Ava knows I love her more than anyone in the . . .' She pulled at her jumper, as though she couldn't contain the ache in her chest.

Detective Mcgraw went over to Joan and helped her up.

'Come on. Let's get you seen to. We're doing our best,' he continued, 'to find her.' He hadn't spoken to me that kindly since my daughter had disappeared.

Detective Mcgraw turned to me. 'The press conference is being prepped right now. Go and get changed.'

I motioned for Anna to come with me. I took it step by step, holding onto the wall for support.

'Ms King.' He stopped me. 'Wait.'

'What now?' I asked.

'Bring a change of clothes.' And then I heard him mutter something about obstructing the course of justice. I realised what he meant and that I might not be coming home. But that didn't change things. It didn't change the fact that my daughter was still out there, and that it was looking increasingly more likely that I might never see her again.

England, December 2004

'Sorry. About last night,' I said to Kaycee. I didn't care now if she reacted or not, I just wanted to say my piece and be done with it. 'About everything.' She was alone with Isabella but she didn't turn to look at me. *'Hush little baby,'* she was singing.

'Fine,' I said. 'I'm going.' I didn't wait for Ben. I picked up my bag, stuffed with the remnants of last night; a champagne cork that Hannah had given me for good luck, five phone numbers on scraps of paper – *as if* – and my silver jacket that I'd found scrunched up in my bag, with an old piece of chewing gum stuck to it.

I opened the front door and Joanne was sitting in the front of the taxi. She looked at me and gave me a half-smile. She looked pale but she'd still made an effort with her clothes. She wore a beautifully pressed green top and navy trousers and had tied her hair up tight in a braid off her face. Just as I was about to get in, Ben arrived next to me wearing a large, black puffa jacket and a snood.

'I'm coming too.' He slung a record bag onto the back seat. 'Joanne rang me. I was just getting food for breakfast but' – he signalled towards the front door – 'Kaycee's fine. She's just . . .'

'It's OK,' I told him, 'thank you.' I wanted to tell him *no, it wasn't OK.* That he had responsibilities but then I realised that some of his responsibilities were with me. After all, he'd built me up. Just because he'd had a baby it didn't mean he could ditch me in the bad times. Indignation rose within me.

'I'm sorry about last night,' I told them both, as we sat in the back seat. The smell of leather and the faint sounds of the radio felt calming. I wondered whether they were going to play my song. I couldn't bear to hear my own voice.

'Please.' I leaned forward and touched the driver's arm. 'Please can you turn it off? Or put on some classical music?' She nodded and flicked the dial on the dashboard.

'Thank you,' I told her.

'Listen.' Joanne looked at both of us with those pale blue eyes of hers. I noticed a faint smudge of purple by her right eye. Remnants of last night. 'Lara. We need to talk to you.'

'I know. I said some awful things.' I started to feel sick. 'I just—'

'Shhhh. Just shhhhh. Let me talk. It's not—'

But I wasn't able to stop. They both listened. Joanne turned from the front seat, twisting her arm so she could pat me on the knee, which just made me feel worse. Ben hadn't said a word, instead just staring straight off into the distance, flicking his middle finger against his thumb.

'So that's it,' I said. 'Now it's been leaked, I'm guessing, damage control? Is that even possible? Or have I destroyed everything? Oh God.' I thought about what the public were saying about me. The awfulness of what they'd witnessed.

'I'm so sorry,' Joanne said. 'They've pulled your performance on *Charity Aid*. I don't know how they heard about it.'

'Oh my God,' I cried. I wasn't prepared for this.

'There's more.' Ben's voice was so quiet that I had to lean my head towards him.

'What?' I asked. I noticed that we were in an unfamiliar part of London.

'Wait. Where are we going? I thought we were going back to mine?'

'We're going down to the police station.' He looked at me again. 'Something bad happened. Apparently. After she took the video. The girl who you hurt last night. Something really bad happened. Joanne?'

'We'll get more details soon but I just want you to know that we're behind you. OK?' I thought back to what I'd done. What if she was dead? Or I'd broken her neck or something? I thought of the thump as her body landed. What if I'd, *what if, what if, what if*. All these thoughts hurtled through my mind and my hands went numb.

'Listen,' he said. 'They just want to talk to you. OK? Nothing else for the moment. Just to talk.'

'OK.' He took my arm and I sensed he wanted to say something, but instead a deep and painful silence fell between us.

'Well, what about my real dad?' Ava had broken the silence first. I could tell something had been on her mind by the way she kept circling her right knee with her finger. 'Was he good-looking too?' I told myself to wait a few seconds before I answered, thinking about my earlier pep talk. *Bonding time*, I reminded myself.

'Well, what do you look like?' I said. 'I doubt someone ugly could have made somebody as beautiful as you.' She was satisfied by my answer and opened her bottle of water, reaching over into the front seat to pass me some so I didn't have to lean over and open mine. I took it, heart swelling at her kindness. We sat in silence again as I drove down Laurel Canyon Boulevard, stopping at a red light.

'Ten o'clock. Think it's going to be too hot to hike in Laurel Canyon?' I asked her. She shook her head. 'Great. We'll go straight there then. We'll pick up a sandwich on the way back and then, hmmm, then what?' I craned my neck around to watch her.

'Ice cream?' she said, eyes wide.

'Yup.' I thought again about contacting Conor. I hadn't yet decided what to do. I was feeling agitated away from everyone. *Come on*, I kept telling myself over and over. This is your and Ava's time. Don't do it. Just keep your promise, but once the thought had entered my head, it became harder and harder to ignore, amplifying, making my body uncomfortable in the way I was sitting. I shuffled in my seat. 'Damnit,' I said.

'What? What's wrong, Mom?'

'Nothing. Just can't get comfortable.' I pulled the seatbelt off my neck just as I accelerated when the lights turned green. 'It's hot and I'm feeling kinda, well, something.'

'Here.' She tapped me on the shoulder. 'You must drink lots. Like you always tell me. Water is good for your skin and replenishes you. It'll make you feel better, Mom, I promise.' I laughed.

'Good girl,' I said. 'That's very caring of you.' I thought again of how thoughtful she was and, not for the first time, how I didn't deserve her. I swung the car out of the main boulevard. I pressed my foot down on the pedal. The sky was a rich blue, it was going to be a beautiful day.

'Look, a hawk,' I said. She followed my finger. I watched it hover above us. In that moment, I decided to quell any more thoughts of ringing Conor, or tipping off the paps.

'Isn't it stunning?' I said, and she nodded. Her eyelids looked like they were getting heavy at that point and I had a sudden thought she might drift off and that I could drive for a bit, alone with my thoughts. I broke all eye contact with her in my rear-view mirror.

I pressed my foot down and for the first time in months, I felt absolutely free.

August 27th 2018

0900hrs

For the press conference, I decided on a pair of white cotton trousers, a pale yellow T-shirt and the yellow espadrilles that I knew Ava loved. Anna, Conor, Joan and Detective Mcgraw all stayed downstairs whilst I got ready. I wore no make-up but I applied a thin layer of moisturiser to freshen up my skin, and some lip balm. I brushed my hair into a loose ponytail and chose a pair of tortoiseshell sunglasses, packed a small bag and I was ready to go.

'I'll go with Conor.' I said, but Detective Mcgraw shook his head.

'Oh no you don't. You come with me. Anna, you and Conor follow behind.'

I needed to speak to Conor and work out a plan of action but for some reason, he wasn't looking at me. Not even when I glared at him, willing him to face me.

'Conor,' I said eventually. 'Look at me.' He lifted his head slightly and I caught a slight frown. 'Look, I'm sorry. About Frankie Spearman.'

'It's OK. I just wish you'd said something. My job has been pretty full on since Ava went missing.' I wanted to tell him that he wasn't the one whose daughter had disappeared. 'England,' he said. 'You just need to fill me in about what happened. With another press conference coming up, I need to know.'

'Soon,' I said. I hoped he'd understand – that I'd tell him the rest of it when I got a chance, although it didn't seem as though Detective Mcgraw was going to let me out of his sight.

'Will I be able to see Matthew?' I asked.

'He won't be coming to the press conference.' Detective Mcgraw opened the door. I heard movement behind me, coming from the kitchen. I couldn't face the idea of Joan alone in *my* house. What if Ava came back? Who would be there to greet her? Joan. The person she wished was her mother.

If only I had told the truth about the pool annexe from the beginning. If I hadn't tried to keep that part out of it. And England. Why had it been necessary? Now I was being taken into the station after the press conference, it all seemed so silly. So pathetic given what had been going on. I remembered someone telling me that one's true colours come out in times of trauma and stress. I felt blanketed in shame.

'Come on,' said Detective Mcgraw, pushing me out the door. I blinked into the bright sunshine. It stung, even with my sunglasses on. I folded myself into the front of his car which was parked just outside the house.

'I'm coming with you two,' Anna said, opening the rear door before Detective Mcgraw could object. She got in and slammed the door. 'Just so you don't play any games with my client,' she said. I'd never felt so grateful to anyone. I watched Conor climb into his black Porsche and swing it round to face the exit. I looked down the driveway, right to the bottom of The Hidden Hills, where I could see crowds of people lined up waiting to see me. How peculiar, I thought, that they should be there, waiting to catch a glimpse of someone in the midst of their fear and grief. Of course, there were those that wanted to offer support. Perhaps light a candle for my daughter. And I was grateful. Then Detective Mcgraw's phone rang.

'Hello?' he answered. My throat tightened. 'Yup. Understood.' He carried on driving, forking left towards the back car park of the station.'Sorry, change of plan,' he said. I could still hear the crowds, shouting my name. '*Lara, Lara.*' I absorbed their chants. 'We're just going inside the station first, before we head back out to the press conference. Just need to have a word with a colleague, about security for the media,' he said, but his jaw had started clenching tight. We drove on in silence. Conor was right behind us. I turned in my seat to face Anna.

'It's OK, I'm here,' she said reassuringly.

When we pulled up at the back entrance of the station, three policemen ushered us quickly into the building. I felt a strange sense of calm come over me. Perhaps in part, this was due to the fact I'd left home. That the station had an official air to it, and I knew that we were being helped. Or perhaps the shock had started to wear off, and the adrenaline could no longer keep up with what was going on. But when we walked into the station, and headed to the reception, I heard Detective Mcgraw shouting.

'Television off,' he screamed. How weird, given we were only going through security. I started to feel more and more uneasy. The girl behind the counter cowered into herself and fumbled for the remote control. She aimed it at a small box in the corner of the room. I caught Anna looking at Detective Mcgraw then her mouth pulled into an o.

'What's going on?' Conor had followed us in and he started to open his arms towards me but he was pushed back by Detective Mcgraw. He pulled me into a side room that had empty coffee cups, doughnut wrappings and coloured sugar sprinkles all over the table.

'In here,' he said. 'Anna. You as well. Conor, you out.' I looked at his face and that was when I knew. When you look at someone's features and you know that within them is buried knowledge of the worst news you could ever imagine.

I heard the television turn back on. The drone of a reporter's voice. Something shifted. Everything stilled. Detective Mcgraw said nothing, because by that time, the sound had been turned right up. He looked like he wanted to kill someone right there and then but of course it was too late because we'd already heard the hurried voice echoing around the entire building.

'Dead body . . . Found . . . Gash to the head . . .' It was then that I started to gag, white spots appearing in my vision.

And still, the voice went on. '*Unconfirmed* . . . Ava King . . . Far from where she went missing . . .'

I felt a hand on my arm. I didn't know whose it was. All I could think was that I'd let her down. The last memories she'd had in this world. She'd never understood them. They'd have terrified her poor little brain. And she would have been wondering why we had not come. Me, or Joan.

Why we had not saved her.

London, December 2004

There was a cup of tea on a worn-down table. I reached out for it in the hope that it might be for me – I'd got used to people bringing things without me asking, but then I saw a smudge of pink lipstick on the rim. Someone had scratched their initials into the wood. I traced it with my fingers wondering what people would think if I etched my name next to it. *Lara King woz ere.*

'I'll wait outside,' Joanne said. 'I'm going to do some work on the more immediate problem we have. Your rep. It's front page and the news reports live are using it as their lead. We're going to have to work on a strategy for you for tomorrow. I think you're going to need to lie low. And then make a public apology on a family TV show. Like *BBC Breakfast.*'

It had only been a matter of months since I'd been interviewed on that show. And now I'd be grovelling, trying to win back the public vote so I could go back to doing what I loved. How could I have been so stupid.

'I've cancelled all your recordings this week too,' she told me. 'Look. I've seen enough of this in my lifetime to know it will blow over. But I need you to listen to me. I need you to do exactly what I say. Do you understand?'

'I do,' I told her. But I hadn't. I just wanted this all to be over. But Joanne had looked at me with such seriousness and intent, that all I could do was agree with her.

'Fine,' she said. 'Look, I'll leave you to it now.' She shut the door and I was left with two police officers and Ben sitting in the corner, slumped over his knees. Good way to spend a hang-over, I wanted to joke but all that came out was the tail end of a breath.

A slight woman, in her fifties or so, sat down with a piece of paper and a clipboard. 'I'm Detective Orla, and this here' – she held out her hand to a sandy-haired man with a square, lined face – 'is my colleague Detective Simmonds.' He nodded at me, giving me a small grin. 'It's OK,' I thought he was saying. But then I remembered all the shows I'd seen. Good cop, bad cop. I turned away from him.

'We wanted to talk to you,' Detective Orla said, 'about last night.' I looked over at Ben who was staring at his fingernails.

It's my fault. God it's my fault, he'd been saying all morning.

'Miss Carys Lockwood,' she went on, 'has filed a serious com-plaint of assault. Would you like to say anything about this?' She handed me a picture of a girl with peroxide-blonde hair and brown eyes. She looked different from last night, in the white glow of the picture. Her skin was clear and smooth, eyes bright. There was a black smudge under her chin.

'She's in hospital.' Detective Orla leaned, back waiting for my reaction. 'She suffered concussion as a result of a fall, after being pushed down a fire escape. And that's not all,' she told me.

'*What?*' it came out as a small laugh but my body flooded with fear. 'What do you mean it's not all?' I told myself that it was all OK. I tried to remember what Joanne had told me. That it would all blow over, but no one answered me and so I asked again, 'What do you mean it's not all?' I tried to sound casual but then I started to feel hysterical. 'Tell me. Please. Just tell me what else.'

Detective Orla passed me a picture. I didn't know what it was at first. All I had been able to make out were black and white dots, forming shadows and shapes, like one of those optical illusions. And then I realised. I looked closer and noticed the writing on the top of the polaroid – just underneath the white border. *Carys Lockwood. 12th September 2004.* That was a date exactly three months earlier. I couldn't breathe. I thought about the life inside her stomach. And then the white rim around her nostrils. I felt desperate, for both of us.

'She . . . she was OK,' I had told them. 'She was fine when I left.' I opened my mouth. I was going to tell them she was coked-up to the eyeballs, but then I realised it would look like I was shifting the blame. I couldn't say anything about the necklace either, and the fact that I thought she'd stolen it, because that would have given me a motive for pushing her down the stairs.

'Well.' Detective Orla rubbed her hands through the back of her hair. 'She's not OK now. She's in the hospital, being monitored and she's had a miscarriage.' I gasped, clutching at my neck. The necklace, I thought. All because of that necklace that I thought she'd stolen. 'Now, Miss King, I'm sure you're accustomed to getting whatever it is you want, whenever you want, but here, when you're with me, you'll be getting the same treatment as everyone else.'

'I . . .' I looked at Ben but he had his head in his hands. 'I'm sorry,' I said. 'Oh God.' And at that moment, I felt like I was watching everything though a thick pane of glass. I was no longer connected to 'me'. I had wanted Ben to say something.

Anything. That he had believed me. But he stayed silent and that's when I knew it was bad. *Really bad*. And that it would help if I apologised, at least for parts of what had happened. But I couldn't. For some horrendous, inexplicable reason, I just couldn't say the words.

Ryans-world.com

Entry: August 27th, 0915hrs

Author: Ryan

There's probably hundreds of us here already, waiting for Lara to make an appearance at the press conference at ten. I'd caught wind of it early. Raced down here in my beat-up car whizzing behind Casey, who was veering from left to right as she did her make-up behind the steering wheel. I thought that was the end of us but she seemed to be pretty used to driving with no hands.

We're all here now. The road has been blocked off and we're waiting for a glimpse of Lara. I'm lucky enough to be right up front. There's a makeshift table with some bottled water and microphones angled like wilting sunflowers. I keep thinking of Lara speaking into one of them, head bowed, begging for her daughter to come home. And then there's the huge screen placed up at the front which is meant to be showing televised clips of Ava but instead, the cameras are panning across the crowd, our faces projected onto the wall.

It's super quiet. Just some people shuffling around. The noise of cars in the background. And then everything went sombre and I swear to God the sky actually went dark. Like one of those eclipses when the world goes a funny color and you're not quite sure if this could be the end of everything. And that's when people stop moving altogether. It's like we're all suspended in mid-air, freeze-framed in our own show. I don't know why. I don't know what's happening. No one seems to know anything. Call it collective unconscious, if you will. If you happen to believe in all that stuff.

And that's when I look over at Casey. She's on her cell, doing this weird gulp thing in her throat. Like a frog on a lily-pad. Her eyes are all bulgy and she can't stop with the throat and she's doing this flicky thing with her line of vision. And I can see her, nodding, her mouth moving. 'Shit', she's saying. 'Shit. Oh God'.

And that's when I know. All of a sudden, the camera pans across the crowd again and everyone starts to wave. It stops on me and Casey. I wave, smile, but by then, I already know.

I look at myself on the screen, my limbs wooden. How I'd cleaned myself up in the past few days, to be on screen. How proud my mother would be if she could see me now. And Granma, if you happen to be watching. 'Tidy yourself up boy', you keep telling me. Well, look at me now. Nice haircut. Looking smart. Taken off all my jewellery. I know I fucked up at drama school but look at me now. And all the time I'm having these thoughts, I'm waving at the camera, waving, smiling.

But I know. I know this to be true. They've found a body. Unconfirmed. But I know it's her.

She's dead.

Twitter: @ryan_gosling_wannabe

LA TIMES ONLINE – BREAKING NEWS: BODY FOUND
BY MANNY BERKOWITZ
August 27th 2018
Posted: 0945hrs

It has been confirmed that a body has been found in Laurel Canyon today by Darren Anderson who was out walking his dog. We cannot confirm anything about the identity of the corpse but early reports indicate that the deceased is a child, most likely, Ava King.

The body was found a far distance from where the initial search had taken place – around six kilometers if initial reports are to be believed – which gives rise to questions about the case itself and what happened to the six-year-old daughter of global superstar Lara King.

Darren Anderson spoke to the press earlier about the moment he found the body.

'I can't say too much at the moment. But the whole area around here has been cordoned off where me and my dog Jasper take our daily walk so we took a different route into the canyon, quite far from where the search had been taking place. We climbed down the rocks. Jasper went down first, sniffing around as usual, until I noticed he was barking and becoming agitated. This sometimes happens when he comes across another animal but when I looked down to where he was, the air was black with flies. My first thought was that it must have been a dead animal. We get road kill around here all the time. But as I stepped closer, I smelled something that I knew wasn't animal. I can't tell you how I knew it was human, because it's not something I've smelled before. But with the heat, the God-awful heat – let's just say that I will never forget that smell until the day I die.'

Anderson is being treated for shock at the scene. The autopsy report will confirm the tragic events.

MORE TO FOLLOW.

I identified the body as that of my daughter, Ava Frances King. Detective Mcgraw bought me a polaroid photograph, and placed it face down on the table. I noticed the pattern in the grain of the wood.

'We have someone here,' he said. 'To help us through this process. She's outside.' But I shook my head. At this point, I didn't trust anyone.

'Fine. Please state your name and relationship to the deceased.'

'Lara King. I'm her mother.'

'I'm going to turn the photo over soon. Are you ready?'

'I'm ready.'

'Is this her?'

'That's her.'

'It looks like she died from an accidental fall. Initial reports suggest that she tripped and cracked her skull on a rock. The way she fell is in line with the gash on her head.'

I stayed in the police station room for over an hour after that, gasping for breath. I think at that point, someone entered the room. Spoke to me for an hour about help and bereavement, except to this minute I could not tell you what was said, or what she looked like. It was helpful, at the time, though. When she left,

Detective Mcgraw brought Anna back in, so he could question me for another two hours.

'We're still trying to shut down the conference,' he said. 'But the press are persistent. Now, what I want to know is why did you lie about being near the annexe on the twenty-third of August?'

'I didn't.'

'Why did you not tell us about Matthew's drug taking?'

'I didn't know.'

'Why was Ava's body found at a distance of six kilometres from where you reported her missing?'

'I don't know. She must have run off. Or it was the car I heard. Drove her six kilometres away. Dumped her. That's what happened. It must have been. She fought back. Got frightened. Someone offered her a lift home and tried something on with her. That's obviously what happened.'

'What? So she ran six kilometres in the space of about fifteen minutes between the time she went missing and you rang the police?'

'Maybe.'

'Or you are trying to tell me that a car picked her up, drove her six kilometres and dumped her where her body was found? Or were you in fact in a different place altogether when you rang us? That seems like the most plausible explanation, Ms King. Doesn't it?'

'Oh God, I don't know. I think I might have got into my car to look for her. I might have driven up the road. Thinking that I would find her a little way up the canyon. Maybe I was in a different place when I rang. I can't remember. I just can't remember, Detective. I was in shock.'

'You can't remember if you got into your car, switched on the ignition, and drove a distance of about six kilometres looking for your daughter when she went missing? You seemed to have missed out that extremely important detail all this time you've had during the investigation and you only think to tell us this *now*?'

'I forgot. I think I did . . . I can't remember . . .'

'You can't remember? That seems very strange, Ms King.'

'Please stop questioning my client now, Detective Mcgraw,' Anna instructed.

'I know this has something to do with the pool annexe, it's all linked together.' Detective Mcgraw slammed his hands on the wall. 'I know. I know. I know. Joan warned me over and over about you. That you didn't care about anything but your fame. That you were totally self-interested.'

'That's not true.'

Eventually I was released on bail with Matthew. But just as we were both about to leave the police station, Conor had started to ask more questions.

'Lara, you need to tell me everything. About England. I don't want to do this to you now. But there are rumours, people are saying you did something. Something that should have put you behind bars.'

So I told him in hushed whispers, whilst we had a moment alone.

'Why didn't you tell me all of this before?'

'Because I killed an unborn child. Please. Help me.'

'Of course I will. You just need to tell me the truth from now on.'

* * *

A woman who had worked with me for years as a lookalike, was called in to help form an elaborate decoy. The plan was that she would go out the front of the police station and drive past the press conference, so that I could leave via the back exit, and grieve in peace.

I passed smoothly through the crowds in an old battered Volkswagen wearing a brown-haired wig and sunglasses. I wished for a lookalike of my little girl too. I wished for her to stand right next to my decoy, so that for one minute I could step outside myself and pretend that this wasn't happening.

As our car pulled up in to my drive, Joan opened the door. She looked pale and washed out. I wanted to tell her to get out of my house. After the stunt she'd pulled with the fob and the things she'd said about me to Detective Mcgraw, I didn't want her near me. But the energy deserted me and I realised I needed her for the funeral. The memorial. I needed her to tell me things she knew about my daughter. Some of the things that she knew and I didn't.

'Oh God.' She held her hands up to her face. 'Oh God.'

'I know,' I told her. 'I will never be the same again.' I started to howl, wondering how I'd go on without her. I couldn't ever imagine resuming my normal life. It seemed unfathomable to me. I hated the thought of anyone even taking another breath without my daughter.

'Why was she found so far away?'

'I don't know.'

'They let you go?'

'Who?'

'The police.'

Not you as well.

'Of course they let me go. Nothing much to go on.'

I thought about what had really happened but I'd be damned if I was going to tell Joan. I thought about Detective Mcgraw. The way his eyes had roamed over me, searching for clues.

'I *know* you know something. I won't stop until I find out what,' he had said. 'We will be charging you with obstruction of justice. Lying about Ava's paternity. And God knows what else.'

'Don't worry,' Anna said. 'We'll get you off. Nothing to worry about.'

'She got lost,' I had told Detective Mcgraw.

'So you're changing your story *again*? You didn't drive for six kilometres after you realised she went missing?' He had shaken his fist at me.

'I don't know anything. I just want to go home.'

Lara King Official Website

Status: Published

August 31st 2018

1530hrs

My dear fans,

I'd like to say thank you, so much, for everything you've done for us. Firstly, your relentless help with the search for my daughter. Secondly, for giving us our privacy when we asked for it. As you know, Ava lived her life in the spotlight and she loved it but we need this time to ourselves, to grieve in peace. We are very grateful to you all for your understanding.

We've had a private ceremony which was beautiful and full of Ava's close family and friends. We played her favourite music and everyone planted a tree in her memory.

The thing that hurts me most is that I will never get to hold Ava's hand again. I will never get to see her grow up to be the most wonderful human I know she would have gone on to be. She will miss out on so much of life that I know she would have loved. Travel, love, laughter. All the things I know she would have excelled at, for her heart was capable of so much.

Thank you, from the absolute bottom of my heart for all the beautiful flowers, notes, poems and presents you have left for her.

The fact I know you are with me, following, supporting and loving me and Ava from a distance means so, so much. More than you could imagine and for that, I'm eternally grateful. It has been difficult since we buried her but I will try and take solace in the fact that she had a good life and that she would have wanted us all to follow her lead in the way she lived.

Please, come and celebrate her life, so tragically cut short. I invite you all to join me, Matthew, Joan and the ones closest to her, in a memorial service dedicated to celebrate Ava's life.

The celebration will be held at Elemeris Gardens, from 2 to 4 p.m. on September 6th.

Wear: Brightly coloured clothes

Bring: A balloon and a donation that will be split between the Missing Children's charity and Hope Sings, a charity that Ava raised money for at school that uses the creative arts to help under-privileged children.

Sing: I will be singing a rendition of 'Amazing Grace' and I would love it if you could all join in for a second rendition straight after. All of us singing for Ava. We'll be recording the song for both charities, and it will be uploaded on to iTunes at midnight September 7th 2018. Recording of the charity single will take place at 3 p.m.

There are six thousand spaces available for the memorial. Please REGISTER HERE for tickets, which will be allocated on a first come first served basis.

PRESS REQUESTS AND ENQUIRIES TO CONOR@ CONOR-PR.COM

England, December 2004

'There's an *opportunity*,' Joanne told me after I'd left the freezing cold London police station. She pressed an American Visa into my hand. 'Go. Take it. Audition as an English host for a TV show. Same format as the one you won. I've sold you well. They're willing to overlook your past because you're exactly what they want. Lovely English accent, very pretty, great singer,' she said, as though she was reading a shopping list. 'The all-round package. I've got a contact there. Conor. He's stellar at what he does. He'll look after you. He went out to LA over a decade ago and knows what it's like. He's going to put in a good word for you. OK?'

'Fine,' I told her. I sounded flat but a spark had ignited inside me.

'Good.' She patted my arm. 'I knew you'd make the right decision. Flight tomorrow. You're booked first class.'

I met Conor when I landed at LAX airport. I suppose it was him that planted the seeds in my brain.

'Joanne's told me a bit about you.' I took a breath, waiting for him to mention the past, but he carried on breezily. 'She told me that you have something. An *indefinable quality* is how she put it.' Phew, she obviously had kept everything quiet. I let out a breath. 'I trust Joanne and now I've met you, I can see what she means. What we need,' he said whilst ordering hundreds of dollars' worth of sushi after I'd signed the contract with him, 'is a total image overhaul. You're great the way you are but you know what's happening at the moment? The good, healthy revolution.' He waved his hands in the air like a magician mid-trick. 'Shed your old image because no one here knows who you are or gives a fuck about your past.' He smeared a large glob of wasabi on his salmon. 'And so that works in your favour.'

'Well, how do I stand out from the rest?' I asked.

'I don't know.' He shrugged. 'Let me think. Have a kid. Do the whole working mum thing. Hell, I don't know. No sex tapes or anything now. They're sleazy and people are bored of them. We need you to be a vision of beauty and cleanliness. I'm sure that will change soon but for the moment . . .'

He carried on talking but his words were like static in my brain because from that point onwards, I did know. I knew how I was going to right my wrong. I knew how I was going to win everyone back. I was going to go all out and totally disassociate myself from my past. I would become an earth mother. And in doing so, I hoped I'd offset the bad. Take a life. Give a life and all that. I thought of the girl, Carys, crumpled at the bottom of the stairs, the life inside her ebbing away. This way, I would make amends. I'd make everyone love me again. I thought back to how I'd tried to make things better in England. The things I'd said after I'd tried to apologise. When I knew then that the future hung on my next few sentences. That somehow, Ben and Joanne had been willing for me to protest my innocence, despite the fact they probably had an idea that I wasn't so squeaky clean. In part, I think they wanted so desperately to believe I had done nothing wrong. And so when I looked up at Ben, and saw the look of disappointment and fear in his face, I knew what I had to do.

'She tripped and fell,' I said. 'I wasn't even anywhere near her and Kaycee was too drunk to see.'

And then my lawyer. 'There were no security cameras,' she told them. 'She had taken footage of my client previously in the hope she'd sell it. I'm sure that goes to show what kind of a person she was.'

Me, going back to Ben's house from the police station.

'You were *so* drunk, Kaycee,' I mocked her as I walked through the door, moving around in an exaggerated fashion. 'I always get *everything* wrong when I'm that pissed. Random memories of things that didn't happen.' I knew that Kaycee had started to question herself, her recollection of the previous night's events and from then on, I was safe. Safe to start anew when Joanne had managed to get Carys Lockwood to sign a non-disclosure agreement following a payout on my behalf from the record company.

Lucky me. I thought about my new life. It was as easy as that, to start again. To wipe the slate clean.

And just like that, I was born again.

Guys, who has their tickets to the memorial? I got mine. As soon as I saw Lara had updated her website, I could feel my pulse whizzing all round my body. I kept refreshing my browser and then the fucking thing crashed and my hands were shaking so much that I could barely type. But I got there in the end. Like gold dust they are and I saw them already trading on eBay for thousands of dollars.

What kind of a sick fuck would do that!

Anyway, I hope you are all doing OK. Thank you, for bearing with me for the past couple days. It's been pretty brutal, I have to say. Like, there's been no media let-up on this whole story. No escape. Constant rolling news, speculation. And then there was that God-awful press conference which Lara never turned up to, and just about broke me and everyone else there.

I've been going over and over it all in my head. I've looked back at the events leading up to that day. Everything that the police told us, everything that we knew from different sources from that whole time.

The fact that Ava's body was found far away from the search. All of it. It's all fucking weird.

I've printed off all the info that came out about her disappearance. I've been staring at it all, driving myself crazy.

But you know, like I told you. She got me through a lot of dark times, Lara did. And Ava. And so if there was anything I could do to help, I want to be their man.

I know. I'm fucking nuts, right? But I'm obsessed. Obsessed with this story and I just want to know what's going on and what the hell happened to Ava King.

Don't you?

Twitter: @ryan_gosling_wannabe

August 31st 2018

1900hrs

I thought back to the chain of events that led me to this moment. Frankie Spearman. That sofa of his. The Hollywood hills beckoning me from afar.

In time, things had gone my way and I remembered when I laid eyes on the initial ultrasound. A cluster of cells. *Now the size of an avocado*, so the blogs had said.

'Do you want to know?' Suzanne, the sonographer, had moved the wand nearer my pelvis.

'Yes, yes, I do.' Despite wanting to forget my past, I needed to cement my future into something more real.

'A little more gel.' Suzanne had pushed her gold-framed glasses up the bridge of her nose. 'You sure you wanna know, sweetie pie? Looks healthy. Everything's beautiful. Heart, you see there? Strong heartbeat.'

'I do.' I had looked at the screen, the limbs curled up. 'I do want to know.'

'OK.' She pointed at the monitor. 'You see there? Look.' She turned the screen towards me. 'You're having a little girl.'

Months later they made the incision, cutting the dome of my belly as my veins had filled up with the meds.

'There you go!' The obstetrician handed me the tiny body. 'A perfect baby girl.' I leaned down, the metallic tang of her head filling the back of my nose and throat.

Part of my spirit, in human form.

I no longer had to face things alone. I leaned down to look at the small person in my arms.

'We're just sewing you up now,' the doctor said, but I hadn't responded. 'It's just you and me, Ava King,' I whispered in her ear. 'You and me against the world. I'll always look after you.'

She turned her head into my chest, and I felt the judder of her breath warm up my skin.

Flashes of her waxy, stiff skin in the photograph flooded my mind. The bloat of her body. The gash on her right temple where she'd fallen.

Detective Mcgraw had been to check on me countless times since the news about Ava's death had broken. Each time he'd asked me about the discrepancy between where I'd said I was and where they'd found her body. I had no answers.

'We'll get the autopsy soon enough,' he warned me. And I told him to stop. That I wanted and needed to remember my daughter as the perfect little girl she was. From the moment she'd been delivered from my body into the world, that's how I wanted to think of her.

Innocent and perfect. I needed to rid my mind of all the gruesome images I'd seen lately. I needed to feel cleansed of everything that had happened in the past week, before I could even begin to think about the fact that my daughter was gone. I needed to realise, somehow, that no matter how hard I cried, or wished, or screamed – no matter how much I beat the floor, and howled, and pleaded – that my little girl was never coming home.

Ryans-world.com

Entry: September 1st, 0400hrs

Author: Ryan

I feel like one of those detectives in a show, with a huge array
of cards and Post-its pinned to the wall, all decorated in different colored highlighter pens and criss-crossed with cotton tape.
So and so was here at this time, so and so said this and this and
this. It's no different really to untangling the source of a vicious
high-school rumor. And as anyone who knew me in our last
year at high school, I'm good at that.

Someone rang me. A source. A real source. Not the ones
from some of the tabloids where the sources are, y'know, made-
up people. 'A pal.' Or the celebs themselves. And I know I'm not
a real journalist or anything so the code of 'never revealing your
source' doesn't count but I'm sure you know me well enough
now to know that I wouldn't lie to you. That all the sources I've
been using so far have been impeccable. And this source is,
well, no different. It's, how do I put it, straight from the horse's
mouth.

So here we go. And by the way, I know I've got this before
the papers (eat your heart out Manny Berkowitz! Hi, by
the way, I know you read this!) but the autopsy report is as
follows: early days, so preliminary findings so far but an
overview:

- It's confirmed that Ava King died from a wound to the right temple with significant evidence showing that she was also highly dehydrated.
- She'd been dead for approximately twenty-two hours when she was found – which means that if she disappeared at around eleven thirty to eleven forty-five a.m. on August 27th she died very soon after. Perhaps she ran off, or got lost and slipped on a rock. She was too far from her supposed original location to have run that distance. Maybe she got in a random car that drove her to where she was found? Maybe Lara King was never where she said she was.
- Ava had an empty stomach, with findings that she had not eaten in the hours that led to her death and had drunk minimal water. Reports state that it is likely the deceased had not eaten since nearly twenty-four hours earlier.

I know that y'all might find this distressing. I've been sitting here for over an hour, wondering how to work with this.

I don't have much more to say, cos I'm kinda devastated right now. I'm just trying to work out how to handle this. Mentally, y'know.

So I'm going to try and work this out and take a break until the papers get wind of this. But until next time.

Here with the latest updates on missing Ava King, brought to you by Lara King's number one fan.

Twitter: @ryan_gosling_wannabe

'Someone's got hold of the autopsy report,' said Matthew. He'd come to find me in the kitchen as Joan and I were organising Ava's memorial service. 'A random guy on the web. It's gone crazy online apparently. I don't know how it got out. I've left a message with the station asking for someone to call me back to find out what's going on.'

'Show me,' I said to Matthew.

'No. Let's wait until Conor gets here.'

'Show me now,' I demanded. He handed over his mobile phone. I read the words in front me.

'Oh God. This must be crap,' I said, relieved. 'I mean firstly whoever wrote this has got it wrong. She ate at the announcement,' I told Joan and Matthew. 'I'm sure she did,' I said, although my voice wavered. At that point I wasn't sure of anything.

'She said she had eaten,' I repeated. 'Joan, when did you feed her?'

'I gave her lunch,' she said. 'Whilst you were having your hair and make-up done. We had a late lunch and then she said she was hungry again later and that she was going to ask you to go with her to get some food that had been prepared for the journalists.'

I thought back to the day of the announcement. Her small voice begging and pleading, asking me to go with her to the table of canapés. 'There's too many people,' she'd whispered. I thought back to her getting ready to sleep. *I'm hungry. I'm hungry*, she'd said. But I'd dismissed her because I thought she'd been time-wasting. *Oh God.*

'She said she had. I know it. I was going to take her for ice cream.' I thought back to my internal struggle at calling the paps. If only I'd called them. They would have known. The world would have known that I was thinking about my daughter. That I hadn't intentionally starved her. Letting the world know I'd made a mistake by being on my phone was one thing. Having forgotten to give her breakfast was another matter entirely.

'Didn't you check?' Joan asked.

'No. I trusted that she had eaten.' I felt the judgement leaking from her every pore.

'Well, Anthony. He normally cooks.' I went silent. 'Anyway, that day, I told her. I told her to wait for me. Whilst I got ready that morning. I asked her to go downstairs. I thought she'd . . .' I trailed off but Joan had left the room. Matthew turned to me.

'This isn't good, you know,' he said.

'Well, you've done things that aren't good either,' I snapped, instantly regretting the words the minute they came out my mouth. He shook his head at me and walked towards the door.

'Don't. Don't even go there. I know you lost your daughter but after everything I've done for you . . .'

'*Done for me?*' We could both hear Joan somewhere near the hallway. He put a finger to his lips.

'Enough,' he said. 'I suggest you call Conor to try and sort out your mess.'

I was left alone then. I didn't want to look at what was online. I refused to let myself, but the longer it was silent around me, the more intense the feeling and the louder the voice in my head became. *Just a quick look*, I told myself. Just to see if you are all blaming me. See what you are saying about me. It had to stop. My reliance on you. I knew it. But it was like an unbearable itch. And it wasn't like you turning on me was going to hinder the search for my girl any longer, which made it even worse. That I was relying on you for my own vanity's sake.

I waited until I was sure Matthew and Joan had gone. I could hear the creak of the floorboards upstairs. It would take Matthew a good forty seconds to get all the way back downstairs and so I got my laptop, which automatically logged in to all my social media.

People *were* beginning to turn on me. I could see that. People who had been so eager to offer their condolences. Mary Mae, who I'd had a public spat with years ago. *'Devastated to see news of Ava King's #autopsy. Starving child. Neglected kid.'* And then I scrolled down and saw a never-ending stream of it. People who had been so supportive of me before Ava had died. How quick they were to turn.

It was OK, I told myself. I would try and keep Ava's name and reputation clean for her sake. Her fans. They would still be onside, and so I logged on to a few Twitter accounts that I knew would be supportive, no matter what but even those had changed their tone.

@Eat_clean_healthy. As a recovering anorexic I find this awful. Lara King obviously making her daughter anorexic for the media #badparenting #autopsy #AvaKing

I scrolled down and down and the comments only got worse and worse. People saying they wanted to kill me. That I didn't deserve to be a mother. That the truth was now coming out.

@team_Kim_Cattrall Let's slay the bitch.

@team_SJP I'm with you. For once. Let's unite.

@Carly_violet Let's all unfollow Lara King. She doesn't deserve our love.

@Jamie_J Done.

The last two tweets had been retweeted forty thousand times already and I had lost nearly fifteen thousand followers. I noticed Conor or one of his team had been tweeting from my account, right up until seven a.m. Tweets about love, grief, loss, finding happiness. He must have scheduled the tweets to go out and forgotten to delete them whilst all this was going on.

People just kept on and on. People I hadn't thought of for months, if not years. I logged on to the news headlines to see video footage of Frankie sitting in his office. The sunlight gleamed through his window, reflecting on the silver, bronze and glass award statues around the room.

'So sad. I just wish things had been different. That I had had a chance to get to know her and look after her.' *Bastard.*

Everyone was disassociating themselves from me. A tightness started to creep around my head. The edges of a migraine. I went to find some Tylenol when the doorbell rang. I looked at the video intercom to see Conor, his face white, his eyes sunken and red.

'Matthew called me.' He walked straight past me to the living room, when I opened the door. 'Told me he thought you were losing it.'

'It looks like the same could be said for you,' I told him.

He sat down and rubbed his face.

'Shit. I don't know how to contain this.' I was glad of Conor. Glad that he was so invested in his job that he wasn't interested in making me feel bad. Glad for me too.

'But we need to. You realise that. Don't you? We need to sort this out before the memorial. And whatever happens after. With you, I mean. I don't want you to have to go into hiding for the rest of your life.' I had no idea he was even considering something so drastic. 'And even if your career ends now,' he went on, 'I have my own reputation to protect.' He stared at me; I was shocked. I knew Conor was cut-throat, but there was some naïve part of me that thought he might have cared about me and my career. Stupid, really. I should have known.

'So what do you suggest?' My mind pulled back to Ava. The autopsy. The gash to her head. Dehydration. I knew what happened to the body in a state of extreme dehydration after I'd done a piece to camera for a Syrian charity. Confusion, hallucination, delirium, kidney failure. I thought of her stumbling around, unable to work out where or who she was. Then I thought about the pathologist opening up her small body. And then I remembered the car journey to Laurel Canyon. Her handing me her opened bottle of water.

'You must drink lots. Like you always tell me. Water is good for your skin and replenishes you.' I had been meaning to give it back to her but I hadn't. I had drunk most of it and then set it aside, despite the fact that the second bottle of water had been right next to me. My heart felt shattered. I had to tell myself to stop, or the guilt would destroy me. I told myself she wouldn't have wanted that but the thoughts kept going, a cattle prod to the brain.

'My website?' I offered. 'Should I write another entry? Like about me being on my mobile? A public apology?'

'No. That won't cut it. It will have to be something more drastic. Something about Ava refusing to eat. This is going to have to be the big one. Trust me on this. The memorial is in what, five days? We cannot afford more people turning. And I'm trying to hold off this other woman selling her story. The one we discussed. The woman who keeps emailing from England.' He looked at me out the corner of his eye. 'She's been contacting the office again. Over and over. Desperate now. Saying she's not going to let up. That she wants to speak to you and if not, she's going to tell the press everything.'

'Fine, well, let me speak to her then.' I thought back to the nightclub. I remembered her face like yesterday, white and ghoulish under the lights. 'She's a coke-head anyway or she was back then,' I told him, furious that she thought she could still hold one over me, all these years later. And then I remembered the forums and the person who had commented on the England thread. I wondered if it had been her too. 'We can do a smear campaign,' I said. 'Get started on that. She was fucked when she was pregnant. What does that make her? What kind of a person?'

'A coke-head? Really?'

'Yes,' I told him. And as I was thinking back to the nightclub, he held up a photograph of a woman. 'Her last email, a few hours ago, had her name and number. I think that she's desperate for contact with you. I've looked her up. There's only one woman with that name on Facebook and Twitter. This her?' He waved the picture he'd printed off in front of my face.

She was about my age, with long brown hair and a smile that sparked something inside me, even all these years later. Her eyes glowed with a kindness that radiated out of the image into the room.

'Kaycee,' I whispered, at the same time that Conor said her name.

'Kaycee, something,' Conor said. 'Hang on.' He pulled out his phone and scrolled through his emails.

'Oh God,' I said. 'Kaycee. It's not Carys. She wouldn't. She wouldn't do this to me just after I lost my daughter?' I turned to Conor. 'It's Kaycee.' I thought of Ben. I thought of myself, young, filled with hope and foolishness, and I sat down and wept.

Grief makes you angry, right? That might explain the way I'm feeling right now.

Hands up who's seen the headlines?

In case any of you need a recap, here goes.

'*Lara is devastated to learn that the public have taken the autopsy report into their own hands. The truth of the matter is something very simple. Ava suffered from intense motion sickness and therefore before any long journeys, whether in the car or on a plane, she would refrain from eating.*'

Who calls bullshit? The press statement wasn't even delivered by her. It was her PR team, who contacted the *LA Times* to set the record straight before any more harm was done.

And I can tell you how I know.

It's right there. In her blog. I give you, ladies and gentlemen, Lara and Ava's entry about travel. I remembered it right away. As soon as I saw the statement about travel sickness. I remembered it because I was taking my cousin on a camping trip, so I read it with interest. For those of you that need a little recap, these are some of the things that Lara said:

Ava loves car journeys the most. Even really short ones. She will pack a blanket, a bag full of toys, a juice box and some snacks which she'll lay out next to her on the back seat. Top tip from the King household is to buy some great audiobooks. We've posted a selection of Ava's absolute faves, right here.

So either she's lying now, or she was lying in her blog. Either way, she's a liar, and that makes me mad.

And she should have the decency to tell us direct. She is too distraught to speak to us but then there were those automated tweets that kept coming and coming as news of the autopsy came out. I should imagine Ava was distraught as she wandered around, trying to find her mother.

I'm getting so angry thinking about it now. Mad as hell. First she was on her phone whilst Ava went missing. Now this. And the fact that Ava's body was found so far away from where Lara says they were. She wasn't the person I thought she was and now . . . now she can't even look us in the eye. Something just doesn't add up. We'd been there for her all this time and I know she's grieving. I know she's a mother who has lost her child but we're all grieving too.

'You didn't know her,' you might say. 'What the fuck have you got to be sad about?' But you see, we did. We did know Ava King. She represented something that many of us don't have.

And so did Lara.

Hope.

And love.

And now, it seems, there was neither and if that means taking matters into my own hands, then so be it.

Twitter: @ryan_gosling_wannabe

'Shall I contact Ben? He was my old manager in the UK,' I asked Conor. 'And he was engaged to Kaycee.' I thought about Ben. His hangdog expression whenever he was tired or hungry. My heart squeezed tight. The last person to have known the 'old' me.

'No,' Conor said. 'Leave it. There's enough going on.'

'Fine. I've got to do some organising for the memorial. I'll speak to you later. Thanks for sorting the autopsy stuff out. Stay here. Make yourself comfortable. I'll send some food in for you.' I shut down my laptop. I hadn't dared to look online since Conor had contacted the press and told me what he'd done. Whereas hours earlier, the pull had been strong enough for me to drop everything, now I couldn't bear to look. It was like I'd overdone it. I felt sick, mentally bloated with it all.

I went into the kitchen where I called a meeting with Joan and Matthew. Chef Anthony had come back for the first time since Ava had died, after everyone had been sent away during the investigation. His presence lent some normality to the situation. He'd laid out a colourful spread of sauerkraut, chia seeds, blackberries, bee pollen, porridge breads and smashed avocado, but in truth, I felt like something loaded with carbs.

'Can you whip me up a plate of pancakes?' I asked him.

'Of course.' He tied up his apron and went for the buckwheat flour. 'Matthew and Joan? You too?' They both nodded.

'Normal flour please, Chef.' He smiled and laid the ingredients out on the work surface.

'Right,' I said. 'Let's call Lily. She's expecting us in five.' I'd arranged a conference call with her about the schedule for the memorial. I saw Joan looking at me out the corner of her eye, her hand spread over the screen of her phone but I caught sight of the headline she'd been reading through her fingers.

Autopsy findings down to Ava's car sickness

She said nothing, just stared at the table, which I found unnerving after her earlier explosion about the swimming pool. I tried to make small talk with her but she would only discuss plans for the memorial. The more distant she got the more I felt the need to connect with her, in some sick and horrific way that I'd never experienced before.

'Look. Lily's done the timetable for the day,' I said. 'Now. Firstly, caterers.' We all went silent, thinking about the last event we'd organised. *The announcement.* We'd chosen to use the same caterers after a lot of discussion and I hoped that they would do a sterling job.

'Now's not the time to try someone new,' Lily had persuaded. 'I know Fantine. I know how she works. It's too late to be risking another company now.'

'Fine,' I said, thinking of the two employees with Bear Productions who hadn't passed the police security checks following the announcement. 'As long as she's sure all of her staff are vetted.

Any security breaches will mean I never use her again and that no one in Hollywood goes near her.'

'Of course,' Lily said without batting an eyelid. 'She's going to do canapés for the three hundred VIP guests you've listed, Lara.'

'Good,' I said. 'And drinks?'

'Well, Chanson have . . .' Lily went silent.

'Chanson have what?' I looked over at Conor.

'They've pulled sponsorship for the champagne,' she said. 'They thought it best in light of the . . .' I heard her hesitate down the phone and then she said briskly, 'in light of the autopsy findings. They thought alcohol wouldn't be appropriate and it didn't sit with their ethos.'

'Fine,' I sighed, pretending not to care. 'Anyone else lined up?'

'I'm looking into it now.'

'Anything else?' I wanted everything to be absolutely perfect, but I was also enraged with Chanson.

'That's it for the moment. The band is booked. And the production company are ready for your performance, Lara. You'll be introduced by the head of the missing persons charity. And then we'll do the charity single straight after.' I started to cry. Everyone was silent, waiting for me to finish. This seemed to happen more and more often, that I'd burst into tears, sometimes for hours on end. This bout only lasted ten or so minutes. I saw Joan and Anthony avoiding eye contact with me.

'Lily, we'll have to ring you back,' said Joan, leaning closer to the mouthpiece. Matthew came over and pulled me into a hug.

'I know,' he said. 'I know. I know. It's OK. I'm sorry.' He pushed back my hair and kissed me. 'Time will make this easier to manage. OK?'

'It won't. But thank you,' I inhaled and called Lily back.

'Sorry about that,' I told her. 'Right. Where were we? Security?'

Lily didn't miss a beat. 'We've got Arrows and I've drafted in another company that deal with the royals in the UK for a double-whammy. OK?'

'Good,' I said. 'Well done.' And I hung up.

'Finished?' Conor said, walking in and reaching over to the plate of pancakes. 'Can I?' But he'd already crammed one into his mouth before anyone could reply.

'It's got carbs in it,' I said, knowing Conor would normally run a mile. He looked like he was going to be sick but then shrugged.

'Fuck it,' he said. 'For today. Listen. I need you in the living room.' He ripped off another section of pancake. 'Now. Hurry up.' He started walking off. I followed him. What did he want? I stopped and straightened a large blow-up picture of Ava on the way. I rested my head on the glass and willed her back.

'Listen.' He ignored the fact that I was broken. 'I've had another phone call from Kaycee.'

'Oh God,' I laughed, relieved. Nothing compared to the autopsy. 'I've offered to pay her to keep quiet,' he went on, 'but she insists she doesn't want the money.'

'What does she want?' I asked. Although in my heart of hearts, I already knew the answer.

'She wants to set the record straight. That's what she kept on repeating in her last phone call.'

'She was wasted. Absolutely hammered,' I told him. 'The reason I was in the bathroom where I got recorded by that Carys girl in the first place was because I had been sent to check Kaycee hadn't choked on her own vomit. She's hardly a reliable witness.'

'Fine. So we can use that.'

'Of course.'

'Why does she think she can add anything new?' he asked.

I swallowed and took a breath.

'Lara?'

'She had sobered up a bit. When I pushed Carys. She'd puked everything up. I think she was pretty with it at that point. She was crying and knew exactly what happened.'

'Oh Jesus, this just keeps getting worse and worse.' Conor slumped back into his chair. 'I'm going to have to think about hiring another agency, Lara. To share the workload. We've been neglecting all our other clients. They're starting to complain that they're not getting enough from us. D'Angelo was talking about moving.' Idiot, I thought. Getting narked because he wasn't getting enough attention, like a spoilt child. As if the press had been interested in anything he had to say of late, anyway. 'Look I'm tired,' Conor continued, rubbing his eyes. 'I'm so fucking tired. I'm sorry.' He stood up. 'I'm so sorry about your daughter. But if you hadn't spent however long lying to me about the things that had happened—' He sat back down again. 'What else have you lied about?'

I looked over at the photograph of Ava. The one next to where he sat. 'I'm sorry. I feel responsible that we didn't find her sooner. I'm worried that Manny's onto this. You know when he went silent? All that shit? I'm worried somehow he's been looking into your past, has got wind of it all and done some digging.'

That got me thinking about Ben. How I could solve the problem and get Kaycee to shut up.

I'd replayed the last moments as I had left their house over and over in the past few days since Kaycee had been contacting us. I had a flash of Ben running after me when we'd left the police station. He had been shaking as he dug around in his pocket.

'Fuck,' he'd said, breathless. 'I'm still so hungover. Here. I nearly fucking forgot these. You gave them to me. Remember? Lavelli's wouldn't be very impressed if you'd manage to toss away millions of pounds worth of gems.' He'd given a small laugh. 'I don't think they're damaged at all. They went straight into my pocket.'

'What?' I stepped forward and held out my hands, the jewelled necklace sparkling in the bright sunlight. 'Oh God. Oh God, Carys. It was all for nothing,' I whispered to myself. 'God. I thought she . . .' I took them from him. 'She didn't. She never had them. You had them all along. How come you had them?' I slipped them into my bag.

'At some point during the night you grabbed them and threw them my way as if they were sweets. You were too drunk to be thinking straight, I guess' He shrugged, 'OK. I'd better' – he looked behind him – 'get back to Kaycee now. She's not in a good way today.'

That had been the last I'd ever seen or heard from him. And Kaycee, Hannah, Joanne, too.

As I replayed this in my mind, I had an idea which I knew if played right would solve everything, and we could all just move on.

'It's OK,' I told Conor. 'I know exactly what to do in this case. Let me speak to Kaycee. Let me deal with it this time. Then you can concentrate on everything else. Concentrate on your other clients. After the memorial,' I'd told him.

'You're sure?'

'Yes,' I said. 'I'm sure.' I started rehearsing everything I was going to say to Kaycee. 'I'll call her back. Can I have her number?' I asked him. He looked unsure.

'Trust me,' I said. 'I was right to come clean about being on my cell, wasn't I?' He nodded. 'So please. Just trust me on this one.'

Guys, thank you. Thank you for asking about me. I'm fine. I'm going to concentrate on the memorial. Getting it over and done with. Paying my respects to Ava. Me and a few other bloggers, Perez, and a few of the other big names (yes, I know! Since I started reporting on Ava's disappearance, I've been ranked up there with the big guns!) are getting together to work on an appeal for a charity working with neglected kids to drive home a point. You know, like the celebs who sit on the board for bullying charities as a big fuck you to their childhood taunters.

I doubt Lara would notice. Or care. (I doubt she's even reading this. She says she never, ever looks online at any of the stuff written about her, or any of the comments made about her.)

But that's our plan of attack. We're all feeling it, you see. Anger, of some sort. I thought it was just me. My affinity with Ava. But it seems not. And the way Matthew got all the shit. For doing what? Snorting some coke! WTAF!

Anyway – guys, I'm still working on my massive spider's web investigation. Tying up threads here and there. I might post a picture of my wall at some point. But, there are a few things that aren't quite right, but I haven't yet managed to pin them down yet. I'm working on it. I'll let you all know when

I've got something. I guess I'll see y'all at the memorial. I'll be bringing you all the latest straight from the event. Thank you, for everything. Love and peace out and RIP to Ava.

Twitter: @ryan_gosling_wannabe

September 3rd 2018

0700hrs

'Look,' Conor said. 'It's two p.m. now in London. It's the right time to call.' I found myself wavering after my initial burst of confidence thinking that everything would turn out all right after I'd spoken to Kaycee. The thought of speaking to her made me want to cry.

'Just do it,' Conor insisted. 'Enough now, Lara.' Before Ava died, I would have berated Conor for speaking to me like that, but now I knew I had no leg to stand on and that thought made me feel weak and powerless.

'Fine.' I took the phone. Conor had already dialled the number and so it was ringing when I held it to my ear. There was a part of me that wished she'd hang up but after a few seconds, the line clicked.

'Hello?' she said, and I was taken right back to that big smile of hers when I'd first met her. *'Ben's told me so much about you,'* she had linked her arm through mine. *'He's really proud of you. We all are.'* And now, her soft tone, like she was fearful of who she was about to speak to.

I let the silence hang for a few seconds.

'Hello?' she said again, this time more forcefully.

'Kaycee,' I managed.

'Lara?' she said. I wanted to ask how she knew it was me but I guessed that she'd see it was a US number and had been waiting

316

for this for a while. I knew I should say something. Anything. Ask her how she'd been but I was frightened of what she was going to bring up.

'I'm sorry,' she murmured. 'I'm so sorry about your daughter.' She spoke so softly that it made me feel guilty. Perhaps she'd just been trying to contact me all along to send me good wishes. But I knew in the silence that followed that, of course, she wasn't.

'How is Ben?' I asked. 'And your daughter. Isabella?' I felt a stab across my chest when I thought about them watching their daughter grow up.

'We're all fine,' she said shortly. 'But listen—'

Here we go, I thought, gripping the phone tightly.

'I've been wanting to talk to you.'

'You've been . . .' I wanted to use the word harass, but I knew I had to be careful with my choice of vocabulary. 'You've been calling. It was difficult when Ava disappeared. To think that you were against me.'

'I'm sorry,' she said. 'When Ava went missing, we thought she'd come back. We thought perhaps it was part of your show.'

'You thought *what*?' I heard a sharp intake of breath. 'That it was a publicity stunt?' I wondered if the press in the UK had intimated that. And then I thought about something that Conor had said to me when I first signed with him. That people's reactions to me were just a projection of themselves, so I had to ignore everyone and just think about myself and my career.

'Don't let anyone get to you.' He'd told me that whenever there had been any negative press. So far, I'd managed. But *this*. This hurt.

'Then I went on all these forums. Followed information about you. Found people who were your fans. I wanted to ask them but didn't have the guts.'

A thought suddenly occurred to me: England. It had been Kaycee who had been posting in that forum all along. The lightning avatar. Bolt Enterprises. Of course. How could I have forgotten. It was Ben's logo. There must have been a part of her that wanted me to make the connection. Stupid me, for not clocking earlier.

'Well, it was Ben,' she said. 'It brought it all back to him. After he found out what happened to that girl on the night out, I told him what you did.'

'You were drunk.' I looked over at Conor who was nodding his head. *Go on*, he mouthed.

'And so were you,' she replied. 'Listen. To be honest, we didn't know what you were capable of. After, well, it's been haunting us.'

'Then why didn't you say anything before?' I held the phone between my shoulder and ear, twisting my hands in frustration.

'It'd be my word against yours. You were everyone's dream. I was . . . I am a nobody. Ben told me not to. That it might harm his career. He's done so well, you know. Despite you. Despite everything. But in truth, I think he had a soft spot for you. I think he was trying to protect you from it all.' I could hear the resignation in her voice. She didn't sound angry, or bitter, or jealous. She sounded kind. Compassionate. 'We were all at the beginning.'

'So why now? What's going on? Do you need money?' I saw Conor lower his hands. He grabbed a pen and wrote something on a piece of paper next to me. *Keep calm*, he'd scrawled.

'I don't want money,' she said. 'We're fine for money. I just wanted to scare you into thinking I'd go to the papers. I wanted acknowledgement for what you'd done. I've been carrying around what I witnessed for all these years.' Her voice started to crack. 'Someone lost their baby because of what *you* did and I knew. I knew and I didn't come forward. What does that make me?' She started to cry. 'I want you to say sorry. I want you to make amends. Say sorry to that poor girl, Carys. I have her in my mind every single time I look at my daughter. You robbed her of that. And now you know what that feels like. I'm so sorry, again. Ava was beautiful. She looked so like you. But now you know. You need to do something. It's making me ill, Lara. All of this has just brought those memories up again and it's getting worse. For me and Ben. I have to think of us. My priority is us, not you. All this time it's been about you. Did you know that? Everything between us has been tarred by your actions. We need to come first now. I need to take charge of that.'

I knew I had to say something to stop her in her tracks.

'The diamonds,' I interrupted. 'It was the diamonds.'

'What diamonds?' she said with a weird laugh.

'I did it for Ben.' I winced at the lie but I wanted it all over. With the public turning so viciously, I had to bury this once and for all.

'But you have to promise,' I said. 'You have to promise not to say anything. If you do, I'll deny it all. If you say something to him, he'll think everything is his fault. It would ruin him. As the person who knows him best in the world, I'm sure you already know that.' I thought about what would happen if she told Ben what I was about to tell her. How confused he'd look, pulling his cap over his eyes.

'That's bull,' he'd say, 'that didn't happen at all. I gave you back the diamond necklace the day after we left the police station,' but before I could think about that any further, I carried on.

'So you see, I want your word, before I tell you what happened. That this goes no further. Just tell Ben you want to put this whole thing to bed. Don't ask him leading questions. Don't make him think there's anything to be suspicious about. All right?'

'I promise,' she said. I knew she hadn't thought about it properly. That she never normally would keep a secret from Ben. I also knew that she'd be too scared to break her promise in case of the consequences.

'She saw Ben with my diamond necklace,' I said. 'Carys. She saw him. She filmed him putting them in his pocket. She said that he had stolen them and she was going straight to the police. I got angry with her. I reacted badly but I was trying to protect Ben,' I heard another intake of breath. 'After all he'd done for me.'

'Really?' she said. 'Really? She was going to do that to Ben?'

'Yes,' I told her. 'She said it would make her rich and famous. More so than me spouting some drunken crap. To think that my manager would be swiping expensive jewellery from his clients. She said she would tell everyone that he had set up a ploy to swipe them and then blame someone in the club. That she had overheard him talking to me about it. So she was going to frame me too.'

'Oh God,' she said. 'But Ben would *never* do that. He's not that kind of person. We all know that. He's such a trustworthy man.' I could hear her getting more and more worked up. 'He wouldn't hurt anyone.'

'I know that, you know that. But when it comes to the public . . .' I stayed quiet. 'I should know. Look, it was a moment of madness. It was a flare of anger at someone wanting to hurt me and wanting to hurt the ones that I care about the most.' I let her digest my use of the present tense but the truth was that if I thought about it, there *was* a part of me that still harboured something for Ben. Nostalgia, maybe. Nostalgia for a time when I could still be myself.

'She was mad,' I went on. 'It was a mistake. I pushed her gently. She must have tripped. You saw how drunk she was, how unstable on her feet. You watched the whole thing. I didn't push hard. And don't you think I regret that every single day of my life? To think that I deprived this woman of her pregnancy?'

I doubted she would have the confidence to tell me she remembered the whole episode well enough. After all, it had been well over a decade ago.

'I wish I'd known,' she said. 'I wish I'd known it was a misguided act of loyalty.' I looked over at Conor and breathed a sigh of relief. 'I'm sorry,' she continued. 'I'm sorry I ever doubted you.'

The more I look back, the more I see it. The staging of each shot ever so carefully styled. The amount of work it must have taken. How it wasn't real. I'm beginning to realise. That shot I showed y'all yesterday on my Insta? The one of all the work I've put into looking at this case? Yeah, that one. It took me hours, and I mean *hours* to style. Firstly to pixelate all the info, making it look pretty. Thinking about what to write. But then again, I'm flying solo. But not for long! I've been picked up by an agency who focus on 'movers and shakers' in the online world. How fucking awesome is that? And now I realise what hard work goes into it being perfect.

But you know what? I realise now, the tide is turning. All this Goop-style stuff online? It's being overtaken by the real parenting stuff. You know. The guys that say, 'I look shit this morning. Here's a picture of me with armpit hair and baby puke all over me and big motherfucking black rings around my eyes.' Because we all know that's what it's like really, don't we? I mean, I'm not a parent but I do like to think that once upon a time, my mother, despite her running off on me, did care.

More and more of you are being honest about what it's really like. And so we have to ignore the made-up shit. We have to ignore the trolls and the haters and unite to change things.

Anyway, what I wanted to tell you all in this post is that after trawling through everything (my eyes are starting to feel like they're bleeding) I found something you guys might be a little interested in.

Lara King's OFFICIAL website.

The one where she and Ava used to post the most gorgeous pictures? So beautiful. I was looking through all the old posts yesterday. My heart hurt to see her, that little girl looking so perfectly into the camera. She did look happy, no matter what Lara was like as a mom.

But then I noticed something in the more recent posts. The posts that have been uploaded since Ava died.

There are two. One when she apologised for being on her cell. The other is from the memorial. I didn't see it at first.

But then I looked closer, searching for clues, here, there everywhere. And there it was. Right at the bottom of the post in tiny, tiny letters.

Posted by user CoN.

Who the fuck? was that I thought. I hovered my mouse over the username. And CLICK!

Author of this blog post, Conor O'Neill.

And I thought, holy fucking shit. She didn't write any of that shit. The stuff about her memorial. Her darling daughter. It was all bollocks. Her PR wrote it. Now I know if I got in touch, asked them for a quote they'd say: *Lara King was too distraught to write to her fans.* I get it. If I lost my daughter I would be too. But to lie about writing about your dead child?

If you ask me, which thousands, THOUSANDS of you have . . . this is some seriously, seriously fucked-up shit.

I'm trying to ignore it because the memorial is tomorrow and I think it's only right that we pay our respects to Ava but I feel like I did when Dallas Masters pulled down my briefs in front of the whole class and everyone laughed. Betrayed. Cheated. Hurt.

Silly. I know. It's not real. None of it's real but y'know. At one time, I could pretend it was.

Twitter: @ryan_gosling_wannabe

'It's OK,' I reassured Kaycee. 'But please. Remember you have to keep this from Ben.'

'I will,' she cried. 'I could never tell him something like that. It would break him that someone was planning to do something so bad. But don't you want him to know? About you, I mean? Don't you want him to know that you aren't bad? That you were doing a bad thing for reasons that weren't wholly bad? I could explain to him in part.' I thought about what she was saying for a minute but I realised Ben's feelings towards me were secondary to putting this whole thing to rest.

'No,' I said. And then I couldn't help myself. 'You could tell him that you spoke to me. That you know I'm not a bad person.' I felt better just saying the words out loud. I felt some semblance of my old self flooding back, layering itself over my endless longing for my daughter.

'I will,' she said. 'Thank you. For what you did for Ben. Thank you so much.'

'I know it's short notice but would you like to come? To the memorial?' I regretted the words as soon as they left my mouth.

'No,' she answered after a short hesitation. 'I think let's let time heal. I'll watch it on the telly. Thank you, though. For explaining. Ben – he'll . . . I think it'll change things. He's been a mess since it happened. Since Ava, I mean. All those memories flooding back.' At last, something I could identify with.

'I had it too,' I told her. 'The minute Ava disappeared. All of my past coming back, pushing its way in. I had exactly the same feelings.' I shut my eyes, swallowing back the guilt at what I'd done and the way I'd manipulated the situation with Ben and Kaycee, but I needed to think about Ava now. About her memory. Raising as much money as we could. Me keeping a clean profile.

'Thank you for ringing and explaining,' she said. 'That's all I wanted, I guess. Just to hear that from you. I'm sorry if you felt I'd been, well . . .' She sniffed. 'Pushy or anything, especially when you're grieving. Despite knowing what you were going through, I couldn't sit there and watch Ben suffer in the way that he was.'

'Tell him I'm sorry, will you? That I still think of him. Even now.'

'I will. He'll be so happy. It'll change everything.'

'I know. Good luck, Kaycee.'

'Good luck to you too, Lara. You are an amazing person.' Guilt slashed its way through me but then I remembered about my little girl.

'Thank you,' I said. I hung up and turned to Conor. 'Are we done? Can I concentrate now on my little girl's memorial?'

'Yes.' He gave me a genuine smile for the first time in ages. 'Good work, Lara. Good work. We can concentrate on the memorial now. Our job here is done.'

I'm on a roll now. I can tell you that with bleeding eyeballs and a wired brain, I think I've found something to do with the disappearance of Ava King. I've been staring at that fucking board all night, my brain whirring, going crazy and then I looked. I looked real close at one of the photographs I had tacked up and a thought entered my brain. I acted on it – just a preliminary look. And it struck me that I think something isn't right with the whole case. *There were lots of things not right about that case*, you're probably thinking, especially after it all started leaking out, like poisoned slurry. But hell . . . this might just blow everything out the water.

But now I need one of you to help. Can any of you step in? A computer whizz who can do something pretty simple, I reckon. And a bit of boring stuff too. Someone who can do something for me in the next twenty-four hours. Before the memorial, basically. I can help. But I'm also working on backing all this up, so it'd be a collaborative effort.

I can't pay you yet. But, I promise that if anything comes of it, your name will be up there and I'll owe you when I can. I promise.

Think of it as, y'know, doing a good deed and I'll use you to upgrade my own website when I sign on the dotted line with the agency (which I'm gonna do).

PLEASE HELP!

And please, send me a DM on Twitter. Do not comment here, as I'm switching this off for a while to focus.

Twitter: @ryan_gosling_wannabe

The sunlight found me as I opened the front door. I stood with my face tilted upwards, breathing in the sweet smell of the garden. I hadn't realised how stale the air in the house had become. Ava should have been running around the pool today. I thought of the earth, now, being fed by her lifeless body.

'Come on,' said Matthew. 'I've got you.' I took his hand and we made our way down to the bottom of The Hidden Hills, past the houses. Something about them made me feel a little uneasy. Their perfection against the never-ending sky. The huge windows, reflecting the sunlight like weird, looming robots on the horizon.

I thought about each step I took. I hadn't worn heels for a long time. I kept my head very still, so as not to ruin my hair, or the make-up that Tavie had worked on tirelessly since the early hours of the morning. I had refused my usual full team, wanting only to be around a couple of select people. Joan and I had been working so hard towards the memorial and I needed time alone. 'I'll be there with you all day and I'll touch up whenever you need,' Tavie said, holding a mirror up to my face. I had barely had anything on my skin for nearly three weeks. The primers, creams and foundations had all felt like paste and I wondered how I'd had this every single day.

I looked different. The set of my features had become harder somehow. Although I realised when I had slipped on my navy Cavalli dress, that I had lost weight in the past three weeks, so that my skin stretched over my cheekbones. I'd spent hours trawling through my wardrobe with my stylist, to find the perfect outfit. She'd marked a few things out that she thought appropriate. Clothes from designers that didn't have any affiliations with anyone or anything politically corrupt, clothes that wouldn't show too much. Because I knew that everything I did today would be closely scrutinised. Even my earrings.

'I've got you these.' She handed me some beautiful ethically sourced yellow diamonds. 'Here. Perfect. You've got everything exactly right. I don't think there's anything about your appearance that the press can jump on.'

'Thank you,' I said. I hadn't wanted anything to detract my thoughts from my little girl during the memorial.

'You look beautiful,' Matthew said, as we had walked to the bottom of The Hidden Hills. When we reached the entrance, I stopped to look at the fresh flowers that had been left by the gates. I'd seen the crowds of people last night from the top window of the house.

They'd left huge bouquets of roses and lilies and, of course, the wild hand-picked ones. Matthew lifted his arm in the air and out of nowhere, a large, black limousine drew up. As we got in, our security detail stepped back, allowing the paps to move forward and press their lenses right up to the tinted glass.

It was a peaceful day on the roads. The traffic seemed to have slowed right down and a smog settled over the city. Ashes to ashes, dust to dust. I thought again about her body in the ground. Decaying. The bones of her skull creeping out from beneath that soft skin of hers. I wanted to throw up but somehow managed to hold it together. We made our way to the temporary stadium, driving down the paved road to the back of the structure.

The crowds were quiet at first. There had been no movement but then I heard the rush of feet, hands holding phones directed at me. I kept my head still and gripped Matthew's hand. I briefly lifted an arm and then froze.

'Kate Middleton,' said Matthew. 'Behave like that. If you do anything else, you'll look too eager, or too sombre, it won't work.' I kept these words in my mind but then I thought, *screw it*. Why don't I just do what I want to do? It was Ava's day after all. I felt stifled after having been in the house for so long. For the past three weeks I'd been able to behave exactly as I'd wanted without fear of press intrusion. Everyone had backed off since the funeral and it had taken me a while to get used to the feeling of not being watched.

'Driver,' I leaned forward. 'Could you open the window?' I felt the coolness touch my face. 'Not too fast,' I told him. And then I leaned my head slightly into the fresh air, and I waved.

'Thank you,' I mouthed to the crowds, and the screams got louder and louder and louder. The car drove right up to the back entrance of a large marquee that would act as a green room and preparation area for the event. The whole structure was huge, like a soccer stadium. I felt nervous at the thought of standing on the stage and singing – I hadn't done that since England – but as we got closer, I heard the band warming up.

The brass instruments tuning for the first note of 'Amazing Grace'. And then Ed Sheeran's 'Supermarket Flowers' cranked up and I heard the crowd singing along.

Matthew and I walked through security and into the tent as fast as we could. Everyone went quiet when they saw us. Lily was ticking off names, wearing a headset. Huge bunches of flowers had been placed around the room. A carpet had been laid across the floor so that my heels wouldn't get stuck. Lily and the production team had thought of absolutely everything.

'Joan?' I said. 'You get here OK?'

'Yes,' she said. 'It's all going to plan. Detective Mcgraw' – she nodded her head over to the corner of the tent – 'is over there. Talking to Conor. Just in case you didn't know he was coming.'

'I did,' I told her. 'I invited him.'

I walked over to where he was standing. 'Detective.'

'Big event.' He looked around. There was something accusatory in his voice. He was perched on a white trestle table, his hands resting on outstretched legs.

'Yes, she deserved nothing less,' I snapped. 'Now I hope you're comfortable. Do let Lily know if you need anything.'

'We've decided to bring in some extra security. Conor and I.'

'Look. I tried to' – Conor shot an unpleasant look at Detective Mcgraw – 'protect you from anything stressful but we've had a few alerts to something online. It's nothing. But we've just got to be careful. Eager fans. You know that kind of thing.' Detective Mcgraw stood up and opened his mouth but Conor walked over and rested his hand on my back. 'Thank you, Detective.' He pushed me into the corner of the marquee and whispered.

'Look,' he said. 'It's nothing at all. Don't freak out. Just concentrate on Ava today. OK? I've got everything in hand. I'm not sure what that idiot Mcgraw had in mind freaking you out like that.'

'What's online?' I felt the pull of finding out what everyone had been saying about me.

'Nothing to worry about.' His upper jaw twitched. 'Nothing. OK? Just, there was an unspecific threat, that's all. That people think you may . . .'

'I may what?' I felt all hot. 'Go on.'

'You may have been covering for Matthew again. So nothing you don't know already.'

'Oh, so nothing frightening?' I rubbed at my earlobes. The gems felt heavy.

'Of course not. Some silly teenager who's a bit over-zealous. Trying to cause trouble and get attention by writing some stupid blog. I think he's just trying to make a name for himself. I asked Detective Mcgraw to station some of his team around. Undercover, of course. We don't want people thinking we're using up police resources either.'

'Fine,' I told him. 'Run me through things again?' He looked at his clipboard.

'Bands. Speech from the head of the missing person's charity,' he glanced down, 'three p.m. for your song and first appearance.'

'OK,' I said. 'I want silence around me in the half an hour leading up to it.'

'Well, you can sit and watch the show. They're setting up projectors of the crowd at the back of the tent, look.' I followed his finger to see a huge white screen being put up. Chairs surrounded the stage with all the VIPs. I saw all the big names there already, everyone beautifully made-up, the paps aiming their lenses right at them.

And then a large metal ring lined with security guards, which separated the crowd from the VIPs. I noticed three white-shirted men, whom I knew must have been undercover cops, their eyes darting across the crowd.

'Good,' I said. 'I'm going to get my make-up fixed. Then I want everyone to sit quietly and watch from here. Just before my performance . . .' I went quiet, thinking about the way I used to sing in front of the crowds. 'I want everyone closest to me – that's you, Lily, Joan, Conor and Fantine, she's worked so hard on this' – I looked over where the head of the events team was standing dressed all in black with her hair in a short, perfectly curled bob, poised with her headset on – 'next to me. Before I perform. I need you just to keep me calm. Then we'll all hold hands in a circle, take a few breaths and I'll go out onto the stage. OK?'

'Fine,' he said. 'Whatever you need. I reckon there'll be over thirty million watching today.'

An hour and a half before the performance Matthew came to find me.

'Let's sit together for this, shall we? Watch the last couple of performances?' He leaned his head against mine. 'I'm here. OK? You're doing great. I believe in you. Look. Everything that has happened. Let's move on. We're a great team.' He squeezed my hand. I looked up to see Detective Mcgraw staring at us. I felt soiled that he'd intruded on our intimate moment. I leaned over to kiss Matthew.

'Yes,' I told him. 'We are. We're going to do this together. Ready?' We both sat down in the of row chairs that had been placed in front of the projector screen.

The camera panned in and out of the crowds with Roy Baggot, the commentator, talking over the footage.

'And look there's the lead singer from "The Kills" in the front row,' he said. 'And now back to the crowds, look at the expression on their faces. Distraught, they'll never get over this, but how amazing to see everyone united in their grief.'

I was pleased that all my celebrity friends had come to support me, especially after the bad press with the autopsy report. And then there was the crowd. A new band that Joan had picked out were playing.

'She heard them,' Joan had told me, 'Ava. They were the support act to that band she loved.' She'd swallowed. '"Little Mix."'

'OK. Book them, when you remember who they are,' I'd told her. 'Speak to Lily. Ask them to perform her favourite song.'

'And this is for Ava,' called the lead singer. 'We loved you so much, we watched you from the beginning and so this song is dedicated to your memory. Please donate.' Her eyes glittered as she scanned the view in front of her.

I saw it then. The look as she absorbed the crowd. It reminded me so much of myself when I had been young.

'Look,' said Matthew. 'They're crying so much. The fans. Amazing. All for Ava,' he said. I looked over at Joan who was biting her lip. My stomach tightened. Not long before I was on stage. And then the camera focused in on someone in the crowds. There was something about his eyes that I recognised.

Then I remembered. He'd been in one of the pictures that Detective Mcgraw showed me from the events company.

I think he'd been one of the employees who had worked at the announcement and whose security check hadn't been cleared. I remembered him because of his ponytail in the photograph. How I'd hoped that it had been hidden under a hairnet as he served my guests. And then I had a flash of him acting strangely. As though he might have been about to ask me for my autograph but he was too embarrassed. Assuming he was the kind who'd had posters of me all over his wall. As quick as I saw him, he vanished. I had a momentary gut-wrench but then I remembered Detective Mcgraw telling me he'd 'checked out', and that there was nothing to worry about. I exhaled, slowly.

'And next,' said the compere, 'the moment you've all been waiting for. We'll have five minutes until the amazing, the incomparable, beautiful, stunning Lara King.' The crowd roared. 'But before that,' he said, 'we're going to have a little practice of "Amazing Grace". As you know, it's being launched as a charity single and I know we're going to sing our hearts out to raise as much money as we can. Is everyone in?' I watched the compère raise his microphone in the air.

'We're in,' came the reply.

I inhaled and stood up.

'Good. Then we're going to have an introduction from the head of the missing person's charity, Felicity Traynor.'

'Joan, Conor, Lily. Come here,' I called. They came and surrounded me. 'Do you think there's going to be any surprises on stage today?' I joked to try and lighten everyone's mood. Everyone laughed.

'Bloody hope not,' said Conor.

'Right. Everyone get in a circle and hold hands. Let's just take a moment. Let's do this for Ava. Wherever you are, darling girl, this one's for you.'

'For Ava,' they said, lifting their hands up and down over mine. I heard the crowds chanting her name. The opening chord of 'Amazing Grace'. Their voices, carrying through the air.

'Five-minute warning,' Conor shouted.

'I'm ready.' I turned to him. 'We've got this. Right?'

'Right,' he said but he sounded pretty unsure of himself. He kept looking over at the crowd and then at Detective Mcgraw, who was at the side of the tent, speaking to a small, compact-looking lady with an earpiece and a dark green uniform.

'Conor?' I asked again. 'Answer me.' I started to feel frantic and I didn't know why.

'Look, it's all right,' he said again except he wasn't looking at me at all. I could only watch as his eyes flickered all over the place, knowing that with thirty million people plus watching me, fixated on this moment, there was nothing I could do anyway.

Thank you for stepping in. All of you. Thank you. After my last post, I was absolutely inundated with offers of help. A couple of you worked through the night to help me out and eventually we got all the information we needed.

I sat on it this morning, and here I am now, singing 'Amazing Grace'. It's beautiful. For those of you not here, let me tell you, it's sending shivers up and down my spine, watching the crowd singing in unison. One of those moments that last a lifetime. It's going to be a beautiful single. The weather too, it's perfect and everyone's being respectful of each other's space. A perfect, peaceful day, just as Ava deserved. She went all out, Lara, that's one thing I can report. We queued for ages this morning and it all went seamlessly. Security was great. Everyone's bags were checked and the marshals obviously knew what they were doing. The bands that played were awesome.

We've all been holding our phones up to get pics of all the VIPs. Here are a couple so far. If anyone has any more that you don't see in the mainstream press ping them here. I'll give you all a shoutout. Here's a selfie of me with my BAE. Anyway, I've been thinking about what to do with all the information I've got.

Word has it that the detective in charge of the case, Mcgraw, is still looking into Matthew, Lara ... some sort of row that prompted Ava to disappear. And now that I've found what I found, it's all fitting together like some sort of gruesome puzzle.

And so I've decided, my dear friends, what to do with the info.

You might be asking, why don't I just go straight to the cops if I've got something worth saying? They could sort it out? Well, I think this deserves a little bit of the spectacular. Don't you? And given she wanted us all to watch her when times were good, all the ins and outs of her life, it's only fitting that you watch this too.

So – I'm going to leave it up to **YOU**, dear friends and readers.

If you say yes I'll do it. I'll unveil the spectacular in about five minutes time. You've got THREE MINUTES.

I've created a poll **here**.

GO.

TRUTH – YES 97%

TRUTH – NO 3%

Peace out.

Twitter: @ryan_gosling_wannabe

September 6th 2018

1500hrs

'Five, four, three . . .' Lily was behind me doing the countdown. I felt the heat coming off her, her breath in short, sharp bursts. She moved in front of me now. 'Two, one.' She shut her eyes, and pushed me forwards. 'Go.'

The curtain parted. Silence. I felt a blast of energy coming off the crowd in waves. And then the music started. I felt the lights right on me. Centre stage. The lights spotting the crowd as you recorded me.

My feet soaked up the vibrations from the floor and that was the moment that I opened my mouth and started to sing. I heard the first note, clear and loud. My body felt grounded and then I heard a wall of noise. Everyone was singing along with me.

I hit the last note, and I watched the flames in the air, everyone holding their lighters up. I held the microphone tight and I lifted up an arm.

I sang higher and higher, louder and louder. The notes floated around the space. Everyone was silent and then someone started walking towards me onto the stage. He looked cool and collected, as though he was in on the act. He waved at the crowd, then brought his hands up over his head, clapping. He was wearing a hooded top, even in the roaring heat, so I couldn't see his face but then I saw them. His eyes. Flinty, green. He had a goatee. Not a proper one. But gentle wisps of hair floating from his face and as he waved, everyone kept waving back.

'Come on,' he said. I saw security stepping back and some of them started to clap. Jesus, I thought. They had been fooled too, and then he pulled down his hood. Instantly, I recognised him. The guy in the photograph. The long-haired dude from the catering company, who'd stammered around me, except he'd cut off all his hair. In that split second, I remembered.

'He's a wannabe actor,' Detective Mcgraw had said. 'Gave a fake name.' *But he checked out*, he'd said. I wish I had asked how.

He came and stood right next to me. I thought at first he might draw a gun and shoot me, but he was standing, staring and smiling, lifting his hands up to the crowd, totally different to how he'd been the day of the announcement. I looked down. He was wearing a T-shirt under the hoodie, and shorts. Absolutely nothing to suggest he was armed, although you never could tell these days.

I looked around for Conor and Detective Mcgraw, hoping they would realise he wasn't meant to be anywhere near me. I could see them both in the wings. Conor was showing Detective Mcgraw something on his phone. Both of them totally engrossed.

'Hi,' he said, right into my microphone. I thought about pulling away, turning around. Screaming. Telling security he wasn't meant to be here but I was rooted to the spot.

Something told me not to move. That it would be better if I let him talk. I looked over again at Conor. *Please*, I pleaded. *Please, just look up*, but they were still totally fixated on the screen. How *dare* they. I thought of what Conor would do. He'd use it to the best of his ability. He'd twist the whole situation to his advantage, and I knew that because I'd learned from him too. So I took a breath and I smiled at the intruder.

'Y'all,' I said. 'Meet ...' And I held the microphone right up to his mouth. For a minute, I thought he might punch me, but then he looked totally shocked and surprised, even gobsmacked, and he leaned down with his arm mid-wave as though he was a rockstar that had just pulled off the performance of a lifetime.

'Nicholas.' He waved. 'My name's Nicholas. And, Lara, I'd just like to say that we've met before.' The crowd hesitated and then he clapped again above his head. 'Come on, guys,' and then there was a roar. 'I worked for you once. Well, I use that term loosely. I served you a few drinks. At your home. The announcement. I'm a jobbing actor. Well, failed actor really. You wouldn't remember my name. That's cos I went by something different that day. But not only that,' he went on. 'I'm also your *number one* fan.'

'Wow. Nicholas, I'm honoured.' Oh God, I thought. Another crazy, obsessed person. But that was absolutely all right. I could manage them. In fact, I'd been doing exactly that for a large part of my life.

'Nicholas. Nice name too. And what would you like to say to the crowd?' I asked. 'Because we don't have very much time until' – I looked at my wrist – 'the audience's recording. For charity.' I decided to shout for Conor, to get his attention but when I looked over, him and Detective Mcgraw had gone. So much for all the worry over security. I remembered asking if they thought there were going to be any surprises on stage. I had been joking. But now, I thought that even if Conor or Lily had seen this guy Nicholas, they might have thought I meant it seriously, and that he was 'the surprise'.

'Don't worry.' He smiled. He had small yellowed teeth. *This is your moment*, I thought. *You'll then make it big and you'll get those teeth changed, mark my words.* I could no longer control my thoughts, they were veering off into hypermania. 'I won't take long at all.' He smiled. 'I just want to talk about Ava.' He put his arm around me and the cheers went shrill. The sun started to look grey. I finally clocked Lily. She was frowning at me, flicking through her notes to find out if she'd missed something obvious and I tried to mouth to her but she was busy turning the sheets of paper as quickly as she could. I watched everyone clapping, some with fingers in mouths whistling, whistling. I felt weak. Weak, and all alone.

So this is where it ends. I don't need to tell you anymore. You know. *Don't you?* You know all this very well because I'm sure you are one of them. Just like the rest of the world. Watching me closely. You might see the flutter of my eyelashes as I try to blink away the blurring. You might see my breastbone, up and down, up and down, as I try and catch my breath. There might be other things you notice too. Conor reappearing. His smile as he looks at the crowd. *Ah, haven't I done well?* he'd be thinking because, still, he hasn't noticed what's going on. You might notice that I want to shake him, right about now. Then you might look a bit more closely at Nicholas.

And you'd realise that you knew him too. Not too well, mind, for he doesn't give too much away and lest I remind you, you haven't known him long. A relatively new friend, let's say.

But, well enough. You know him well enough.

LIVE BROADCAST

Ya'll. My name's Nicholas but you know me as, well . . . Ryan Gosling Wannabe. I know, I know, hands up. I look nothing like the Gos. I know I look like that dude the new big cheese Timothée Hal Chalamet. I look the spit of him. Especially before I went and shaved my head recently. Anyway, I'm to be known henceforth as . . . everybody wait for it . . . Nick Nack Says. You like? Great. Anyway, I'd like to thank you so much for taking part in the poll just now. Y'all know what I'm talking about, don't you? You guys at the front there. I see you, with your phones, thumbs up. Yes . . . y'all know. Ninety-seven per cent of you, an overwhelming ninety-seven per cent of you said that you'd like this to happen. Lara, you hear that? Ninety-seven per cent of people I polled just now out of a total of millions, they wanted to see this happen, right here. Right now. So don't think I'm alone in this. Anyway, I can see you over there, looking a bit edgy. I'll get on with it, then Lara can do her stuff. We can do our stuff. Together. Raise money for Ava. Right?

So, I'd first like to say, you can tweet me at my new Twitter handle which is at Nick Nack Says. And I'd like to thank you all for your support.

Now. Ava. We loved her, didn't we? Like she was our own sister. Our beautiful baby sister. You see, Lara? Look at the joy she brought everyone. Look at how many of us are here. It's scorching hot, and the world is here, with you, Lara King. Lara, I can see you nodding away in that beautiful way of yours, like the sunshine is literally up your backside.

So let's take it back to the beginning, shall we? There was the leaked 911 call. TMZ. Happens all the time. I've listened to all of them. Prince. Brittany Murphy. Bet you all have too. Sick, I know.

What struck me in that call is that, Lara, you said you were listening to Katy Perry. Did she love Katy Perry? You were singing along to Katy Perry on the radio you said. 'Yes,' you say? 'Yes, Ava adored Katy Perry'? I bet she did. Who doesn't love a bit of Perry?

So, I was thinking about Katy Perry whilst I was working the other night. I cranked up my iTunes. Found her name. I was singing away. 'Firework', in case any of y'all are interested, when I suddenly caught sight of a still of the CCTV footage of Lara and Ava King, when they'd stopped at that red light at Laurel Canyon. You know the one where it looks like a Chanel advert? All beautiful, and then my heart stops when I remembered what happened after.

Beautiful picture, wasn't it, Lara? I bet your heart could barely take it when you saw that. The last real public sighting of your girl. What's that you say? 'Yes, you miss her so much.' I bet you do.

Let's go on, shall we? Who here listens to Classical Tunes? On the radio. Hands up. None of you. Thought as much. Oh, Tom Banks over there, your hand's up, sir, is that correct? Good.

And then my mind wandered. Because I'm kinda obsessed with Ava and Lara and most things celebrity, I thought to myself, gosh, I wonder what radio station Lara and Ava listened to on their special out together before Ava disappeared? Would it be Kids Ahoy? Or something a little sophisticated. A bit more adult. But then I enlarged the car dashboard from the CCTV footage. You know there was a real clear picture of the dashboard. All these brightly lit dials and buttons and whatnot. And there I saw it. Classical Tunes, 86.6 FM. Wow. It didn't surprise me. Not at all. Lara and Ava. A classy pair. Get you, Lara. Classical Tunes. But then that got me thinking and I'm sure you've all caught up with me now.

Classical Tunes, Katy Perry? Doesn't really fit, does it? Nah.

Of course, Lara could have just changed the radio station, I hear you say. She could have just said it as a figure of speech. Weird figure of speech. I don't think so. It's quite a random thing to say, and quite specific when your child is missing. Don't you think? Looks a bit out of place. It's in the semantics, really, isn't it?

So that's why I got my friend – Kyle? Where are you, Kyle – there you are – to scrape all the radio listings from the six hours before Ava went missing. Nope. No Katy Perry in all that time. Believe it or not. Nothing. Sorry, Katy. I hope you're not sad about that.

So, you know. There's her first big lie. And what next? You know, you can look into this but I don't think Lara and Ava were having a jolly old time in that car after all.

We were listening to Katy Perry on the radio. Are you sure about that, Lara? Are you sure you weren't taking us for a ride?

Trying to fool us into thinking you were having a lovely old time with your daughter?

Because of course that's what you'd think, isn't it? With that choice of language? *Katy Perry. Me and my daughter grooving along in the sunshine.*

And then all the other lies she told. You can find them all listed on my Twitter. They should be uploading right now. As we speak. Remember: at Nick Nack Says.

Oh fuck. Lara's security. Wait, hear me out. Wait. Someone's on the defensive, aren't they, someone's lying. Trying to get us to look the other way. The police, bet you they had no idea about all this. Looking for a kidnapper. Or Matthew. But there was something going down right there in that car that day. Please . . . Don't hurt me . . . Don't fucking hurt me. Lara, you had a kid. You fucked it up. You deserve this. I never had a mother. She did. You fucked it.

I'm trying to help.

Don't you fucking understand. Ava.

I'm trying to help.

It's at this point that I think about running. I think about where I'd go. You're all watching me so closely that there's nowhere to go. But if I was alone, I'd race back up our cobbled drive, lined with shiny cars. I'd perhaps curse the palm trees, forcing me to weave my way around their silvery trunks. I'd ignore the burn of lungs until I reached the security key pad and front doors to my home. Mine and Ava's home. And I'd try and think back to where it had all started, my throat swollen with the catch of my breath.

I'd of course try and ignore you all. Forgive me, for being rude. I've always needed you. But now, as I watch you all in front of me, I realise I can't go anywhere. I'm trapped. Oh, the irony of it all, by *you*.

I think of Nicholas, who'd just been on the stage. He called himself a fan. Of mine or Ava's I can't remember. Funny fan, to turn on me like that. But he'd got me. And now, there's nowhere to turn, except to you.

You go slow at first. I see you, hands moving towards your back pockets. Some of you lift your screens up towards me, lights flashing. I open my mouth to sing again. But I stop mid-way. And then I think of Ava. The goodness that radiated from her.

I once read somewhere that your child's DNA passes right through you during pregnancy. That it gets absorbed into your own DNA. I hope that was true of Ava. That somehow, I'd got her goodness, somewhere.

'Shall I sing?' I asked. But everyone was silent. I was desperate. My body started to shake. 'Guys?' But no one spoke. I saw the bright white lights burning into me. 'I'm here. We've got to sing the song. For Ava. The record for charity. Come on. Don't do that. I thought you were all going to raise money?' I laughed, injecting a breeziness into my voice, but I felt you turn hostile. I thought I heard hissing from the front seats. I tried to get you back. I opened my mouth and started to sing again but none of you were paying attention.

'Ava.' I tried to switch attention but I heard the hisses get louder. 'Listen,' I shouted. 'Listen. Can't you respect my daughter? This is her memorial. All for you to pay your own respects.' But a rush of noise started filling the air.

'We loved Ava,' I heard someone shout, above the hissing.

'Stop,' I shouted and I looked down into the pit in front of the VIP row of seats and moved my hands, trying to get them to start up the music again but they all stood there, mouths open and holding their instruments in mid-air.

'Listen to me.' My voice got higher and higher, but I had lost you. I thought back to the moment in the police station. Ben. Joanne. How I'd managed to pull you all back when I'd moved to the US, because no matter how hard I tried, once I'd had you, there was no way I would live without you. And then I start to feel very angry. My daughter. She's dead, and you're behaving like this? Every cell in my body vibrates. Listen to me. Are you listening? But you're all busy, staring, recording like I'm some sort of exhibit.

And I'm trying to get you to listen. But you aren't. You aren't listening. I think about running. And I think about how after this, I'm sure as hell going to get put inside. And that's pretty inevitable when I tell you what happened. So this is it. I might as well go down on a high. It might as well come from me. The unfiltered me. I feel bad. Really bad. Because, well, this is the beginning of the end.

And with nothing to hide behind, I have to give you the real me.

Ladies and gentlemen, I present to you:

Lara King.

'It was me,' I shout. 'I did it.' The rush floods back in. My blood slows. Every single head is turned to me. 'It's my fault she's dead.'

You're all silent now. I see Conor on the side of the stage, hands clasped to his face. Detective Mcgraw is next to him staring at me. I put one hand out, ready for him. The other holds the microphone, so you can hear every single word I'm saying.

'We'd had a row,' I tell you all. You are transfixed. Glassy-eyed. 'After the photoshoot with Matthew Raine. The day of the announcement and our engagement.' I go quiet. You move forward, desperate for more. 'So, Detective, you were right about that. Ava was not hot on Matthew at the time, for whatever reason. She was asking me about him. That started things. But I won't go into that now. Maybe it was something to do with all that Dare or Die stuff.' I'd lead them down the wrong path with that one.

I thought about Matthew. I saw him behind Conor leaping up and then freezing, shaking his head. Don't worry, I whispered. *That secret would always stay safe with me.* I would never, ever betray him with that. It was a mental life sentence, what he'd done – let alone being put behind bars for good if he'd been caught out. I thought of the things Ava and I had seen in the swimming pool annexe. The things that had traumatised us both.

I replay them now, the images that had flashed from the projector onto the black wall of the pool annexe. The force of Matthew's muscled arm as it connected with another man's head. The man falling. The sound of his skull, cracking on the stone. The whites of his eyes. And then, blood, trailing from his ear.

'It was me,' Matthew had told me last night when I'd brought it up with him after the shock of the autopsy. 'I killed that man in Perth. My dad covered for me and went to jail. Told everyone it had been him. I'd just got my first film part. Dad wanted me to be big. Ever since Mum died.' He'd swallowed. 'I paid the bar owner to give me the CCTV. Quarter of a million dollars. He kept asking for more. I've had to put a stop to it.'

'Why were you watching it?' I had asked him. 'That day. In the pool annexe before the announcement.'

'To punish myself,' he'd said. 'The drugs aren't enough, you see. To dampen the guilt. If I keep playing the video, over and over, then it reminds me of the person I am. You and I were about to get engaged. I had to remind myself of the person I really was, before something good happened. Do you see? And then you caught me. The day of the announcement. The door, to the annexe. I usually lock it. I'm usually so careful. But that day, well, I'd had a heavy few nights. Couldn't find the key so I just shoved a chair under the handle. Didn't realise I hadn't done it properly.' I thought about the Dare or Die video and how Matthew's heavy nights manifested.

'You aren't a bad person,' I'd told him. He'd told me he'd taken the video footage to Jenna's and had asked her to keep it hidden. But I'd gone over and destroyed it.

'You nearly got there, Detective Mcgraw,' I carried on. 'Good work. So we argued, like all couples do.' I took a deep breath. 'In the car, Ava was whining. Whining about Matthew. About her real father. We drove.' I think of her voice now. *I'm hungry. I'm hungry.* 'We drove to Laurel Canyon. Somewhere deserted.' I look at Detective Mcgraw. He's there, on the edge of the stage, unable to break the spell, and then I look at all of you. I'd certainly got you back again with this. I can feel the energy crackling around the audience.

'She told me, she leaned forward in the car and told me she was going to tell. Her teachers. Tell them something that she'd seen earlier that day. Something she had witnessed in our indoor swimming pool. Of course, I'm not going to tell you exactly what that was. Suffice to say it was unpleasant. She said she would tell everyone everything if I didn't tell her who her real father was. Six! I know! She is . . . she *was* only six. I don't know how she thought of that kind of stuff either. We screamed at each other then. She told me other stuff too. Stuff she knew would wind me up.'

I think back to the moment she'd threatened me. 'Joan will help me,' she'd said, her eyes all watery. 'Or my teacher at school. She said I could come to her with any problems.'

'No!' I'd shouted. I carry on looking at you all. Your mouths open. 'You come to me,' I told her. 'I'm your mother. Don't you understand?'

'I'd been scared then,' I carried on, my voice slow and sad. 'Tired. I was so tired. She'd been in my ear, all morning. Still asking for Joan. Joan? Where are you? Happy now? And still going on about her dad. And the funny thing is, you all know, don't you? Now you all know who her father is. It would have taken me two minutes to tell her. But a lifetime to explain. And in truth, well the real truth of it is that I wanted her all to myself. I didn't want her looking anywhere else for love. For affection. She was mine. I was scared, if you will. I know. I should have had more confidence in myself as a mother. Don't worry. I'm not excusing any of it. I know it's wrong. Anyway. Don't let me get distracted. So her real father. And Joan. She kept asking for them both.'

Joan. I think of Joan. My heart breaks.

'*Joan*, she kept saying. And I kept telling her, *Ava. I'm here. I'm your mummy. You don't need Joan. You don't need your teacher.* But she just wouldn't listen. She was crying then. Telling me I was a bad mother. *Bad. Bad. Bad.* You don't care about me, she had been screaming. You just care about your fame. I want Joan.' And then I remembered how she'd pulled her golden card.

'*I heard Matthew,*' she said. '*I heard him say to someone that you only ever had me to get famous. To kick-start your career. That I was like a show-pony.*

'*Who did he say that to?*' I had asked, thinking how that couldn't possibly have been true.

'*Conor. They were laughing about it. Matthew kept making neighing noises.*' She had cried then. Really cried. *You're not my mummy*, she'd said. *You are not. You don't love me. It's true. What they said is true. That you'd be nothing without me. Just a washed-up has-been. That's what they called you*, her eyes flashed black. *I remember now. That's what they called you. Matthew said you were soon going to become a washed-up has-been if you weren't careful. And that you needed him more than he needed you.*' I had felt something inside me, like the snap of an elastic band in my gut. I thought about how I'd covered for him. How I was also implicated by the fact I had known about it but hadn't said a word, so I could never say anything.

'Heat was rising in my body and I felt as though I couldn't really breathe. Washed-up has-been. I thought of Matthew too. How untrue it had been and at that point I didn't even know if Ava had been telling the truth or not. I know what you're thinking. That she's too young to think of words like that. But I wondered if she'd heard them from one of the kids at school. You know. That perhaps their mothers or fathers had been talking. And she was just repeating the things she'd heard. But I felt like I was going to pass out with anger.

'And so I pulled over. Somewhere where nobody was around. *Get out*, I shouted. She didn't, at first. She didn't get out. But then I opened the door and I pulled her out the car. *Go. Go. Go.*' I shut my eyes. I can't bear to look at you all right now.

'I think of her face. The defiant set of her mouth, but she'd been scared at that moment too. She was normally such a good girl. But she'd been angry. And really scared. She knew she had pushed me too far. I saw it in her eyes. The light, seeping into her pupils. The quiver of her mouth. The place had been empty. Miles of emptiness. Air, thick and heavy with dense, suffocating heat. Gloom, despite the bright sky. She didn't like being alone. And then I really went for it.'

I watch as you sob in front of me, hands up to your mouths.

'*Get the fuck out*, I was screaming. I don't know where that came from. I don't. But she did. She got out. And I drove off.'

I let the words sink in.

'I thought she'd stay there. Just a little warning. That was all. You know how you do? Five minutes. The naughty step. Time out. Whatever it was. All the stress from the announcement, you guys watching me and Matthew, big changes. After everything I'd given him and that's how he repaid me. All this time, I've had to pretend I didn't mind. So that no one would suspect we'd rowed. Matthew, see?

'Anyway, I told the police she'd fallen asleep. It was my word. That was all they had, apart from parts of the routes I had taken, that had been found on CCTV. They saw me drive all the way back to the Boulevard.

'*She was asleep, lying in the back all that time*, I told the cops. But she wasn't. It had just been me, driving. And then I had turned to go back and get her. When the rage had calmed.' The sun shifts for a second and then seems to burn brighter than ever. 'Twenty minutes it took. I turned back to where I thought I'd left her. But I couldn't remember. I honestly couldn't remember. The paths, the roads. They all look the same. I was frightened then. But I knew she'd be OK. I knew she'd be fine. That it would just take me a bit of driving around and I'd pick her up, sooner or later. It took me twenty minutes to get to the Boulevard. Twenty minutes back. And then I got out the car. I was screaming, shouting her name. But all of a sudden, I realised

I had no idea where I'd stopped the car. I was tired. I told you.' I start to laugh. Hiccuping. This was such a relief. 'And so I knew it had been a long time then. I rang Matthew. Despite my anger with him. I rang him. He was the only one I knew would help me. Because of course, he does need me.' I looked over at him, thinking about all the other things I knew about him that I'd kept quiet.

Some of you are moving towards me now. And some of you are backing away from me. Like you cannot believe you'd be in such close proximity to a monster.

'Matthew came. I called him sometime around ten to eleven and asked him to come and find us. I told the police I had been talking to him on the phone. About our day. Instead, I had begged him to come to me. Made him stay on the line with me until I calmed down. I told him to turn his phone off after he hung up. He drove fast. Towards me. Told me to calm down. *We'll find her*, he told me. *We will. Just fucking keep calm.* I was screaming that I didn't know where I'd left her. And I'd just like to say to you all that at that moment, we believed we would. We really believed we would find her. Just a little blip. Forgot the kid. You surely must have read about it loads. I thought we'd find her and she'd run into my arms. Hot and sweaty but there she'd be and I'd say sorry, stroking her hair. And no one, and I meant no one, was going to find out. Except she didn't come back to us. We couldn't find her. She was gone.

'After it had been a while since I'd left her – about an hour and forty-five minutes, Matthew told me . . . *you have to ring 911.*

'*We can't,*' I said. '*They'll find out. That I dumped her. That you knew about it.*'

'*Shhh*,' he said. He shook me then but I was still screaming and sobbing and then he shook me again. Ferociously, by the shoulders. '*Shut the fuck up and listen.*' I did as I was told.

'*Here's what we say*,' he said. And then together, we went through the timings, second by second. We rehearsed it over and over. That I hadn't dumped her. That she'd gone to the loo. I couldn't tell the police that I'd left my daughter in a rage, could I? I just couldn't. We obviously did a good job. No one cottoned on and we vowed never to discuss it, even in private, after that.' I silently apologised to Matthew. Better I drop him in it now, I thought. He'd at least cut his prison time then, I thought.

'*Make the call*,' he said to me, after we'd perfected our alibis. I shook my head. I still believed she was going to walk right out in front of us like a mirage. But he made me. I remember the thickness of his voice. The way he almost growled at me. He dialled the number. Held the phone to my ear. I did it. And then the police. They arrived. It took them about fifteen minutes, because I couldn't find any landmarks. None. It was just empty space. So, by that time . . .'

I think back to how long she'd been alone for. My body drops. I kneel down, still telling you the story.

'By that time it had been coming up to two hours that she'd been gone. Like I said, I always believed in my heart of hearts she'd be back. You did too. Didn't you? You gave me hope. You always did.' I think of Matthew. 'Please. Don't blame Matthew,' I say to you all. 'I know he did some bad things. But deep down he's a good person.' I think of the video footage again. How I had ignored it. 'He tried to help me. He tried to help Ava. I know . . . you'll wonder why he didn't go to the police. Because

I told Matthew I'd blame him. He's a great actor, isn't he? But there are bits of himself he'd want to change. His past. His history. His father in prison. He wanted to erase certain things so of course when I told him that, he covered for me. He did his best to pretend everything was normal. See? But the fact is that like me, he believed that she'd turn up. He never thought it would get to this. He'd never thought his lies would have such big consequences. And, you know, once you're in too deep it's hard to get out. Isn't it?' I turn to Detective Mcgraw.

'Here,' I shout. 'I'm ready.' I turn my head from the sun. It's a beautiful day. Mcgraw walks up to me. Takes the microphone from my hand and sets it on the floor. I feel the cool of the metal around my wrists. I watch him, the shape of his mouth. I can't hear him much, though, the words searing into my brain, like I'm underwater. Something about things not matching up. No footprints. Forensics.

'You missed it,' I tell him, my voice quiet now. 'You see, you were all looking the other way. Like it or not, you too, Detective Mcgraw. I know you had your suspicions. You were nearly there. I'd rowed. She'd heard and run off. Close. But not quite. And you couldn't help but be blindsided by it all. Me.'

I feel the metal tighten even more around my skin, followed by a sharp click.

And the funny thing is I know now that when I get locked away, you will want me even more. You won't be able to get enough of me. I'll be sentenced and I'll still be with you, right by your side.

I'll write my memoir. I'll work with Conor, ready for when I reappear into the outside world. No matter how long it might take. I think of it all again. The television appearances. The concerts I'll give once again.

I'll be a new woman. And, Ava, I'm sorry. I'm so desperately sorry. I was meant to be your mother. But the truth of it is ... well, there was some truth in the words you said to me just before you disappeared. The words you said you had overheard. That I was nothing without you. And that's why this happened. Because the truth seared right through me. You were right. I was, I am nothing without you. And that's where all you lot come in. Do you see?

Anyway, the truth was that I was never meant to be a mother. But despite all that, despite the fact I had her for the wrong reasons, there was a part of me that had grown to love her. Really love her. The shape of her mouth as she smiled, widening her face into a splash of joy. The way she jumped up and down and clenched her fists tight when something really excited her. Oh, this is making me so sad.

And, Ava – when you were born I was meant to protect you. I failed. I'm sorry. Maybe I will have another chance. Make amends. Matthew had been worried about if you'd been found. How you'd talk. *It was my mother,* you'd say ... she left me. But I told him he didn't need to worry. That you'd protect me, in just the same way I hadn't protected her. I rub my wrists against the metal. Were they really necessary? I was hardly going to hurt anyone, here in front of you all.

Joan ... I'm sorry too. I'm really sorry.

And, bear with me. One last apology. Or should that be thank you? Matthew. Thank you. For covering for me. I think about what he'd done, searching the canyons, sweat shelfed on his top lip. Wiping it away with those beautiful hands of his. *I won't tell*, I think. Your biggest secret. Somethings would stay just between us. Because you, you all know enough now. I would never let you in on that. Because you're all going to go away thinking he's the hero of this story, aren't you? Despite the things he may or may not have done. You're going to think he was trying to protect me. That we'd find Ava, no problem. That the bonds of love lasted strong between us.

Oh no. It was *him*, he was trying to protect himself. But, Matthew, you kept quiet all this time. I'll do the same for you. I think about how enamoured you'd all been by us. The way you'd followed our relationship. That first heady date we had had in Nobu when you went more crazy for us two together than we could ever have possibly imagined in our wildest dreams.

And then I think back to the first time Matthew and I had *actually* met. Away from the cameras. He'd introduced himself in the hallway of my home, his shadow stretching across the tiles.

'Nice to meet you, ma'am,' he'd said in his soft voice. He'd walked through, looked around my living room. 'Your house, it's rad.' I remembered looking at Conor, a small frown on my face, the edges of laughter rising up my throat. Then he'd told me he liked my art and I can't really remember what he'd talked about next.

'Thanks,' I'd told him. And then I'd left Conor and our lawyers to sort out all the paperwork. 'Come on,' I told him. 'Let's go into the kitchen for a bit.' I'd liked him. But not like that. He wasn't really my taste, you see. In truth, he's too clean-cut. Too young-looking. 'Let's just leave them to it,' I'd told him. 'They can hammer out the details of our . . .'

'*Relationship?*' he'd held up his fingers in air quotations.

'That's the one,' I'd said. 'Our *very* special and falling in love at first sight relationship.'

'Let's get to know each other anyway,' I had told him. 'And I need to tell you about Ava. She's my daughter. And no one is to know about this. Not her. Not her nanny, Joan. No one. Just you and me. Do you understand? I do not want any of this coming out, ruining my reputation. Because together.' I had taken a deep breath. 'We're going to build a strong brand. OK? We're going to rule the world and I'll be a decoy for all the other stuff you don't want . . .'

'I'll drink to that,' he'd said before I could finish. He reached into my large silver fridge and pulled out a screw-top beer, flicking the lid into the bin.

'Cheers.' I had clinked his beer bottle with a small, crystal glass I'd filled with cucumber water and ice. 'I'll drink to that too.'

Shame, really. We had been destined for such good things together. The press, onto his father's past. Someone sniffing around about his partying ways but, in truth, we had actually grown to love each other, in a weird, dysfunctional way. At least, as far as I knew what love was. We were a good match. Conor was absolutely right, as usual, and he chose well. We had really grown to rely on each other, bound together in our loneliness, I suppose. And of course, things had happened in our lives that had been more similar than I could possibly have imagined. The things we'd worked so hard at to keep secret.

And you, I could sense you were getting ever so slightly bored of me and Ava. Restless, let's say. The comments, they'd kept coming thick and fast. But you'd needed something else to grab your attention. Not much. Just a small change. A bit of optimism. A bit of hope. A fairytale happy-ever-after ending. That everyone can find their one true love. Because despite all this female empowerment stuff these days, you all still want that, don't you.

And now, you.

You wanted me when you thought I was good. Now, I pray, you'll still want me when I'm bad.

You built me up, and then you broke me.

I don't blame you. I still love you, I still *need* you. Even as you watch me, eyes squinting from the bright rays, my wrists bound in metal being walked away.

And as I say goodbye to you for the time being, I can tell you this. We will meet again. I can't stay away from you either. I will see you soon. As someone new. A different Lara King. I'm good at that.

So, please, give me another chance.

I will not let you down because I am yours.

Unequivocally, shamelessly, perfectly.

I am your guilty secret.

This piece was originally intended for appearance in the paper during the time of Ava's disappearance, but due to sensitivity over the case, the LA Times *postponed the article. We've taken the steps of publishing the transcript in full. For more of Manny Berkowitz's commentary on the interview and details surrounding the interview, please sign up for access to our* LA Times *members area.*

I'm sorry that you didn't get your story before Lara King was arrested. That you worked so hard at getting me to talk and no amount of money could get me to change my mind. I'd signed an NDA too. Not that I care about that. Too long has passed. It's good to see the back of her. But now. I'm ready. Now she's gone. She can't do me any harm. You see, I was scared. Shit-scared. I know Hollywood's a powerful place. Who knows what would have happened. I mean . . . you can't speak out, can you? Power, it goes in all the wrong hands. Look at all the Weinstein stuff. I mean, there's one of me. I was never sure my voice would be enough, you know? That to speak out against another female, whether that would go against some sort of, well, *code.*

But anyway – now I can say my piece. Tell you my thoughts on Lara King. I only met her once many years ago. *But it was all I needed.*

She was lonely. I could see it in her eyes. The fame. It had already got to her when I met her. I couldn't ignore her. There was something in her eyes in the club that night. Lost. Lonely. Cold? I don't know. But she looked right past me that day. I did my best. Told her how great I thought she was.

You know she was quite new on the scene. I mean, she was no one that special in that moment. I thought she'd like hearing how great she was. And I think she did, at first. But then something flipped.

She seemed disconnected. It freaked me out. And I felt it. That she thought she was so much better than me in that moment. Projection? I don't know. But it was like she was lost in her own glorious world and nothing else mattered.

I'm going to get you back, I thought. Perhaps it was me, you know. Perhaps it had been a long time coming. Perhaps I'd been so dejected by the way she'd dismissed me earlier. So when she came in and spoke to me like that, well, I lost it. Totally lost it. And then she was going mad too, and I had it in my head just at that moment. Like a flash of lightning. I shouldn't have videoed her. Should I? It was bad. Then she pushed me. I only felt the pain afterwards. She hissed something to me before she did it. Something about a diamond necklace. I didn't know what she was talking about. But I felt the words slip out, the cold air on my skin.

My body slammed down the metal steps and then I was on the stone cobbles. I watched someone get her in a taxi. A shaven-headed guy. I just about managed to lift my head up at that point. He looked like a bit of a geezer. But then he looked at the woman Lara was with and held his hand out to her. And they both got in the cab with him and zoom, they were gone.

Never saw them again. I lay there on the concrete. My body screaming in pain. I was black and blue. Never showed my boyfriend when I got home. He would have downright killed her, and by that point, I'd started to think about who I was going to contact with the video of her screaming at me. But then I grew angrier and angrier. I thought about the headlines. Who I was going to call. And I did. The next day. I still don't regret it to this very day.

I remember seeing her in America after that. Her and Ava. The perfect mother and daughter relationship. And now look. Poor, poor little girl. Dead.

The police asked me if it was true. Whether I had baited her into saying and doing those things. They came to see me the day after. But like I told you. It would have been me against the world. This rich, powerful woman. And who was I? A nobody. I was a student at the time. I didn't have money for legal fees and the rest. I could have made a mint from selling that video but I didn't.

Maybe I did push her into it. The things I said to her before I started recording.

You see, if I did bait her, well, it was because I was in a bad place. I was in a really, really bad place.

I didn't know what I was doing.

You see, and now this is the truth. It's been needling me all this time. Years I've been thinking about what it would be like coming clean. Getting all this off my chest. My baby. I'd started to bleed. Heavily. That night. In the club. Just before Lara came into the bathroom.

The pains had started early that morning. I knew. It had happened one too many times before. I was familiar with the form. Wear a sanitary pad. Take some strong painkillers. And I was in so much pain. Mental pain. Emotional pain. So I decided to blot it all out. I took drugs to forget. Snorted a few lines. Sniff, wipe nose. Forget.

But this time, the timing. After she pushed me, it was too good. I went to the hospital the next day. Told them and the police everything. 'She pushed me,' I told them. 'I landed right here.' I pointed to the small protrusion by my waistband. I had been sobbing. Hysterical. 'And right after she pushed me,' I told them, 'I got these pains and I started to bleed.'

And then I had shown them my body. I remember the gasps at the hospital when I told the nurse who it had been.

'You never,' she had said, inspecting my legs and then the doctor, parting my thighs, the cold speculum inside me.

But really, it wasn't her. All that time I wanted to tell someone. I just wanted to get her back for the things she said. I guess I wanted someone to blame. We'd been trying. Me and my boyfriend. We'd been trying for a while. It was easier to blame Lara King than to accept that, well . . . I've always thought that perhaps she had Ava to relieve her guilt at what she'd done to me. You know. Perfect mother. Wipe away the shitty stuff you've done in your past. Or to build up her reputation. Distract people from looking at her past. *Ooh isn't she wonderful, with her beautiful kid. So maternal. She would never have put a foot wrong.* But you know. She was a person before she was a mum. Having a child didn't make her who she was. No. That happened long before.

Anyway, whatever it was, look what's happened now. And I never got to be a mother.

It wasn't enough. Was it? It wasn't enough for her that she hurt me the way she did. She had to carry on.

It never is.

It's never enough.

I know I've been a bit silent of late. It's been so freaking sad, reading Manny Berkowitz's profile on Lara King. They were right, the *LA Times*, to postpone the piece. Especially after that massive exposé with Carys Lockwood. (Chapeau, Manny. You will always reign supreme.) Before I go on, I just wanted to say one thing. Ava – you told Manny on the day of the announcement that you didn't think your mom loved you.

I wanted to let you know that wherever you are, we loved you. You were loved. You were. And I'm glad Manny told her – Lara – I mean, how special she was. That she was to be cherished. I'm glad she knew, even if she didn't act on it. She needed to know how lucky she was.

But with all of that, after watching Lara King go down . . .

SOME GOOD NEWS, PEEPS!

After my big stage debut (for those of you who went to high school with me and accused me of always hiding behind my computer, who would have thought?) my phone was literally going off the freaking hook!

Mad! Non-stop. My granma, she couldn't believe it.

'Finally.' She pulled my ears and kissed my cheek. 'Finally you've been recognised, I'm so proud of you.' And it felt good, y'know? It felt good that I'd believed in what I'd done. That I'd followed through on my instinct. Failed actor one day, successful superstar blogger the next.

Boom!

And so, kids, my message today – always believe in yourself. Always trust in yourself. Cos we ain't got much else in this life.

And right now, I'm delighted to say that I've signed with none other than the famous PR guy himself, da, da da . . .

Conor O'Sullivan! He said he's going to make me ***big***. Says he can see 'something' in me. Whatever that is. First things first, work on my image. That kind of thing. He's even arranged for me to get my teeth done. First session tomorrow. Watch this space.

Nicholas! Over here! Smile!

Zing!

What goes around, comes around, Lara King.

I love you all. Thank you, for championing me, for reading me, for giving me this chance, because really it's all down to you. All of this. My amazing fans.

My support network who've followed me all this time, through thick and thin.

You made me into who I am today.

The readers of my posts that kept me going and built me up and up, and up. Right to the top.

Right to the stars.

I love you.

No, really. I do.

I love you all.

So take a bow.

This one's for YOU.

Thank you, goodnight and God bless.

X

Acknowledgements

I'd like to thank Nelle Andrew for absolutely everything. Your unfailing support means the world to me.

Laura Williams, Sophie Orme, Jennie Rothwell (alongside the editorial notes, thank you so so much for taking my panicked phone calls and emails towards the end, and for being so calm and reassuring), Margaret Stead, Jon Appleton and Alex Allden. And Jett Purdie, for my last front cover. Thank you so much for all the collective work you have put into the book.

The Redfern Gallery: Richard Gault, Richard Selby, Paul, Michael and Maya. And also to my friend Paul Gould from the Faber Academy *Write A Novel* course.

To my friends who have supported my first novel and have had to put up with my second-novel struggle both in terms of friendship and generosity and also answering endless inane, brainstorming questions. My heartfelt thanks go to, Nick Matthew, Chloe Sarfaty, Alison Hitchock, Clarissa Ward, Alanna Clear, Edwina Gieve, Anna Van Praagh, Daniel Cavanagh, Mahim Qureshi, Lynn and Josh West, Zoe and Rick Harris, Kathryn Usher, Elly Walsh, Nerissa and Sammi Martin, Emilie Bennetts, Henrietta Wheal, Maria Riachy Guven, Caroline Hall, Cara Randell, Sarah Wheeler, Liz Barnsley, Esther Walker, Vikki and Olly Sloboda.

Thank you to Chris Missen and to Rick Harris for the introduction. Thank you also to Damon O'Sullivan for the police procedural info. And to Rumena Mahbub and Bridget Robson for your amazing childcare and life-lessons.

Also a massive thank you to Dr George Paolinelis. I'm extremely grateful that you held your nerve to save mine, and am forever grateful to Lynn West for the introduction.

The Bonnier crew, with special thanks to Ayisha Malik (I'm sorry, Mallers. One day I'll stop . . .), David Young, Graham Minett and Chris Whitaker.

Izzy Benson, Elizabeth Day, Caroline Jones, Liz Thornton, Lynn West and Charlotte Wilkins – thank you for being there for me, unfailingly – at any time of day and night. I really couldn't do any of this without you. You inspire me and make me laugh so much and have given me so many happy memories to cherish. Thank you.

Huge thanks go to my fantastic in-laws, Karen and Ellis – I am incredibly grateful for everything you do for us, and to Nick and Zoe, and my very cool and amazing nephew and niece, Jamie and Carly Spero.

And, of course to my husband Olly, my parents, Emily and Matt, Chester, Jasper and Alia. And to Cyrus, who is much missed. You are all brilliant people (and dogs). Mum and Dad for being the best parents ever, Emily and Jasper for imparting your supersonic wisdom, thoughts and humour to me on a regular basis. I feel very lucky indeed.

My lifelong best-friend Asia Mackay – this one is for you. I really cannot thank you enough for everything. For your never-ending support in both writing and everything else.

Olly, Walter and Dominic – my favourites. For putting up with my writing! And the rest.

Want to read
NEW BOOKS
before anyone else?

Like getting
FREE BOOKS?

Enjoy sharing your
OPINIONS?

Discover

READERS FIRST
Read. Love. Share.

Sign up today to win your first free book:
readersfirst.co.uk

For Terms and Conditions see readersfirst.co.uk/pages/terms-of-service